Emilie

Hope you'll enjoy this book
recommended by radio!
(NPR's book critic)
love!
Dad

FICTION

ATLANTIC
MONTHLY
PRESS

MOUNT'S MISTAKE

MOUNT'S MISTAKE

LEW McCREARY

THE ATLANTIC MONTHLY PRESS
NEW YORK

FIRST EDITION

Library of Congress Cataloging-in-Publication Data
McCreary, Lew.
Mount's mistake.
I. Title.
PS3563.C3526M68 1987 813'.54 87-12608
ISBN 0-87113-174-9

Design by Laura Hough

Published simultaneously in Canada

Printed in the United States of America

The Atlantic Monthly Press
19 Union Square West
New York, NY 10003

First printing

For Pete McCreary
1953–1979

The author thanks the following for their vital contributions to the nurturing of this book: his wife, Mary Prosser; DeWitt Henry, director of *Ploughshares*; Kathryn Kramer; Richard Pisano; Bonnie Thompson; and Patrick J. Sheehan, head of reference at the Motion Picture, Broadcasting, and Recorded Sound Division of the Library of Congress.

1

YOUTH: SLOWLY, SOFTLY

Everything has had youth. The two old dogs were lifted into their baskets lined with wadded rags. If the old dogs were set down wrong, if their legs were folded too severely underneath them, the legs would fall asleep before the dogs did, and in the morning the dogs would collapse when lifted out and set upon their nerveless, bloodless feet.

Father and Mother Mount were watching Jay, the boy, their Jay, play with old Phantom, the spaniel, and Phantom's wife, Canasta. Phantom was sixteen, Canasta fifteen. The boy was six. In his early youth he was enjoying the old age of the two dogs.

He took Canasta's muzzle in his hands and pried her mouth open. Then he looked inside. He put his face right up to her teeth; she stared at the ceiling, gummy eyed. He hummed a little song into her mouth and listened to the sound of his voice ringing around in the hollow. Canasta's tongue struggled up and down with a dry smacking. He forced her mouth shut, catching a tab of pink and black lip between two yellow teeth. Canasta whimpered. Phantom lifted his head from the grimy rags. With three smart taps, Jay patted Phantom's head back down. He grabbed Canasta's tail and made it wag. His mother and father laughed. The boy smiled.

"Good girl, good girl," said Father Mount. Canasta wagged her tail in earnest. After the boy had gone to bed, Canasta would gaze at Phantom and growl softly, Phantom growling softly back.

When he was seven Jay first heard Diamond Falls. His family stood behind the house and buried Phantom beyond the rhubarb. Canasta sniffed at Phantom's box, and Father Mount nudged her nose away with his foot. Jay heard Diamond Falls that day for the first time, hissing up through the trees beyond the meadow. His father told him Kickham Run was joining the east fork of the Jasper River a hundred yards below the splash of Diamond Falls.

"Soon the water is leaving Ohio and going to Indiana. At Diamond Falls it gets up its head. And that's what you hear."

But Jay thought the noise was Phantom hiding from him, burrowing under leaves and breathing hard. "I know what Phantom means," he told his mother once. She said, "It means an old black dog." He said, "I know."

One evening at dinner, after Father Mount said grace, Jay stopped moving when his fork was halfway between the plate and his mouth. "Wait," he said, and his eyes closed helplessly. The lids fluttered; his lips trembled. Mother and Father Mount stared at him for half a minute until he opened his eyes and opened his mouth and finished the movement of the fork. He hadn't dropped a single bean. They thought he was a mysterious child. He never explained, but he was hearing the sound of his father saying grace, a familiar echo from a great distance, turning the world on its side.

When Jay first went to play at Diamond Falls he was seven and a half. Mother Mount watched from the back door. Jay got smaller and smaller and smaller. At the far side of the meadow she watched his head and shoulders drift into the trees. Birds flew up. She began to follow. She shut the door so quietly. She walked across the meadow with her skirts lifted above the grass. Father Mount stood at the window of his workshed and watched her go. She drifted into the trees.

Jay sat on the giant rocks above Kickham Run. The rocks were warm and smooth; the heat went through his pants. He took off his clothes. He moved from rock to rock to find the one that fit him best. On the one known as Orchid Rock he lay belly down. The rock was shaped like a shallow bowl. He peered over its rim and looked downstream to Diamond Falls where spray rose up like a gas. Mother Mount thought he looked like a salamander sunning itself. The edges of his skin were blurred in the brightness of the light. He seemed so soft that he might have had no bones at all. He ran his hands over the rock. His round muscles tensed and relaxed in a slow repeating rhythm. Where she was crouched in the ferns, the shoots reached high and tickled Mother

2

Mount. And Father Mount was sneaking up behind her. The sound of Diamond Falls was rushing through the woods, and all the hands of all the Mounts were moving.

One morning at Goodspeed Normal School, Jay lifted the lid of his desk and closed it; lifted it . . . closed it . . . lifted it . . . closed it . . . slowly, quietly, fanning changes in nice Miss Dawkins's voice, the soft aspirations of a goose in flight. Inside his desk the books were moving by themselves, dull colors crossing and rising, pages blinking in the wooden basin. Jay was scared to reach inside because a book would crawl to his hand and bump against it, like a cat's hot forehead.

He heard the other children's voices crying in the grainy air of the cold room. He heard his name said slowly, echoing: "Jjjaaayyy?" Someone gripped his hand. He felt a tug and was taken outside; hands were waving. In the hall Miss Dawkins knelt in front of him. Back in the classroom some of the bolder children tiptoed up to peer beneath the lid of the desk. Miss Dawkins touched his face. Then she pressed her hands against the sides of his head, rubbing soft circles. It felt so good.

"Is that better?" she said. "Is that better?"

In the schoolyard he leaned against the school. This time each day Paul Pilers, Health Instructor, placed him there to stand. It was his spot. When he pushed away and took three running steps, Paul Pilers scowled and hunched his shoulders. Jay returned to the side of the building, which was cool and blue with shadows. His classmates ran and chanted. Every few days a new club was formed. A member was sent to tell Jay that he would not be allowed to join. The member waited. Jay opened his mouth slowly and his teeth came into view, shining wet.

Miss Dawkins watched from the window above. She was concerned. Jay's head was very much deeper than wide, his hairline low. She stared straight down at the top of him, which rested as still as a target. Some of the children saw her and pointed. The children watched Miss Dawkins carefully, her lowered eyes in the large window casement. Paul Pilers threw a ball so high in the air it tried to lift Miss Dawkins's eyes, but it could not. The children's faces were raised to the sun like flashing coins. Slowly the ball descended.

Through his town of Bolusburgh, Ohio, Jay followed people at a distance. Ahead of him they crossed each other's fronts; they whirled

3

and clutched and scattered, and then came back and continued on. They reached down and picked up and threw in any direction. They blurted out and laughed and stumbled. Holly Frieda noticed Jay and whispered to Jerry Bolus. The whispering went up into the trees. Jerry Bolus turned and stared, turning Jay.

From the time the people he followed passed a house, Jay would count until he passed the same house. Maybe seventeen. But sometimes he never arrived. He would unexpectedly turn left and left and right, and soon he would be where he never designed to be, slowly climbing the mountain ash in front of Leonora Clawson's house, Leonora staring silently from the parlour window. He picked it clean of empty locust skins, filling his pockets to bulging until they crackled when he walked. And walking home he walked them into dust.

Leonora sent a note on eggshell-colored stationery: Mr. and Mrs. Mount, your son was in my tree again. You should have him checked. His physical skills are so very poor. Above a certain height I worry about him. Yours, Leonora C.

There was something called Old Music.

Once a year it came to Bolusburgh. Bolusburgh was much too new to have Old Music of its own. The Old Musicians in their colorful outfits came by barge down the Bolusburgh Canal from Lake Erie, twenty miles northeast. Mr. Tyrus Portman Bolus, Sr., who was the father of both the canal and the town, many years before had invited the Old Musicians to visit Bolusburgh at the end of every spring. No one knew exactly what day the Old Musicians would arrive, only that the time was drawing near. The banner was cleaned and stretched across the terminus of the towpath: *"Bolusburgh Old Music Days Festival—Every Year In June, So Far Without Fail."* A prize was always given to the first person to hear the Old Music, and that person was always Father Mount.

Jay sat in the sun outside his father's workshed. He listened to the fastening and unfastening sounds his father made just inside the door, assembling and taking apart. This day it was a small machine, lumpish, roundish, the size of a skull. Another day it would be a large machine. What did the small machine do?

"With all my heart and mind, young Jay, I just don't know," his father told him. But still Jay heard the tumbling click of tiny parts. How could his father fix a machine if he didn't know what it was?

4

"All I can see with a thing like this is the basic go-together and the soundness of this or that part of the whole appliance . . ." He held it into the light. "These teeth are something, here . . . you see these teeth? I can turn this cam and the two rows of teeth . . . see? They are parted and something here pushes from in back? Now I go the other way and, see? They are come together again, like a mouth . . ."

Jay squinted. His father was still in the dark of the shed, but the two long arms reached into the sunlight and held the small machine with its teeth and cam that worked like a mouth. One of the hands went off to the side and pointed back. "This tiny clip in the corner here, it was bad and I had to make up another. The clip kept the fluid from leaking out; the fluid kept the machine from running rough. That fella Ty Howser brought it up from the ropeworks. So I guess it might be a tensioner of some type, where these teeth grip and let go and grip and let go and grip and let go . . ." The hand that had been pointing was squeezing now like a claw. Jay laughed.

But suddenly there went his father, flying out the door of the shed and dropping the small machine in the dirt in front of Jay where it rocked and chattered. Jay heard the pounding of his father's feet already around the corner of the house and heading up the street to the center of town. There was only that day this time last year (and the day the year before that and, vaguely, the year before that) to which Jay could compare this event. Now, in the slow accumulating progress of his learning, he whispered to himself: "Father's heard the Old Music first again." He listened hard, above the lingering clicking of tiny parts in the small machine, to hear the same music his father had heard; but it wasn't coming to him yet.

Instead, the bell at Bolus Hall began to toll and soon, everywhere, there was a slamming of doors and the rush of citizens flocking, voices calling, garments brushing together. And Mother Mount was scooping him up and making him run ahead of her, around the corner of the house where his father had disappeared.

Then finally he heard the Old Music, deep and slow, flowing through the streets of town like the brown spring cresting of the Bolusburgh Canal. The old cautious drumbeat rattled windows and rustled the leaves of the twenty-year elms. The worried strings and solemn horns slid heavily between the cracks, the loosened spaces and swaying shapes. The

5

sounds were balanced: pleasure and sadness, the wild holy moan of the sudden festival.

The four sons of Tyrus Portman Bolus, Sr., carried him ahead of the Old Musicians in a portable woven chair, one at each corner. The skin of his ancient face was wounded with an old brown smile, and the slow opening and closing of his worn teeth reminded Jay of the small machine, the tensioner, which he wished he had thought to bring along.

Behind the Boluses, and just in front of the Old Musicians, came Father Mount. He smiled and held his prize aloft. Mother Mount lifted Jay until his head was lost in the lower limbs of the twenty-year elms. But through the leaves he could see his father's prize: the bust in shining bronze of Tyrus Portman Bolus, Sr., hot in the sunlight. Jay smiled until his teeth ached, and a buttery, green-tasting leaf poked into his mouth on the breeze blowing up from the Old Music drifting past.

His mother squeezed his thighs. He could feel her arms trembling. He was nine years old and growing bigger, nearly too big to be lifted up anymore. He reached higher and grabbed the next limb and climbed away from his mother's hands. As he felt her cool fingers slipping off his feet, he noticed the other children higher up.

When he was twelve, Jay guided Freddie Blackhage down the road and lost him. They set out together on an overcast Saturday afternoon. Jay held the six-year-old Freddie by the hand; their arms swung. Freddie's older sister Norah reported the sight and substance of their going: the easy movement of the two connected arms, the sound of Freddie's small voice chippering up at Jay, calling out the names of things and Jay saying calmly, firmly, "No . . . no . . . no . . . no . . . ," while staring down at Freddie's head. Norah saw the clouds of insects gathering farther down the road, a willowy grayness forming in and out of almost human shapes.

The wind was from the northeast, out of Canada, running down the Bolusburgh Canal then straight through town and curving suddenly, caroming from the ocher brick facade of the ropeworks and heading west, following Wooden Miser Road and blowing up the backs of Jay and Freddie. Jay smelled the telltale smell of the northeast Canada wind, what his father said was the oily slick from dying lampreys stuck to the barges in the canal. It was heavy and sour, and drifted right to the edges of the cornfields that rustled softly south of Wooden Miser Road.

The low Ohio sky was silvery gray, like powder on the wings of a moth. They walked and walked. Freddie and Jay were seen together for the final time by one of the men from the ropeworks. He saw them three miles west of town, standing on the bridge where the road crossed over the east fork of the Jasper River. He said hello to them. The small boy raised his hand to wave, and the older boy went after it and caught it like an escaping bird. The man from the ropeworks clicked to his horse and it went across the bridge, shaking the planks and causing the seed and dust and pebbles to leap and fall. As the man rode farther away, the two boys watched the switching of the horse's tail and the rising of its flies. When the man was gone the boys began to walk again. On the western side of the bridge, where the corn continued, Jay turned from the road and Freddie followed. Into the corn they went, Freddie's shorter legs moving faster.

In the corn they wandered up and down the rows, across the rows, in and out among the stalks, the heavy leaning ears, the bending tassels. They went quietly, turning and turning, listening to the steady sigh that came from no particular direction. They peeled back husks and flicked the worms away with their fingernails and watched them sail like spit. They startled crows as big as turkeys, mean and yellow eyed. The crows flew slowly up and out of sight, but staring behind themselves and calling harshly underneath their wings. Jay found two ears of wormless corn and offered one to Freddie. Freddie took it silently and ate. One of his infant teeth came loose and stuck between the kernels. Jay dislodged the tooth and put it in his pocket to save for later. Freddie cried when he saw the streak of blood that stained his corn. Jay traded with him and ate that ear himself. After they were done he hurled the empty cobs above the tops of the stalks and heard them land, scattering crows.

In time they found a spot, a balding of the field where seed had failed to take. They sat crosslegged. Jay grew ever more certain, having brought the boy along, that they were friends now. They had come to this spot together, and Jay could feel how special it was. "This," he said to Freddie patiently, "this is Ohio. We are living here in Ohio. This good ground is the ground of Ohio, and we are Ohioans and we will never leave. This corn is Ohio corn, and it has a special taste. So many good things can happen here." Jay nodded over his words, considering the many good things. Freddie was quiet, small and hunched. His face was joyless and chalky with anxiety.

7

"Never leave?" he said.

Jay lay back, sighing, and stared at the sky, at collisions of sober grays, a rainless August glowering that promised only a swollenness of shade. He became contented and still. He lay and stared and listened to the hissing of the corn. Everything was mixed together, dreary and slow and lazy, as though falling from the clouds in an unanticipated arrival of Old Musicians whom Jay was finally hearing first. He swayed in his shallow trough of earth, and was completely alone because Freddie Blackhage had crept away.

Two days later Freddie was found in Glory Ledge Ravine. He was in a "condition of utter brokenness," according to Milan Mastergeorge, the physician, who would say nothing further except to the Blackhage family. But the party of searchers who had discovered the body would explain in hushed private that the boy had bent in the middle when lifted and had been determined thereafter to be bendable in hundreds of unnatural ways in the course of moving him home for the final time.

He had fallen from Glory Ledge, perhaps while wandering alone in the dark. And in voices touched with a curious modesty, people suggested again and again that a barrier should be erected there. And it was. But Glory Ledge was soon imbued with a morbid atmosphere that transformed it from a place of beauty and serenity to a haven for illicitness. No one with unimpeachable intentions ever went there except by accident. And even then persons encountering the anomalous fence would find themselves turned away without quite approaching, chilled by its presence there.

Finally, Jay, the only child of Fletcher and Corinne Mount, was seen in retrospect as a lifelong villain for having taken the Blackhage boy away from his home. His history of childhood oddity was made more powerfully cumulative by this act of neglect. "Never take a walk with Jay" became one of the anxious codes of the standard Bolusburgh upbringing. The saying implied a peril darker by far than that of "Stay away from Diamond Falls" and "Don't bother the ropeworks men" and "Don't ever let me catch you swimming in the canal." Even after Jay Fielding Mount had left Ohio, the use of his name continued in the general context of advising against any walk with any stranger.

But when Jay, on that watershed afternoon, sat back up in the cornless patch of cornfield and saw that Freddie Blackhage was gone, he searched until the nighttime came, weaving in and out of the corn and back and

8

forth along the banks of the east fork of the Jasper River. He was made especially uneasy by the feeling that the boy was not really lost but was only hiding from him instead. He cried and hollered and tantalized the darkening afternoon with blandishments shouted to the missing Freddie: of better and longer walks on brighter days, of the trading of prized possessions, of games to be played in vacant buildings and of the immediate return of the lost tooth. But Freddie heard these all with the nervous sensitivity of the hunted, backing away from a darkness in the voice itself, broken sounding and shot with phlegm; backing away from that darkness and into another that was accidental and unexpected. He had lost himself by moving away, and Jay had failed to find him. But in Jay's pocket remained the tooth that he would always keep, small and warm and white, the summary of something nearly had.

Ultimately, the shame of the Mount family was offered up to the town for expiation on a September afternoon in 1891, when Jay was whipped in public by his father under the nodding gaze of Tyrus Portman Bolus, Sr. The great strangeness of the event was accentuated by the phenomenon of Jay's cries of pain, which didn't escape his lungs until many long seconds after the striking of the lash. In these spaces of silence the onlookers of Bolusburgh were themselves breathless and ashamed. When the whipping was done, Jay went silently to Diamond Falls, where he lay in the sun and let his cuts be puckered by the heat.

His father, for the rest of his life, never heard the Old Music first again. And his mother began giving birth to Jay's brothers and sisters with a ferocious regularity that was aimed at diminishing the power of Jay and his place in the family's heart. The babies' crawling smallness filled the house with new horizons. The cramped rooms were stretched as they raised their faces, quizzing whitely for love. Thinking of Phantom and Canasta, Jay watched them and said not a word.

But his life went on.

He found himself a friend. The name of Jay's friend was Douglas, and he was more than forty years old—older, therefore, than Bolusburgh, which was younger than most of its citizens. Except for those hot summer days when the canal was rank, the town always smelled like something brand new, as though the wood of the clapboard houses hadn't quite fully cured and the plaster walls inside them hadn't yet absorbed enough of the atmosphere's must to give it back in the form of aging, stale secretions. Around evening the town often smelled like good fresh food of a fairly uniform kind that, from house to house, seemed to have sprung from a single agreeable recipe no one much cared to change.

Douglas had arrived in Bolusburgh on an evening in the fall when roasting chicken filled the air and sweetened it with the scent of softening rice and celery and nutmeg stuffing. He was brought by a black wagon driven by a religious man who was on his way to Missouri, which was known as a Methodist place. From where he sat he called up to the preacher, "I'll be getting off here."

The men from the ropeworks were walking past in the other direction, going home to supper in the Ropeville section of town. Some of them looked at Douglas like they knew for certain he'd be working next to them one morning soon. But he never was.

This had happened fourteen years before, and the twenty-year elms were just then beginning to give tiny circles of shade to Main Street. Jay was ten months old. Mother and Father Mount would lay him down on the oval rag rug and stand over him pouting and widening their eyes. Phantom and Canasta would come to sniff, pressing their cold black noses against his bare stomach, which he hardly seemed to notice. Lying there on his back, he moved like a slow swimmer confused about which direction to swim in. That particular evening, Mother and Father Mount looked up together and saw Douglas walking by on Erie Street in the dusk. He had a carpetbag and was observing everything carefully.

"A stranger," said Father Mount.

"He looks like a thief," said Mother Mount.

Both she and her husband immediately crouched down so the stranger wouldn't see them looking through the window at him. Jay picked this instant to sit up by himself for the first time without rolling over to do so. Because of the timing, the whole family bumped their heads together and the dogs ran off to their baskets. There was a lot of commotion, and Douglas heard it out on Erie Street.

Douglas was tall and narrow framed and unusual in his habits. Wherever anyone went in Bolusburgh, Douglas was liable to be there, watching but never speaking. He showed no sign of reacting to what he saw, and people often said that this, second only to his bodily stink, was the thing that made them most uneasy about him—the feeling that he was percolating terrible thoughts while standing as nearly inert as something growing slowly in the damp between the knuckles of the willow roots that crept across the towpath. If he gave an impression of menace at first, his stillness kept the menace from blooming. People finally just looked away and went on about their business.

When in motion, Douglas neither walked nor ran. He crept. He crept without shame, with each foot meeting the dust at the very tip of its shoe's toe, his ankles and knees like liquid and his progress much like floating. Up and down the forthright streets of Bolusburgh he made only the smallest of abrasions; grit whispered beneath his tread.

Moving against the sides of buildings, he darkened windows as he passed with his arms out crucifixion-style, fingertips and heel of palm caressing panes of glass. And, like the end of an eclipse, his wake brought a freshened breeze that stood the curtains out and slammed the doors in upstairs rooms. Neuralgias flared and diminished. Objects lost were found, and things forgotten were remembered.

But if he had a salubrious role to play in the life of Bolusburgh, it went both unacknowledged and unappreciated. And if there were a soul in Bolusburgh charitable enough to entertain the thought of asking Douglas home for chicken dinner, that thought perished as soon as the asker entered the wide orbit of Douglas's stench—a breathing up of the very deepest odors. These hovered about him constantly like the memory of life's most dreadful meals and bitterest disappointments. Even in repose his face was never fully released from this ripeness; on his worst days his mouth was curled at the corners and his eyes were creased from cringing. Some people found this expression poignant because it suggested he was able to smell himself and find himself no less disagreeable than others did.

He was made more noxious in the heat. On hot August afternoons he competed with the worst the canal could offer. On such days his creep subsided to a shuffle as he sought some quiet place to hide. He would move away from Bolusburgh like an exile. On his way to the edge of town he was watched from behind windows that—even in such heat—remained closed until he was out of sight. The trees at Glory Ledge enfolded him in their listlessness as he leaned against their trunks. He became quieted in the wrapping of leaves, breathing less, almost sleeping, the smell drawn back inside.

This was Douglas's condition on the day he was found by Jay Fielding

11

Mount, the boy having followed him to Glory Ledge. Jay watched patiently as the branches closed around the man like wings and the eyelids drifted shut. In that moment of ease Jay could feel that Glory Ledge was sighing. Only then did he dare to come out from his concealment, creeping softly in a flattering imitation of the man (of whom he had already made a distant, long-term study), creeping like the smaller shadow apprenticed to the larger one—which suddenly cracked open its waxy left eye and regarded the boy who watched him.

"Hello," said Jay. "I believed you were asleep."

Jay smiled and Douglas smiled back. The branches parted at Glory Ledge and out he came. As the man stepped forward, Jay saw his hands were shaking and his eyes were wet.

At times that summer Douglas would be seen with his arm draped across the shoulders of his acolyte, whispering what were presumed to be nauseating things as the two of them crept through town in unison, the boy carefully scrutinized by Bolusburghians for signs that he was secretly revolted to be so close to Douglas. But the boy would turn his face to the face of his older friend, and only a fraction of distance remained between them as Jay uttered some nauseating thing of his own and the two of them laughed. Bolusburgh grimaced in Jay's behalf— after all, he was one of their own by birth—and observed as summer turned into autumn how the skin eruptions spread across his face like nature's vengeance.

They went everywhere together. Douglas would accompany Jay to Glory Ledge and wait just beyond the fence while Jay climbed down into the ravine and stood at the spot where Freddie Blackhage landed. When Jay climbed back up to the top, his face would be red and his lips pressed thin against each other. Douglas would help him scale the fence, a help that was not unnecessary because Jay's movements after climbing up the ledge were jerky, as though his muscles were angry.

Sometimes they sat in silence at Diamond Falls, bathed in the rush of cool air that flowed along the surface of the water. Mother Mount would be up in the ferns, watching for signs of the vanished softness to settle again upon her boy, and seeing nothing but his sharpness. His head would turn and his eyes, catching some flash of motherly color brightening out of the shadows back up the ridge, would nail her in the greenery. Or she, anyway, would feel that this was so, taking the fixity of his gaze as proof that he was seeing something more than shaded vegetation. He was seeing her, and she drew herself down deeper in the ferns.

She watched the other one—the lunatic—sit shirtless in the bowl of Orchid Rock and bounce on his haunches like a boy on a wooden horse. Mother Mount laced her fingers like a sling beneath her swollen belly and palpated its tautness for the feel of something moving. She was growing her fourth child, but still watching her first. Douglas wagged his head, and she watched his ragged, graying hair beating back and forth.

She remembered that she once had seen him take a living cicada between his teeth and, by squeezing gently, play its keening like an instrument. She remembered the final squeeze that broke the bug—how Douglas grinned and spat and how the cluster of witnesses turned away from the pulpy orange smear of his teeth. This was when Jay was very little. And now he and that man were friends. It made her sick, and she felt her belly move.

But she stayed where she was until the smell of Douglas finally reached her, somewhat softened in the coolness. Then she snuck back through the ferns and across the meadow to home. In the window of his workshed she saw Father Mount in profile, holding up an object that, by the familiar low-browed squint of his perplexity, she could tell he had not yet mastered well enough to begin repairing. She heard her babies chattering inside the shed with Father Mount. She believed he could keep them safe in the zone of his aptitude for repairing things. They would grow up seeing wrong made right, and that was the finest lesson they could learn.

When Jay turned seventeen, Douglas had been dead for nearly a month. His death was a terrible accident objected to by almost no one. Even Jay now seemed to feel little more than an ache of loneliness. The lightning bolt should have claimed him, too.

The episode had been swift, instantaneous and total. There was nothing anyone could have done. In the aftermath there were only ashes surrounding something solid and small, which was then removed. Over Bolusburgh, the guilty sky floated past, dark and dry and bruised. The sudden vacuum was filled with nervous whistling as people regarded the spot where the accident had taken place.

In the public imagination, the occasion of Douglas's death had been so often longed for—never in great detail, exactly, but always with the generalized hope of someday being without him. The future would be one of uninterrupted clarity, of shadowless days, of nevermore finding oneself downwind of his smell or caught in his unblinking gaze. The possibility stayed vaguely in the back of many minds, like the hope for a cure to a minor ache that can be endured but that still causes too much waking restlessness and fitful sleep to be forgotten entirely.

When Douglas's death actually came, a long-sought flatness swept through town and stayed. In a single instant the probabilities of life in Bolusburgh were refigured and all the rhythms restored to an evenness. The air itself changed, becoming less complicated.

In his office at the ropeworks, Tyrus Portman Bolus, Sr., saw the flash and heard the thunder simultaneously. He turned to the open window and said to himself, "By God, but that was close!" And when the flash was drawn back into the sky, the changed air flooded his office with its new consistency—thinner and simpler—and the light of day took on a gracious dimness. He breathed it all in, breathing easier, and was entirely satisfied.

"Yes," he laughed, "yes, that was *close* . . ."

It was better than close; it was perfect. Jay had been twenty feet from Douglas when the lightning struck, and the collateral energy had thrown him outward from the point of the blast, which was more or less the top of Douglas's head. Jay's last awareness was of the overwhelming smell that rode the shock wave like a helpless projectile. It was the signature of Douglas's end, himself released.

After that, Jay lay unconscious, covered with a fuzzy, crackling aura that danced on his skin and was the splintered offspring of the main force that had struck his friend. The aura went away, leaving tiny red lightning-shaped burns on his flesh.

In a matter of days the burns faded, but he lived the following weeks as if he were an empty barrel. He was speechless and apparently thoughtless. He heard nothing but hollow cracking sounds, as though the bones of his ears were being broken over and over again, opening fissures out of which the air was released in periodic bursts.

Milan Mastergeorge, physician, could only shake his head. For days he monitored the patient's condition, recording strange machinelike cadences in all the body processes. Taking the pulse, he felt a force that

14

was less like the beating of a heart than like the sharp reciprocations of an engine, each stroke bulging beneath his heavy fingers like a small explosion. Placing his vegetoid ear alongside Jay's slackened mouth, he heard the puzzling rush of air that was unlike any breathing. As he listened, he felt Jay's shiny eyes just floating there beside him, and he felt how utterly empty they were, identical silver coins. Slowly he turned and met them with his own eyes and regarded the wonderful cleanness of the look, the bleached echo of an adolescent gaze, struck pure by residues of the flash that killed the other man. As a doctor he knew this rule so well: what kills can also cure. Electrical force was full of mystery. One time it stood your hair on end, another time it knocked you flat, and still another time it killed you. Maybe the boy would be changed for the better. A bubble of appreciation formed between the doctor's lips. With tenderness he touched Jay's cheek, and a hissing sound arose from the windpipe.

"Boy," he said quietly, "you sound like a damn contraption . . . I've done all I can do. Now maybe your half-wit father can fix you." With that, snapping shut his case, Milan Mastergeorge stood and left the room.

Jay sat on the chair, next to the chair where the doctor had sat, and listened to his ears break. The lightning struck again and again, like waves. It was loud and perfect every time, and Jay wilted away in its brightness. The ugly smell seemed to burst inside him like a sac, releasing gas to vent through his breaking ears. He sat there with his arms dangling, and his slow fingers played chords in the air just above the floorboards. Once again there was Old Music, and his empty eyes filled up for the vanished dead: two old dogs, a broken boy and a lout. His insides flowed out into the room.

In bed one night two weeks later, Jay heard his father coming down the hall. The door opened slowly. In the shallow light from the lamp he carried, Father Mount's face was scared. But he came to the edge of the bed and softly touched Jay's shoulder. Jay lay still and stared at the ceiling, where a single spidery crack in the plaster had recently been flashing down to the bed.

"You come with me," said Father Mount, taking hold of Jay's bicep like a handle and leading him out of bed. They went down through the dark house and into the yard out back. The crickets paused. Jay waited while his father unlatched the workshed door and lit the lamps inside. When the wicks were right, his father beckoned to him. When Jay didn't come, his father patiently fetched him and ushered him in.

"Sit there on the bench," said Father Mount. "Go on, hop up." A place had been cleared in the clutter of parts. Jay did as he was told. Father Mount stood back and stared at his son and nodded. He peered through slitted eyes. Jay, staring back, could see that his father was preparing to make good on something, an old unspoken promise.

"Don't move, young Jay," said Father Mount. "I think I know your trouble, and I'm going to try to fix you up."

The workshed glowed, and Jay stayed just as still as a large machine. He set his eyes on the rows of wooden-handled tools that leaned from racks on the opposite wall. And he listened to his father's delicate whisper, which was like a prayer uttered over the dead or nearly dead. The lips were very close to Jay's ear, and the sound was full of hope for the quickening of certain mysteries. Then he felt his father's arms as they slowly wrapped around his shoulders and began to squeeze with a force that warped his ribs and took his breath away until the glowing of the workshed blotted out to blistering pins of light, like insects winking off to sleep. And Jay could feel the magic working, making him almost as good as new—as good as his father could want him to be.

In the morning Jay awakened in his bed. He felt much improved. The room was quiet and the air was changed. The terrible smell was gone. Through the open window he heard his father's hammer striking something iron, and he heard his mother singing to the babies, the babies singing back like birds. Getting dressed, he put on the nicest clothes he could find, which were black pants and a red shirt with a belt that was brown and shoes that were brown. He had the wonderful urge to go outside and walk through town, to find some people and let them know how different he'd become. He left without telling anyone. Going through the gate in front of the house on Erie Street, he did not creep. He put his foot down heel first, then flat, and then the other foot, and so forth, until he began to run. It was a warm spring day in Bolusburgh, and the people stopped what they were doing just to watch him running past. He was having a good time.

* * *

16

But by the time Jay turned eighteen, Bolusburgh had died in his heart, as though its glaze of likeability washed away in the rain one afternoon. A powerful energy took him over, filled him with movement and sent him walking in anger. The simplest, most familiar sights were difficult. A tree: he decided he detested it, and his stomach agreed, frothing and bloating until he turned his eyes away from the limp, disgusting leaves. He cast his angry thoughts down upon the street like bones, marching everywhere alone and muttering as his feet slid back and forth beneath his lowered gaze. He was watched and he was worried over. Mothers held their children, and fathers, knowing all they needed to know about the mysteries of anger, held their tongues when they saw his eyes.

He threw dirt at clothing hanging on a line; earth struck two shirts like a breeze and made them flutter dirtily. A dog brought a stick to him and dropped it at his feet; he pretended to throw the stick for the dog, and when the dog ran after the phantom toss, suddenly there was the stick hitting its head. The dog squealed and kept running.

Jay walked past Goodspeed Normal School and listened unmoved to the slamming of desks and the blowing of whistles. Paul Pilers, Health Instructor, stood in the midst of two dozen hopping children and held a ball beyond their reach. Looking down at the children, he turned in a circle and grinned, spreading disappointment. Miss Dawkins leaned from her window, wearing black, and studied the scene of the children playing. Jay stopped and threw a stone. It was a very good throw, since the stone struck the ball and tipped it into the throng of screaming children. Miss Dawkins turned her head and noticed Jay. He almost waved at her. Then she called to Paul Pilers and pointed. Paul Pilers, making fists and pumping his forearms, stalked slowly in Jay's direction. Jay ran around the corner, half sideways like a dog, and knocked things over in his wake. Some children cried, some children laughed. Miss Dawkins moaned, and Paul Pilers chased as far as the edge of the schoolyard.

Along the towpath the barges lay empty, riding high and bobbing easy. Bales of hemp and large wooden spools of finished rope waited in the sun. Tired for the moment of walking in anger, Jay dangled his legs in the soupy canal. His feet disappeared in the murk. He suffered the unseen attentions of slippery things bumping against his feet. He didn't much care what they were, and he was even vaguely happy that his feet were there to be bumped. For a while, then, he just sat.

The day was warm and quiet, and from the belly of one of the barges he heard the sounds of a man and woman doing noisily something that, by the silent example of his father and mother, he knew was meant to be private and soundless (except that sometimes, by accident, there might be a sound). It was probably a man from the ropeworks and a woman from another town. Mother Mount said there was a town like that not far away from Bolusburgh. Jay felt bad about listening, but he couldn't help himself. So he sat there and wondered what it looked like, violently shaking his head at each conjecture as though he was mad at himself for even thinking.

Then, all of a sudden, he heard it—worse than ever—filled with terrible sorrow and remorse, arriving earlier than ever, arriving a whole two weeks before it would have been time to stretch the white linen banner and wash the cobblestones that began where the towpath ended.

There was no mistaking the sound. As soon as he heard it, Jay was on his feet and running, his still-wet bare soles smacking the cobbles that were hot and sometimes sharp. Twice he stubbed his toe on the granite curbing but kept on going, running along the bricks of the Main Street sidewalk until he dashed up the steps of Bolus Hall where, bursting indoors, he startled his former classmate, Jerry Bolus, who was now an apprentice clerk in the Office of Deeds and was carrying a ledger across the lobby.

"Where your shoes, hey?" Jerry Bolus cried to cover up his fright. But Jay ran up the spiral iron stairs on which he left a little blood from his injured toe whose big pink nail was torn half off.

At the top he reached for the length of rope that hung from a hole in the ceiling, and he rang the big bell that announced the Old Music. He rang it until the people came running. Through the window he watched them come, and smiled to see it. They ran past Bolus Hall straight down to the end of the towpath. There was shouting all over the building. Below him he saw Jerry Bolus and two of his older brothers rushing out of the lobby with the banner. They were having trouble not wrapping themselves up in it. He heard one of the secretary ladies shouting that "someone should get to the ropeworks and fetch the old man."

Jay held the rope and let the weight of the bell lift him off the floor and set him back down again. Finally he allowed it to stop. Then he ran downstairs and into the street and back to the canal in time to see the barge with the Old Musicians drifting in to tie up.

The music they played was truly sad. Jay recognized the tune as "Hog Goes Flying Up To Heaven," something his father sometimes sang in the shed. The Old Musicians played while some of the people helped to tie them up and the rest sang along, adding the words to the music.

> *Hog goes fly . . . ing up to hea . . . ven*
> *Hog goes fly . . . ing up to hea . . . ven*
> *Hog goes fly . . . ing up to hea . . . ven*
> *Wipe the knife and see him gone.*

The song went on like that for dozens of verses, all the same except for the one last line in every verse. Everyone knew how it went and in what order. Jay sang too. He looked around the crowd and saw his father and mother at the back edge with the babies. He could tell his father was waiting to learn who had heard the Old Music first and rung the bell. Jay was so proud of the moment that would come as soon as the music ended. They would all have to wait for Mr. Bolus. Jay cupped his hands together at his waist to practice how he would hold the prize, the little bronze bust that his father had said got smaller every year, just like its model. Jay could already feel the heaviness, but he decided he would try to hold it up now and then the way his father had always done when the parade was going through town.

The music ended just as Mr. Bolus arrived. He was carried by some of the ropeworks men—Jay heard people near him say they carried him roughly, but they all seemed to be smiling. They seated him in his woven chair, and after he'd adjusted himself he called out the ritual question: "Who heard these people coming, I wonder?"

Jay was nervous, but he stepped forward through the crowd toward Mr. Bolus and said as loud as he could the ritual answer: "I did, sir!" Mr. Bolus looked at Jay for a minute and then said something Jay hadn't heard before in the ritual. "Okay, kid," he said, and then jerked his head to one of his sons, not Jerry but Clive, short for Clivus, who handed Jay the prize. Jay held it up and turned in a circle, grinning. There was some fluttery whispering before the crowd began to break up, at which point Tyrus Bolus, Sr., said quickly, "Let the parade commence!" which was part of the ritual. Jay thought a lot had been cut out—some of the formal remarks about having "ears like a rabbit" and "legs like a deer" and "a heart for the good Old Music." But he didn't care; he figured it was all because everyone had been caught unprepared. Except him.

His father came over and patted his shoulder. There was a funny look in his eye, but Jay didn't have time to think about it because the music struck up right then and the Bolus sons lifted the corners of their father's chair and stepped off up Main Street. The Old Musicians played "Our Old Canal Brings Everything," the special Bolusburgh anthem they had written for the town so many years before. The tune was lazy and dark like the water, and you could only march very slowly to it. Jay had a little difficulty matching his pace to the music. He had to take a step with one foot and sort of tremble to a stop before taking the other step. After a while it struck him that the thing to do was creep. The music lent itself to creeping. He hadn't crept in over a year, but that's what he began to do, sending his feet out like insect feelers and slowly planting a toe in the soft dust between the hard cobbles. Creeping felt good save for the pain in his nail. For the first time in a long while, he thought about Douglas.

Behind him Jay could feel the instruments swaying back and forth. The deep drumbeat thundered into his back; he noticed how it seemed to make his shirt quiver. He thought he could almost lean back against the beat, and he did just that, the backward slant of his body sharpened even more by the creeping.

On either sidewalk he heard spectators hissing as he crept along. He found it difficult to keep the rhythm going and still hold the bust in both hands. So he hooked the head between his right upper arm and ribcage, finding it most comfortable if he could wedge his muscle in where the jaw of the thing narrowed to neck just before the base. He did that and heard still more hissing. The people were displeased with him, but he decided he didn't really care. He felt fine, and the music carried him along. The face of the bust looked down upon the cobbles.

Up ahead of Jay, in his woven chair with his sons at the corners, Tyrus Portman Bolus, Sr., flopped his head from side to side in time with the music. Once, finally, the head failed to reappear above the back of the chair. Jay thought the old man had fallen asleep, but it turned out he was dead. The traditional picnic had to be canceled, but the Old Musicians played on for days. They stayed until after the funeral.

* * *

Jay left Bolusburgh when the Old Musicians were finished there. He followed them, learning their mannered scornfulness and their casual treatment of the music they played. These attitudes shocked Jay at first, but he slowly accepted them. The Old Musicians helped the process along by paying him hardly any attention except in public. When they were not out in public, they told him they didn't care beans if he came with them or not. But when they were performing, they made extravagant displays of their high regard for his having heard them first. Jay's confusion over these two extremes of behavior finally gave way to the view that much of life amounted to elaborate pretending. As badly as he wanted to think the Old Musicians were only pretending to be indifferent to him, he knew that wasn't true. They were always reminding him how well they'd gotten along without him before they met him. Jay would say, "I know, I know" in a way that made them say it again and take him by the shoulder and show him how he'd stacked the instrument cases wrong. "I know, I know," he'd say, and it would just go on like this until everyone tired of the game.

They were players and professionals, and they made him earn his place with them by carrying and fetching. Apart from occasional spells of awkwardness and puzzlement, he was able to carry and fetch very well. When they played at the funeral of Tyrus Portman Bolus (1809–1897), Jay was useful in several ways. He helped to carry the instruments to the graveyard. And between the playing of "O, Take Him To Your Big Safe Arms" and "Gone Away So Sadly," he helped by shaking the spit from one of the tubas.

So he went where the Old Musicians went, slowly westward from town to town. He learned all over again, in his new pretending way, how to moan and sway and crinkle his eyes, and do it without really carin' anything about the tired old tunes that, despite himself, he conti to love.

The Old Musicians traveled in three big wagons. Jay w find out that they didn't go everywhere in barges and ' unsuitable for going most everyplace but Bolusb fact, that when the Old Musicians came to B' was stash their wagons a couple of miles u to the towpath, leaving an old man to t' thieves. As with everything else Jay lea these practicalities scrubbed away at the special delight he had always taken in the coming of the Old Musicians (who, as Jay slowly realized, were not even especially old).

In truth, he also had trouble accepting the fact that the Old Musicians visited other places at all. Until he had actually gone along with them to a few other towns, a Bolusburghian jealously lingered. Finally, though, he came to feel himself allied with the Old Musicians more than with his old town. And as the weeks went by, he found that he joined the Old Musicians in their private amusement at the depth of feeling they aroused from town to town. Now and then, however, being so new to scorn, he would laugh too loudly in the wrong place or at the wrong time, and earn himself a sharp look, a cuff to the head or a day of short rations. But he never complained, and he was always just as ashamed of himself as it was hoped he would be. Though sometimes if he moped for too long, one of the Old Musicians would have to come over and put a hand on his shoulder.

"Cheer up, kid," the Old Musician would say. "Just think how bad you'd feel if you was still stuck back there in B-burgh."

And that was true. He remembered how happy he had felt when the barge started to move away from town. He stood at the stern and waved at his father, who'd come to see him off. Father Mount walked along the towpath for a while, squinting in the bright morning sun and saying nothing, so Jay had to stop waving and, in fact, began to think that maybe his father would follow him everywhere and never let him go. But eventually Father Mount stopped walking and then turned back toward Bolusburgh. Jay watched him get smaller and smaller and smaller until, as the barge went around a gentle curve, all he could see was the left sleeve of his father's white shirt, that gleaming whiteness broken at the bicep by the black armband worn in memory of Mr. Bolus.

And that was that. Jay was ready for the world. He turned around and sat down on the deck with his legs folded around the old carpetbag that had once belonged to Douglas. He opened it up and looked inside. He plunged his hands into its depths and moved them around among all the cherished possessions he had decided to take from Ohio. He closed his eyes and felt the textures of all these things, and the difficulty of telling where one left off and another began. They all belonged to him. His hands went deeper until, at the very bottom of the bag, they found the bronze bust of Tyrus Portman Bolus, Sr., and extracted it and set it down on the deck. When he looked at the bust shining there in the sunlight, at the sharp and delicately wizened details of its face, he was exhilarated to feel that his years of formative youth were done.

From that point on, he belonged to something else. He looked up and saw the Old Musicians staring at him. He decided that what he saw in their eyes was a heartfelt congratulation. He stared back at them, smiling, until one by one they looked away.

A month later they abandoned him in Fort Wayne, Indiana.

2

ON A TYPICAL DAY
IN FORT WAYNE

On a typical day in Fort Wayne, J. Fielding Mount began by coming home from work. He worked all night in the asphalt shingle factory up in North Fort Wayne piling grit upon moving screens and carrying heavy loads around. Asphalt shingles were the newest thing in building materials. Everyone wanted them. Men came off the streets to watch the houses going up. They left their friends or families standing on the sidewalks or the gatepaths and they approached the stacks of shingles lying in the sun, running their fingers across the smooth-yet-rough texture of these new things. For a moment they were entranced and silent, openmouthed and thoughtful. "What're these here?" they asked. They bent over and smelled them, smelled the sharp, sweet creosote and felt the warmth coming off the grit. "Them're shingles, mister," someone always barked in a way that expressed how much work there was to do and how little time there was for answering questions like that, how little patience for laymen's fascinations with a novelty already worn thin amongst the tradesmen. "In five years there won't be no other kind."

There was always a job open in North Fort Wayne. Even two twelve-hour shifts a day weren't enough to keep up with the business. They were always looking for new men to replace the older, slower men, the men who got sick of the smell or collapsed on the job, the men who drank, the men who complained, the men who refused to do enough work, and the men who couldn't carry a hundred-pound weight fifty yards without stumbling or dropping the load.

To get hired you only had to see Mr. Amory Malmsborn, the son of the owner. He would ask your name and age, weigh you on the big scales and turn his back on you and then spin around real fast, leaping and screaming, trying to scare you to see if your nerves were shot. Then he asked you to take down your pants and cough and to spell New Jersey or say who was president. If you could do most of these things, and if you were heavy enough and not too jittery, then the job was yours. Ten dollars a week to start, which was not bad except that you had to give back a dollar every Monday to cover the rental of your safety gear: a pair of long-cuffed gloves, a pair of gaiters, and a leather collar to keep your neck from being spattered with hot tar. But after you showed you were okay, then they let you have the stuff for free. About a month, say. That was considered to be your first raise. Amory Malmsborn himself came and gave the dollar back to you with a big smile. "What's your name, man?" he asked, and then, before you quite answered him, said, "Okay, fine." He walked away smiling and patted someone else on the back or shoulder and swung his arms around to suggest that work that had never even stopped should start again. Then he went and weighed some more new men.

J. Fielding Mount was doing all right. He'd been there for about two months. Mr. Clement Norman—the supervisor, known as Mr. Clem— noticed right away that Mount would do almost anything. And Mr. Clem valued a willing worker. At first they had Mount cleaning the mixing tanks, which was something the new men were assigned. The older new men were always glad to see a fresh new man arrive since it meant that someone didn't have to clean the tanks anymore. Mount wore a wet rag tied around his nose and mouth and went down into the tanks with a scraper. Another man watched from the catwalks above and set up a holler if Mount passed out. Then a couple of other workers would run and pull him up by a rope that was tied underneath his armpits. After the fifth time Mount was rescued, Mr. Clem decided to give him another job. This was too bad since Mount had been much more thorough than anyone else, even right up to the instant he passed out with a hollow bonging sound. He pushed himself to the limit. In some of the tanks you could see the copper shine again after ages of nothing but rough black crust.

Once they'd gotten Mount out of the tank, the men would carry him unconscious into Mr. Clem's office, lay him on the floor in the corner and leave him be. He stayed out for about five minutes. Then someone would walk by or just happen to look over, and there he'd be, standing at the door looking out at everyone through the glass, eyes glazed and smiling like a drunk. The smell of the tanks affected your brain for a short time after—some men had even gone and committed crimes the next day and said they didn't know why. Mr. Clem had also noticed a change in the pitch of a man's voice, which seemed to get higher the longer he stayed in a tank. So he made a rule that no one could stay in a tank for more than five minutes—someone was supposed to blow a whistle. It was part of Mr. Clem's job not to sicken a good worker if he could help it, though he tried on purpose to wear down the ones who drank.

But Mount was doing okay. He came on time and gave good value for the money he was paid. Except for being solitary, he had no moods as far as Mr. Clem could see. He didn't talk or joke, and no one seemed to be his friend. He took his meal break away from the rest, stretched out on a wagon piled with bags of grit. Mr. Clem noticed that if you walked near him while he was eating, he would shield his food from sight as though there was something shameful about it. All Mr. Clem could think was that Mount was eating mice or muskrats or something scavenged from the brush. But what a man ate or how he acted when he ate it was none of his business. As long as it didn't interfere with the job. Except for the thing with the food, Mr. Clem wished he had more men like Mount.

When the shift ended, J. Fielding Mount would stand in the gravel yard at the foot of the factory steps as his fellow workers surged past and climbed aboard the big flatbed wagons that would carry them—along with braces of still-cooling shingles—into the center of Fort Wayne, from there to return with the men of the day shift. Because the wagons rolled at a speed not very much faster than a man could walk, and because there was sometimes rough competition for the space already taken up by the load of shingles, Mount preferred to go home on foot.

He would wait in the darkness until the wagons were out of sight, until the light from the swaying lanterns—hung on poles at the wagons' corners—no longer crazed the trees and fields with leaping shadows. He would wait until he couldn't hear his fellow workers anymore. Once there was darkness again and quiet, Mount would set out along the road, moving away from the warmth and light of the factory building and the thick, sweet smell of asphalt. It was like sailing away from a shore, and, in his very first steps, Mount often felt the tingle of an adventure.

Walking home from work, he took the long way. At the start of his walk it was always still dark—often pitch black like the sides of a dirty mixing tank—and there was no one around but cats. He couldn't always see the cats, but he could hear them and feel them there in the bushes of the yards of the old dark homes along Oberdine Avenue. Sometimes he heard their feet running fast across the wide verandas, one cat after another like members of a tribe. He grew to hate them because he couldn't see them and yet was sure they were very near him. He believed there were some he had never seen, and he hated these the most. One time he stepped right on a cat that was sleeping; it was like a soft, squealing mush, and the sound it made almost stopped his heart. He vaguely thought other cats might have put this sleeping one in his path, that there was something deliberate going on. For the next few days he stuck to the other side of the street, but there were just as many cats over there, some of them probably the very same ones.

On Oberdine Avenue, on still nights, he could sometimes hear the sounds people made when they were sleeping. In summer all the windows were left open. Mount stopped to listen now and then, not always sure what he was hearing—whether the watery sound of feet swishing under sheets was really that or only something else, like the sleeping flutter of a caged canary. All that prevented him from sitting down on the grass and the knuckle roots under a tree were the cats he knew were always following. Up in a window one time he saw a woman's silver hair above a shadowed face. He couldn't make the face out, but the hair moved back and forth in a rhythm, as though the woman was singing or listening to someone else's singing. But when Mount couldn't hear a song he stopped listening and moved on. He decided on second thought that it hadn't been a woman at all, only a white wig hanging from an unseen cord. The woman whose wig it was was someplace else, in bed in another room with a small dog asleep between her feet, the dog's fisty head across one of her shinbones. He could almost feel how light the dog was, almost as light as the wig, and probably the same color. What a good dog, he thought. What a good dog to sleep so soundly and stay inside the house.

Those times when Mount stopped, the cats also stopped. He won-

27

dered why they paid him so much attention. It was almost as though they waited on purpose for him to come along. He hated them, and he wished they would just sleep quietly on the porches or crawl through the diamond-shaped spaces in the latticework beneath. He would rather not be followed. It was that simple. Sometimes he turned without warning and stared back into the darkness. He could feel all the little low eyes stopping, eyes that if something was shining in them would shine back unnatural orange or yellow and would not blink. He moved his head back and forth like an angry teacher; his hands were on his hips. The cats were waiting. Slowly a clock bonged six in one of the houses, each of the strokes like pudding—thick, dark and shuddering. Then Mount turned again, using the clock as though it had spoken for him, as though it had said enough to put things in their place, and he walked away from the unseen cats.

The farther he went on Oberdine Avenue, the more he heard the river up ahead. That was the Saint Joseph, the Saint J. If he went all the way on Oberdine, he would come to the river and have to stop. He could look, but that was it. The river. Down close to it, Oberdine got small and shiny, browner, softer, wetter . . . where the river sometimes squeezed up into the tracks and polished everything smoother. The road finally lost control and just went down very steeply and was gone—no road anymore—eaten by the quiet left-to-right of the brown water going straight into town.

But before Mount reached the end of Oberdine, he took the right turn onto Stiffney Street, which ran parallel to the river. He noticed that he seemed to hear the river louder the lighter the sky would get, as though there gradually came to be more space for the sound to spread out in. On Stiffney Street the houses were smaller, closer together and set right next to the road. There were dogs on Stiffney Street instead of cats. But the dogs never bothered Mount. Two or three would sometimes walk him up the street a little ways and then turn back. He liked best the small round dog with the big lump on its hip. As it hopped around his ankles Mount could feel the hot breath on his socks or up his cuffs. He tried to remember always to carry pebbles in his pockets, and he would drop them one by one on the head of the small round dog with the lump. It seemed to enjoy that. Mount named it Tiny. The other dogs were jealous and tried to get in front of Tiny, but Mount would only drop pebbles on him.

On upper Stiffney Street as the sun was rising, he stopped by some of the houses and stared in the windows at the furniture. He liked the way the light was at that hour, how it slowly brought out only half the color in the fabrics that covered the fat sofas and chairs. He could see in without even standing on tiptoes. Sometimes he let his nose touch the cold glass, then his forehead and a little bit of his hair. He closed his eyes and opened them; the furniture was empty. He liked the peacefulness of empty rooms. There was something nice about a thing not being used. Even a clock. When he looked at a clock he deliberately ignored the hands. His mother used to go around the house in Bolusburgh just touching things, not using them but putting her hands on them and sliding her fingers slowly across or around them with her eyes closed, sighing or humming, pretending she was not aware of the boy there watching.

She would pick something up and look inside it, blow in it, squint as dust came out, then touch her cheek against it. "Don't look, Jay," his father said sometimes. "Don't look." But he and his father both looked, and his mother could go on like that for a long time until she finally broke something, dropped it, leaned too hard against it, squeezed it, bent it backward, sent a small piece rolling across the floor. Then she would look at Father Mount and shake her head, blinking like someone waking up. "Can you fix it, Fletch?" she'd say to him. "You know I'll try," he always said. Then Mother Mount would go and take her nap, and his father would take the broken thing out to the workshed, where it would remain until it was fixed.

On Stiffney Street Mount hardly ever saw anything broken. The rooms were filled with delicate objects, always there in their places—never missing. The house in Bolusburgh had various empty spaces from which things were absent—one day one thing, the next day another. Occasionally Father Mount took an object outside just to let it sit in the sun awhile. "We'll like it better when I bring it back in," he told Jay when Jay asked him why he'd done it. And Mount recalled it was true he felt better when a broken thing was fixed and returned to its place. From this he learned that nothing was ruined forever. And whatever went away, with only a few exceptions, came back.

Even his mother came down from her naps with a new kind of look on her face, her gray eyes brighter and quicker moving and the black hair settled closer to her temples, not floating in space so much—even now Mount couldn't completely explain the changes he would see in her. But when Father Mount came in from the workshed, he always went over to her and touched her slowly and thoughtfully, the way, it seemed to Jay, his mother touched the things around the house that, finally, she sometimes broke. "Don't look now, Jay," she would say. "Go stare out the window at the street."

But he always watched everything they did. Mother Mount would sit there in her favorite chair as Father Mount's hands went up her shoulders, her neck, the sides of her head, then down the back of her head and the knobs of her spine, down to the seat of the chair. She smiled carelessly. Her mouth would slide open and her lips lose their usual shape. She seemed so happy. He never saw her teeth except at times like this when they would shine wet at first and then dry slowly in the open air until they were finally dull and big. "My father and mother," Jay would think, watching their two faces—his tall and serious, hers soft and falling toward the open collar of her dress.

Then Jay would go to the window and see if there was anyone in sight on Erie Street. He sometimes wanted to call people in to see them, to watch his mother and father the way he watched them, and to test whether others would understand his parents the way he understood them. But Erie Street was quiet and empty. Jay felt they were all alone. He turned away from the window.

On Stiffney Street he never saw another living person. He expected to look through a window one day and see someone looking back angrily, perhaps two people starting to move toward their door to come after him. Instead of seeing people he heard them. Sometimes he heard a door closing, water running, or a toilet emptying. These people were beginning the day Mount was already ending. When he started to hear their waking sounds he would move away from the houses and go to the middle of Stiffney Street, walking in plain view and at a purposeful pace like a man who has nothing to hide. Anyone seeing him from an upstairs window would hardly have given him a second thought—a solitary man out early.

The thing he feared the most was the chance of finding a baby in the bushes, a baby in a wicker basket crying with a blue blanket wrapped around it. What would he do? Would he walk right past? The newspapers carried these stories all the time. Poor people, unmarried girls, people down on their luck—they brought their babies to nicer neighborhoods and left them in the bushes. They hoped nice people would take the baby in and give it a better chance in life. What they should have known was that most of the time the baby was given over to the French Sisters who ran the Catholic orphanage in Churubusco.

Mount figured that since he was out the earliest, he was likely to find the baby first. What would he do? Would the baby be sick or healthy? What would he feed it? (At home he had oatmeal, sour milk, a loaf of bread, a pound of raisins, two lemons and an egg.) With the exception of the people who gave the babies they found to the French Sisters' orphanage, Mount believed the law said that if you found the baby you had to take care of it, and if you did a bad job they could put you in jail until you either paid for its youth or the baby was old enough to care for itself. And if you found the baby, picked it up and looked at it but then put it back where you had found it, you were liable to be charged with the same law of abandonment that forbade the mother to leave her own child in the bushes in nicer neighborhoods. The finders-keepers law, Mount thought it was called.

In the paper about two weeks before, Mount read of a baby found on Oberdine Avenue. The baby was taken in by a Mrs. Dean Davis Prouty, a widow whose Irish housekeeper found the baby in the forsythia bush to the left of the veranda. What interested Mount was to read how lonely Mrs. Prouty and the Irish housekeeper were and how they thought what a good thing the baby might be for them and what a good thing they and Mrs. Prouty's eleven cats might be for the baby (who would be named Dean Davis Prouty II even though she was a baby girl). Mount counted up the eleven cats on his hands and recalled that sometimes when he heard a cat in the dark it would sound to him like a baby crying. Now when he heard what could either be the crying of baby girl Prouty or the mewling of an unseen cat, he was bound to be less certain which was which. This troubled him.

He was more on his guard for abandoned babies on Oberdine Avenue, especially since the story had been in the papers and people with babies to abandon might naturally think of the lonely and accommodating Mrs. Prouty and her Irish housekeeper (whose name was given as Nora and who might want a baby just for herself, a baby to call Nora that would grow up with baby girl Dean), until there might be as many babies as cats, all crying together in the dark and crawling softly out of the forsythia . . . whatever that was.

31

Mount suppressed his breathing when it suddenly went faster, which it sometimes did in the midst of thoughts that could have gone on forever without reaching some clear conclusion. What in the world would happen if he came upon some baby that had failed to survive its night in the bushes? What would he do if the baby wasn't squirming and moving its mouth open and shut the way a live baby did? That would be the end right there. He would turn the baby over and walk on quietly, but he could never stop thinking about it, the front and back of the unmoving baby he'd found in the bushes. If you had only one baby to find in your life, what if it turned out to be the one that didn't survive the night in the bushes? Never mind what to feed it or where it would sleep or whether it could stand the smell of asphalt in its life all the time. If Mount had his choice, when he found the baby the baby would still be kicking and squirming, maybe smiling. But he could see how it would be best if the baby was found by someone else, Mrs. Prouty or some of her neighbors, or even the people he'd never seen on Stiffney Street, the people who took care of Tiny the dog. Whoever left the baby in the bushes didn't imagine for a minute that someone like Mount might find it, didn't take into account that an asphalt shingle workman passing by on his way home would be the one to find this baby left in the nicer neighborhood—especially since he himself was headed for one of those streets that people took their babies away from in wicker baskets in the dead of night. So, for these and perhaps other reasons he would someday think of, Mount dreaded finding the abandoned baby. He didn't know in advance what he would do. He wouldn't know until it happened. It was nothing like a fly landing on your forehead just above the eyebrow: you automatically hit yourself in the head, and that's that. But with the baby, that was different.

He calmed his breathing by dropping down to one knee and wrapping his arms around the opposite shoulders and squeezing himself so hard that he almost passed out. He had to do this once or twice a week when a thought slipped out from under him and he ended up either repeating and repeating or else chasing it like a blown hat. When the thought got so out of control that he was unable to make a simple decision or speak when spoken to, or to go forward with the practical matters of life—that's when he went down to one knee.

On this latest of Fort Wayne mornings—when Tiny the dog with the lump stayed with him much longer than ever before, bouncing and panting around his cuffs until upper Stiffney Street had given way to empty fields on both sides of the road—Mount dropped to one knee and squeezed himself so suddenly that he nearly crushed the head of Tiny the dog, who ran home yelping. Mount had imagined that in just a few seconds another person would come over the rise where Stiffney Street legally ended, and that that person would be Father Mount coming to tell him serious news about Mother Mount, or else Mother Mount coming to tell him serious news about Father Mount. He had felt both their presences strongly in the houses on Stiffney Street whose empty rooms he had just gazed into, as though he and she had been there behind a couch or in a closet or on their way down the stairs, their feet fast coming into view as he turned and walked away. That was why they were suddenly on his mind.

So, Tiny the dog was running home crying and Mount was down on one knee at just the moment when another person did come over the rise at the end of Stiffney Street. She stood in front of Mount and looked down at him and shook her head, doing something squinty and sour with her face. Mount had started to sway from side to side, an effect of squeezing himself so hard, and to keep him from falling she reached down and touched his shoulder. But he fell over on his side anyway.

"Come and eat breakfast, Mount," she said. He opened his eyes and looked up at the hem of her robe.

It was Hin Lin. On a typical day in Fort Wayne, halfway home from work, Mount stopped for breakfast at Hin Lin's house, a squat bungalow with thatch on the roof and a constant fire in all weathers, with different-colored smokes coming up the chimney. It was a mystery how the thatch never caught on fire and burned her house in different colors.

To get to Hin Lin's house, Mount took the path that sloped downhill through the meadow of goldenrod and other weeds at the end of Stiffney Street. The meadow led to the right-field fence at the Otis Dye Nolan Memorial Ballyard, where the Fort Wayne Jesters played. Mount followed eastward around the fence and then, in back of the first-base grandstand, descended into a shallow, wooded ravine where the ground was often squashy underfoot and where there was always a sweet ripeness in the air from the many thicknesses of decaying leaves. A few baseballs—like big dirty eggs—were halfway embedded in the muck.

Mount had a place in this ravine where he liked to sit, a cool, smooth, impressive rock with vein-blue seams and fissures all through it. On those mornings when he was in no hurry to eat he might spend as much as half an hour sitting on the rock in the trough of the nameless ravine, doing little more than breathing and staring, one by one, at the dirty, red-seamed baseballs.

If he was hungry, though, he would walk right across, down and up, jerking angrily at his ankles when the muck swallowed his shoes. Emerging from the trees at the top of the far side, and looking both ways to see if anyone was near, he would blow twice forcefully into the tight hollow chamber of his two hands fitted together. The two owllike whistles were his signal to Hin Lin that he was coming for his breakfast. Then he would wait concealed until he saw the red smoke from her chimney that meant he was welcome to enter.

On a typical day in Fort Wayne, Hin Lin would be kind to Mount, feed him a lovely breakfast that he thought was much too good for him, then send him home. Leaving, he would drop fifteen cents into the hinged top of a tiny brass temple replica on the table by Hin Lin's door. Sometimes, seeing the fifteen cents of her other visitors, Mount would feel curious and jealous. Who were they and what did they look like? When did they come to eat? Why did he never see them come or go?

From Hin Lin Mount had received his first pineapple, first coffee cake, first French toast. She had given him his first eggs scrambled with cheese, diced green onions and thyme. She had given him his first tiny Swedish pancakes served with powdered sugar and raspberry jam. And she had given him his very first orange juice, the bright color of which originally frightened him.

Hin Lin was Chinese, but Mount took little notice of the fact. She spoke with the usual flat accent of the Indiana region. She had been so long in Fort Wayne that her oriental clothing, which she could not replace, was nearly threadbare. Even though Hin Lin was only ten years older than Mount, her old-looking clothing made her seem older still. But Mount liked the way she looked. Most days she wore red, a very long robe with golden threads in it. When she didn't wear red, she wore blue. Every so often she wore regular Indiana clothing, dresses with tiny flowers in them and dresses the color of the sky or the color of corn. Mount always told himself he didn't care what people wore. His own clothes were so normal and so much alike that it seemed as if he only had one of everything when in fact he had three or four more, including one pair of brown shoes and one pair of black (to go with the droopy black bowtie his father had given him three Easters before in Bolusburgh—"Tie it like Daddy showed you, Jay," his mother told him, "and see if you can't make it hang like the Cross").

Mount couldn't help noticing that Hin Lin kept long sticks in her hair that held it exactly where she wanted it. Sometimes he thought about pulling one of the sticks out just to see what would fall and where. But he didn't because he knew it would be as though she undid his belt without asking. Almost more than he noticed the sticks in her hair, Mount noticed that Hin Lin smelled like her breakfasts. What clung to the walls of her house clung also to her, to the folds of her robes, the backs of her hands, her hair, and the very fine white powder on her skin. The smell wasn't any one thing, but all of it, all of the days of breakfast that had taken place in her house. It reminded him of—but was better than—the smell of the ladies who worked in the Bolusburgh library. When they walked through town in the afternoons, behind them you could smell the hundreds of books, and you wanted to sneeze from it. (They were known as the ladies who could make you sneeze, and Jay sometimes used to follow his father following the library ladies with some of the other townsmen.)

The smell of Hin Lin and her house could make Mount's stomach growl. It could cause other changes in him as well. When he came into the house and she walked him to the bright corner where the table sat between adjacent windows, he often felt more clear in his mind and would know what he wanted from life, both to do and to eat, and he was glad that there were experiences he'd never had that would finally be his if only he kept on coming to breakfast and going to work and going to sleep at the close of the day, which, typically, was around ten-thirty or so. In the presence of Hin Lin, Mount believed that his life at the moment and his life in the future were promising. In the course of breakfast, smelling Hin Lin, smelling her house, it was clear to Mount as at no other time that his life in Indiana was very good. While breakfast cooked he sat with his chin in his hands and stared, seeing nothing, into the deep brown grain of the table where the welling mystery of all his promise floated without ever quite showing its form.

Mount was aware that Hin Lin was sacred in her attitudes toward breakfast, but he took little notice of the ceremonies of preparation that she observed in her own precise way, holding her inverted cupped hands over steaming eggs and then carrying the caught steam across the room to release it exactly above Mount's head. Mount neither cared nor didn't care. Hin Lin often told him how much she admired his indifference.

"I'm very glad you let me do these things," she said. Mount stared at the two clouded-over yolks she had sprinkled with grated cheese and Italian liqueur, which she suddenly set on fire as he watched. The heat and fumes burst into his nostrils, and he felt the tiny hairs withering and dying. "Okay, eat," said Hin Lin. And as he reached for his fork she began to chant. She always chanted softly while he ate. The chant seemed to Mount like an oriental lullaby for the eating of food.

It was Hin Lin who discovered Mount, and not, as with most of her clients, the other way around. She saw him coming out of the trees behind her house one morning. She was taking a white linen tablecloth from the line, and he became visible to her as she folded the fabric smaller, his figure flashing into view with each shake and creasing of the cloth. He likewise watched Hin Lin appear, and he stared at her in such a way that she could have believed she had made an impression on him. Before she turned to go inside, she tried to hold his gaze. But he lowered his head and hurried on.

The next day she waited and called out to him, asking if he was hungry. She smiled nicely, but he shook his head without looking at her and didn't stop walking. Shy, she thought. She saw that his back was hunched forward as though he expected an object might fall from the sky and strike him. The day after that, she set breakfast out in the grass and simply stood over it beckoning and smiling. It was waffles with strawberry sauce, encircled by a dike of sausage links. Mount came slowly closer and crouched above the plate. At Hin Lin's urging he began to eat. Softly she chanted. Every now and then he would look at her, just look. With his fork he accidentally pierced a bee that was hovering over the strawberry sauce. He almost ate it, but Hin Lin reached down and pointed at the fork where a daub of black and yellow fuzz was quivering in the tines.

"Oh, thank you, ma'am," said Mount. He began to like her, but someone watching him eat made him nervous, and he held his hand over the plate like an umbrella.

Mount didn't go every day to Hin Lin's house. On the days when he didn't stop there he would sneak around the ravine or crawl on his hands and knees so she wouldn't see him. He was ashamed not to go, as though he was disappointing her and she was waiting there with worried creases in her face, a special batter in a crockery bowl or some smoked crabs from who knew where in the world.

But it was not a typical day when Mount didn't stop at Hin Lin's house. It was probably a day when his stomach hurt or a day when he needed the fifteen cents to take his shirts and pants and sheets to the Chinaman named Grady Ho who did wash on Tonowanda Street. Or else a day when he figured he needed not to see Hin Lin because he didn't want to leave her house with his stomach full but his mind in a turmoil of thoughts about her.

The truth was she seemed to control him sometimes, as though her voice crawled inside him along with the food and stayed there. The food would be placed before him and he would eat with the chant in his ears, and want to interrupt her, ask her questions about why it tasted so good, whether anything she did was special for Mount alone. Some days he would think about the others, about whether Hin Lin, while chanting, was thinking about another who was coming soon or one who had only just left. Did she cook them all the same breakfast that day, or did they each get something different? Did she know what he liked? Did she think about him after he left the way he thought about her? While he was walking the dark blue shadows of Dillabaugh Street, was Hin Lin lighting the eggs on fire of a man named—Mount wondered what the man was named.

Did Hin Lin notice things about him that she would never say she noticed? There were large brown moles on the rims of his ears. Did she see them and think they were strange? Or did she care about the popping sounds his knees made when he was happy and he moved them too fast? Or the way he forced air through the cracks between his teeth when he wanted to say something he couldn't think of? Hin Lin never let on.

While she was chanting and Mount was eating, wanting to ask her these questions and more, her control was so great that he never did ask. He only ate and smiled up at her as her voice clutched at his thoughts. When she chanted her eyes were closed, and he sometimes thought of slapping her and of the red mark his hand would leave on her cheek. Then he ate some more, taking the mark away, feeling bad. He was always hungry.

Every day the food was different. When he finished eating he always thought to himself, "I want the same thing tomorrow." But it was always different. And he never regretted the variability from day to day. He only waited for the time when things would begin to repeat, which he knew would finally come. The waiting was like believing in death, but still he wanted to tell her, "Hin Lin, I don't care. I just don't care at all if it's the same thing two days in a row, or two weeks." It would have taken some of the pressure off and some of the fear away. But Hin Lin was in charge, and he sometimes wanted relief from her.

Some mornings his heart pounded in his temples as he climbed out of the trees. One day as he was about to whistle he simply lost consciousness and lay half in and half out of the ravine. Three boys found him and were going through his pockets when he started to squirm. They ran off barking like dogs and making fun of him. Days later he caught one of them and beat him badly, rubbing a dirty baseball in the boy's face and barking back at him over and over again. The boy's two friends were watching from a distance, taking note of the large anger in Mount, each standing very still in a way that said they were learning something scary that they would not forget. Mount stood up and looked at them both, their serious narrow faces, tiny mouths and straight hair. He wanted to befriend them, all three, to meet them sometimes and show them he was nice when he wasn't catching them going through his pockets. The beaten boy stood up and ran toward his friends and beyond them. Then the other two backed away slowly and suddenly also ran, back in the direction of the baseball field. Mount dropped the baseball and walked up to Hin Lin's. Almost as soon as he whistled, red smoke came from the chimney.

"Come and eat breakfast, Mount," she said to him as he lay on his side in the path at the end of Stiffney Street. She had come to find him. Something told her to cross the ravine and skirt the right-field fence and fetch him like some lost animal—a goat or a working dog or a deaf-and-blind old horse that only children would miss. He was late, and she had news for him that she couldn't wait to tell.

"Guess what, Mount?" Mount was on his knees brushing himself off. Dust from the goldenrod he'd fallen against was flying in the air. Hin Lin refused to wait for him to guess.

"I've found a baby in the grass outside my house," she told him. "A

Chinese baby boy. There was a note on his blouse and it told me I should keep him and call him whatever name I liked because he was so young he didn't know any before whatever I would call it."

She held up the note in Chinese. To Mount the writing looked like streets of tiny black houses. He saw the pinhole where the paper was fastened to the baby, as though the baby had come with instructions.

"Come and eat breakfast, Mount, and see the baby."

Mount went with Hin Lin and saw the baby up close. It was almost red, it was so young. It squinted. Hin Lin held it in the crook of her arm wherever she went and whatever she did, cooking breakfast for Mount and serving it. When she chanted, she chanted as much to the baby as to Mount or the breakfast itself. Mount ate and wondered how long the baby would survive without a fifteen cents of its own.

"What'll you call it?" he asked her.

"I don't know," she said. She frowned. "I've got the goat for milk, but I still might have to give the baby to the French Sisters. They can name it whatever they want."

"This happens all the time," said Mount.

The baby was a good one. It had a dozen or more expressions, and it switched them from one to the other the way a mockingbird switches its songs. Hin Lin and Mount just watched it silently, and Mount, when he left, left an extra ten cents for the baby, whatever its name would be and wherever it finally came to rest.

"I might send him to my sister in Chicago," said Hin Lin. "She has a permanent room in a good house there because she saved the wife from drowning. She has no work to do; she's just there. It would be a perfect situation. I'll think it over." She sat there and nodded as though she was just then thinking it over and about to decide.

Mount stayed much longer than usual. Hin Lin let him hold the baby, which he was very good at because he didn't tighten his fingers around it, but left them loosely curved like a basket. After an hour or so he heard three sharp whistles from somewhere outside. He wanted to look, but Hin Lin drew him away from the window. She took the baby out of his hands and sent him through a door he'd never known was there, down a path that was also strange but that led eventually to the same path—by a winding spur that dropped down close to the river—that he usually took toward home.

* * *

Home was a house with a red door called the New Harmony Lodge for Men. It was run by the sisters Margaret, Marjorie and Martha Chastine, who wore identical sweaters no matter what the weather.

Mount shared a bed with a man named Harry S. Rabchenuk, a salesman of medical textbooks and instruments. Harry Rabchenuk slept in the bed at night and left the room at seven in the morning. His smell lingered on, an especially brisk and cleanly smell that was caused by astringent spirits in a blue glass bottle in which flakes of many various herbs and spices drifted like black snow when the bottle was shaken. For a minute after Mount entered the room in the morning, his eyes would smart and his nostrils twitch. Sometimes, as though to punish the bottle, he would lift it up and shake it, watch the black flakes float and ponder emptily about nothing, his eyes going blank.

Mount slept in the bed during the day and was seldom in the room past five, though by rights it was his until seven. Before he left for work, he would stand by the window in the northwest corner of the second floor, staring at the street. People walked by who couldn't see him and wouldn't have cared at all if they could have. Nobody lingered on Anthony Street. Nobody even walked slowly. Across the street was the Blaze Defiant match factory. Chickadees flew in and out of the ivy that grew up the bricks. There was always the smell of the sulphur blends and the piles of aging lumber. Because of the danger of fire, the factory had its own fire station right on the grounds. During the day bells often rang for drills. If people walked fast on Anthony Street, Mount figured it was because of the matches. Anything might happen, and no amount of bell ringing would help.

Some afternoons, standing at the window, Mount saw Harry Rabchenuk come home early carrying his two cases, the one with the books and the other with the surgical tools. Mount watched the top of his head come up the walk, a burnt red spot in summer and a pale white patch in winter where some of his hair was gone although he was not yet forty.

Because Harry Rabchenuk was always smiling, Mount was scared of him. He had knives so sharp, Harry said, that an ant that crawled across the blades would cut itself in half before it even knew it. Then he smiled. Mount felt sick when he looked at the silver instruments on blue velvet. Just touching the cases he shivered, as though the things inside might leap through and cut him. Harry Rabchenuk gave a talk one night to the other men and the sisters Chastine and showed them everything.

It was a Sunday when Mount was off. Mount stood in the parlour doorway, half in and half out of the room. Where the parlour rug abutted the hallway rug, he felt himself suddenly on a blade and staggered back. Harry Rabchenuk looked up and smiled, holding in his hands a complicated thing that he said was used to hold layers of flesh apart so that surgeons could reach the deeper things inside. The other men and the sisters Chastine nodded. Mount went up the stairs, turning slowly as he went to make sure there was nothing coming behind him or in front of him or from above or below. His skin felt crawly, and he thought of the harm that might come to him.

Rabchenuk kept his sample cases and other gear against one wall, and Mount kept his carpetbag at the foot of the bed. Lying in bed, he felt as though he and the bed and the bag were an island or a boat. Somehow he would finally fall asleep for the four or five hours that were all he needed. He wrapped a black linen sash around his head to cover his eyes. Someone who saw him asleep would think he had just been executed.

Harry Rabchenuk had half a dozen photographs of his family on a table next to the bed, and Mount would stare at these before he went to sleep. Rabchenuk himself was in some of the photographs, a large smiling face, a small nose—Mount could count his teeth. These were the first private family photographs he'd ever seen. There was something about the photographs that Mount liked. He wanted to take the Rabchenuks out from behind the glass and hold them in his hands. They were like small living things stored this way until someone needed them. Mount would have given anything for plates of his mother and father in their favorite clothes, doing what they were happiest doing, which was often just standing in the sun between the back door and the workshed thinking of things to say to each other or what to have for supper that was down in the cold cellar.

Mount was anxious sometimes to show people that he had a family he remembered. He was sure that in the two hours between when he left the room and Harry Rabchenuk entered it, some or all of the sisters Chastine visited to dust or change the linens or simply to inspect—as it was their right to do. And he believed that they would probably pick up and shake the blue glass bottle of herbal astringent spirits and would stare together at the photographs and make comments about the Rabchenuk family, wondering how the young girl in the long skirt with the accordion pleats could have gotten the dark spots on her face and whether the tops of the other Rabchenuk men's heads were also balding like Harry's.

Mount wished the sisters could have looked at Father and Mother Mount. If they'd been able to, then on Saturdays when he handed Margaret, Marjorie or Martha his room and board, they would have seen him differently, knowing where he came from—Fletcher and Corinne's boy. They might have smiled instead of just staring down at the money book and making the green ink line through his name. They might have seemed to like him better. Possibly they would have also asked him to join their singing.

The sisters Chastine often sang together and led the men in song some evenings in the parlour. They were known around the neighborhood and were even hired to perform at parties celebrating christenings and confirmations, or parties where the children from the blind school learned new songs from them and then had cake. When the sisters Chastine led the men of the New Harmony Lodge for Men in song, they treated them like the children from the blind school. Martha would use her own special teaching method where the pupils held the fingertips of their left hands to their lips as they sang, to show them how to make full instead of half sounds and to form each musical syllable distinctly. Some of the men cooperated and some did not; some babbled instead of singing, and a few of the rudest made sounds with their mouths so coarse that the sisters pretended not to notice.

There were twenty-six men when the house was full. When, finally, they just let loose and sang, the choruses were so robust that the room would seem to shake. With Margaret on piano, Martha and Marjorie swung their arms and smiled, pink or yellow or blue in their matching sweaters as they mouthed the lyrics widely, urging the men on to finer and finer phrasings. At some point Sergeant Blaney came in off Anthony Street and held his hat over his stomach and listened, staying for exactly three songs and telling everyone briefly what had happened so far in Fort Wayne that night.

But Mount experienced none of this. The sisters led the men in song on Wednesdays after supper, when the dishes were dried and the cats let back in. Mount was then always busy making asphalt shingles, but in the empty parlour on Thursday mornings he could almost feel what was left of the tunes, a slowly fading vibration still coming off the walls as though the music, like an army, was marching farther and farther away.

42

During the later daytime, when Mount was half asleep, he could half hear the practicing of the sisters, their voices riding light across the rolling chords of the baby grand. When he slept their music was like an ocean surrounding his bed and slumber. It slid through his dreams along with the bells that were rung all day at the match factory. He would awaken with a crust in the corners of his eyes, the taste of sulphur trapped in his mouth, and, in his mind, sweet, religiouslike melodies he was sure he'd never heard before.

In fact they were many of the same melodies known and played by the Old Musicians who had brought Mount out of Bolusburgh with a dollar in his pocket, his carpetbag and a vague knowledge of the way back home. The sisters knew these melodies because each of them had once been married to one of the Old Musicians, whom they had met when the Old Musicians were in the habit of wintering in Fort Wayne—where there was always plenty of Old Music to choose from, three or four good rehearsal halls, and many reputable piano tuners and instrument dealers. When the Old Musicians abandoned Mount in Fort Wayne, it was the one named Calvin—a drummer—who told him hurriedly, "Go down to Anthony Street, young man. There's a place there run by some sisters, and they'll fix you up real good."

The sisters Chastine were even all still married to the three Old Musicians, but each of the parties had long ago agreed what foolish and youthful mistakes the unions had been. And now they jointly pretended that nothing had ever taken place and that all that had been exchanged between them were chords and harmonies and sheaves of sheet music instead of weeks or months or (in Martha's case) just over a year of matrimonial life. The couples lived in the big house on Anthony Street that the sisters' father had left them. Only later, once the last husband was gone, did it become a boardinghouse, after the sisters held a meeting and decided that they were used to having men around and used to having them suddenly leave or keep to themselves for days at a time, curse and argue, slam the doors and leave the bathrooms in a wet mess with rings of shaving stubble stuck to the basins.

Nowadays the sisters cleaned and cooked and practiced their singing, saving the rest of their free time for the knitting of identical sweaters. In the morning, before he went to bed, Mount sometimes watched them knit. They sat in a three-sistered circle with their three balls of

43

pastel yarn in the middle and their legs outstretched to keep the yarns from rolling out of the circle. For a while they talked, and then for a while they didn't. Mount sat in one of the corners at one of the tables—where the men sat in the evenings and played cards or wrote letters to the homes they'd left—and pretended to play checkers with himself, jumping willy-nilly, clicking the black and red pieces and hearing the matching clicks of the sisters' needles.

When the sisters spoke to each other, they spoke in a code of their own devising. Sometimes after a statement was made, the two sisters Mount could see would smile or scowl or grimly shake their heads. Mount found himself helplessly imitating the facial expressions of the sisters. Once he laughed out loud at something Marjorie said that Marjorie hadn't meant to be funny, and all three stood at once and asked him to shush or leave the room.

Mount liked them best when they knitted in silence, their three heads down at the very same angle gazing at the lengthening rows as their hands clicked along like a chorus. Spontaneously they might begin to hum. Though it seemed they began together, it was really a case of the other two leaping in so quickly to join the first that almost no time had elapsed. This was nice for Mount, who needed to be reminded how weary he was at the end of his day. As the sisters hummed and knitted, his eyes grew heavier and he thought of going upstairs to shake the blue bottle and stare at the Rabchenuk family pictures and wrap the black sash around his eyes.

"Goodnight, everyone," he would say to the sisters after piling the checkers in same-colored stacks. The sisters, pausing neither in their humming nor their knitting, would raise their shoulders slightly in what Mount took to be a friendly shrug of farewell. Mount didn't want to disturb. To him they were beautiful humming and knitting like a womanly machine. And when he had left the parlour, softly closing the rolling doors behind him, he sometimes imagined the sisters jumping up from their chairs and running around the room like crazy women, laughing and pounding the walls, happy finally to be alone. But the truth was they only sat there knitting, feeling the lightness of the room and the near-emptiness of their house, which seemed to empty more as Mount fell asleep.

3

TROUBLE

There was going to be trouble. Mount knew it. True, he hadn't known all along, but then suddenly it struck him. One afternoon in the early summer when he had just stepped out of bed, he told the sisters Chastine. There was a rumbling pain in his guts—as though from bad cider or perhaps from poison—and just the one word was on his two lips: "Trouble." He said it in front of the mirror. He watched his face move in the glass as he spoke. "Trouble," he said. There was a dropping motion, his nose seeming to lengthen, his lower teeth showing almost completely and then sinking shyly out of sight. He could see little beads of sweat on his forehead, cold and hot on his skin at the same time. He said it again: "Trouble." He felt pretty bad.

He moved up closer to the glass. His breath showed in two foggy spots that got bigger and littler. The dark holes in the middle of his eyes were smaller than ever, and he wondered how any light got in to keep the molds and mosses from growing inside. No matter how he widened and narrowed them, his eyes stayed exactly the same. He recalled Dr. Mastergeorge of Bolusburgh saying that the holes in the middle of the eyes were the chief portals of all illumination—even of knowledge and even the Lord—and that a person with tiny holes would be damned and stupid all his life, in addition to being more likely to trip and fall over unseen objects that suddenly appeared in his path. The business of the molds and so forth, that was something Mount had learned on his own. He just seemed to know about it.

But the sisters Chastine said they weren't worried. He found them in the hallway not far from his door. They were together. He thought they were exercising, possibly jumping over each other in turn. The hallways on the second floor were soft and long. You could land without hurting yourself. Mount worried about the hallways hurting Marjorie especially, who was frail and had a diamond-shaped face and was known to sneeze in fits that lasted for longer than you could hold your breath or the time it took to run to the corner for kerosene. It was possible that Marjorie wasn't allowed to jump since she wasn't allowed to carry the laundry past the second-floor landing without help from either a boarder or from one of her sisters.

When they saw Mount come into the hallway they composed their faces and stood motionless in the strange positions in which he had found them. They didn't laugh. "Trouble," said Mount, entranced with the sound of it. The sisters looked at each other. Martha's forehead was full of beads of sweat and deep creases that Mount thought might hide deposits of grime from all the cleaning she did. Her legs were trembling and she was breathing hard.

"Oh, yes?" she replied.

Mount nodded. "Yes'm," he said.

"What can *we* do?" said Martha, gesturing toward her sisters but also partly including Mount in case he wanted to be included. She had a tremendous amount of tact. It was obvious to Mount that she was speaking on behalf of her sisters; he saw the other two cast little looks of thanks in Martha's direction. Then they tugged at the sleeves of their sweaters that had ridden halfway up the veiny, work-sharpened muscles of their forearms.

"I don't know yet, if anything," said Mount. He put his hand on his belly in order to press back something that felt as if it might suddenly burst. The sisters waited. Martha said she wasn't sure if he was referring to a trouble that was his alone or one that affected everyone. She stood on her tiptoes and tried to see over or past him into his room for evidence of the trouble. But the door was only half ajar and Mount was blocking the way.

"What kind of trouble?" she asked.

"Don't know that either," said Mount. He should probably never have mentioned it. He tried to smile, but all he could think of was the deep, deep pain in his viscera, so the smile was only lips and teeth and he could feel how wrong it was and see it in their faces, the sisters

46

standing before him with all the patience of saints, but also with a worn kind of look that was sad and sour at the same time.

"Trouble," said Mount. "Just trouble, is all. Make me just about want to cry." Martha frowned a little. Mount felt the sympathy.

Mount liked Martha best, but he never told her. He hoped she would be saved from the trouble, whatever it turned out to be. He hoped everyone would be saved, but it was Martha he thought about when the trouble crossed his mind. Martha was the biggest of the three and she could smile when you found her alone, which was often when she was on her hands and knees in some corner whisking grit from the darkest shadows where Mount would never even have noticed it. "As long as it's here," she said about the dirt, "I'd somehow know, and feel it." When she was down on her knees like that, with her broad back stretched out straight so the sweater was tight across it, Mount had the urge to touch her, to run his hand down her spine like a dog and say nice, gentle things to show her he understood why she was down there, and all the good she was doing for everyone. He felt about this unknown trouble the way she felt about unseen dirt.

If Mount had known exactly, he would have come to her privately and told her where the trouble was coming from so she could prepare.

"Well, try not to think about it, Mr. Mount," said Martha. "We're not worried, and we don't think you should be worried either. When the time comes, everything that needs to be done will be done. And that's all we can ask. Just take a measure of comfort in that, and say grace to the Lord."

She smiled, and her forehead flattened so that Mount could see the three lines of grime unfold from her creases. He liked her very much.

"Don't worry," she said again.

"All right," said Mount. He meant to try very hard.

"We're going now," said Marjorie. And Margaret nodded solemnly. But they hadn't actually moved by the time Mount finally stepped back into his room, closed the door and felt the silence on either side that lasted only an instant. "Trouble," he whispered, and his lips brushed the cool varnish of the door. Then he heard the sound of rough tumbling in the hallway as the sisters began to move again.

"Be careful," he said, shaking his head. Then he went to the mirror and said it again, watching his lips move slowly and carefully, ending in a hush.

47

* * *

When he left for work each afternoon, he took everything. This went on for several weeks. Seeing his worried fretful face, people looked around themselves for whatever might have caused it. On the days when he didn't work, he took everything anyway and went elsewhere. Finally he returned, bringing everything back, feeling foolish, finding nothing changed—no trouble, no news of some disaster he had escaped by having left with everything. He rounded the corner slowly, ready to see the tragic emptiness, the deep crack in the street, the rubble, the woeful, distraught survivors.

His carpetbag bulged like a sausage and his arms grew longer, he believed, with each week. He could hardly get over the fact that he had so much property. It weighed as much as a brace of shingles. He was proud just to lift it. He wanted to stop strangers on the street and think of some reason to have them hold his bag. He gave a boy a ginger ale to lift his bag for thirty seconds. He stood to one side and watched the boy's forehead strain and his eyes start to plead. Mount let it go on to almost forty—he hoped to see the bag drop—before he said okay to the boy. Then he watched the boy drink the drink and told him he could have another if he drank the first in under three seconds. But the boy was already drinking before the challenge was out of Mount's mouth, so Mount just bought the boy another one anyway.

He had a lot of stuff. The heaviest thing was the famous bust of Tyrus Portman Bolus, Sr., and the lightest thing was the feather that Father Mount used to use to tickle the feet of Mother Mount. Jay had just plain stolen it from them the day he left home. The feather was the only thing he had that was theirs, and he sometimes sat and tickled himself with it, thinking of them both. He figured they were smart enough to know he'd taken it—since it surely turned up missing around the time of his leaving—but he wanted to think they didn't mind. They had probably gotten another to replace it. He imagined them talking about it once or twice a month and laughing. Everyone in Bolusburgh probably knew about it now and told their children, "Don't take our feather the way Jay Mount did. Don't you dare!" And then they all probably laughed and hugged and held up the feather to admire it.

In between the feather and the bust was everything else, the shoes and shirts and pants and suspenders and two books, and all the rest. There was a pair of black gloves that he kept his money in—coins in

48

the left hand and bills in the right. And there was a ball of some kind that Rebecca Dinsfriend had put in his desk one day at the Goodspeed Normal School. It was his now.

Everything fit together in the bag just right. He put each item in in the same order whenever he packed—which at present was every day—and said the name of each thing as he put it in. One Sunday afternoon late, when he was getting ready to give up the room to Harry S. Rabchenuk, he permitted Harry to stand in the doorway and watch him pack. Having a person watching pleased him. Mount said the name of each thing and held it away from himself for a second before he plunged it into his carpetbag as though he might never see it again. Harry watched and said nothing. Whenever Mount looked up, there was Harry smiling. His eyes were wide, the holes in the middle deep black and large, and the white parts surrounding as perfect as if they were painted.

"I'm not coming back this time," said Mount. Since he'd just then conceived of the plan, Harry was the first person he had told. "You can have the room all the time from now on, or else you can ask the sisters to get you another like me. But you won't see me again. I'm not coming back." He was tired of packing every day; he was tired of feeling the trouble approaching as strong as ever before, coming closer like something hot above or around him and sending him every ten minutes out to the hallway privy then back again—tingling, trickling and burning, an ache in his lower stomach descending deeper until it reached to his legs, spreading like a rash gone inward.

"Where are you going?" asked Harry.

"I'm going to Belinda Meadows, Arkansas, where my sister Rosalie lives with a doctor named Ephraim Savage who has a back condition and can only crawl around the house there. I'd like to take them something." Mount looked around the room.

"I'd like to take them this." He pointed at the photograph of Harry S. Rabchenuk's sister and brothers and Harry himself. "I know they've never seen anything like it in Belinda Meadows. And I'd gladly trade you this ball." Mount held up the ball from Rebecca Dinsfriend. He didn't care about it at all. He would have given the ball away because when he packed, its roundness allowed it no particular way to come to rest.

"But those're *my* people, Mount," said Harry. "What good are they to you?"

"I don't know," said Mount, thinking this over for the first time. He pointed down toward the legs of the gathered Rabchenuks. "I imagine there's a dog in there somewhere named Brandy or Jeff. What say?"

"I'll take your ball," said Harry, "but let me give you this instead." He went to the mantel and took down the blue glass bottle of astringent spirits. "Here," said Harry. "They haven't seen this in Belinda Springs either."

Mount took hold of the bottle and shook it the way he had a hundred times before when Harry wasn't there. As always, the flakes of herbs and spices drifted blackly.

"Belinda *Meadows,*" said Mount. "I'd rather take the picture, though."

Mount had never told a deliberate lie before. Oh, sometimes he wouldn't know the full truth or even know the truth at all. Or sometimes he would only be confused, and it would turn out he was wrong. But there was something about a deliberate lie that felt good. Every now and then he would look over at Harry just to see what a person looked like believing a fabric of completely untrue statements. Harry had a sudden stupid look to him, the look of a person who could be slapped in the face and not do anything back. Mount felt his hand want to slap Harry's face, but it didn't, and Mount was proud of everything about himself just then. He wondered if there really was a Belinda Meadows or Belinda Springs. The name had come to him so easy that he believed it might have been sent, like a sound in the night that you wake up hearing—but minutes after it's gone, so you think the sound came from inside you.

"You go away now," said Mount to Harry, "so I can finish up and take my leave in peace."

"Okay," said Harry. He took the ball from Mount's hand and left the room, closing the door behind him. "I'll be downstairs," he said through the shiny wood.

Mount felt good. His hand was still in the form of the ball, trapping a globe of warm air that he didn't care about and that he suddenly made a throwing motion to be rid of. And it was gone for good. As quickly as he had decided to leave the New Harmony Lodge for Men, he decided to steal the photograph of the Rabchenuk people and take it with him. Plans had never formed so fast in his head before, coming like children chasing over fences. Mount imagined a bed in a different boardinghouse, and a table beside the bed with a lamp on it softly smoking and the photograph sitting in the realm of the lamplight, the texture of the velvet dress of the sister surrounded by her brothers, the nice deep walls behind them, another whole room beginning off to the left and a light on a table deep in that other room with the foot of someone else just showing, toe leather blurred and shiny. And there was always the unseen friendly dog, whatever his name was.

Harry would know he'd taken it. That was a problem. The plan wasn't perfect. He asked himself did he care, did he want to stop? No, he didn't. He wanted the picture, so he took it. He breathed on the glass; it clouded and cleared, and he breathed again. He took it frame and all; he slid his thumb across the glass where he had breathed and found it slick, sliding his thumb until the slickness was gone and his thumb just stuck and unstuck, squeaking. He reached down into his carpetbag and parted the clothing in the middle, inserting the picture so it would have padding on either side. Then he moved the other pictures around on the table to hide the vacancy. With any luck the missing picture might go unnoticed another three days. And Harry would think it was gone to Belinda Springs, Arkansas, when in fact it had gone somewhere not even Mount himself knew or could have predicted.

So he shut the bag and forgot the theft and went to the window to gaze out one last time on Anthony Street and across to the match factory where the ivy fluttered and the birds flew in and out.

It was a good time of year to go. In the sudden heat of early summer that would be coming any day now, the windows would be left open over in the match factory and the birds would fly right in to take matches to use in making their nests. Some of the house fires in that area of Fort Wayne were surely caused by matches in the nests of birds in the eaves of those houses. There was quite a local hatred of birds on that account. Mount joined this hatred and, seeing birds, would wish them dead— sometimes nearly shaking his fist—and want to see them fall straight down and crash. In windows around Fort Wayne, women sat with slingshots and fired capless acorns at birds here and there. But the sisters Chastine, when they talked among themselves and Mount was nearby to overhear them, spoke very kindly sometimes of birds and spoke sometimes of their absent husbands in the same breath in which they spoke of the birds, their talk trailing off into a satisfied kind of quiet, as though they had all just eaten a very good meal. Mount didn't know what to think. But now he saw birds flying in and out, and all he could think of was the danger they posed. If they didn't mean any harm, that was fine; but if they did it all the same, what was the difference? It was a good time to leave the Anthony Street vicinity. He nodded out the window. The birds proceeded heedlessly, in and out, a match, two matches, three matches, bird after bird.

Mount went. He went as though he would always come back, again and again, every day packing and unpacking. He said no goodbyes except to Harry S. Rabchenuk, who caught him in the foyer and took his hand and pumped it kindly, smiling and making vigorous chat about the pleasures of having shared a room and been clean and thoughtful and punctual and never a problem. Harry let go of Mount's hand and went backward deeper into the house, getting smaller and darker with every step, his voice growing fainter until the lips hardly moved at all.

"Goodbye, Mount, goodbye," said Harry, "goodbye—" And Mount had almost forgotten he was leaving.

The sisters Chastine were not in sight. They were either upstairs or in the kitchen—from which came a warm, potatoey smell—or they were in the cellar washing or slaughtering chickens in the yard, one sister holding, one swinging, one watching and moaning. Wherever they were, Mount didn't seek them, didn't think of telling them he was off never to return, or of asking them to sing him the song of godspeed they sometimes sang when a boarder left, holding the boarder's two hands and making him part of an unbroken circle, swaying and looking up at the ceiling or the sky or the lines of linen bleaching in the sun. That was the sisters' way, that was their fondness; men came and went, and they marked the occasions with a song.

Mount left. He held his position in front of the New Harmony Lodge for Men for several minutes, uncertain how to proceed. He put his bag down on the walk and stood pretending to count possessions on his fingers so as to seem to be thinking of what he might have forgotten before he had gone too far to come back and fetch it.

On Anthony Street, people in not the best-quality Sunday clothing went back and forth in family clusters, or clusters of men together or women together. Mount thought he might fall in behind one such group and follow it, just to get himself going until some direction took hold of him and he went along unassisted. The world beyond Anthony Street stretched forth, and Mount was gripped for an instant by a sweet sense of optimism such as would grip him when he read in the newspapers stories concerning the building of steel ships, the three new treatments for pellagra or the attainment by deserving men of higher ranks in banking or the military. Mount felt anything could be done, and any-one—even those who hadn't done the actual doing—could reap the benefit. And no one like himself would be left behind cruelly waiting and waiting. That was how the future looked at that moment, with no thought of trouble to cloud it for the first time in many weeks.

He glanced up at the window where his room had been for one last look. He imagined only emptiness behind it, a curtain blowing back softly into whiteness, no walls, no floor—nothing to focus on. But instead Harry Rabchenuk was looking down. That is, Mount saw man-like creases of movement and believed it was Harry, moving his lips, waving slowly, sighing.

Harry Rabchenuk looked down at Mount moving off along Anthony Street. He scowled. Mount had stolen his photograph and Harry was prepared to get it back and to see that justice was done.

What was the photograph to Harry? The photograph was *his*, is what it was. His sister Rita and his brothers, one of whom, Barnet, was dead now and only alive to his memory in the picture Mount had stolen: a face, a smile, one shoulder lower than the other—his brother Barnet. The photographer had come at the invitation of his parents, Karl and Ruth, to the house on Boothby Avenue in Dayton. It was an amazing day. The man's name was Evans Whittlesy, and he came from New York City. He had four large cases and two assistants, and all the family crowded in as the cases were opened and equipment set up. It must have cost plenty. Harry's father Karl was a doctor and was interested in the chemistry of the process—the silvers and acids and powders. He asked questions endlessly about the optics and how did the light and chemistry interact, how was the image preserved until the chemistry was readied later? That sort of thing. The photographer could not or would not give answers to these questions, moving his hands in the air like birds to indicate that fogs of mystery shrouded all parts of the process, that there were no answers to give.

The posing itself was endless. Muscles ached from remaining still. Whittlesy talked inscrutably in single-syllable codewords to the two assistants who moved around the room like gnomes in swift, crouching bursts, either expanding or compressing arrangements of family members, apparently at Whittlesy's direction. Whittlesy himself was like an oracle, gifted and serene, waiting and waiting for what he suggested by his manner was perfection—of his tableau, not of its members. The assistants moved here and there expending great energy, sometimes breathing hard. Afterward they were spoken of by the Rabchenuks as "the monkeys." For days and days the house smelled like explosions from the flashpowder. Harry recalled that the smell had aroused him greatly; for hours at a time he would sit by himself in the living room, breathing deeply, staring blankly, hearing nothing around him and feeling a not unpleasant tension growling in the pit of his stomach like a hunger for everything. Three months later two enormous wooden crates arrived. Inside them were the photographs, framed and floating in excelsior.

Harry's father spread them out on the living-room floor in orderly rows, and moved among them like a commander of troops, approving, smiling, saying nothing. Then he divided them up, solemnly, ceremonially, in a kind of divestiture—so many for each of the children, so many to be kept in common, so many to be kept in reserve, in a safe place away from the house.

"You will always have these," he finally said. He was almost in tears, Harry could hear it in his voice. "Always," he said. "We will have that day forever. This was how we were." At the time, Harry, his sister and brothers found this all both peculiar and touching. A silence hung in the air. Furtively they looked at one another.

Harry watched until Mount turned the corner. It was as though he had stolen a piece of those two days in Dayton, a piece of the fascination and happiness, of the solemnity; a piece of Rita and Barnet and Karl, Jr., and Willy and Harry himself. It was as though something belonging to them all was cruelly missing, and they could have no peace until it was recovered.

Harry thought of Mount placing the picture on a table somewhere, staring at it, his mouth slowly opening at the vision of Rita's velvet dress. Harry's face flushed. Breathing carefully to slow his heart—as his father had taught him—he ran his hands through his thinning hair and decided on the path he must take. He would find a policeman and make a complaint—he would not take matters into his own hands. He would do this immediately. And he would have the photograph back before nightfall.

* * *

Carefully Mount picked people to follow. He looked for certain things, a kind of hat, a stride, a color of cheek, a pumping of elbows. Nothing, though, had seemed to lead anywhere. Most of the people, it turned out, were going only a short distance, and he had had to find others to fill these sudden vacancies. Sometimes the others were taking a direction opposite or greatly different from the one Mount had recently come, but it was better, he reckoned, to change directions than to stand still for too long or to follow the wrong person just because he was going in the same direction. The wrong person was anyone who, for whatever reason, Mount didn't want to follow. Maybe it was someone who walked too fast or too slow, or someone with a limp or with a friend who limped; maybe it was someone who looked like he might not want to be followed; and maybe it was someone Mount thought someone else was already following. Frequently he saw people he was sure were following other people—which did not surprise him but only made him look elsewhere.

The consequence was that Mount had not traveled very far at all. He had seen the river twice—he wasn't sure whether it was the Maumee both times or the St. Joe's or each of them once. Water was water. But people were not crossing, not over the bridge at Swift Avenue or on the ferry that ran all day between Two Rocks Point and Dexter Fields, and Mount lacked the certainty to do it by himself, though he had the patience to wait until he could. He had passed the county courthouse twice and two bakeries three times each, following one of the people he was following into one of them once and buying the same thing the person he was following bought—a stiff pastry horn filled with sugary cream—and then following the person back out and in the direction he had come from, past the courthouse again and left in Wayne Park, where there were many birds milling aimlessly and many people deliberately not feeding them but kicking at them instead, hollering and grunting, milling also. Mount then joined this mass and stayed with it briefly, milling and grunting, eating the pastry horn, until he followed someone away from Wayne Park and back in the direction of the other bakery and down toward the other river—whether the St. Joe's or the Maumee—then going left on Carriage Street all the way to the carriage-works and just beyond, where the person he was following went into a house and there was suddenly no one else to follow. A lull. Mount went over to a tree and leaned against it and let his bag slide down to the ground, where it teetered on a root.

What Mount hadn't noticed for almost an hour was that there were two people following him. They were having a time of it, too. It was one thing following someone who was going somewhere, but it was another thing to follow Mount. One of the two was Harry S. Rabchenuk. The other was Officer Paige of the Fort Wayne Police Department. Officer Paige was having the time of his life and trying to convince Harry Rabchenuk that it was worth delaying the arrest because the subject was acting so strangely that there was a high probability of an additional crime being committed, perhaps another petty larceny—which was what, to Harry's annoyance, Officer Paige had termed the theft of the photograph.

"Never mind," hissed Harry. They stood in the shadow of one of the great brick columns forming the gate of the carriageworks. It was getting dark, and Harry wanted his picture back. Mount had stopped for five minutes or so outside the house into which the man he was following had disappeared. When two women and a dog came out of a house on the other side of Carriage Street, Mount began to follow them—back toward Harry and Officer Paige. It was then that they had ducked into the carriageworks entryway.

Harry had long ago begun wishing he'd simply gone after Mount alone. By now he would have the photograph back and Mount would have his black eye and his lesson, and that would be that. But, no, he, Harry, had had to do the right thing, and now he was under the official governance of Officer Paige, who kept trying to buy Harry's cooperation with the promise that the two of them could "dust up" Mount once the arrest was made.

They were moving again. For what seemed the hundredth time, Mount switched his bag to the other hand and shook his relieved shoulder. Harry knew how heavy the bag was with all the stuff Mount had in it, and Harry's picture, too. They had to walk slowly because the two women were having to stop for the dog, a big dog like the one his family had in Dayton—Prince, a yellow hound with breath like something dead.

"Oh, when?" Harry pleaded.

"Not yet," said Paige. Paige was tall and overweight, formless and

56

hulking with the voice of a lighter, shorter man. At the sound of his voice, Harry had at first found himself looking at Officer Paige to make sure his appearance hadn't suddenly changed.

"Something's going to happen," the policeman said.

And Harry agreed it looked as though something might indeed happen. What Mount was doing was most strange. He didn't seem to be going to Arkansas at all; he didn't seem to be going anywhere. Harry tried to think whether he had ever done anything similar. When he took his sample case around to the doctors' surgeries he was sometimes shown the door more quickly than he had anticipated, and then there was time to kill and he might wander. But this following business, this was what was strange.

Mount switched his bag to the other hand again and worked the shoulder around. Harry felt halfway sorry for Mount now that he and Officer Paige were stalking him like game and nodding gravely to each other, saying things like, "I know he's gonna do something else."

Then the two women suddenly turned around and both spoke brightly to the dog as though to enforce the turning, and the dog came along happily, running past Mount without stopping to sniff or be patted. The two women came along behind, also walking past Mount and taking no special note of him. And Mount himself kept walking, back up Carriage Street toward the center of town, only even slower than the women had gone, as though the bag was dragging him down and he hadn't a clue what to do. Harry suddenly thought—he had been so stupid—there is no Arkansas, no sister, no doctor. It was pathetic.

"Officer Paige—" Harry began.

"We'll take him now, sir," said Paige. Harry went along as Paige turned his formless hulk into what Harry took to be attacking speed—a faster walk, twice as fast as Mount and also faster than Harry could go. Soon they were right behind him, Officer Paige with Harry two steps back. Paige said, "Stop, sir!" And Mount stopped dead, without even an extra shuffle or two, the bag just slipping from his hand and hitting the ground with a soft but dense concussion, seeming to bounce slightly.

Mount turned around, and Harry could see the confusion in his face and then a smile, and then more confusion.

"Harry?" said Mount.

"Uh, yes, uh, Mount," said Harry.

Officer Paige filled the awkward moment.

"I think, sir," he said, "you're in a bit of trouble."

"Trouble?" said Mount. "Oh, trouble . . ."

There was no lawyer. The fact was noted. No one stood beside him. He was led to a railed and varnished enclosure where there was a very soft seat with a high, hard back. The softness of the seat was owing to a red velvet cushion, and before Mount sat he picked up the cushion and held it and squeezed it. The courtroom was quiet while he did this. No one said a word, but Mount had the feeling there were others present who would have liked to squeeze the cushion. Then he sat. He saw people were looking at him. He returned their gazes, touching each face. He smiled. Then he didn't smile; then he smiled again.

A man told him to state his name; he stated his name. He stated where he lived. He gave the address on Anthony Street. Whenever he said anything, he noticed the quiet. He disliked how his voice sounded, and he wished others were talking amongst themselves here and there in the room; he would have felt more normal. The man who had asked him to state his name held up the photograph of Harry Rabchenuk's sister and brothers and Harry himself. Mount said yes, he knew the photograph. He was about to say how much he liked it, but the man asked him another question: did he steal the photograph?

Mount couldn't believe they didn't already know that, but he said yes, he did steal it, yes. He said yes twice more, hoping to settle the issue once and for all. The man who was asking the questions suddenly stopped and said that he thought it wasn't necessary for anyone else to testify since the defendant—he pointed at Mount—confessed the crime. But then he went on to relate what two other witnesses would have said if they'd been called, and the judge interrupted the man and said it wasn't necessary to say what these others would have said if they'd had the chance to say it, and if the man *wanted* them to say it he was free to call them and they could say it themselves. The judge asked, "Does the state wish to call additional witnesses?"

"No, Your Honor," said the man.

"Then rest your case," said the judge.

"Defendant may stand down," said the man to Mount.

"Defendant may *stay where he is,*" said the judge. The judge sounded angry. Mount looked at the judge. The judge looked at the man.

"Your Honor?" said the man. The man looked confused.

"Will the state allow the defendant his defense?" asked the judge.

"Oh, uh, yes, Your Honor. Certainly."

"Then, rest your case."

"The prosecution rests," said the man. He went back to a table and sat, apparently, thought Mount, to rest. The judge turned to face Mount.

"Mister . . . Mount," said the judge. "You are here without counsel, and you have been exceedingly generous and cooperative with the state, I will say. But you may still present a defense. And I may ask you questions, and the prosecution may respond to what you say by questioning you further on the substance of what you may say. Do you understand so far?" Mount nodded.

"Now," the judge continued, "you have said that you took the thing, the photograph, in question. Can you also offer statements likely to mitigate the taking of the thing, to make it seem either less serious or more understandable than the prosecution has made it seem? Do you follow me?"

"Well," said Mount, "I took it because I wanted it and I didn't have anything like it, and he had others."

"Did you intend, after having it for a time, to give it back to its owner?" asked the judge.

"No, sir," said Mount. "I wanted to keep it for myself."

The judge looked at Mount for a second or two and then said, "Well, I commend you for your honesty here, but you know I'm going to have to find you guilty, Mr. Mount. And unless you can give me a very good reason I'm going to be forced to send you to prison for a time, some length of time I have not decided yet, and you may not—no, I think you will not—like being in prison, since it is a very different experience, no doubt, from life on, what is it, Anthony Street?"

Outside the window of the courtroom there was a terrible rain. Mount looked out through the rain, wondering if Father and Mother Mount could imagine where he was and in what a serious situation. He had stolen a photograph. Aside from the feather belonging to Father and Mother Mount, this was the only thing he had ever taken that wasn't his to take. And now he would pay. At the end of the paying, though, it would be just as if he had never done it, and he would then feel better for having paid. But he agreed with the judge that he would surely not like the paying itself, only afterward when there was that relief.

The prosecutor stood and asked the judge to sentence Mount to a term of eighteen months, so that a message might be sent to those who would "scorn an unlocked door and disrespect an open trust." He said, "I for one want to live in a Fort Wayne free from these anxieties and in the hope that I, unlike the unfortunate Henry Rabincheck, won't have a thing as precious as a dead brother's memory spirited away from me." His voice rose at the end, scaring Mount considerably.

"And what about you, Mr. Mount?" asked the judge. "What do you think I should do with you? You can make an argument against the recommendation just put forth by the prosecution, which I will say I consider quite immoderate indeed."

"Well," said Mount, "you could let me go free." A couple of people, including the prosecutor, laughed at this.

"No," said the judge. "I don't believe I could go that far. But I'll tell you you seem like a nice enough fellow, and you are a young fellow whom I think will make the best use of a shorter term than the state recommends and then not be in any further difficulties in after life. Don't you agree? And, so, with that in mind, I will sentence you hereby for the crime of larceny in a value lower than fifty dollars, otherwise called petty larceny, to serve a term of not more than nor less than thirty days at the Allen County House of Penal Detention, said term to be served forthwith. Stand down, sir."

The judge banged his gavel and the next case was called. Mount watched the rain scrub down the window glass and felt his wrist be taken hold of.

4

STIR

First of all, it smelled. And Mount himself smelled. He smelled himself and everything else. Everything else smelled as bad as he did, and he wasn't sure whether it was him smelling outward into the air or the air crowding in and smelling him up. But the fact was he wasn't used to it yet.

"You'll get used to it," said someone he couldn't see, someone cells away with a voice like cotton, not friendly and not unfriendly—no name, just a voice. "You'll get used to it." A flat statement. Mount hoped he wouldn't. Then he changed his mind and hoped he would.

"I hope not," he said. His own voice sounded like cotton. He smelled, and he sounded like cotton. "I hope not," he said again.

The food came. He heard the cart rattle through the heavy door, the heavy door swing open and move the air, moving the smell back and forth until it settled again and was around him very still, unchanged. Twice a day the food came. A warder brought it who said his name was Joseph. "*You* call me Joseph," he said to Mount, as though he told other prisoners to call him other names. Mount said, "Thank you, Joseph." Joseph didn't say anything else. His face was soft and white, and he was younger than Mount.

In the morning came coffee in a tin cup with the handle broken off and a loop of leather lacing tied through a hole punched in the rim; a bowl of thin and steamy grits with a blood gravy that was not blood-colored but brownish, maybe old blood or blood cut with something like a spice. In the morning he ate the grits and drank the coffee because he was hungry and thirsty. There wasn't anyone who didn't eat. Then, afterward, he heard people at their buckets making sounds almost like crying. Joseph came along the flats with his cart, collecting the cups and bowls. Once the heavy door was opened and shut again, moving the smell, it was quiet as could be. After a few mornings of feeling the quiet fall so suddenly, Mount heard himself thinking, "Now we can be ashamed." He lay on his bunk and felt ashamed until the coffee sliced through him and he swung down and hunched to his bucket, making sounds almost like crying.

In the late afternoon the cart came back, pushed either by Joseph or by a second warder who said less than Joseph and was rough with the food, making sure some spilled—as though he didn't care—and keeping his eyelids half closed and his lips squeezed tight. He frightened Mount. Mount never said anything to him but only took the food and suffered it to be slopped over the rim of the tin plate onto his hand as he reached for it. Joseph was better. Mount ate whatever was on his plate.

The first three days were like one long day, raining and dark. When he let himself sleep he would think, "When I wake up the rain will be ending." But when he woke up the rain was still falling. He refused to leave his cell, and he was allowed to stay there. No one minded. The other men went past—to and from what, Mount didn't know—and they looked into his cell, seeming to think something about him but not saying it, not saying who they were, not asking anything. It was a place where people didn't speak.

Mount didn't even know where it was. With other men he had been taken there in a thing like an omnibus. Black horses pulled it, the horses wearing black blankets with white borders and cockaded harnesses, the brushes black with silvery ornaments. Inside, the omnibus was black as a deep pocket. He sat on a bench on one side with some of the other men, opposite a bench on the other side with the rest. In the dark there was only the sound of their breathing and the nearness of their warmth. It was eerie feeling alone like that; the other men were like distant cities. The box was cold inside because of the cold June rain that he had noticed first in the courtroom, through the window, as the cases before his own were called and heard.

So he didn't know where it was. The omnibus had gone along for a while, jouncing and creaking, leather and wood and iron. Mount's body was thrown this way and that, but, strangely, never touched the bodies of any of the other prisoners. And Mount sometimes wondered if he was, after all, alone; and he wondered if the others, also touching no one else, wondered the same thing. But still he felt their warmth, even in the cold, and still he heard their breathing and one of them coughing and another, sometimes, praying.

He didn't know who they were. He was sure he had been in the courtroom with some of them when their cases were called, but he had not paid attention. He had only sat and watched the rain and looked back into the gallery where there were some of the citizens of Fort Wayne, but no one he knew—no one until later, when Harry Rabchenuk walked in and wouldn't even look at him. Harry sat in the very back, directly behind someone tall. Mount tried to see him, but he could see only the top of Harry's head where the hair was missing, and that only sometimes. Mount didn't think much one way or the other about Harry being there, and not at all about Harry being there to give testimony against him. Something about the sight of a familiar face just made Mount wish he could see it better. He wished he still had the photograph. His neck began to ache and he let his gaze drift back to the window, which was tall and wide, framing the rain that flattened the view so it had no depth. Mount almost fell asleep before they called his name.

When the omnibus first stopped, Mount thought that was it, they had arrived wherever they were going. He started to stand—he was so afraid of everything that he wanted to get it all right, to do everything promptly without being told—but they had not arrived. Mount fell when the omnibus lurched ahead. Even in falling he still touched none of the other bodies, and none of the other bodies seemed to take any notice of his falling. He lay there for a while and absorbed the silence of the others not reacting. Imagining he could see them, Mount looked from one to another, all around the black box, believing his eyes could turn to beams and show him their faces or their jittering knees, something human about them just to make him less afraid. It was so dark. He lay there, his weight on his elbow, his elbow bouncing on and off the floor, as the omnibus jounced and creaked. He heard the breathing and other sounds and felt the warmth of the rest of the men. The rain sounded softly on the roof of the box. He got up slowly, on hands and knees, and crawled back to the bench, touching no one.

The omnibus rolled to a stop for the second time. This time it had arrived. Everyone inside sat still, breathing quietly and listening. The rain fell softly on the roof. Outside there were sounds of things being done to horses, of sharp footsteps on wet stone and, finally, of the wagon's door being unlatched. When the door opened, Mount looked at the other prisoners' faces, which were blank and cold—not grieving but only tired, as Mount then realized he too was very tired.

And so the thirty days began to pass. Imprisonment was more tedious than Mount could have imagined. The first three days were like one long day, and then every day thereafter was like three. Tin cups and plates came and went. Darkness was constant, rising up suddenly from black to gray and then settling slowly backward like a change that failed. In the mornings Joseph, after he had given out and then taken back the cups and plates, came along to collect the wastes from each man's bucket.

One morning Joseph said to Mount, "You are sick." There was a silence while Joseph stood there waiting, his face split twice by bars.

"What?" said Mount after a while.

"Sick," said Joseph. "Sick. You have to come see the doctor now."

Mount stared at Joseph and Joseph shifted back and forth, one foot to the other, his face doing something like deciding.

"The doctor, when I take up the buckets," said Joseph uneasily, "the doctor tells me I am meant to look in the buckets and report to him if I see anything that is strange. And yesterday I did, in yours. He said you were sick. That's all. And now you've got to go see him. Dr. Church. I don't know what, but he says you're sick with something."

Joseph took his keys and unlocked Mount's cell. Mount followed him out, but Joseph turned and faced Mount and walked backward along the tier with his hands stretched out to keep Mount distant. It would have been easier for Joseph if Mount had walked in front and Joseph had held him from behind by the waist of his pants. But Joseph was trying not to catch what Mount was sick with. Mount understood. He began to feel sick. But then he thought, I'm not sick at all.

Dr. Church tried to change his mind. Dr. Church was in a heavy coat in a cold room. You could see his breath; he wasn't used to the cold. Mount's own breath was invisible, and so was Joseph's. Joseph left Mount with Dr. Church. The door closed with two clicks and a kind of sigh. Dr. Church nodded at Mount.

"You're Mount," said Dr. Church. And Mount said yes, he was. The room turned out to be even colder than Mount's cell, and soon Mount could see his breath in the air. Dr. Church remained silent, watching, and Mount began to want to cry for help or to run.

"Undress," said Dr. Church finally.

"It's cold," said Mount.

"Undress," said Dr. Church.

"I want to go back to my cell," said Mount. "I've only got twenty-three days."

"Undress for me, inmate Mount," said Dr. Church. So Mount undressed. He piled his clothes on the floor of the cold room and stood on them; under the soles of his feet the clothes were still warm. Dr. Church, leaning against the wall ten feet away, just stared Mount up and down—the sharp knees, the hairless chest and belly, the bony frame, the watery eyes and the matted, reddish-brown hair. He also looked at Mount's thing. When Mount saw the doctor looking at his thing, he couldn't help looking down himself. It was cold and small.

"Turn around," said Dr. Church.

Mount turned around.

"Keep turning." Mount turned again, and again. He wondered what day it was—a Monday or a Tuesday, or what? What day? His mind was going through the days. He kept turning. Each day was like a box that he knew what was inside. He was dizzy. It was Sunday. Or it was Wednesday. The visit to the doctor was completely unexpected.

"Stop," said Dr. Church. Mount's back was turned. "Plessy's Syndrome," said Dr. Church. Mount heard a loud snap and felt a sharp stinging pain below his shoulder blade. He half turned around and saw Dr. Church stuffing something into his pocket quickly.

"Never mind, Mount. Turn and face me." Mount turned. His back still stung. He tried to reach back and rub it.

"Jump up and down," said Dr. Church.

Mount jumped up and down on his clothes. Each time he landed a pain shot up the front of his left leg, straight to his knee. His clothes got colder and he felt the fleshy parts of his feet hardening and getting more tired.

"Now crouch and turn your head from side to side as fast as you can."

Mount crouched and twisted his head back and forth as fast as he could. He felt pains on both sides of his neck straight up to his ears, the bones in back of his ears.

"Stay crouching and open and shut your mouth as wide as it goes, and make a loud sound only when your mouth is closed. You understand? Only when it's closed, not open? No sound at all when it's open."

And Mount did this, too, hurting his teeth when he snapped his mouth shut. The hard part was making the loud sound only when his mouth was closed. Twice he failed to do so, and twice the doctor angrily made him start over—though it seemed strange to Mount that there was a starting point at all, or a fixed duration for such an activity or a goal to reach that would be its natural ending. So how could he start over?

But Mount did everything Dr. Church told him. The procedure reminded him of Mr. Amory Malmsborn hiring men at the shingle factory (and Mount, remembering his job, wondered if he could ever have it back). Dr. Church continued to lean against one of the cold walls, never removing his coat—which was made of dark fur—and never coming over close to Mount to examine him in the way a doctor usually did.

"Are you growing tired?" the doctor asked him after a while.

"Yes," said Mount, "and I'm very cold."

"Now. Stand up as straight as you can. Very straight . . . That's it . . . Even straighter . . . Yes. That's good . . . ." Dr. Church came toward Mount very fast and slapped him hard across the face and brought his knee up into Mount's groin, which caused Mount to buckle forward and caused the doctor to spring away so that Mount, in falling, wouldn't fall on him.

Then Mount was on his hands and knees—coughing and his eyes watering terribly—and Dr. Church was also on his hands and knees near Mount, and they were like two dogs sharing garbage or about to sniff each other. Mount was conscious of his thing hanging down in the cold and how the thing itself didn't hurt at all but the sack part hurt all the way up to his throat and down to his ankles. He wanted to go right back to his cell and stay there for twenty-three days without moving, but he knew he couldn't leave the room until the doctor let him go.

"Do you know why I do this, Mount? Do you know why I've done this to you?" asked Dr. Church, his mouth very close to Mount's ear.

Mount shook his head. He could smell Dr. Church's coat right next to him; he could feel the soft cold touch of the bristles of fur. He could smell his own ugly smell reflected back in the smell of the coat and the smell of Dr. Church, whose breath was steamy, sour and liquorish.

"I do it because I like to. And because I can. That's all. I ask them to bring you to me and they bring you to me and I do what I want to do, and no one cares. I'll do it again tomorrow if I want. And I am paid all the same, no matter what I do. I tell you, Mount. It's a great thing possessing freedom like that . . . and it's a terrible thing to be like you and not possess any. Inmates should all have the most pain and unpleasantness possible; you should never get the idea you will be cared for here. Then maybe you will be fully improved and learn some lesson and not return here . . . Am I right? Yes?"

"Yes, sir," said Mount. His eyes were squeezed shut, but his breathing began to feel more normal and his stomach stopped sucking in and out so fast.

"Am I sick?" asked Mount. Dr. Church reached out and patted Mount's head and put his cold hand on Mount's back, which he used to help himself up. When he was standing again, he kicked Mount in the left shoulder, and Mount pitched over slowly onto his side on the floor. He ended up staring at the toes of the doctor's shiny brown boots, which he hoped were done with him.

"Just a little blood in your shit is all. It's only the change in diet. You'll be all right. Now put your clothes back on."

Mount put his clothes on. Dr. Church had returned to leaning against the wall. He looked tired and disappointed. While Mount was dressing, the doctor kept his head down and turned it slowly from side to side. Mount thought he was probably thinking of some music, maybe singing to himself silently. For a long time after Mount had finished dressing, nothing further happened. Mount only stood and waited, frightened even to make a sound. His body hurt all over. To help the time pass, he concentrated on each of the pains, one at a time, making their acquaintance.

"Go away," Dr. Church finally said without looking up. And Mount simply went away. That was the last he saw of Dr. Church.

Late one night Mount woke up and started screaming. The sound kept pouring out. Other prisoners shouted for him to be quiet, but he continued screaming. Part of him was thinking, What am I doing? But the rest of him screamed. It was loud.

Others had done this before him. There was a prison name for it; it was called bleeding. Someone would say, "God help us if so-and-so goes bleeding again." Just two nights after Mount arrived, a man on the third tier bled. The screaming lasted about an hour, maybe longer. It seemed longer. Mount thought how crazy it sounded. He tried to block out the noise by covering his head with his blanket. He wanted the screamer to die suddenly or to run out of energy—which was called bleeding to death.

Now Mount was doing it himself. Louder and louder, the noise came out like water from a bucket. What am I doing? part of him thought. The rest of him was terrified and did what it did without thinking.

For a long time no one came. Some of the other prisoners threatened him, but that did no good—and they knew it would do no good. Still others began to scream in much the same way as Mount was screaming. They added their loud, shrill sounds to his, and in the short spaces when he was quiet himself—trembling and gasping for breath and wiping his nose with the back of his hand—the other voices made the screaming continuous.

Soon after these voices joined in, a gang of warders ran onto the wing. The warder on duty at the desk by the door had gone to get help. They spread out quickly through the tiers, going cell to cell with brass fire bottles under their arms, cursing the inmates and spraying into the darkness. The solution in the fire bottles had a portion of vinegar added, and it stung to be doused, especially in the eyes. By the time a warder reached his cell, Mount had mostly quieted down. He was sprayed less than some others—the warder outside his bars cursed sharply when the bottle was empty. It was like a dream of punishment—Mount only half saw the dark face of the warder moving in darkness. From somewhere below there was torchlight, but it leapt dimly and Mount could identify no one. He heard men crying out in pain; he heard warders calling other warders to help them.

Two inmates on the tier above were taken forcibly from their cells and moved to another wing that was supposedly smaller, with smaller, darker cells that you could only crawl on your hands and knees in. Mount was ashamed that he had started all this and caused so much harm. He knelt on the floor of his cell and prayed to be forgiven. He prayed out loud, but not loud enough to be heard by the other inmates. There was no answer, and he was unsure his prayer had been received. There had never been an answer before, but Mount kept on hoping and sometimes he felt certain events that happened later were meant as a different form of answer than people were generally accustomed to.

The next morning, as the other inmates filed past his cell on their way to wherever they went, someone poured urine from a tin cup through his bars and whispered that that wouldn't be the end of it either. But it was. Nothing else happened after that. The warder named Joseph brought Mount a mop and a bucket of lye water, and Mount cleaned the urine up, thinking that it was much like his own. As on every other day so far, Mount refused to come out of his cell, and no one minded. He stayed there all day and whistled, sometimes hitting his knees with his fists and pretending he was whistling actual words that another person could understand and reply to in wordlike whistles of his own.

When it finally stopped being cold—people said this was the coldest June in anyone's memory—it began to be hot. Suddenly it was hot. Inside the wing the changing of the seasons hit very hard. There was no in-between. Nobody was cold anymore. The change occurred virtually overnight, and now everyone who before had had too little clothing to keep warm in was almost too warm to wear anything at all. Men sat inside their cells uncovered, letting go of their modesty, and on Sunday the minister, whose name no one knew and who came to bless the men one by one and to say kind words and deliver and take away mail, made a stern announcement from the doorway to the wing:

"Gentlemen, until you are all well covered, for Jesus' sake, I will not pass among you with the good word and will not give my benediction or leave the mail. So be it, and you may believe me."

But the men just sat there and sweated and did not cover themselves. All energy had gone out of the place. From the door, finally—after a warder had checked each cell and found many men still unclothed—the minister called out a blanket benediction: "May the peace of God and all his mysteries be with even you, the undeserving, until we are met again. Amen." And from the cells there were slow amens said mushily, a buzzing like that of the very slow flies that were now to be seen everywhere. The big door banged shut and echoed. The hot, smelly air quivered, and the slow flies hovered in it, seeming to swing. It was quiet. It was Mount's second Sunday in jail. Nothing else happened.

* * *

The next day, Monday, he had a visit. After breakfast he sat on his bunk and sweated. The warder Joseph unlocked the cells and let the other inmates out. Mount kept to his habit and refused to leave his cell, but no one cared what he did. He watched the other inmates filing past on their way to wherever they went—to the yard or to the stitchery, where they made burlap sandbags for flooding season. They didn't even look at Mount anymore; no one was curious. They just accepted that he was in there, refusing to come out. Sweat rolled down his forehead. He didn't move. There were hundreds of flies in his cell, floating slow in the air like dust. He began to count.

After everyone was gone, Joseph brought him a book. The book was the Bible. Mount held it in his hands like a baby and looked at it; the book was cool and black. Mount opened it. There was dense printing on every page, and the pages were like tissue. Several flies flew in closer.

"Pick any page," said Joseph as though performing a magic trick. Mount refused. He shook his head and closed the book; the flies darted outward. A drop of Mount's sweat landed on the cover. He rubbed the sweat away with his thumb.

"*You* pick a page," said Mount. He handed the book back through the bars. Joseph took it away and came back later with checkers. Mount refused to play. He had only played with Father or Mother Mount, or else he had watched the two of them play. He decided he could not play in prison. He explained this to Joseph. Joseph held the checkerboard like a tray; he had already set up the checkers on it. Mount could see he was disappointed.

"Let me see your teeth," said Joseph. Mount opened his mouth and showed Joseph his teeth. He could feel the warm air blowing through his mouth and making everything dry, and a few of the teeth began to hurt. Some, he knew, were so loose that he could move them with his tongue.

"Okay, enough," said Joseph. "Everybody smells bad in here. Me, too, I think. Do you notice?"

Mount shook his head. Joseph seemed satisfied. Mount was too busy noticing his own bad smell to notice Joseph's. But maybe someone at Joseph's home had told him something.

"I think I do, though," Joseph said. Mount nodded. Then his visit came. Another warder Mount had never seen before interrupted them at the bars.

"He has a visit, John," the other warder said to Joseph. "This is Mount, right?"

Joseph nodded. He took the ring of keys and unlocked Mount's door. The two of them led Mount along the tier and down a flight of stairs to the flats, then out of the wing and through long, dim corridors that were cooler than Mount's cell but still hot. Some of the flies followed. As Mount walked he felt the halves of his ass sticking together. He was brought to a room where there was a long table with a board standing up in its middle and running the length of the table. The board had face-sized holes cut in it. There were chairs on Mount's side of the table; he couldn't see what was on the other side. It was impossible to know who was visiting without bending over and looking through a hole to see if a face was there. When Mount found the right chair to sit in he saw Hin Lin's face through the hole.

For a minute he didn't remember her. She smiled. Mount moved his face up to the hole. He could smell Hin Lin's good breakfastlike smell. It nearly overpowered him. Through the hole she passed him a shining bun with raisins and white icing. Mount was so eager for the bun, he scratched her finger by accident when he grabbed for it. Hin Lin smiled, but Mount thought she could never imagine how good it was at that moment to have a bun like that. She gave him another, which he ate less fast. His teeth hurt and he was having trouble breathing. Then she gave him another one. He was about to start eating when a warder came up from behind and snatched it away for himself. Mount frowned and saw Hin Lin frown; he heard the soft, chewing sounds of the warder eating the bun. The theft made him so mad, but there was nothing he could do. His eyes and mouth were watering—from anger and from hunger. Then Hin Lin gave him another bun, and he ate it as fast as he had eaten the first. Sweat rolled down his nose and onto the raisins and icing.

"Oh, God," said Mount with his mouth still full. While eating the buns he had fallen behind in his breathing; he could hardly breathe. "Oh, God . . ." He thought he might never catch up.

Then the visit was suddenly over. They had no chance to talk. Hin Lin's small face got smaller as she backed away from the hole in the board. Mount was secretly glad. What would they have talked about? He waved through the board. "Thank you," he said. There was icing on his fingertips.

"Let's go," said the warder. Mount imagined the taste of Hin Lin's pastry in the warder's mouth. "Let's go," he said again, and Mount detected that the warder's voice was fuzzy sounding, as though there were raisins and pressings of dough caught up in his teeth and on the roof of his mouth. This made Mount sad; something special had been lost to him.

He stood up and felt dizzy—he was breathing hard and sweating, and the heat was intolerably still. The flies hung in the air, rising and swaying and dipping down like the ones in his cell; when they touched his face they hardly touched it at all—the contact as soft as could be.

"Goodbye, Hin Lin," he said. He wondered about her baby.

Two days later he received a letter from Hin Lin. He could see by the date on the opening page that she had written it near the time he had been sent to jail. Perhaps the letter had lain around somewhere and been read out loud by warders putting on and taking off their uniforms in the changing room. The seal had been broken and the letter itself was soiled and wrinkled as though it had been much handled. It was said these things happened frequently. Having the letter was good nonetheless. Mount read the words over and over again.

Dear Mount,

I saw all about your trouble in the newspaper. No one should have such trouble. It was bad of you to do it. But it was bad of them to send you away. I will miss you mornings at my table. Even so, I know they had no choice. In Qingdao they would heat your hand slowly over a thick fire until it swelled and burst or until you lost your mind. Then they would set you free and you would be ordered to tell your story to children for a certain number of years. After a time, you might be considered wise and they would let you be a merchant. But you would always have your bad hand, and for the rest of your life you would wear a small brass bell around your neck. By this, your customers would know your past, and they would always pay you less and more slowly than they would pay other merchants. But never mind. I am sorry for you, dear Mount.

Now that the weather has gone so cold, my fire is always going. But it was like this in China too in the time between spring and summer. I try to do here what I always did there. I move very swiftly, even inside the house. I start and stop as fast as I can and I do not sit still for long. This can be done in the smallest of space, and I commend such a measure as this to you for use in the small space where you must now be kept. I am sorry again about this.

My baby has been lost, and I have been more lonely. The mother came to take him back. She was sorry. She told me her story. Her heart had been slowly changed. Her own mother had kept her in a closet to find out what she had done with the baby. Finally she confessed, thinking she would be released from the closet. But her confinement continued. The family wanted more from her. For many days she drank fish soup in the dark and thought very hard, and her mother and the others in her family would come and whisper things at the door of the closet. At some point her heart had changed. Without even sleeping she would dream that the baby, as large as a dog, was waiting outside the door of the closet. Over and over, she would ask how the baby was. After a while the family knew her heart had changed. They released her. Right away she came to ask for the baby back. What could I do? She was sorry, but she had to have him. He was lying on his back in a basket on the table by the window. Outside the window was one of the mother's brothers staring in at me with a dark expression. When the mother asked me what name I had given the baby, I told her another name than the one I had chosen. She said she would call him by that name in my honor, but I know she will give him a name of her own liking.

The letter went on for two more pages, but whenever Mount read it through he would stop at this point and close his eyes, feeling himself completely outside of his cell and outside of his time in jail. He remembered the deep green color of the grass in Hin Lin's yard and the perfect odor of sausage or ham floating in the air like a soft fabric, floating through his own interior body as he breathed in. This was what he missed. He remembered the silence of Hin Lin as she carried a plate of food. The silence combined with the swishing sound of her garments and her feet sliding across the floor. He remembered the sound of his fifteen cents falling to the bottom of Hin Lin's brass temple. Afterward, when there was time to linger, he sat in the grass outside and listened to his inner organs muttering their thanks.

How sorry I am he is gone. At first I was not sure I liked him. When he looked at me and would not look away after only a short time, I was uneasy. My sister would have liked him right away, and I thought of sending him to her in Chicago. But then, after several days, I began to think of new ideas. I changed the rooms around, taking a chair and a rug and reversing them and moving where I slept from the front to the back of the house. In that smallest room off the kitchen I painted elk and dogs and bears and yellow birds on the walls around the two windows. Someday you can see them. I cooked new things with new ingredients that I bought at stores I had never entered before. At the end of the day I would sit with my feet near the fire and hold the baby in my lap. The baby would lie there not quite sleeping and not quite smiling, and I would look down and think he was giving me these new ideas through his half-opened and half-closed eyes and mouth. Then he would make a sound, and we both would laugh. It was so warm in my lap. I named him . . .

Something was written here and blotted out after, a dense black coffin of ink half a thumbnail wide.

Now, Mount, you must swear you will not be in more trouble. It will be sure to shorten your life and take away energy from all the time that remains. In Qingdao the criminals were all unhappy. Sometimes in the mornings they would meet in an empty hut near the baths and complain to each other. You could hear their sour voices, and people walking past would frown. Then they would come outside together and complain to random people on the streets who were only going about their business. The citizens would strike out at the criminals and insult them openly, and the criminals would moan unhappily and shrink back into their own little circle. Then they would retreat to their hut and complain further among themselves. It was a bitter life for them. In Qingdao there was no honor to crime as there seems to be here. There was no Jesse James. The criminals were sad and bitter. They were ashamed.

So, Mount, I will come to visit you. If your spirits are low, I am very sorry. But it will only be a short time. As far as the world of light is concerned, you are fully in the dark now. But when your term is over, you will spring forth with absolutely total brightness into this land of freedom. All the world will welcome you then, and we will pray for your new beginning. So, there, Mount.

As a signature there were two little houselike symbols of oriental writing, which Mount assumed were a Hin and a Lin but could have been anything. Below these two symbols was a postscript stating that the letter had been written by "the Scribe and Notary Public Wm. J. Hallissey, of Rumsey Avenue, entirely from the spoken words of the signatory, Miss Hin Lin."

After Mount had finished reading the letter he stared again at every page in no particular order. Then he brought the pages close to his face, exploring in the most minute detail the paper and ink until the characters were blurred and the sweat was flowing all over his body. He sniffed the pages to see whether breakfast or Hin Lin could be smelled; but they could not. He did whatever might help to prolong the life of each reading of the letter. For instance, he thought up conversations between himself and the brother of the mother of Hin Lin's baby. In these conversations the two of them talked about what a nice house Hin Lin had, and sometimes they just stood outside in the yard and looked in through the window at the baby in the basket on the table—which Hin Lin finally picked up and slowly handed to the mother. Then the brother said something Mount could not make out, but when Mount said "What?" the brother was already trotting away around the house to where his sister and the baby would come out. And Hin Lin was still in front of the table by the window, staring down at the empty spot and not looking very good.

Then Mount, as Hin Lin had suggested in her letter, began to do everything swiftly, stopping and starting in a single motion and swatting flies in midair with such force that they slammed against the walls of the cell and plummeted to the floor, where he could smash them under his fast-moving feet.

Then he read the letter again.

On a Wednesday, Mount was released from prison. For many days before, whenever someone went past his cell, he would call out, "Is my time over yet? Is it thirty days?" Without even slowing down, people said, "Your job . . . keep track . . . your time." Mount kept on asking. In the heat his slow voice sounded more and more like cotton. The warder Joseph would smile and scratch his head and pretend to count his fingers. Mount believed Joseph knew or could find out, but wouldn't tell or wouldn't inquire. There was a happy meanness on his face, and he would go sideways, back and forth, moving his feet in a funny sliding way in front of Mount's cell and counting and losing count and saying, "Maybe" and "Who knows?"

Then one night it was the Fourth of July. Warders ran through the wing lighting off crackers and throwing water and raising hell. Out the window Mount could see the sky getting pink and blue and brilliant white. He heard the heavy thudding from Fort Wayne, and he said to himself, "The time is got to be near." But the truth was he had lost count somewhere along the line, and when the Wednesday—what later proved to be a Wednesday—came, he was not prepared. He thought it would be the day after the day after that. He thought in any event they would come and give him a kind of certificate and say, "You'll be leaving us tomorrow, Mr. Mount." And so forth.

He was reading the letter again, pretending it was the first time through. His face was following along in a high dramatic way— expressing pleasure, sorrow, anger and surprise. He suddenly heard the warder Joseph laugh.

"What are you doing, Mount?" asked Joseph, who was just staring into the cell like someone idle and lonely, all the other inmates then being out of the wing for their two hours of industry and exercise. Mount was startled. Joseph had come up quietly.

"How long you been here?" Mount asked Joseph. Joseph didn't say anything. He half smiled. Mount wondered if Joseph had been there from the start, when Mount spread the pages out sideways on his bunk and stood over them happily as though each was a house and yard and he was waiting for the people to come outside and carry on their various lives. Joseph wouldn't have known then what he was doing.

Mount looked close. Joseph had a cat with him. The cat was on Joseph's shoulder, perfectly still and wicked looking. Flies were sailing around the head of the cat. The cat was staring at Mount.

"Hey, there, look at the flies," said Mount, pointing.

"Yeah," said Joseph, turning his own face up toward the face of the cat. "Them flies're imagining this cat is a dead one." Mount imagined the same thing.

"I was just reading this letter again," said Mount.

"Well, that's okay, you just go ahead," said Joseph. "You can do that all you want and I won't stop you. I got all day long."

"Thank you," said Mount. He waited for Joseph to go away, but the warder stayed put, half smiling. The cat kept staring with the flies still sailing in rising and dipping circles around its head. The whole business made Mount feel funny. As Hin Lin had taught him to do, he began to move swiftly, stomping and spinning, shooting his arms to the sides and jerking his head back and forth in the air. Droplets of sweat were flung away from him.

"Whoa-ay, Mount!" said Joseph. "Whoa, then . . . wait a minute, wait . . ." The words, as Mount heard them while moving fast, were like taffy stretched hot and sagging. When Mount slowed down, Joseph was still there saying them, and Mount tingled as he listened. The cat was gone, but the flies remained in the air above Joseph's shoulder where the cat's head had been.

"Okay, then," Joseph said, "okay. I'll tell you the truth this time, I will . . . okay? You're going home. There. You're getting out right now. I mean it, Mount. It's true. You only have to go with me to Master Horrigan's office and then you can go wherever you like and be done with it. What do you say?"

In Master Horrigan's office they had Mount's clothing in a crate of the kind tomatoes came in. Up and down the slats of raw, rough wood were bits of old fruit skin stuck there in dry pink dabs. Mount's clothes were in there too, the things he had had with him thirty days before. He put his hands down in the crate and felt what was there: shirt, trousers, suspenders, vest; brown hat, coin purse, shoes and socks. They were just as he remembered. Master Horrigan swept his hand above the crate to get Mount's attention. The crate was on the corner of a table on which there were also pieces of paper for Mount to sign and a pen and ink for him to sign them with. Master Horrigan pointed at the papers, the pen and ink.

One of the documents said that he was the same Mount who had been sent to prison thirty days before. He wasn't sure if he was exactly the same, but he signed it. Another said that he had received in good condition the things that had been taken from him thirty days before. He signed that too, after first pretending to count and be satisfied with the value of the coins in his coin purse—he couldn't truly recall how much had been in it, but what was there was all right with him. Then he signed two other documents. He didn't care what they said. But Master Horrigan told him they released the county from any claims on its liability unless he, Mount, stated then and there what his claims were. The other paper on the table was to be signed by Master Horrigan and given to Mount as proof that he had fully discharged his sentence. Mount told Master Horrigan that he was in no doubt he had done it start to finish, but he was told by Joseph the paper was like a school diploma when you went from sixth grade to higher.

"Thank you," said Mount as he took the document, "thank you," though something inside him told him his thanks were not expected. Master Horrigan handed him an onionskin envelope that Mount could dimly see a dollar bill showing through. The second he saw the money he thought he would go and buy himself a pie with a top crust that had been brushed with milk and melted butter and a filling made of something in season in the month of July in Indiana. His mouth watered.

"Thank you," he said again. But the business was not yet done. Master Horrigan presented him with a slender book with cardboard covers and laces that bound the pages inside. Mount opened it.

"Written by me," said Master Horrigan. Mount saw the name, Walter C. Horrigan, under the title, "Lessons To Guide Thee—Verses and Homilies for the Newly Penitent."

"A gift for everyone who leaves here," said Master Horrigan. "Compliments of Allen County and myself. May the spirit of goodness that dwells in all living creatures, and slumbers in some, find its full waking supremacy in you, Mister Mount, evermore. Amen. You may go now. Good luck and godspeed."

And, after having him change from prison clothes into his own, they let Mount go. A big door opened and shut, and he was expelled into brightness and heat.

5
ELECTRICITY

The jail was a dark thing back behind him.

Mount squinted at first. The sun was high and powerful, bigger and brighter than he had ever known it. His weak eyes watered, owing to the sudden change from such darkness. Tears rolled down his cheeks, growing larger, combining with the sweat that was already there. The weather was hot and sticky. Mount walked with his head down, his shiny face pinched and stunned by the outdoors after his thirty days in the dark.

But he was happy.

"I'm so happy," he said aloud.

Two gray birds flew right over his head, one next to the other, both flapping and whooshing. He shielded his eyes and looked after them. The two birds curved left and were soon out of sight among trees that welcomed them in and hid them. Mount took this to be a powerful sign of whatever it might later come to mean to him. Only time would tell. But the birds were his very first greeting by the outside world, the first greeting of himself in his new, free condition.

"I'm so happy," he said again. He had a dollar in his pocket and a book and some coins. Anything was possible.

But he didn't know where he was. So he asked a stranger who came out of a woods in which Mount could see a small house—maybe the stranger's house. The stranger said, "Canada that way," and pointed, "Chicago that way, Bolivia that way, Oklahoma that way," pointing in all directions.

"I want to go into Fort Wayne," said Mount. And the stranger told him that he, the stranger, was going there, too, and he would be glad to lead Mount straight to Fort Wayne without stopping.

"Tell me who you are," Mount said to the stranger. But the stranger acted highly mysterious and wouldn't say, and Mount had the thought that this man was an agent of Master Horrigan of the jail, put there to test Mount's penitence right off the bat and lead him back to prison if he failed.

"Just call me Bill, or some such thing, and leave it at that," the stranger said. Mount was satisfied. He knew what a person wanted from him.

"You can call me Mount," said Mount. But the stranger didn't say anything further and only walked alongside of Mount, a little bit ahead where Mount could see almost all of the stranger but the stranger couldn't see all of Mount. They both seemed to like it that way because it lasted as long as they walked.

Every so often, Mount looked back over his shoulder at the Allen County House of Penal Detention. The building was set in a clearing half encircled by a forest, and looked like a hidden castle. There was not much else in the vicinity that anybody knew about, and Mount wondered if the woods were full of warders waiting to catch whoever escaped.

"Do the warders wait in the woods?" Mount asked the stranger.

"They do," he said. "They come by and they ask me for cups of coffee, and they ask me to come out and pass the time with them."

"Do you do that?" asked Mount.

"They can have that coffee if they want," said the stranger. "I don't mind that. They can lean against my firewood and talk to each other if they want. They don't bother me as long as they don't bother me myself."

After a while, when Mount looked back over his shoulder there was nothing to see, the road having slowly curved and the trees having closed in and reared up and made of themselves a solid wall. There was no more reason to turn and look, but still he felt the prison back there lingering— not the people inside it but the walls and the damp and the way it smelled, its color and its dark and its weight, the animal character of it.

"You smell pretty bad," the stranger said.

"I do," said Mount. "I know that's true. I picked it up on the inside there." But Mount smelled the pine trees, too, and the one smell was scrubbing against the other, and he felt as though the world itself was cleaning him and making him better as he passed on through.

"I guess it'll go away," he said.

With the stranger just that little bit ahead of him, Mount could study the way he walked; he passed the time observing the stranger and practicing swinging his arms in different ways and at different speeds and rising up on the balls of his feet with each step, which he was sure would cause deeper impressions to be left in the dusty road and thereby confound whomever might follow along behind, if anyone.

"Go ahead and ask me where I work," the stranger told Mount.

"Where do you work?" asked Mount.

"I work for Mr. Edison's company making e-lec-tri-city," said the stranger, drawing the word along slowly like cars of a train. "It lights the lights along Washington and Jefferson and Clinton, and the lights in homes and businesses, and wouldn't you be surprised what all."

Mount said he would, and he waited.

"There is a ship somewheres," said the stranger, "and it carries lights so bright they scare the fish and everything else. It's got its own isolated dynamo. You can see it fifteen miles at night."

"You like that e-lec-tri-city," said Mount, picking up on the way of saying it and on the way the stranger liked it so much.

"I surely do," said the stranger.

The two of them walked a long time. They were going from the country into the city. At first there were hills and trees. Then hills that were almost flat, but were hills all the same; the water would have run down them. Then the trees slowly disappeared, becoming odd and solitary, so far apart from each other that they were bent and frail and frightened looking. In the opposite way from the trees getting fewer, the houses increased until they seemed to belong together, their sides and eaves in each other's shadows, their windows thrown wide open with curtains hanging half in and half out, the voices of the people inside them such that Mount couldn't tell which houses they came from until—complaining of the heat and coming to the windows and leaning out—these people would sigh so the sound carried across the lawns to where Mount and the stranger were passing, walking into town. The people appeared tired and red faced just from being alive in such a heat.

"Are we almost there?" Mount asked. But the stranger didn't answer.

This was a different part of town; Mount didn't know this part at all. He could hear no rivers and he couldn't smell the asphalt shingle factory that made the whole of North Fort Wayne smell the way his clothing used to smell when he worked there—the way the world seemed to smell at that time, a better smell than the one he had brought from jail.

"I can get you a job if you need a job," said the stranger. "I can get the ear of the manager because he likes me. And I can make him take you on just because I say so."

"Why should you do a nice thing like that?" asked Mount. Mount thought it was funny the stranger mentioning a job just when Mount was thinking of shingles. Things were going along pretty well. Here was Mount in this uncertain position, and answers were falling on him out of the blue, and all he had to do was walk half a step behind this stranger. He almost had to remind himself he had just been let out of jail, that he had come to consciousness that very morning by the act of a stick being banged sharp against his bars and by the warder Joseph saying to him, "All right, you Mount."

"It ain't just doing a nice thing," said the stranger. "It's only nice if there ain't no use for it. But I say there's a use for it. There was a fellow at work, name of Milo or Philo, that walked off yesterday and just left his shovel there leaning up against the bricks like some old drunkard. Well, it was probably the heat that finished him off. But whatever it was, we need new meat all the same. That's what the use is of asking you. You look like new meat to me. And that other guy won't be back. So, don't go just thinking it's nice. Even though there is a great opportunity there whenever you go to work in something new like this where who knows where it can lead. You can thank me some day when everyone calls us both sir."

"Well, how about that," said Mount. "Well, how about that?" He was back in Fort Wayne. He could hear the rivers somewhere not far away.

Bill, the stranger, talked to the manager. Mount waited in the background shifting from foot to foot, both of which were tired from all the walking he and Bill had done. The boilers and machines were so loud Mount couldn't hear the two men's voices; they were just a couple of mouths moving in the heat of the place, which was also very bright or

82

very dark, depending on where you stood—near the boilers or near the machines, the latter being brighter.

The manager would look at Mount then listen to Bill in his ear, look at Mount again, then back to Bill. Along the walls were lights that didn't flicker, lights that were not flames, glowing instead of burning. E-lec-tri-city, thought Mount. The manager shook his head and stuck a finger in one of his ears and shook his head again; then he offered his ear to Bill, which Bill said something into. The manager said something back, and Bill patted the manager's shoulder and said something else, which was just his mouth moving. Then Bill came over to Mount and shouted in Mount's ear, "Okay, it's all set." Bill's voice hurt deep inside Mount's ear, and he jerked his head away and shook it, sticking one of his fingers in the ear until it felt better.

Bill took him to the shovel that was leaning against the bricks where Milo or Philo had left it like a drunkard. Bill took the shovel and put it in Mount's hands. Mount's fingers closed around it; he could feel the whole music of the place trembling in the hickory handle as though it was alive with e-lec-tri-city.

"Thank you," he said. He didn't even hear it himself. Bill laughed, with his mouth just opening up and staying open long enough for the unheard laugh to disappear. The shovel tingled in Mount's hands.

After his first day of working for Mr. Edison—who was never there in Fort Wayne himself but had associates running things for him—another stranger, not Bill, took Mount round to Mrs. Collamer's boardinghouse. She lived on Bilge Street close by the power station in a house with little peaks and points and angles and cut-out pieces of trim stuck to it. The man who brought him knocked hard on the door and then, before the door was answered, left Mount there to wait.

Mrs. Collamer came out slowly and stared at Mount through the big beveled pane of glass. He could tell right away she didn't like him and he didn't like her. She had a strange expression, raising one eye and drooping the other and letting her mouth go slack. She looked mean and afraid at the same time. The look made Mount want to protect her and protect himself in whatever way was possible that would not suddenly make things worse. He returned her gaze.

"Okay," she said through the glass. "Okay." Mount liked her a little better.

When the door opened, though, the smell burst out like the devil himself escaping. It was German food, Mount realized, salty and sharp, the way he remembered the smell coming from every unstoppered opening in the tidy blue Dutchy houses on Luther Street in Bolusburgh. Mrs. Collamer led him inside and laid down the dozens of rules that everyone resented: no this and no that; no spitting in the rooms where signs were posted; on time for each and every meal; the bedding placed outside the door on Monday mornings; always pull the long chain hanging down from the tank in the bathrooms, and always use the matches provided there for odor.

There were many more rules, but Mount didn't even listen. He had just about had enough. He closed his eyes and lolled his head back. He could still smell the warm electricity of the power station mixed with the coal dust stuck to his dirty shirt and his cheeks. That, in turn, was mixed with what little was left of the terrible prison smell of himself that the long day had covered over. The whole accumulated business softened the smell of the kraut, or whatever, that infested Mrs. Collamer's parlour.

"Sign here," she said.

"What do you mean?" said Mount. He opened his eyes. In front of his face Mrs. Collamer held a document printed in scrolly black letters. The paper was a list of all those rules of the house, the same as she had just finished speaking, set forth in legal form. It stated at the end that the undersigned understood and agreed, and assented to quit the dwelling-house if ever found to be in violation, and to forfeit without a claim any monies already paid for any room and board not yet received. There was a line for Mount to sign on and a line for a witness—in this case Mrs. Collamer, since none of the boarders were handy. She signed in the same scrolly hand as the script on the rest of the document.

"There you go," she said. She put the document between two fat books in a glass-front bookcase. "Overnight, it'll flatten out good, and then I'll take it to the bank tomorrow and you and me'll be jake then. Okay?"

The tired-out Mount said "Okay." He said "Jake."

Mrs. Collamer took Mount to show him his room. The room was three flights up. When she opened the door he saw right away that the evening light was peculiar; honey colored and thick as smoke, it made his stomach churn. He said something respectful about the room, but

84

Mrs. Collamer only said "warm," and "nice," and crouched down to pick at something invisible on the gray-green coverlet that was so worn you could see right through it.

"Nice for you," said Mount. He went to the window. All he could see were other houses, other windows. Everything was opened up in the terrible heat and the burnished light. He put his head out and quickly drew it back in. He felt the inside and outside blended unpleasantly, wrongly, with no proper boundary keeping them apart as they ought to have been. He imagined cats coming over the sills as he slept, padding across the floor and spraying the corners, the legs of the bed. He touched his back where it hurt from shoveling. All in all, summer was a torment. His fingers dug in hard astride his spine, grinding up and down. He groaned.

Mrs. Collamer waited patiently, quietly. There were four kinds of flowers on the walls and some wheat and barley, all painted in a shaky old hand with pale colors that had run here and there, connecting some of the flowers together with pastel threads that Mount knew didn't belong there but liked anyway. He ran his finger from flower to flower, following these accidental rivers.

Mrs. Collamer stayed and watched Mount go around the walls. She said nothing, except every couple of minutes she coughed and said, "Well?" Mount didn't answer. He pretended her voice was coming from one of the other houses, from a person he couldn't yet see but who any second was going to walk slowly past a window and take a long look at him before looking away.

"Well?" said Mrs. Collamer. Mount turned around and stared at her, wide as the door with her hands on her hips. The kraut smell had come all the way upstairs.

The next day he went to see the police. He had to get his carpetbag back. Officer Paige, who was the one who had arrested him, was there. When Mount walked in he saw him fussing with something on the wall, a round black bug that was crawling sideways. Officer Paige would stop it with his finger and make the bug move in a different direction. The bug would take a few steps, but then would start to circle around and try to go in the direction it had been going before Officer Paige put his finger out. Then Officer Paige would turn it again. Mount got the idea he was trying to keep the bug from crawling up on the portrait of

President McKinley that was hanging nearby in a place of honor. Officer Paige reached out and put his finger smack in the path of the bug.

"Hello," said Mount, and the shock of a sound coming from the direction of what until then had been Mount's pure observant silence caused Officer Paige to spin around fast, a startled paleness in his face. "Who are you?" he said. He was large and formless and very white. Mount liked him.

"It's me. It's Mount. Remember?" Mount stood very still and let Officer Paige stare directly into his face for as long as it took. "I'm here to get my things back, all my personal things that were in my bag along with that one thing, the photograph, that belonged to that other fellow whose name was Harry and who was with you when you caught me that time. Back then. It was over a month ago. I just got out."

"Oh, yes, Mount," said Officer Paige. "I think I remember now. You're the one that never once said he didn't do it. Though, of course, how could you, since we caught you with it?" Behind Officer Paige the bug had crawled up on President McKinley's face. It crept across the cheek and the bridge of the nose and entered one eye; it left the eye and crawled across the forehead and, finally, lost itself in the hair.

"No hard feelings, Mount?" said Officer Paige.

"No, sir," said Mount. "Just my bag back is all. I'm finished with everything else. Everything's behind me now."

"That's good," said Officer Paige. "You wait right here and I'll go get your bag." He went through a door and shut it behind him. He was gone for a long time. Mount walked over to the wall and reached up and ran his hand across the hair on President McKinley's portrait, capturing the bug. He dashed the bug to the ground and crushed it under his shoe, where it made a small noise and left a brownish smudge that he scuffed away. Then he sat on a worn wooden bench and made friends with the stationhouse dog, a big yellow thing that smelled old and acted like it wanted to sleep all the time. But Mount kept getting the dog's attention and taking its paw and scratching its bony yellow back until his fingers were tired and dirty feeling.

"Okay," said Officer Paige when he finally came back through the door. "This here's your bag."

Even at a distance Mount could see the bag wasn't his.

"This is wrong," he said.

"No, it isn't," said Officer Paige. He thrust the bag at Mount. Mount thrust the bag away and Officer Paige thrust it back with an angry look that was chiefly in the narrowing of his lips. Mount took the bag and looked inside. Not a thing in it belonged to him; this was obviously the stuff of someone else.

"This is someone else's," said Mount. "I could go to jail again for this. Lookit here." He started taking things out. The trousers had longer legs and all the shirts were blue. He held one up.

"Lookit this," he said. "These're *blue*." The yellow dog looked up at the shirt and went back to sleep. There weren't any shoes or stockings either, and there was no famous bust of Tyrus Portman Bolus, Sr., that dated back to Bolusburgh. There was a book, though. He took it out and opened it. The book was a training manual for constables called *Doing Your Duty*. "Ex Libris," said the inside cover, and below that, "G. Fletcher."

"These're G. Fletcher's things," said Mount.

"Aw, dammit!" said Officer Paige, slapping his forehead. "Then that means G. Fletcher must have yours."

With the address Officer Paige had given him Mount went to see G. Fletcher, a man about the same age as Mount, only taller. He lived in a house of his own off Hiawatha Lane, a new house that Mount could see right away had asphalt shingles.

"I probably made some of those shingles myself," said Mount as he knocked on the door. When G. Fletcher opened up, Mount said again what he'd said about the shingles.

"Who are you?" G. Fletcher asked him.

"I've got your things," said Mount, "and you've got mine." Mount held up the bag. G. Fletcher invited Mount in and offered him coffee. While the coffee was on the boil, G. Fletcher went into another room and returned with Mount's carpetbag. Everything was there.

"This is wonderful," said Mount. He shut his eyes for an instant and felt its weight in his lap; it cooled him. The smell of the coffee filled the room. He reached inside and drew out the bust of Tyrus Portman Bolus, Sr., and held it to the light of the window by the table where they sat. It shined dully. Mount tilted it back and looked up the darkness of the two tiny caves of the nose.

"Who's that?" asked G. Fletcher.

"My father," Mount lied.

87

"I wish I had something like that of *my* father," G. Fletcher said. "Now he's died and I can hardly recall what his head was like. Though I remember his voice all right."

"Mine's still alive," said Mount.

G. Fletcher went and got the coffee. He poured through the piece of muslin and then went out the door and spun the muslin around his head so the coffee grounds were flung to the winds—except that in the morning's heat and stillness there weren't any winds.

"It saves me a lot of washing up," he said, coming back in the door.

Mount went on talking about his father and holding the bust of Tyrus Portman Bolus, Sr., in his hands, but standing it on its cut-off neck on the table when he took up his coffee cup to drink. Then it was as though there were the three of them there.

"That's nice," said G. Fletcher after every story Mount told him about Father Mount, only some of which were true. "No wonder they made him that statue there."

"That's right," said Mount. "He saved the lives of seven boys in the town, including mine—without which I might have spent the rest of my life in one room, just sitting there letting the food run out the side of my mouth. And one of the other boys he saved twice from terrible fires in two different houses in the same year. After a while they began to say he could hear the crackle before the match was struck."

"Was it always fires?" G. Fletcher asked. But Mount suddenly tired of talking. He shrugged. The coffee was making his brow sweat. He cradled the head in his hands.

"Well, he's a handsome man," said G. Fletcher.

Mount looked at the head and then put it on his shoulder next to his own. "Do you see how we look alike?" He could feel the cold bronze ear touching his cheek. G. Fletcher nodded.

"I suppose so," he said. "It's not often you see two generations on one set of shoulders like that."

Mount nodded. "I should go now," he said. "I've got to go to my job that I'm already late for."

"Oh, what job is that?" G. Fletcher asked. He stood up. Mount stood up, too.

"I work for Mr. Edison down at the power station. I work with that e-lec-tri-city which lights the lights. They say there's a ship at sea and you can see it from here to Ohio it's so bright. Scares everything away."

"Well, what do you know," G. Fletcher said.

Mount stood silent in the room a little longer, inhaling the sour burnt-coffee smell and looking slowly in a circle so as to pick out things to remember later, such as the shiny yellow-pine color of the wood the walls were made of or the skinned rabbit hanging upside down from a string tied to the handle of a cupboard door.

"I'm sorry I got your things," he said. "I've been sent to jail for that before."

"Well, it isn't your fault," G. Fletcher said. "I got yours first, after all. By accident, of course. But I just picked it up without thinking. I didn't even look. Why, you could send *me* to jail for that."

"I know," said Mount. "But I wouldn't."

"Well, okay then. Things are fine between us, and no one can say they're not."

"That's right," said Mount. He put the bust of Tyrus Portman Bolus, Sr., back in his bag and strapped it shut. The weight felt good at the end of his arm and he was glad to have it back where it belonged. Regaining his possessions left him almost completely recovered from prison.

"Thank you," he said. "Thank you."

"Someday soon," G. Fletcher told him, "I'm going to be a constable. So, if you ever need my help you can come see me and I'll arrest anybody you say, and I'll go to court and testify to whatever things you tell me and make sure they're sent to jail. But only if they truly did the bad things you said they did. Understand?"

"I do," said Mount.

"You should see me in my outfit," G. Fletcher said. "I'm your ace in the hole."

"I appreciate it," said Mount. He stepped out the door and heard it bang shut behind him.

From G. Fletcher's house he walked to work, switching the bag from one hand to the other, feeling the shoulderbones draw apart and the ache that he had from yesterday's shoveling turning into the ache that he had from today's carrying the bag—a better ache because it signified his reunion with his things, and would last for as long as it took him to get to work and resume the shoveling that would make him ache some more, and so forth. The hard leather handle grew damp with sweat. Mount began to whistle in time with the walk. And walking, he felt the head rolling freely inside.

When he got to the factory the other men were already working. He was more than an hour late. The other men went on with their work, not saying anything. But Bill, the stranger who had found him on the road from the prison the day before, scowled at him. And the manager came up behind him and struck him lightly on the head—not enough to hurt him but with the clear intention of straightening him out so that it would never happen again.

"I promise," said Mount. But the surroundings were so loud that no one heard him, and Mount had the idea they were happy just to have another body there to shovel with and make the circle larger.

So he went straight to his shovel. Already it felt like his own, as though it was waiting there just for him and had forgotten all about that fellow named Milo or Philo who had walked out and not come back. The handle was as warm as the air, and his hand fit nicely around it. The shoveling motion came to him naturally. Stoop and slide, lift and walk. He started moving coal from one of the big black piles into one of the yellow-mouthed boilers. He and the rest of the men took turns, going in a shoveling circle to and from the pile and the mouth of the boiler.

After a while they went to another pile and another boiler, and another and another after that, an engine of men circling inexhaustibly, no one stopping as they fed the bigger business of the place, playing their parts accomplishing what Mr. Edison had been pleased to set in motion from far away. The work was the hottest Mount had ever known. But, as he heard one of the other men saying later to someone else, "Look at it this way: in the wintertime it's a dream."

Mount thought he might wait for winter; then again, he might not. He thought about it and had a vision of electric lights shining out upon snow, yellowing the chill. He liked the electric lights but not the chill. In Bolusburgh in winter, the lampreys froze clinging to the sides of the barges in the Bolusburgh Canal. In the spring, seemingly no older, they slipped back into the water, leaving the shape of a circle there on the hulls to stink in the warming air. Mount hated the wintertime.

"I might not stay that long," he said, stooping to shovel. But no one heard him. All day long the piles grew smaller.

* * *

Mrs. Collamer chose not to like him. She watched him coming down the street. He must have seen the curtains moving, because his eyes met hers; she shivered from her heels to her hairline, once up and once down. God bless the rest of my men, she thought. I'm as safe as I can be.

Mount came in the door. He had his empty oilskin sack from the lunch Mrs. Collamer packed for her men. She went to get the week's money from him.

"Here it is," he said. He gave her the money and the empty oilskin sack. She couldn't complain, and she didn't.

"You're good for another week," she said. Her shivers came back, but not as strong. The August days were long and always warm, the windows left open around the clock like an invitation to anything. That very afternoon a pigeon had come in an open window and soiled the dining-room rug. Mrs. Collamer chased the bird around the house with a broom until it broke its neck against the shiny blue door of the second-floor bathroom. She put the bird in the dirty pillowcase from Mr. Hosford's room. The wings had still been trembling.

Mr. Mount continued to stand there in front of her, annoying her by the way in which he always seemed to expect something more from her, forcing her to guess what. Often her solution was to release him in some formal way, to say, "You can go wash now," as though she was his mother. Otherwise, he would simply continue to stand there for hours as she was coming and going. Literally for hours, as though he was some kind of tree or a horse that slept standing up.

"You work hard, don't you?" she said to him. Immediately she wanted to bite her tongue. He might get the idea she liked him, and then, as sure as snow follows snap, he'd be expecting even more than he did already, maybe going so far as to ask to play Shotgun or Whist or Grimaces with her, and cracking his knuckles gruesomely over the cards in the middle of shuffling.

"Well, I do the work that's there to do," he said. "I'm obedient." There were grimy, tearstain streaks on his face caused by sweat running down the patina of coal dust. "But I guess it's hard enough, all right."

Mrs. Collamer nodded. The sound of water trembling in the pipes in the walls from someone upstairs washing gave her an idea.

"Before you go up to wash, Mr. Mount, I need your help in burying a bird." She was glad to see his face hardly changed; he didn't seem to object. She touched his shoulder to signal that the chore was about to commence. "Well, good," she said. Otherwise, he might have just stood there waiting, as she had seen him do before.

She took him outside in the yard and fetched the shovel from the shed by the rhododendron bush. With her toe she defined the dimensions of the plot she wanted. She handed the shovel to Mount. He took the handle in a way that showed his experience, checking its weight and its balance and putting the toe of his shoe to the metal, making it ring. She saw how thick his back was.

"This is fine," he said. The ground was soft. He sunk the shovel into the dirt, and it seemed to go in easy. Mrs. Collamer was pleased.

"I'll go and get the bird," she said. By the time she returned the hole was dug and the dirt piled neatly beside. Mount was peeling two green twigs to make the cross.

"It's a pigeon," she said. She held out the pillowcase. Mount took it and looked inside.

"I think I know that bird," he said. "It's one of the ones from up between those gables." He pointed up, and Mrs. Collamer looked where he was pointing and saw the other pigeons looking down from the steep-pitched slate up there that was almost the same color as the birds themselves. Seven or eight of them perched in the gables' shade. They were making soft, womanly, fluttering noises, lifting and lowering their feet one at a time, slowly and methodically, with no clear purpose that a person could make any sense of.

"This bird?" Mrs. Collamer said. "Why, yes, I suppose it must be."

The two of them buried the bird.

"Should we unwrap it?" she asked. "Or should I bury the pillowcase, too?"

"It doesn't matter to me," said Mount. "Except unless you put it back on my bed sometime."

"It was in Mr. Hosford's room," she said. "But it might get mixed up in the laundry by Emmaline."

"Then bury it, too," said Mount. Mrs. Collamer nodded, and Mount let go of the pillowcase so it dropped straight into the hole he'd dug. The linen settled in a circle like the petals of a flower; in the center was the blue-gray bird.

"Ashes to ashes," said Mount. He shoveled the dirt back in and tamped it down. "When the grass grows again you'll notice the change and think of that bird," he told her. She tried to smile. "You'll never forget where it is," he said. She heard the scratch of the pigeons' feet on the slate up above.

"I'm much obliged for your help," she said. "You'll find something extra in your lunch next time." She was thinking she would slice him the full six inches of summer sausage, instead of five.

Believing that the chore was finished, she expected him to move. But he stood there staring down at the hole that was now covered over and dirt brown. He took his wobbly cross and bent down and stuck it in.

"Amen," said Mrs. Collamer helplessly.

"The name of that bird was Dave," said Mount. She watched him shut his eyes. She stood there waiting in the warm evening air for everything to be over. Above them the rest of the pigeons flew up from the dark between the gables. She was startled. She turned and watched them settle on the roof of one of the neighbors, each about a foot apart. With his head still down, Mount raised one hand like a minister. The tips of two fingers jutted into the slanting sunlight.

"Amen," said Mrs. Collamer again, this time more loudly so that Mount would see it was time to end. The pigeons cooed, and she found herself thinking, "Dave, Dave, Dave," and wondering whether the others had names, or was that only something of Mr. Mount's.

The sun was setting. Its light was the color of honey, and she thought how she would like to be near the ocean and mix the honey with the blue and stare off into the distance believing anything she wanted, thinking of her brother Gus in Germany or some man she hadn't met yet who would take her anywhere she said and buy her a silver cream and sugar service that he would never touch himself.

"That's too bad, Dave," said Mount in a prayerful voice. His hand came down against his thigh with a slap, and he lifted his head. Mrs. Collamer said amen one final time. Now she could go inside and have tea and slice the cabbage thin with the one good knife. She reached over and took the shovel from Mount. Then she returned it to its place in the shed by the rhododendron bush. When she came out of the shed, she looked up and saw that the pigeons—that she had often called *her* pigeons—had come back to roost between the gables. And that was fine with her. She heard the screen door slam and saw that Mount had just gone in. And that was fine, too, being by herself all of a sudden. She stood there near the shed by the bush in the honeyed air; a blood-

93

pumping sort of noise—one that was almost constantly a distraction in her thoughts—shut off and left silence inside her.

Ah, good, she thought.

The colored girl, Emmaline, came out the lean-to door from the cellar and began to take the linen off the line. Mrs. Collamer watched Emmaline going up on her toes and down, watched the smooth brown leg muscles changing their shape, watched the blue cotton dress swinging and working.

"Thank you, Emmaline," she said, just to let Emmaline know she was there. But the colored girl kept on working, the white line bouncing in the dusk.

Mount listened to two of the other men talking. The president was dead. McKinley, shot on September 6, 1901, had died September fourteenth. Mount thought back to the portrait and the bug on the police station wall. He wondered what it would be like to be a victim for a week, then die. He wondered how it would be to lie there thinking one thing and another: Maybe I'll live and Maybe I won't. Then having those doctors hovering and the relatives coming in and out, whispering uselessly. The candles and the shades, the smells of the wound, the bandage, the dirtying bedclothes. This was the president.

"It's terrible," he said. He took a bite of his summer sausage.

They were sitting in the yard, in the shadows of the mountains of coal that lay just beyond the tracks where the little hoppers circled out, around and back into the power station, bringing fresh piles of coal to shovel. For the time being, the electricity was taking care of itself—the boilers burning hot, the armatures whirling, the current climbing up the coils and into the wires that were strung up high, wrapped once around porcelains and then sent out through the walls to wherever the power was used.

A long time ago Mount had gotten over the awesome feeling of mystery when he looked at the wires. Now when he saw them, all he thought was: the power is flowing through them. For an instant he would feel the same old tingling in his arms, and then he would go back to doing whatever he'd been doing. Such as eating. He finished the sausage.

"Let's have a moment of silence," he said. The two men who were talking stopped and looked at him and looked at each other, and both seemed to agree to bow their heads in silence. Mount watched them. Everyone else went on eating, which, if not exactly silent, was in keeping with a moment of respectful observation, whether or not it was observed deliberately.

"Okay, that's good," Mount said, and the two men started talking again in a tedious way, insisting over and over that they were "worried as heck about the country" and shaking their heads woefully, the one who was keenest on McKinley lamenting that history itself was deranged by acts like these and the people were set adrift.

Mount couldn't see it. He felt bad about McKinley, but he didn't feel bad about anything else. He hoped they hanged the man who did it. The man was a foreigner, on account of which, Mount supposed, he might not be entitled to a regular trial. Mount imagined a crowd of people could shout from the street near where the man was confined, and he could be brought out where they could hang him up quick from a telegraph pole. Maybe the thing had been done already. The rope belonged in a museum somewhere, and people would go and pay to see it, still knotted, still in the shape of the foreigner's neck.

He reached in his oilskin sack and pulled out the bunch of grapes from Mrs. Collamer's wobbly arbor, early purple grapes that were sour and still too firm. He squeezed their greenish insides into his mouth, sucking the juice from the skins, which he then tossed over his shoulder onto the coal. He swallowed the insides whole, not removing the seeds or chewing down on the pulp, to avoid releasing the sourness that was held deep inside and ruining the sweetness sucked from the skins. He wondered if the seeds would float right through him completely intact and come out in the morning where he could see them before he pulled the long chain and lit the match there for the odor. And how did the liquids know to go one place and the solids another, especially in a case where liquid and solid were combined in a single item of food?

Mount heard the St. Mary's flowing on the other side of the mountains of coal. He heard the whistle of a boat and he thought to himself: that's the *Rosemary B.* Whatever the *Rosemary B.* was. The whistle blew again and the two men were still talking about the dead president when the manager stood up and stretched and reached down and tapped the stranger Bill on the shoulder and jerked his head toward the inside of the power station, meaning that lunch was over and work was supposed to begin. Everyone stood up, and the ones who had been sitting on overturned buckets took their buckets back inside while the rest dusted off the seats of their pants as they were walking. Mount was among this latter group of men, slapping and patting themselves and leaving little black coal-dust clouds in the air behind.

Bill, the stranger, was a fine teacher who knew about a lot of things, and Mount listened to him endlessly, Mount smiling and squinting and generally displaying all the respect he felt in his heart for someone who knew so much and was willing to share it—no matter who with. Mount would listen on and on, wishing he could save it all, everything a man like Bill would say to him that was good and smart and might come in handy someday, if only he didn't completely forget it. And it was probably the strain of thinking he ought to remember, and knowing he could not, that made him squint and smile in the nervous way that later tired him out so that he wondered why the day seemed so damn long. But he couldn't stop. Not that, nor the habit of putting his whole hand underneath his nose so that breath coming out the holes made a soft and likeable hissing noise on the topmost finger. When he did that Bill would reach over and forcibly take the hand away, saying, "I like to see the whole face of who I'm talking to."

They were sitting in the lowly tavern on Shipstad Street that was down by the river and had flood markings on the inside walls with the dates that the water rose that high and the number of people killed. The year 1884 was next to Mount's shoulder. The number 42 was next to Bill's.

"At first they buried the wires hereabouts," said Bill, "in iron pipes insulated with hot asphaltum poured inside. But if there ever was a problem you had to go open up the trenches to find it. And if a horse went over, and maybe there was water on the ground, and there was a break somewhere in the line or an air bubble in the asphaltum, the horse would rear up and throw the rider or go tearing off with a wagonload of something that ended up spilling all over the place. I know for a fact that some people got killed. Not here, but in Chicago. You can't see it, but e-lec-tri-city can come up out of the ground like the devil and go right through your shoes and roast your flesh and insides 'til the smoke comes out your ears."

"It's the wave of the future," said Mount, smiling and squinting.

"And now they string the wires *up* instead," said Bill. "And if it snows real bad or the wires ice, they snap and fall and dance in the street. The same exact e-lec-tri-city as they buried underground, only now it's up here with the rest of us, hanging over our heads like a clothesline or a telegraph wire. I can tell you, it's a sight when a squirrel hits a bare spot running along overhead—hiss, kee-rack!"

"I'll bet it is," said Mount. Bill drank some beer. Mount drank some too.

Bill told Mount he was writing down everything he learned about "the stuff," which is what he called it when he didn't call it e-lec-tri-city. "I'm writing a book," he said. When Mount heard about this book he told Bill how much he admired him being able to write down even a single word about something impossible to see.

"But people write about God," said Bill, "and they can't see him." Mount nodded, but Bill cleared this business up by saying no, he was dead wrong about that because people imagined the face of God. "So, maybe you are right," he said. Mount nodded. He closed his eyes and saw God looking like Tyrus Portman Bolus, Sr., only alive, with a bigger head and blacker, sharper eyes that could see right into your heart where all the regrets and the unkind thoughts were kept.

"I see him now," said Mount.

"I know," said Bill. "But you're right about that. It's not like e-lec-tri-city at all. With that, instead of what it looks like, what I write about is what it does and how it does it, and who likes it and who doesn't among the people. After all, if this is the future and some of the people don't want it, what does that mean? Why would anyone stand in the way?"

Mount shook his head. "I sure don't know," he said. "I was struck by lightning once, and it was terrible."

"But you're still here," said Bill. "That's the important thing. And you like e-lec-tri-city nearly as much as I do, don't you?"

"I do," said Mount. But he really didn't. Or, the truth of it was, he didn't care one way or the other. He just felt like it was something that was there, something bigger than him that he would have to live with because it was the wave of the future. And Mr. Edison's head—which he thought was also a godlike head—was connected to the whole enterprise; for that reason alone it was going to succeed to the point where no one would be without it.

But the major thing to Mount was that he stay friends with Bill, so he said whatever he had to to keep himself in Bill's good opinion, smiling and squinting and trying to remember everything Bill said.

"I want to meet Mr. Edison someday," said Bill.

"Me, too," said Mount. But he really didn't. When Mount saw pictures of Edison's forehead and eyes a chill ran through him. There was a portrait in the power station no bug would crawl across. It hung over the doorway into the room where the men washed up after working all day. Mount thought a portrait ought to smile down upon men who had worked so hard. But it didn't. The face just stared straight ahead sternly, like the light on the front of a train searching for cows to bump off the tracks.

Bill reached across and took Mount's beer because his own was already empty.

"Go ahead," said Mount. Bill was slugging it down.

On Mount's day off he stayed in his room like a hermit. Or he climbed out the window so no one would see him go. It depended on what he wanted.

There was no lack of things to hold on to while he descended. It was that kind of house, trimmed and tatted and textured with every imaginable decoration accenting its slopes and slants, which were like the unexpected variety of the rocks that rose to the top of Diamond Falls.

He climbed down from one gadget to the next as though that's what they were there for, holding tight with his hands while he felt with a foot, delicately, knowing the top of the trellis was near.

"Be careful," Mr. Hosford said one day, looking out his second-floor window. Mount, all concentration, was startled and almost fell. Rose thorns encircled his ankle and ripped at the skin as his leg trembled. It was October, and the thorns were hard and sharp.

"Oh, yes," he said, "I will."

"Well done, Mount," Mr. Hosford said. "Always doing it the hard way. Bravo to you!"

From the trellis Mount leapt backward into the yard, bending his knees on impact and flinging his arms to the sides. At exactly that moment Mrs. Collamer was setting two kraut-and-caper pies to cool on the porch rail. She heard him thud.

"What's this?" she cried.

"Never mind," said Mount. Mr. Hosford clapped his hands and

whistled. A neighbor dog barked through the privet hedge. The pigeons flew up from between the gables, went to another roof and then returned.

"Don't tell me never mind," she said. "Stay off that trellis, you hear?" Twin plumes of blue-green steam came out of the kraut-and-caper pies, carrying their terrible smell to the world. Mrs. Collamer stepped down into the yard and examined the climbing roses and shook the trellis for signs of damage. The roses nodded like heads; some of their petals fluttered off. She turned and faced him.

"No Sunday dinner today for *you*," she said. "I won't have steeple-jacking up and down my house. I won't. And disturbing the neighborhood. I won't." She pointed at the other houses. She pointed at Mr. Hosford leaning out his window. He waved politely.

"I'm so sorry for this, Mr. Hosford," she called to him.

"It was nothing," he said. "Never mind about it. Really."

"Don't say it was nothing," she told him. "Don't. This goes on always, and I'm so sorry." She shook the trellis some more; the roses bobbed.

"*Look* at this!" she cried. Mount began to back away. The wood of the trellis smacked against the side of the house. Whole roses fell.

"No, really," said Mr. Hosford. "It was nothing."

"I'm *talking* to you!" Mrs. Collamer cried after Mount. But Mount was moving, walking briskly. He heard a piece of the trellis splinter and the shriek of nails being bent and pulled from the cool wood.

"*Look* at this!" More wood was splintered. He didn't dare look. He passed the dreadful pies, with their crusts as white as peeled potatoes. Their smell reached down inside him, and he began to run.

"No *dinner*, Mr. Mount!" she hollered. He heard the pigeons flying up, wings battering the air. He felt the shadow of the house above him, towering.

He hated her. The people out walking on Bilge Street turned and watched him as he ran.

"Look out," he called. The words flew back behind him, and he could feel the very likeness of his own e-lec-tri-city churning on inside, a runaway pain no pie could cure.

6
HIN LIN

Christmas came. The people who dressed as angels filed up and down Bilge Street in the dark, surrounding each house and singing like terrible children; singing with colds and bad tempers; singing endlessly through their noses. They threw pebbles up at the windows and wanted money thrown back down. Either they were poor, or they were collecting for the poor who were too weak and lackadaisical to collect for themselves. House by house they were louder, the same songs over and over again. Finally Mount heard the desperate pebbles stinging his window. He blew out the lamp and searched his trousers for something to throw that would sound like money. But all he had was money. Coins. Nothing else. He raised the window. The singers circled the house, holding candles, the candles guttering and the singers swaying, their cold breaths steaming up bright.

"Here's something!" Mount hollered. He threw down a coin. It disappeared into darkness, and he didn't hear it clunk on the frozen ground or see an angel go after it. He threw another. Same thing. It disappeared. The angels kept singing, some of them stopping to throw up pebbles. The circle seemed to reach all the way around Mrs. Collamer's boardinghouse. Some of the other windows were going up, and arms came out and threw money down that disappeared and couldn't be heard hitting the ground and didn't cause angels to scramble after it.

"Here's another!" Mount shouted. Nothing happened. The angels' voices were sharp and sour. One of them reared back and threw a pebble at Mount's window, but since the window was open the pebble sailed

100

past Mount's ear and smacked the wall on the other side of the room. It rattled to the floor in the dark. He threw another coin as hard as he could, hoping it would hit someone and hurt. Then he shut the window. One song turned into another and another. More pebbles hit the glass, or missed the glass and hit the wood around it. Mount lay down on his bed. Whenever he recognized a song he sang along softly, adding his own small voice to the big sound welling up around the house.

When the singing stopped Mrs. Collamer came out and addressed the singers, commending their singing and thanking them for coming, and giving their leader a dollar and a basket of her holiday biscuit cookies dotted with poppy seeds. Then she went back in. Mount heard the thick Christmas bells bang against the door as it shut. He got up from bed and went to the window. Below him the angels were down on their hands and knees picking up the coins.

"Here's one!" cried one, holding up a coin.

"Here's another," cried a second. They crept along with their candles in their fists. Mount heard some of them coughing and sneezing. Their leader went among them taking the coins as they were found and dispensing Mrs. Collamer's poppy-seed biscuit cookies. Mount saw one of the angels take a bite and spit it out and throw the rest of the confection up at Mr. Hosford's window, where it broke to bits.

That was Christmas Eve.

On Christmas morning there was oatmeal and cream, with a stalk of cinnamon wrapped with red ribbon standing up in it. By each man's place there was a shiny dime.

"Merry Christmas, men," Mrs. Collamer said, pouring coffee from the big tin pitcher. The men lined up for coffee before they went to their places. They remained standing until all were present. Mrs. Collamer led them in a short prayer for the Christ baby.

"Bless that little newborn baby, men," she said.

"Amen," the men said.

"And bless you, too, and keep you safe," she added.

"Amen," the men said. They sat and ate. They looked closely at the dimes and put them in their pockets.

"There's more of everything," Mrs. Collamer said.

Mount didn't quite know what to do with the cinnamon stalk, but he cleaned his bowl and had two cups of coffee.

* * *

Later on, a Chinese boy came around with a message to come to Hin Lin's house. Mrs. Collamer wouldn't let the boy in. He held up a folded paper with Mount's name on it that Mrs. Collamer read through the glass. She called to Mount from the foot of the stairs. He came out of his room and looked down over the railing. Her wide face tilted up at him. The sight gave him the urge to spit; he felt his mouth fill up.

"A messenger!" she said. She waited there as Mount came down. "It'll be the Hebrews next," she said. "Go look."

Through the two doors' beveled glass Mount saw the boy bounce up and down in the cold. His breath would hit the outside glass and bloom, and his face would disappear and reappear. Mount went through the first door and opened the second.

"Hello," he said. The boy handed the folded paper to Mount. Mount gave the boy a penny and told him to buy himself a ginger ale. Mount knew it cost more than a penny. The boy ran away. Mount unfolded the paper and read: "Come here right now and we'll have Christmas."

Mount wore his scarf. The day was cold. The streets were nearly deserted, all the people inside with one another. There weren't even any dogs or cats in sight. Walking along, he smelled the smoke from the fires of all the houses burned down by the candles of their Christmas trees. In the distance he heard the clanging of the fire pumpers rushing with their tanks full of river water. The sky was dark with floating soot, and Mount felt Christmas all around him.

He didn't have to knock. Hin Lin was waiting at her door. She opened it so that Mount could walk in without stopping. The house was decorated. The sharp corners of the room disappeared behind various-colored soft paper flutters moving in the warm currents from the black stove near the door.

"Merry Christmas, Mount," said Hin Lin. She bowed to his back.

The house was blazing hot. Mount turned around. Hin Lin was wearing only the lightest covering, a long white gown that touched the floor and hid her feet as she walked toward him.

"Merry Christmas," she said again. Mount found he couldn't say it back. He took his scarf off, then his jacket. He was hot. The room was as hot as the power station. He took off his gray sweater and had it half over his head when Hin Lin put her arms around his chest. He could see the top of her head through the knitting. The room was ablaze with heat and light, and he saw her black hair shining.

She squeezed him sharply. "Merry Christmas, Hin Lin," he said, feeling that the words had been squeezed right out of him. Hin Lin let go and backed away. She took his scarf and jacket and sweater and put them in another room. When she returned she carried a present wrapped in Chinese paper with symbols that looked like delicate houses painted in red and green.

He pulled the paper off, tearing some of the symbols. Inside was more paper, noisy tissue surrounding something floppy that turned out to be a pair of black pajamas the like of which he had never seen.

"Thank you," he said. They were black as coal. The pants had a braided black drawstring to make them tight at the waist. The shirt had no pockets. He loved the pajamas right away.

"Thank you," he said again. "I'm just sorry I don't have a thing for you." He wiped his hand across his forehead. The house got hotter and brighter every minute. He started to unbutton his flannel shirt.

"It's all right, Mount," said Hin Lin. She pointed at the pajamas. "Go put them on," she said.

"Well, I don't know," he said. He looked at Hin Lin in her long white gown. He hadn't even sat down yet. He imagined the two of them together, black and white. Hin Lin went and put more wood on the stove. The pieces of wood had festive ribbons tied around them. The ribbons went in with the wood. The stove roared until its door was shut. Mount took off his flannel shirt. His chest was clammy. He stood there in his shoes and pants and undershirt. He bent down and unlaced his hard black shoes with their toes like the shiny shells of two box turtles.

"Go ahead and do it, Mount," she said. "It's much too hot for you in here now." She smiled. He saw her bad brown teeth. She bowed her head. Every surface in the house had candles on it, the floors and the tables, the sills and mantels and shelves. Their light was so full that Mount could feel the flickering in his eyes, as though the flames were inside him shining out. Hin Lin was also shining. Her eyes and skin had an extra wetness—though it might have been from anything. It might have been nothing but sweat from the heat. When she smiled her teeth were shining, too.

"Go in that other room and put them on," she told him, smiling. "One and only size fits everyone."

Mount undressed in the other room; then he put the pajamas on. He tightened the drawstring and tied the knot, pulling the hanging loops out larger. The circle gripped his waist. He looked down at himself as best he could: He was black and white, the white skin mottled with blood in the heat. He came out of the room in his bare feet. The floor was hot. He picked his feet up one at a time where he stood. Hin Lin was putting more wood in the stove. Mount saw the red ribbon catch and curl up yellow. She closed the stove door; the roaring shrank down. He couldn't leave his feet on the floor for long. He picked them up and put them down. Hin Lin had another piece of wood in her hand. This didn't make any sense. It was already hot.

"It's warm enough," he said. She acted like she didn't hear him. She opened the stove door. She was singing. Mount thought something must be wrong. The yellow flames licked out and roared. The fire was so hot there wasn't any smoke. She let her hand drift into the flames. The wood went in, and she closed the door again.

Hin Lin turned around. She was singing a Chinese song. The song's melody carried her voice up and down the way the currents of air caused the paper flutters to wave like noodles. She stopped her singing and looked him over. She smiled and clapped her hands and rolled her eyes.

"So *nice*, Mount! Very good," she said. "It fits you absolutely right." Mount sweated and squirmed. The black linen clung to his skin. He felt like the kind of fish that would swim in heat instead of rivers. He wiped his forehead.

"So, why is it so hot?" he asked. He was amazed Hin Lin could stand on the floor in her bare feet without squirming.

"This is a ceremony, Mount," she said. And as soon as she said it, everything made sense to him, and the heat and the sweat stopped feeling so wrong and troubling: it was a ceremony.

"That's it," said Mount. "It must be." Right away, to make his own contribution, he spat into his left palm and rubbed the other on top of it to kill the devil in the house. Then, imitating what he had often seen Hin Lin do, he made a chamber out of his hands and whispered some old secrets into the chamber before he broke the hands apart and placed his palms on Hin Lin's ears, where he left them resting and where she let them be.

"Merry Christmas," he said, believing that the words would travel through his arms and come dimly out his palms where she could hear them. All of this was part of Christmas Day. All the heat that was swirling around the house was part of the planned celebration. So were the soft yellow candles, the black pajamas, the paper decorations and whatever else was coming.

"Then, after the ceremony is done," said Hin Lin, "you can help me burn the house down." She said this very loudly. Mount's palms were still on her ears.

"All right," said Mount.

Everything was done to prepare the house. More and more wood went into the stove. The candles began to melt from their bottoms or go limp and start to bend. Mount tried to straighten them, but the candles could not be fixed in the heat. So he decided to let them droop. What did it matter? One way or the other the house was going to burn.

Hin Lin told him the ceremony was because of the abandoned baby being taken back by its mother. The period of her life that included the baby and was barely started had been prevented from going forward. She believed a change was necessary.

"I don't even know if I loved him," she said. She tried to describe the baby's face, but she couldn't remember it.

Mount smelled smoke. The paper flutters were starting to scorch. He went and put two more pieces of wood in the stove. Its sides were glowing. He pulled the decorations down and put them in the stove with the wood. Their colors colored the flames and then they were gone. He shut the stove door.

Hin Lin was leaving Fort Wayne to be with her sister in Chicago.

"I won't leave anything behind. Just the place where the house was standing, where, because of the fire, no grass will grow. The heat goes far down into the ground and stays there for years. Long after I'm in Chicago and happy."

The kitchen was cooler and they went there for relief. The room had many windows that the cold air rattled through.

"Later, will you take me to the train?"

Mount nodded. There was nothing to eat on the kitchen shelves. There was no food in the house. Hin Lin told Mount that to her Christmas meant not eating. From the night before until the day after, no food at all.

"Since when? That doesn't sound right."

"Since the time I first knew Christmas. Since when it was 1881 in San Francisco, the Year of the Snake."

"Okay," said Mount. It didn't matter. He was too hot to be hungry, anyway.

The purpose of the ceremony was to let the house heat up inside and warn it of the coming fire, so that any spirits living there could prepare to leave when Hin Lin left. They could go with her to Chicago, or they could stay behind in Fort Wayne in some other house. It was their choice.

"They might like to come with *you*," she said to Mount. And he felt like someone who might be liked by someone else's dog even more than that dog liked its owners. He wondered if that could happen.

"Oh, I don't think they would," he said. He smiled. He asked Hin Lin if she thought there really were spirits in the house. She shrugged. She said it didn't matter what she thought.

"If any are here, then it's right to do this."

So they set about doing the rest of the things. The house became hotter and hotter. Just getting near the stove was all it took to burn Mount's hand; when he started to put the last piece of wood in, the flesh turned shiny red and taut. He hadn't even opened the door. He wrapped a rag around the hand and tried again. With one end of the piece of wood he banged at the stove door until it swung open on its hinges. He tossed in the wood.

Hin Lin said, "Leave it open now. Now we go the other way." It was time to let the house cool down.

This final step took hours and hours. The color of the fire changed, and the stove itself made creaking noises accompanying the wood that snapped and sparked inside. After a while the fire was more orange than yellow, with a spot of blue the size of a thumbnail that shimmered in its midst and moved here and there as though restless.

Hin Lin went around to all the windows and spent a considerable time at each, saying something in a low voice about what she saw. When the air became merely warm, she went into the other room and after a while came back fully clothed and prepared for travel. She stood at one of the windows like a sentinel, not blinking. The sun went down.

At some point Mount began to follow her, going to the windows himself and seeing what she had seen. But doing this didn't mean the same to him as to her, and he found himself standing there counting to a hundred, to a thousand, remembering things that had happened to him in other places and years before. He couldn't hear what Hin Lin was saying. The sound of her voice was small and tight. The house was growing cool. In the spaces between the limbs of the trees that jutted out of the ravine behind Hin Lin's house, the sky was violet, then gray, then black. Mount went and put his clothes back on.

In the other room he saw Hin Lin's packed bag. It lay on the bed closed up, brown and thick. On the floor some of the candles still shimmered from pools of wax, burning like accidents. Mount touched the bag and felt its fullness: A life was in it, leaving. He looked out the window and saw it was snowing. Slow. Floating. Each bit by itself with darkness around it.

"It's snowing," he said to Hin Lin when he came back into the larger room. She was at the final window. The room felt cold.

Starting it was nothing. Hin Lin told him, "You do it, Mount." Mount had never done such a thing. He was afraid of fire. The house was dark except for the one last lamp Hin Lin was holding. She had taken everything she wanted. It was the middle of the night. They had sat on the floor with the lamp between them and waited until the sides of the stove were cold and black. Then Hin Lin had made the decision to go ahead with the burning.

"You want this house?" she asked Mount out of the silence.

Mount thought about it. "No," he said.

"You can have it if you want," she said.

He shook his head. He felt the house slipping away.

"Okay," she said. Her knees cracked getting up in the cold.

She got the several other lamps and poured their oil around: on the walls, on the poplin curtains, on the bed in the other room. She blew the last lamp out and poured its oil on the yellow pine floor. The oil spread. Mount heard it flowing across the wood with a whisper.

"Now, light the match," she said. She went to the door and waited there. Mount held in his hand the box of Blaze Defiant matches and the rough tin striker.

"Go ahead," she said. He lit the first match. He felt his face flare up and smelled the sulfur. The yellow tip of flame was reflected in the lamp oil on the floor. He dropped the match and watched the two tips meeting swiftly. The match just hissed in the oil and died. He lit another. He crept backward and crouched at the edge of the oil and touched the tip of the second match to the spot where the dry pine and lamp oil met. The burning started there; the pool leapt up and formed itself, a blot of fire just awakening, licking up and snapping softly like silk in a breeze.

Mount ran backward. Hin Lin was quickly out the door. Mount followed. They stood together in the snow. Soon they felt the heat come back. It warmed their faces. The fire spread. The snow on the roof was melting, running off. The snow on the ground was melting, too, the heat creeping outward from the burning house.

"It's going," said Hin Lin. She cried. The fire began to roar and climb. The flames came through the walls and broke the windows, consuming and growing until the air was bright. Close by them, the snow stopped falling. But they could see that it still fell beyond the circle of the fire's effect. Before long, the roof was breached, and bursts of sparks shot straight up into the sky until the wind caught and carried them, and they were darkened where the snow began falling again.

Soon the walls were gone, and what was left were glowing timbers, a skeleton dissolving. No one came. No fire pumpers, no spectators. In the depth of the night, the fire was theirs alone. Mount thought: I did this. This is mine. He remembered the striking of the match, the small beginning. So much had happened since. One of the timbers snapped and fell, eaten through to its middle; a dense swirl of sparks rose. Other timbers followed, collapsing in on the center, shattering into embers dancing up in light.

The house became a heap. Mount thought: Mine.

"Okay," said Hin Lin. "Now we go." The sun was coming up; not the sun itself but its light shooting crosswise through the clouds the way Bill the stranger said e-lec-tri-city shot through water.

"Here it comes," said Mount, meaning the morning, the next day after Christmas. The new light silvered the snow. The light came in behind the heap of embers and took something from it, making the fire smaller in the sky and against the day. In this light the heap was sad. Mount squinted. He thought of saying something like what a minister would say. What would a minister say? And what could he say that would be like that?

"This is terrible," he said.

"Here, now," said Hin Lin. "Let's go." Smoke rose and snow fell, the fire no longer keeping it away. Hin Lin put a hand on Mount's elbow. He picked up her bag; how full it felt to him. They went down along the top of the ravine until its two sides joined in a shallow, treeless swale that pointed them straight into town.

"Now, please, you take me to the train," she said. The snow was blowing at their backs, and their visible breaths went out ahead.

The station was empty, vast, echoing. Its benches were slick and dark. Walking in, Mount switched the bag from one hand to the other. His shoulders ached from carrying, but he had refused to let Hin Lin take a turn.

"This is yours," he told her. "I've got it."

The station had no white people in it. The clock said six past six o'clock. There was a tall colored man in one corner, leaning and staring, beginning his day or ending his night, it was hard to tell. Mount watched him eyeing Hin Lin and Mount.

"Never mind," Mount told the colored man. The sound of his voice swam around in the emptiness as though disturbing a dense sleep.

"Never mind never mind," the man shot back. Mount ignored this. The sound died slowly; the colored man stayed where he was, his face shadowed and still. The man was poised to wait.

"Never mind," said Mount again. The sound was like mush.

Hin Lin walked on ahead, into the midst of the long, dark benches that all faced in one direction like pews in a church—toward the clock, facing the double-wide doorways that led to the platforms where the trains would come. The only windows were high in the walls, half circles aswirl with snow, snow both rising and falling, confused. Hin Lin chose a bench and sat. Fatigued, she let her head sink back.

Mount came and sat beside her. She felt the cold come off him as though he carried the outdoors along with her bag.

"Thank you, Mount," she said. "A train will come. No need to wait with me."

But Mount waited. He put her bag between his feet. A long breath escaped him. He felt his flesh warming to the bench, the bench warming to his flesh. His cold blood told him: Stay. He listened for whistles and heard none. Daylight angled down through the windows, through the snow outside.

When the longer hand of the large clock moved, it clicked mightily, each minute the snapping of an inch. The hands became nine minutes after six. Then ten. Between these clickings of the clock the station was quiet. The snowfall sealed the quiet inside. It was easy to think there might never be another train, that the clock would continue circling inch by inch without bringing forth a new event. And the waiting would be until Judgment Day. The trains would be out there, dead, white mounds.

"I'll wait with you," he told her. It was thirteen after. Her eyes were closed, her breathing deep and slow. "You're going to miss me," he said. She didn't move. He stood up and walked to the corner where the colored man was standing. He stared at the man and the man stared back, not afraid.

"What time's the train gonna be here?" Mount asked this man.

"Never mind," the man said.

"What's your name?" said Mount. "My name is Mount."

"I'm Bill," the colored man said. Mount thought he might not be telling the truth.

"I already *have* a friend named Bill," said Mount.

"Then you best leave *me* alone," said Bill, "and go on about your business." Mount stayed where he was. Bill stood there looking over the top of Mount as though there was something on the far wall. Mount looked behind and saw nothing going on, only the wall itself.

"What're *you* here for?" he asked Bill.

Bill jingled a ring of keys on his belt and then pointed around at everything, as though the whole place was his.

"What time's the Chicago train?" asked Mount.

"Whenever it get here," said Bill. Bill laughed at Mount.

Mount walked away and came back. He wanted to smile. In the high windows the snow was thick. He looked over and saw Hin Lin with her head sloped down to her shoulder and her mouth wide open in a circle as though she was surprised at something happening. But she was only asleep. She looked old.

"What time's it due?" he asked Bill.

"It's due seven thirteen every day but Sunday," said Bill, "which today isn't even but a Thursday."

"In the night or in the morning?" asked Mount.

"In the morning," said Bill. Mount looked at the clock. It was six nineteen.

"Then it's coming in less than an hour," he said.

"Lest the snow don't set it back," said Bill, making little falling, fluttering streaks in the air with his long black fingers.

Mount nodded. Another man came into the station. A white man. Snow blew in behind him, skidding dry across the floor. Mount knew the face of the man from somewhere, maybe from the bakery where Mount often bought something sweet to keep in his room to eat after those dinners at the boardinghouse when nothing tasted good. He always had something hidden at the top of the closet where Mrs. Collamer's short arms couldn't reach. This new man looked like a man who would eat a cake, or a bun with candied fruit.

He nodded at Bill. Bill said, "Good morning, Eldon."

This Eldon went to a door that didn't look like a door but like a part of the wall; he unlocked it and disappeared into the wall. Soon, a sliding window went halfway up behind the grille where the tickets were sold for the trains. Mount heard the pop of gaslight lighting. He saw the pale hands of Eldon moving in the light, the hands doing setting-up chores like two kindred animals darting back and forth. The rest of Eldon was hidden behind the half-raised window whose glass was milky white.

Mount watched. Bill told him, "I'm always the first one here." Mount listened to Bill's thick, slow voice that seemed to have many parts combining to make the sound.

"Some days it be longer than others before another soul come in," said Bill. "I likes that quiet time by myself. And I hates the very first peoples that comes. Say, didn't I look at y'all like I hated you and that old China lady?"

"You did," said Mount. "I know you did."

"That's right," said Bill. "And if no one come in before Eldon do, then it's Eldon I be hating. But today it be you and that old China lady that comes. So I hates you. And by the time Eldon come, that part of the day be over when my peace and quiet be busted up. So I look at him and don't think one way or the other. Eldon just be Eldon, that old white fool."

"Well, how about that," said Mount. He was surprised to hear of a colored man hating anyone at all. He always thought they were peaceable and quiet, and were content for people to pick on them and hate them without them doing anything back, because that's just the way it was.

"You hate *me*, then?" Mount asked Bill.

"Oh, yes I do," said Bill. He said it like he meant it. Mount was perplexed, since he hadn't done Bill any harm.

"But if Eldon comes in first, then you hate Eldon?"

"I hates him for just that time," said Bill, "then I gets over it as the day go along. We gots to work together, y'hear."

"But, what about me?" asked Mount. "And her?" He pointed at Hin Lin. She was still asleep.

"Can't say right now," said Bill. "The day gots to go along a little. One thing, though . . . It don't be nothin' you can do for. Time take care of time, is all. You can ask me later if you wants."

Mount nodded. He walked away and came back. The clock said six twenty-six. Eldon came out of the wall and started taking down things that said MERRY CHRISTMAS in big red and green letters strung along the wall. There were three sets.

"*You* shoulda done this," he called over his shoulder to Bill.

Bill snorted at Eldon's back.

Mount came up close to Bill. "I burned down a house today, Bill," he said. He smiled and waited. Bill snapped his head around and looked hard at Mount, who saw the respect coming out of Bill's eyes.

"I saw the smoke," said Bill.

"That's right," said Mount. "That was it." And he left Bill just standing there.

Hin Lin woke up a while later. It was almost seven. She asked Mount what he was doing. He told her, "Waiting." Her breath after sleeping was sharp as smoke. In fact, smoke from the fire might have been inside her.

"Don't wait," she said. "Go on." He smelled it again.

"I'll go to work," he said. "It isn't that far. I'll be there before the others, and it'll be quiet for a minute."

"Then go ahead," she said. "But do this first." She held out money for a ticket. Mount took the money.

"Chicago, Eldon," he said through the bars. Eldon looked up.

"How'd you know my name?" he asked. He didn't look happy about it. Mount was always happy when someone knew his name.

112

"Bill over there told me," said Mount. He jerked his head.

"Who's Bill?" said Eldon. Mount pointed at the colored man. "You mean Clarence? He's no Bill."

"Then never mind," said Mount. "One way to Chicago." He had the money in his hand.

"Three dollars," said Eldon. He began to write out the ticket. Mount waited. He asked if he could have a set of the MERRY CHRISTMAS letters. Eldon looked at him.

"I want to remember this year," said Mount. "A lot's happened."

"We use 'em again, mister. We use 'em every year," Eldon said.

"Okay," said Mount. "Never mind about that. I'll get my own some day."

But Eldon went away and came back and gave Mount an R through the bars. "I got extras of these ones," he said. "You can get the rest yourself." The R was green. Mount was sorry it wasn't red, but he didn't say anything. Eldon finished writing the ticket.

"Train'll be late some," he said. "There's men out shoveling in the yards, but it's going slow. I'm hearing seven twenty-five, seven thirty, okay?"

Mount said he guessed so. He gave the money through the grille. Eldon slid the ticket out to him.

Mount gave the ticket to Hin Lin. She was sitting there crying. He didn't know what to do.

"Train'll be late," he told her. She smoothed the ticket on her lap. "Seven thirty or so," he said. She nodded. Tears fell on the blue ticket making darker blue spots.

"I'm leaving, Mount," she said. He already knew that.

"I know," he told her. She seemed to want to say more. He put his hand on the top of her head. It was hot. He imagined it was going through her life, recalling events up to this point in a certain order— such as happy things first then sad things, or alternating the one with the other—and this feverish effort came right to the top of her head. But with his hand there she didn't say anything else. And that was good, at least. More tears fell silently, and she was kept within herself. Mount was sure that his hand was in a good place. Soon he took it away. She lifted her head and looked at him.

"Be careful, Mount."

She stood. The ticket fell to the floor. She brushed her hand after it and then let it be.

"I have the feeling about you that you are not always careful," she said. "And anything can happen to you before you know it. Am I correct?" She put her hands around his wrists like cuffs and brought herself closer to him. Her hair smelled like smoke.

"I don't know," said Mount. But he did know something.

"One thing just leads to another," he said. "An incident comes around. I'm always there for what happens. And that's what life is. Life is always going forward and doing whatever it tells you to do. Then something comes along. And then another thing. Like the train to Chicago, or anywhere else."

He stopped and listened in vain for the whistle from down in the yards where the roundhouse was or for the sound of the men out shoveling, the scraping of the blades one after the other.

"I guess so," said Hin Lin. "But, anyhow, be careful."

"Okay," said Mount. These were two things people said: Be careful and Okay. She let go of his hands. They felt better not being held.

"Goodbye," said Hin Lin.

"Goodbye."

Mount closed his eyes for just a flash and thought about all the breakfasts she had made him. He had a whiff of some of their soft, sweet aromas coming back to him as though they were life's great rewards hanging right in the air he was breathing. Then he opened his eyes and she was walking away.

"Thank you," he said.

He heard the whistle, starting soft and growing louder, blowing twice, coming closer and closer, joined by a bell. He caught her by the time she got to the double-wide doors, where the colored man Clarence was swinging them open, slicing arcs in the snow. He spun her around.

"Here," he said. And he gave her the big green R. "So you'll remember me."

He heard Clarence laughing.

7
FLIGHT

Whatever is powerful enough to induce a man to leave Fort Wayne, Indiana, got into Mount one afternoon early in 1902. Fort Wayne looked as tense as a wire under a harmless dusting of snow, and the houses on Bilge Street had little white highlights on their cornices and gables, around the gray slate shingles and on the green copper flashing atop the cupolas. Little white highlights everywhere, an appealing display for the eyes of just about anyone. But not for Mount's.

He looked at the harmless dusting of snow and thought he would perish for certain if he didn't get out of town before nighttime came and the sky turned dark and made the slender lines of snow glow like bones in the moonlight. He had been at his window all the night before, whispering against the cold glass, brushing it with his lips in all the places where the bones of snow showed through. The street had spoken back with white messages of flight. The spell was in him.

A spell like this could come over him either fast or slow. It might accumulate, the way a dripping faucet took weeks to grow a blue-green stain in a porcelain basin. Or a spell could strike like lightning, first catching him unawares then departing before he knew what happened. If something in the spell told him *Move,* he moved; if something told him *Sit* or *Stay,* he stayed or sat. The thought was liable to become the deed as soon as it became the thought.

One day he had tripped a man running down the walk in front of Mrs. Collamer's boardinghouse. The man flew through the air and landed on the bricks, skidding along and tearing up his knees and elbows, forehead and nose. Mount was surprised at himself. He glowered at his foot as though it was a bad dog that had bitten someone. The highest authority in all the world were the twitches of instruction inside him that sounded like doors slamming blocks away.

Sometimes the things his body did were a terrible mystery to him. He remembered how his foot hovered low in the breeze above the bricks that day. The injured man had crawled back toward the guilty foot, moaning, shaking his head.

"Why, why?" the man had said. "Why?"

Mount told him he was sorry, put the foot on the ground and turned to go inside the boardinghouse. He believed he didn't deserve to be out in the sun by the picket fence in the sight of other people. When he felt like that he assumed anybody seeing him could look right in and observe that his dark insides were bad.

"I'm going to fetch a constable!" the man wailed at Mount. But no constable ever came.

This lightninglike spell had occurred the summer before. The present one was of the slower, blue-green stain variety, having taken some weeks to build to the point where an action was finally necessary. And now Mount stood at the front door looking out at the disturbing snow and decided he wanted to drink some water as quick as he could. He went to Mrs. Collamer in the kitchen and asked her for a glass. Then he told her he was leaving.

"Well, that's all right, Mr. Mount," she said. "You're a very unusual man. I think I can tell you that now that you're going."

"Thank you, Mrs. Collamer," he said. He left the kitchen carrying the glass, which was empty because he had never filled it with water. Yet he thought only that he had drunk it faster than ever before.

He went upstairs to his room and put his belongings in his bag. And doing this, he noticed something strange. Always before when he had packed his bag, his belongings filled it completely. But now there was room at the top even though he had just as many belongings. Feeling through the contents he assured himself that everything was included; and lifting the bag, he found that it was just as heavy as ever. So why was there so much space at the top? He didn't know. He sat on the edge of the bed for almost an hour, mentally stretching the bag and shrinking his belongings until their scale was in agreement with the present outcome.

* * *

Mrs. Collamer listened as Mount descended through the house, heard the whooshing sound of his carpetbag as it brushed against the floral-papered walls. She heard three doors close: the one to his room, the one to the vestibule, and the final one at the very front of the house. The doors rattled; air flew around in his wake and settled finally into a deeper peace than it had known when he was present. He was gone.

And now that he was gone, Mrs. Collamer realized with a shudder that he knew where she lived. The change was like the difference between standing behind a man with a camera and standing in front of him. She wasn't really scared, but, all the same, it was funny she had thought of this.

She ran to the dining-room window to see what direction he would take with his bag in his hand. She saw him head south along Bilge Street, out of town. And in her heart of hearts she wanted to tilt the street downhill to hurry his departure from her sight. She didn't know why this was, exactly, only that so much history of a disturbing nature had passed between them. The dead bird. Long, motionless silences that entrapped her. His return of a smile she had never smiled at him, at moments when she was just in the midst of thinking something terrible. He struck her as an accidental sort of person, and she believed he would always be somber and unhappy, and would perhaps always have the effect of making fundamentally satisfied people experience a gnawing, indescribable discontent whenever he entered a room or came toward them on the street.

He disappeared behind a tree, and the breeze that followed him shook a thin veil of snow from its branches. As far as Mrs. Collamer knew, he was utterly gone.

When the manager of the Fort Wayne Isolated Edison Power Station noticed he was missing, he replaced J. Fielding Mount with a boy. The boy worked as hard as a boy will work, and the manager was satisfied in the conditionally satisfied way of all managers and bosses. For himself, the boy was glad to be in out of the cold, even if this meant working.

The manager could see the boy was not as good a worker as Mount was, but the boy was there and Mount was not (though the manager would wait a few days before telling the boy he could be permanent). And the boy would work for much less money than the loss of Mount's labor would cost in lost labor. Two boys would work for two-thirds of Mount's wage and accomplish three-quarters of his labor. And three boys would earn the full wage paid to Mount but produce—if a good third boy were found—one-and-a-quarter or more times the labor.

Or the boys could eventually be dispensed with altogether and a very stupid and gullible, though well-muscled, man could be hired to work twice as hard as Mount and for only one-half his wage. Of course, finding that man would take time, and the boys would do nicely in the meanwhile. But the loss of Mount was neither surprising nor calamitous, and not felt as much as the full loss of a full person might be. Even Mount's friend Bill made a joke about his being gone, and people who had worked with him for all those months laughed heartily. The boy took over Mount's shovel and felt that the fit of it was good in his hands.

And during the lunch break, this borrowed boy scrounged off the street filled the place of Mount as though it had always been only as big as the boy, or as though the same Mount who was now, as the day's lunch was being eaten, many miles from Fort Wayne had never quite been able to fill the place now occupied by the boy. And the manager was stirred by the face of the boy, which was so pleasant seeming even through the coating of coal dust, and he thought that it was as familiar as the face of anyone in the circle of men—all of whom were being sociable and polite with the boy in a way that they had never been with Mount, who it seemed was not at all missed by any of the company.

The manager bit a pickle in half and patted the boy on the shoulder. The boy smiled a lovely smile of inclusion. So what if Mount was gone? the manager thought.

He was traveling like a prisoner on the run, as though dogs were after him. Whatever induced a man to leave Fort Wayne, Indiana, had gotten into him so strong it motivated his limbs as if they were the armatures of a dynamo. He didn't know why, but that's the way he felt. He was a man running, hiding out in the daytime and moving on at night. While it was dark he was filled with an energy he had never known in any daylight; and when the sun came up, his exhaustion was correspondingly profound.

He was headed south.

Along the way, scattered people thought they saw something—him—a blurred slash of fabric passing between trees caught in the swinging light of a carriage lamp as someone led a buggy to the barn, or a shadow, thrown by moonlight, leaning across the stubble of corn in the southern Indiana farmland. He was out there. But he was never truly seen; he was only almost seen, and his passing made scarcely the smallest difference.

J. Fielding Mount—the accidental man—was discovering in himself a fugitive spirit which bloomed in his gut like an ache and made no place seem fine or welcoming. Probably this came from his nocturnalism, from feeling often as though he were being glimpsed, when something crossed his face—a beam of light or an unexpected breeze. The spirit came from seeing the pretty amber glow in the windows of distant houses, and the figures moving back and forth inside, lighted by comfort. Sometimes the smoke from a chimney would curl around in his direction, and the sharpness of it would nuzzle against him; his nostrils would quiver and his eyes would widen. And then he would move away, as though the smoke were an outreaching filament of whatever was making him run. It might have been anything; it might have come from anywhere. (He remembered a tall drinking glass, aglimmer with fungus, left on the floor in a corner near his bed at Mrs. Collamer's—something growing, dusty blue, in his memory, speaking across a hundred miles, two hundred, five hundred miles. It might still be there growing.)

, He had a general direction, but no destination. The destination would reveal itself only when the urge to stop running came over him. A feeling of recognition would suddenly be there one morning when the massive orange sun was rising in back of a dark silhouette without windows, a blackness with an aureole. A bird would cry in the thicket behind him. At his feet he would see something strange to eat, a cluster of dark berries surrounded by dull leaves. Or a reddish, butte-shaped morel. The wind would die, the air becoming perfectly still, smelling like nothing at all. His feet would ache; his hands would tingle; his cloth bag would seem to be fuller, heavier. His heart would beat more slowly. The voice inside, sounding like miles away, would say *Stop . . . Stay.*

But for now, J. Fielding Mount, who was still on the run, never even broke his stride in the cool of the night that he sped through. He was already in Tennessee.

They collided north of Memphis: J. Fielding Mount, the accidental man, and his counterpart, Malvina T., the accidental woman. She was headed north and he was headed south, and the switching systems that operate in the senses of these fugitive types failed somehow in the darkness.

They passed each other on opposite sides of a tree before both of them stopped. They were both surprised. Malvina T. imitated an owl, and J. Fielding Mount began to snort like a pig, and they went around the tree for a tiresome length of time in flight and pursuit before Malvina T., who turned out to be somewhat less accidental than Mount, reversed direction twice in rapid succession and caught him. By the throat.

"Gotcha!" she said.

"Oh, God!" said Mount. The face of Malvina T. floated darkly far at the other end of her arm. The cold fingers of her large hand squeezed him by the neck, chickenlike, and he waited for the blade to swipe through.

"Oh, God!" he said again. These were the first words he had said out loud in weeks. He had been running south in silence like a spooked horse with its senses shattered. "Oh, God!" The words just naturally came out strangled sounding. Whatever it was—whatever it could be—had finally caught up with him. But from the wrong direction.

Malvina T. was tall and tough. He hadn't seen her coming. She was dressed in dark clothing, dungarees and a heavy black sweater. She wore a wide-awake hat, and when pieces of moon struck its slouchy brim they trickled bony-white light onto the lower half of her dirty face. He could see her dark lips moving. She was hissing something. She had long thin legs, the legs of a runner, and she looped one around behind the knees of J. Fielding Mount and forced him down to the ground.

"Whooer you?" she whispered. "Whooer you?" She pulled at his ears. Her sound went back and forth inside him. He could see her pretty well now. She was headed north and he was headed south. They were in a woods in Tennessee. There was part of a moon up in back of her head, high over the trees. She blocked it like a building. The light hit her and ricocheted sideways.

"H-how do you do," he said. "My name is J. Fielding Mount . . . uh, Mount." She was sitting on his belly, and he was surprised. Their breaths collided. She looked at him for a long, long time, and she was like a puffing statue.

"Hold still," she finally said. Her hands were busy. Something accidental was beginning to occur, and he wasn't sure what. But he became both hot and cold, and he worried that all those circles he and she had run around that tree had ruined their directions. And later, after this was over, he would find himself returning north without meaning to, and feel the distant thud of her footsteps running back south. And this one sudden accident would turn out to be exactly where he was going all along—the end of everything.

"I'm on the run," she said. Her voice was different, less breath and more voice. He was feeling good on the ground. Little things were crawling next to his ears. Leaves were crackling and tipping under the weight of insect feet at the ends of legs like crooked hairs.

"And so am I," he said.

"That's good, mister, that's good. I knew it right away. So . . . tell me . . . where you all . . . headed . . ."

"South," said Mount. "Not sure yet . . ." He felt good.

"Me neither," said Malvina T.

He looked at her face with the moon behind it. There was a white light in her eyes, like the white moon shining all the way through. She opened her mouth and the light came out. It hissed from way back in her throat like a private, inside creature. Something was happening. He had come to a spot on the trail like one of those locations where someone was known to have been murdered, or a mound of built-up earth where dozens of Indians were buried with their potteries.

He felt his muscles getting tighter.

She reached up and yanked her hat off and held it down over his face, pressing the back of his head into the twigs and bits of stuff on the ground. He smelled her head inside it and the roasted smell of the leather band. He breathed in like a hungry, stalking animal getting closer to something good to eat that was dead. Inside the hat was everything that he wanted then; the hat was a good dark dome. It was warm. He reached up his hands and took some of her tough hair into his fists, and he pulled the top of her body down close enough to know that she was there. The warmth poured down.

She was twisting and talking. He heard her mouth outside the hat. He heard her saying words out loud that he had only thought of under his breath when he'd been running all that time before they met. These words had no known meaning and were of a kind he thought wasn't possible to say deliberately because they were only the careless sounds that something running makes.

121

She pulled away, but then he pulled her back again. Closed up inside the warm smell of her hat, he was happy. The happiness spread in every direction, surprising him all the while. He listened gladly to the barking, slicing spell of her unknown words until something—like horses' hooves—made a sound outside of the hat and pounded down next to his head. And he knew she was gone. It was quiet. He might even have believed it was snowing and the snow was closing down around him.

She let him up.

"Get off of me!" said J. Fielding Mount.

"I am," said Malvina T.

"That's good," he said. He stood up with her hat in his hand.

"Want to do it again?" she said to him.

"Do what?" he said.

She decided to rest her clothes for the night. She would let them sit somewhere else, in a pile away from her, and take whatever shape they wanted. He took the blanket from his bag and watched as she dropped her dungarees and lifted the sweater over her head and let that drop too. There was nothing underneath, only bits of whiteness floating. The moonlight hit her skin in the shape of the spaces between the branches and leaves. The rest of her was dark. She moved around as if he wasn't there. He felt the sounds inside him stopping slowly; the gallop in his blood was dying the way the current dies in the wires when the dynamo arms stop churning.

She dropped her hat on top of the sweater, and all of her clothes lay on the ground looking like herself collapsed. Her hair was longer than anything he'd ever seen in the way of hair. There were souvenirs caught up in its ends, little pieces of all the places she had traveled north through. They dangled and swung when she moved, catching the light or bumping against her elbows: dried bits of cotton plants, a hickory leaf, a seed pod, strands of grass, a tiny bone, a long blond splinter of wood, some twine, a thumb-sized ball of paper.

She went ten yards away and squatted down and let the water run out of her with a hiss that was like her whispering. A ragged diamond of moonlight settled in one of her eyes, which she aimed at him. The sounds inside him started up again. He released a warm, expanding puff of vapor into the atmosphere, and she followed it back. It was the middle of the night. A whistle blew some miles away, and both of them felt it, but at different times—once as a train and once as a riverboat, one headed north and the other headed south.

She lay down on the blanket, and he wrapped it around her. It was gray, and where the moon struck it, it looked its exactly perfect color. The air was chilly. All around them hidden animals were expelling visible breath. He could hear them. Tiny plumes of it rose up from the leaves; the earth was ventilating.

Mount leaned back against the tree. He had this conversation with Malvina T.

She told him her name was Malvina T. She said she came from Louisiana. Her father had reminded her many times that on the night she was born he lost his tiny crop of okra to the bugs. It was a coincidence, he told her, and that was why he had named her Malvina T. But he always refused to reveal to her what the T. was supposed to stand for. She finally gave up wondering, and that made her happier.

Her mother fainted every morning after breakfast. Food unsettled her. She would wake back up and swear that flies were hatching inside her. Three weeks ago Malvina T. was sitting on the porch shelling peas into a pan. Every third pod had a family of tiny worms. A dog was hurrying toward her with a rabbit in its mouth. The dog appeared to be smiling because of the way it carried the rabbit. Her father's boots were sounding on the steps inside. Her mother was in the outhouse humming godly music that came out through the crescent vent. A sickly old blue heron in the top of the tree that rose out of the hollow was flapping and crying. And even though Malvina T. couldn't see clearly quite so far, she had the impression the heron's eyes were stuck shut.

The sun was making Malvina T. sweat. It came down on her through the space where a board was missing. Her hair was hot. Where it was parted in the middle, there was a seam of special heat. When her father came out the door, he stopped by her chair and put his hand on the top of her head. It felt so heavy there. Her mother stopped humming, and the door of the outhouse opened. She swayed in the brilliant sunlight and made a cringing face. The dog came up on the porch and dropped the rabbit. The rabbit was still alive, and the dog licked a raw spot on its back. Her father lifted his hand from her head and grunted. He stepped over the rabbit, past the dog and past his wife, and continued to walk out of sight, down into the crusty, muddy hollow where the creek ran by with its trickle of cloudy water that carried the spiders for a ride.

123

Malvina T. put the peas aside and went into the house and up the stairs to the sleeping loft. The shiny palmetto bugs on the cedar slat walls hardly stirred; she didn't believe they ever even breathed. When she finally came down again, she had everything she wanted to take tied up in a rolled canvas tarpaulin. Her mother was washing the dirt from eggs. When Malvina T. told her mother she was leaving, her mother began to hum. The humming changed by small degrees until it became a swoon. Her mother moaned and fainted, slipping down slow and easy. The dust blew from underneath her. Malvina T. was out the door before the dust had even ceased to move, before her mother was fully flattened on the floor.

Her last recollection of home, she said, was stepping over the rabbit and seeing the sickly heron fall from its perch. The dog began to race toward it, and she hoped the heron's eyes were still stuck shut. Its terminal squawking followed her north.

J. Fielding Mount sat propped against the tree, as absolutely still as the victim of a massacre. He was awake, and his eyes were open. Malvina T. lay quiet in the gray sandwich of the blanket. She had spoken her piece and then fallen asleep. Her feet, still shod, drifted out from under. They twitched sometimes like running feet, and Mount interpreted this as Malvina T. already beginning to leave for the North.

The moon was setting. The night became darker. Nothing else breathed or moved. But up in the sky there were wisps of vapor—not quite clouds—whipped along by unfelt winds, still lighted by the falling moon and casting shadows that were small and dim, like the shadows of fledgling birds. The air was sweet and dry. Mount felt himself adoring it and blending with it, the pores of his skin yawning open to let the inside out and the outside in until nothing was kept apart anymore and all of it was easy and still. He was happy at heart to be there and could not let himself sleep for fear that the calm that had come to be a guest inside him would flee as soon as his eyes drifted shut. So he stayed that way all night, noticing everything that changed around him while keeping the calm from changing within him, his body almost afraid to move and break the spell of perfect satisfaction that warmed the blood in his veins and kept his fingers feeling like pillows floating.

Deep into the night, when the sky had faintly begun to gray, Mount touched the blanket. Malvina T. stirred and opened her eyes and led herself through the slow process of wakening. Then she looked at his face and recalled him, smiling. He felt her eyes upon him and put his hand to his face to touch what she was seeing. All night in the dark his face had changed, becoming smooth and careful instead of sharp and chipped like crumbling shale. The air breathed in and out of him softly. This was a change; he felt the change.

"Oh, go ahead," she said. Her arm came out. "Come over here, you Mount . . ." And that was what they did. The odors of North and South combined between them, and what they did together ended in the slowly changing light in which, for a minute, they saw each other's faces.

Malvina T. departed at dawn, taking something from him to keep in her hair: a wooden button from his sleeve. She said to him, "Come along with me," but he told her, "No, you come with me." She shook her head. The button dangled, pointing north like a compass. He watched her going, her body rising steadily into its stride. She ran. He didn't go to sleep until her feet kicked leaves too far away to hear. When he first lay back he held his breath and listened hard; but there was nothing. She was gone.

He slept all day in the leaves, dreaming dreams that disappeared as soon as he had them, as if they had never come. His head pointed south. Five horses and riders passed him by that day, close enough to count his fingers, though none of them even saw him. He was becoming himself again. Two foraging squirrels ricocheted from his hip. A spider crept into his ear and out again: no one home. It was happening.

While he slept, his accidental aspects were restored to him, having grown stronger, weaker, tighter, looser, angrier—more resolutely wrong. They invaded his every part with defect until, when he awoke and the night was coming on again, nothing he saw looked the same as before. He had forgotten everything. The echo of Malvina T. was a weather disturbance on the far sides of distant hills. When he found that a button was missing from his sleeve, he searched for it on his hands and knees until darkness persuaded him to quit and go on. He headed west instead of south, not knowing the difference. He was up to his waist in the Mississippi River before he suspected his direction was wrong.

He was wet. Things bumped against his ankles underwater. He stood there as still as a piling and tried to imagine what they were. They swam around between his legs, learning to love his presence there. Sometimes they swam straight to the surface and leapt out not quite high enough to be identified. But they were things, all right.

He stayed in the water all night long, shivering and talking nonsense. An unpleasant kind of smile blinked on and off across his face. He had never before been so thoroughly accidental as he was that night. The soft river bottom welcomed him downward by degrees. His carpetbag was a sodden weight, an anchor at the end of his long left arm. By the time the sun came up, hissing and rumbling, only the head of J. Fielding Mount could be seen above the surface of the water. His mouth was moving; sounds were tumbling out. The river rushed south beneath his chin and carried the sounds away.

Malvina T. was just then crossing into what she was sure was the North. The air was lighter, the trees less lush, the ground not quite so cushioned. Deep in the chamber of her left ear blood was beating, the hard squeeze of her runner's heart. The land bounced up; smooth brown boulders were shining in the morning light. She smelled the North in her hot nostrils.

J. Fielding Mount felt the pounding of her feet in his temples, and the river wet his whiskers. He began to wave his right arm. A south-bound barge was coming, pushed by a boat. The barge bore down on the frightened, addled melon of his head. The prow advanced like a sweeping black beam. The whistle blew; startled birds flew up. The colonies of things that hovered near him darted away. He saw, above the whispering prow of the barge, a great gray elephant staring down at him. His eyes widened; he waved and waved. The sudden blackness of the sweeping beam erased the day.

He grabbed hold of the approaching dark and was off—though his boots stayed stuck in the mud and the bust of Tyrus Portman Bolus, Sr., rolled out of the bag and sank.

Far to the north, Malvina T.'s left heel came down and crushed the tunnel of a mole. Up and down the river the day was beginning.

8
GUARDIANS

When the barge hit the body the circus wagons shuddered slightly. The pilot shut his eyes and listened: Was the body bouncing underneath, being battered in its drowning? No. The sound of the barge said no. The body had either been knocked to the side or was holding on to the prow. The freaks, who were then in the midst of their morning practice, rushed forward hoping to see something. The elephant Chloe reached down with her trunk and dragged the body aboard; the tip of her trunk felt the cold hand, then crept up the arm to the shoulder delicately, looping beneath and encircling it, then lifting. The body came from the water limp and slow as Chloe raised her head. The freaks watched silently: a machine was working. Water dripped from the body—the man whose mouth was open, whose eyes were shut.

Chloe lifted her head higher, and the man hung dripping.

"Put him down!" said Semple Groves, the circus proprietor, from the doorway of his wagon. He emerged wearing the green silk dressing gown with the map of the southern states sewn on the back in different-colored patches.

Chloe lowered the man to the deck slowly. His limbs first bent then straightened as he came to lie there face down. Chloe's trunk released the shoulder. The man coughed and breathed.

"Good girl," said Semple Groves. He looked at the man on the deck and thought of the old saying: "Like something the cat dragged in."

If rescuing the man from the water had made an impression on Chloe, she failed to show this right away. But he lay there, a figure in her fist-sized eye, and she saw him.

The comforting woman he later came to know as Mother Danilecki was kneeling by Mount when his eyes first opened and he felt as though he'd just been born again. He saw her old yellow face that was round as a cheese. The face was coming closer, breathing hard upon him. He closed his eyes and coughed. An indescribable happiness bloomed in his stomach and spread throughout him, buzzing like a cicada, until it went just as quickly away and he coughed some more.

The blot of his shape soaked wetly into the deck. And there he was: something had come along. Something always did. He heard the soft voice inside him whispering: *Stay.*

It was a circus. For days Mount went about discovering it, going freely where he wanted, helping out and seeing how things were done. In Memphis the wagons rolled off the barge, across a chattering plank into streets where people were waiting to cheer.

Mount joined the circus parade and followed along. His first few steps were difficult. No one was near him, and he felt like he was just floating strangely among others who were also floating. But no one told him to go away, so he stayed there, going step by step. And soon the walking itself took over, and there was a rhythm to it and plenty enough to see and hear as the people at the sides of the street hollered and whistled and clapped.

There were strange and beautiful sights, as when Claire, the albino woman, came out of a hole at the top of one of the wagons and danced by herself in a gem-studded gown on the wagon's roof. The crowd grew hushed. The wagon turned a circle slowly in the street to keep her in the people's view. Mount walked over near the wagon and looked up at her, shading his eyes. In the midday sun her skin was bleached as paper; her yellow-white hair was shocked out sideways with light. To Mount, she looked like the ghost of someone pretty. On her fingers she wore tiny bells that jingled out the music she danced to. After a single turning of the wagon, she disappeared down through the hole she'd come up from. The wagon went straight again, and people cheered and wanted her return. Mount himself applauded, wondering how he would ever describe what he'd seen. For a minute he followed after the wagon, smelling something trailing in the air from her skin, a sharpness that hung there.

Semple Groves took up a speaking trumpet and enticed the crowd, telling them they could see more of everything if only they would come out to the fairgrounds that night. Mount heard some people holler back that they would and others holler back that they wouldn't on a dare. Then Semple dared them all in a good humor. And he said, "Bring your money, too. And bring all your wives and children, young and old, that can stand to stay up late and see what they've never seen before."

The elephant Chloe raised her trunk and shrieked. And Mother Danilecki, dressed like a gypsy, pulled a rock dove from deep in one billowing sleeve and let it loose. The dove flew up to the cornice of a nearby building where it scattered the other doves already there. Then, suddenly, the rock dove burst into flames and flew off, leaving a trail of thick smoke and ashen down that winked like embers and drifted slowly. The spectators gasped for a moment before they cheered. And four blocks farther along, the rock dove fell from the sky, cooked and enfolded. A clown raced ahead and retrieved it, and held the bird up until it burned him and he tossed it back and forth from hand to hand comically. The dove's catching fire was the strangest thing Mount had ever seen an animal do. Weeks later Mother Danilecki set him the task of capturing birds to be used in this way. When he asked her how he might tell which birds would be able to do the trick of catching fire, she laughed at him and reached out to scratch the top of his hair, which bristled under her touch, seeming to raise itself to her fingertips.

Mount went farther and farther south with the circus, town by town, by way of the river. He noticed the way Semple Groves's voice was changing over time, becoming slower and more Southern, so that words of one and two syllables grew longer as the days grew longer, Semple's thin, hard smile growing looser as the nights grew warmer, the dark air deeply scented with blossoms. There was more liquor drunk more appreciatively by more people, and at night on the deck of the barge—at those times when the circus was traveling and not performing—there were stories told round and round, most of them by Semple. Mount remained at the edge of the circus's circle and listened as well as he could. No one outright invited him to come in closer, but no one told him to go away, either. So things stayed roughly the way they were, which was pleasing enough.

One night Mount found himself near Chloe. Her warm smell was strong and sweet, milky and complicated. The smell drifted down around him, and he was sure that if the sun had then been shining, Chloe's shadow would also have fallen across him, as heavily gray as her skin.

Semple sat with his circus surrounding him and directed the yellow crock of sweet liquor around the circle as though it was a child who should meet all its elders and please them one by one. As the crock circled, he told his stories—including the present, most solemn one relating to the terrible death, in Vicksburg the year before last, of a foolhardy roustabout named Hector who had tried to do something difficult and dangerous all by himself, without waiting for others to help him in the way he had been taught. The man ended up both crushed and pierced. Lantern light leapt in Semple's face, and Mount could read the lesson there: be careful. The crock went silently from one pair of hands to the next. And Mount felt half a sadness for the unknown death, the careless man.

"Some way or another," said Semple Groves, "we summon these misfortunes to ourselves." Mount imagined whistling for an angry dog that comes running from far in the distance.

It was then that the elephant lay her trunk on his shoulder. The trunk settled there so gently that it did not startle him, the weight of it so much less than he would have guessed. He turned his head and there it was, the dexterous tip of it seeking something, moving deliberately and slowly as it tried—or so Mount thought—to learn essential, inward facts about him that no other living creature (excepting, maybe, Mother Danilecki) would ever have a way of finding out. He thought of trying to keep his secrets to himself, but the trunk crept here and there insistently, the gray flesh crinkling and rippling, extracting what it seemed to want. And Mount could feel the inward flowing outward, all his hidden light and energy, everything he might someday have wanted to share with his dearest companion, one such as Mother Mount had been to Father Mount. He gave this up so easily, without thinking, without wondering why it was wanted, without uttering even a sound. The short bristles of Chloe's trunk scratched him warmly as the organ curled near to his throat. Then, slowly, the trunk withdrew, sliding back as it had come, flexing and breathing with a whisper across his shoulder, then gone, the slight weight lifted.

Mount had a lightness in his head and felt like he was known right down to the last detail. Then a sound came from deep inside Chloe, the sighing of inky realms of gas. And Mount thought: That's her thanks. That's something I've done for her.

Then someone's mouth was clicking at him, and he saw the yellow crock being handed back, shining dully in the dark night. The barge hissed south through the river. Mount reached out and took what was offered.

He spent more time with the elephant. Her handler's name was something Gendron, and Mount couldn't remember the first part because no one called him by it—the same as no one called Mount by anything but Mount, if they called him anything at all.

He fetched buckets of water and stretched up the long-handled brush that swished around and scrubbed the water she blew onto her back through her trunk. Gendron told Mount he could see Chloe liked him just fine. He said that he, Gendron, could read all her delicate feelings—however much she wanted to hide them—because he was not just a handler but a trainer and an expert. And he told Mount right off about the two men she had killed. "Not here," he said, "but with another outfit." Mount looked at her and wondered how. Was it the trunk squeezing the breath out and letting none back in, or did she push you against a wall and lean with her full gray weight?

"Mostly," said Gendron, "it's the males that kill. In their must time when their blood goes cloudy. You see the yellow comes into their eyes and you right away double chain them and leave them be. There's no getting close, no matter if they loved you yesterday. They forget they ever saw you, the males. But all we got is Chloe here, just a lady with a mean streak."

Mount spent the first day standing back and looking at her. Her head stayed interested in him, following Mount as he moved around in the grass like a planet circling as close as it would ever get. When he switched his orbit, she did too. Gendron watched this and asked if Mount would like to help him. Whenever someone said help, Mount always said yes, until he was sorry about it later.

Gendron liked Mount's being there, and he told him so instead of paying him anything. Gendron's legs were bad, and he liked best to sit in a chair and direct the tasks performed nearby, whether or not the tasks were his own or someone else's.

"Chloe likes my voice," said Gendron. "So, don't you talk to her. I'll be the one to talk. You just do what I say to do, and she'll treat you like it was me."

Mount learned to lead her, where to stand and how fast to walk so not to get ahead of her. From a single spot they went in a circle that grew larger and never crossed itself. Gendron spoke out firmly through the speaking trumpet, his voice rising sharp in Mount's ear. This made Mount feel like an animal doing the trick of leading an animal; and so he did. In a while they were almost to the big top, and Mount could hear from inside the sounds of the acrobats and clowns and bareback riders practicing—people who were so exalted and gifted that they were frightening and slow to take notice of him. Some even stood by the drawn-back flaps gazing out, and their faces clearly showed that they saw hardly anything worth seeing, that any second they might turn back and look into the preferred inner darkness, where someone was sure to be flying or flipping or falling.

The farther Mount moved from where Gendron was sitting, the more he wanted to talk to Chloe in his own voice. But he remembered what he had been told, and stayed mute, though Chloe tempted him by swinging her trunk so it brushed the backs of his knees, one knee at a time, as he was walking precisely where Gendron had instructed him to—one foot in front of her forehead and on her left side, where he could feel on the nape of his neck the air pushed forward by the fanning of her ear.

Without Mount noticing, the man named Jase who played the part of a colored man in the sideshow came up alongside and tried talking to both Mount and Chloe. But Mount stayed mute even then, since Gendron had told him not to unveil the sound of his own voice in Chloe's earshot—she was meant to think he was only the physical embodiment of Gendron's voice.

"My instrument," was how Gendron put it, placing a cold hand on the back of Mount's neck and pushing him forward toward Chloe, who was chewing something noisily.

And this Jase—almost as young as Mount—who had only asked a

stupid question to pass the time and was still waiting to have it answered, said to Chloe, "Well, this man won't talk to me, will he?" Mount wished he could answer, but he couldn't. Then Gendron himself tried to shoo Jase away, but Jase just ignored him and transformed his voice to sound like a colored man, making it high pitched and strange and sorrowful. And Mount was amazed at the difference. And something in that colored voice annoyed him, like a bee buzzing too near his face, so that a sharp emotion of wanting to hit out at Jase sprang up in him. Then right away Chloe swung at the side of Jase's head with her trunk, and he fell back on the ground with a stunned expression. Some people came running.

"Hey," he said.

"Never mind," said Mount, forgetting his pledge to stay silent.

And Gendron rushed over, limping up and down on his bad legs, and reprimanded Jase for coming so close to getting killed. Then he cuffed the back of Mount's head, and Chloe shrieked—which startled Gendron.

Jase picked himself up and said he wasn't hurt. But then he sat back down again because he was dizzy. He reached out and patted Chloe's leg, but the elephant paid him no attention.

"Don't touch her," said Gendron.

"I always did before," said Jase, "and you know it. I think it's him that did this, that caused this." He pointed at Mount.

"Maybe so," said Gendron. "But all the same, you should leave her be from now on since she did this to you. She's got your face in her eye now, and that's all it takes."

Mount wanted to say he was sorry, but he held himself back, not wanting his head to be cuffed again. Several people were looking at him, and he knew they wouldn't forget him now, whether he said anything or not. He reached down a hand to help Jase up, and Jase took it firmly but held onto Mount's face with a wary eye. Mount shook his head.

"You mute?" Jase asked.

"He don't never talk near Chloe," Gendron said. "I talks, he walks. So, don't take it personal. All of us here is just sorry, so let it go and don't come near Chloe again. You can count on this, that you were lucky as aces this time and you mayn't be so lucky again."

"Okay," said Jase. "Okay twice, and forget about it."

He walked away shaky, and the rest of the people also drifted off until all that was left was Mount and Gendron and Chloe. Gendron made Chloe bow, speaking in a hard voice as she bent each of her forward joints. And Mount stood back and watched Gendron tapping sharp at her knees to keep her coming. Her head went lower like a dog's.

"Get on," Gendron said to Mount. "Your reward for being a fool on earth is getting to spend a few minutes closer to heaven."

So Mount climbed up on Chloe's back, and Gendron walked them straight to where his chair was waiting. But instead of lowering Chloe again, he just sat in the chair and stared at Mount and Chloe for a while, twisting his face in a smile that betrayed he was getting no fun at all out of what he was doing. And Mount didn't say anything—for he thought that it must be a test of his discipline to keep quiet. Instead he passed the time by looking as deep as he could into the Mississippi forest surrounding the field where the tent was pitched, and he imagined men in Southern gray uniforms hiding in the trees watching everything and planning to burn the tent late at night. Or he imagined that, if they were not men, they were children running from angry uncles with steaming Bibles. Or they were strangers just like Mount himself, looking for a place to be and something to do until they found where they were going. And while he was sitting there, Chloe raised her head and curled her trunk back slowly toward him, the tip working as though it was pulling itself on the air between them. He reached out and patted the trunk, saying nothing. Gendron watched this, smiling no more. Then Chloe began to lower herself without Gendron telling her to, and Gendron, springing out of his chair, rushed to give her the order to bow and leapt in to tap at her joints, which she folded gracefully and gently beneath her until she was low enough for Mount to climb down easily.

None of this was lost on Gendron, who was not accustomed to hearing the sound of "beware" in his thoughts. But he then resolved that he would treat Mount carefully, recalling the way Chloe's trunk flicked out at Jase, a tease of a blow that did no more harm than it meant to.

"Come into my wagon for a drink and a bit of bread," he said to Mount after thinking this over for only a minute. "I can see you've a way with her right off the bat."

Mount followed Gendron silently, proud of not talking. He was starting to like the man.

* * *

134

In secret he talked to Chloe in his own voice, whispering in the dark where her legs were hobbled and chained to a spike driven deep in the ground near vine-wrapped bales of grass that the circus boys were sent out to gather every evening, so she and the other animals could eat their fill without having to wander.

Mount swished a path through the dew on the ground. Chloe's shape stood out like a blot, spreading more the closer he came. Gendron was in his wagon sleeping. And now Mount slept there too, in a blanket roll on the floor. Each night after he blew the lamp out, Gendron talked on tediously to Mount about the seven other circuses he'd been with and all the people in them who were stupider than he was, and all the women and girls in the towns where they performed who came to his wagon after the show when he was a younger man, and let him do it. ("Now no one come to this wagon," Gendron said, "but you.") When he asked Mount where he was born, Mount told him a lie: Sandusky, he said. Then Gendron laughed and said he'd been in a show that played Sandusky "just about nine month before you was born there. An' I met your mother that night, an' she let me do it. So, I guess that mean I must be your own father." Gendron laughed and hit the wall of the wagon, which rattled.

Mount could hear him drinking from a flask in the dark ("It take the twitch out of my legs so's I can sleep"), a suction being created when he nipped on the flask's small, cold mouth. After a while the talking just stopped, and sometimes Mount heard the rest of the liquor dribbling out on the floor about the same time Gendron started to snore. It was then that Mount crept out.

He was struck by the strangeness of opening the same door night after night and finding a different place outside, situated differently on the ground, so that the stars themselves were seen helter skelter from one night to the next as what was home kept moving while staying the same. This changing but not changing could be a bewildering thing. If he was planning to see Chloe, Mount tried not to fall asleep first. It wouldn't do to fall asleep and then wake up and try to remember where you were; you were just somewhere, in a town in the South or on the deck of the barge, somewhere creeping out to find the elephant.

Chloe seemed to hear him coming. Mount wondered when she slept or at what depth of unconsciousness. She always stirred when he came near, with what was almost a creaking of her enormous skin, as though whatever rest she had settled into was rippled like the surface of a calm pool. Then he heard the air sniffing in and out of her trunk, the trunk reaching toward him from the growing blot, giving it depth. And still he wasn't to her yet. The dark of the night grew denser as her shape consumed it.

"Hello," he said, the human greeting. He smelled the milky smell. He still had a few feet to go.

It was like drawing near to a house, right up to the side of it, and listening for the life or emptiness inside, as he had often done on summer nights in Bolusburgh, putting his ear directly to the clapboard—still warm from the sun—and hearing something: a footstep, two footsteps, someone coughing or laughing or singing. And so he put his ear to Chloe's side, never minding the short, straight bristles, and heard her own calliope of inner harmonies, digestive and mechanical, all keening and bubbling together. Her skin was warm. When he took his ear away the sounds were muted; when he put it back, they sang. She stood still and let him do it. And soon his own stomach began to sing, sounds that arched like shooting stars, that sailed and dimmed and waited for an answer. And he talked to her softly, leaving his ear at her side so that his words hissed back into his head, adding themselves to the sum of his and Chloe's combined sounds.

Mount felt that the link between them was growing strong.

Gendron planned to put Mount in the ring with Chloe. He taught Mount how to place his head beneath one of Chloe's feet.

"It's Chloe's trick," he said, suggesting that this was something Chloe had learned to do with the human head, but not something Mount might learn to do with Chloe's foot. At first, Mount practiced only with Gendron, putting his head on the drum-shaped wooden platform, one ear to the wood.

"You got to smile," said Gendron. "Whoever can see your face got to see it smiling." Chloe was out in the meadow, hobbled and chained.

Mount smiled and waited.

"Good," said Gendron. "Now, imagine the foot coming down." Gendron took an old pie tin and lowered it slowly to Mount's up-facing ear. The tin felt cool.

"If the pressure grows past this," said Gendron, hardly pushing down at all, "pull out. She'll squash it like a grape. But when you pull out, jump up smiling like the trick is over, not like it just went wrong and you almost was killed."

"Okay," said Mount. The pie tin was on his ear, and he could feel the warmth of Gendron's hand coming through, the sensation seeming more and more what it might be like to have Chloe's foot there.

The next day Chloe was brought in and Mount was told not to speak in her presence.

"Here's peanuts," Gendron said, handing Mount a bagful. "Go give her some. It'll make her feel more friendly like."

Mount spent a few minutes giving Chloe peanuts. She acted like she didn't know him. He thought maybe she'd been sleeping because she acted a lot like Mount did when he'd first got up, all slow and unhappy and quiet in herself. Every seven or eight peanuts she blew one up in the air where it sailed like a high-hit baseball and fell.

"Some of 'em she just don't like," said Gendron. "Which I can tell." He had Mount gather these rejected ones, which he said he saved and ate himself. "It's nothin' wrong with the nut inside, it's the shape of the shell she don't like."

Then he had Mount walk her around the ring in both directions. Each time her foot came down Mount thought of his head being underneath. One time he'd had a horse step on his foot, and all that weight came down as if the horse didn't even know, and he had to beat on the horse's side and shout in the horse's ear. He was surprised at the weight. He multiplied to imagine Chloe's weight. Gendron rolled the drum-shaped wooden platform into the center of the ring.

Gendron talked in two different voices, one his human voice, the other his Chloe voice. With two choices, Mount should have liked one of them, but he didn't. The Chloe voice was sharp and nasal, and the human voice was soft and wet, like something growing in old food. The worst part was that, since Chloe was there, he couldn't answer Gendron at all, and the only spoken sounds were Gendron's two bad voices mixing back and forth.

"Now, watch me," Gendron said. Then he started talking to Chloe, bringing her near to the wooden thing. It was Gendron's voice that made her take unnatural baby steps, halfway at a time, then smaller and smaller, each bite of ground a dose of discipline. He stopped her with a wave of his hand. She was right up to the wooden platform. "Now, watch . . ."

Gendron got down on his hands and knees like a man at the guillotine. Then he lay his head on the center of the platform, a happy smile on his face, which he aimed at Mount.

"See?" Mount nodded.

"*Chloe! Step!*" barked Gendron.

Mount watched her raise her foot, for all the world like she didn't want to do it and couldn't understand why it was necessary. But she did it anyway, getting her foot up to the height then stretching it forward until it hung over Gendron's head, waiting. The foot was perfectly still.

"*Down!*" said Gendron.

The foot came down like an old lady sitting, the space between it and the head closing slowly. Mount crouched and watched it lower and lower until the clearance of air slimmed down to just a sparkle of light from one of the torches outside the ring that shone at the rim of Gendron's ear. And that was that. The foot stopped moving.

"*Hold!*" said Gendron. The foot was barely resting there. Chloe threw her trunk up and blew out a shriek that rattled around the canvas. Gendron was smiling relentlessly, but Mount thought this looked less like a smile than a grimace that struck him as small and hopeless what with the elephant's foot above.

"*Go back!*" said Gendron. And Chloe did everything exactly in reverse, with the same slowness and the same steady, half-stupid expression in her eyes that called attention to her just being an animal—which after all was the beauty of the trick, since why would an animal do this in the first place, except for food.

"Now you clap!" said Gendron to Mount in his human voice. So Mount clapped, feeling in his own eyes the same stupid expression he had seen in Chloe's and doing it because he worked for Gendron for food and for a place on the floor.

Gendron leapt up and flung his arms in the air and limped in a small circle until he had faced in all directions, where now there were only near-empty bleachers and some clowns lying on their backs resting and paying no attention.

"Okay," Gendron said. "It's your turn." He led Chloe some distance away from the platform and then motioned for Mount to position himself.

Mount went and lowered himself to his hands and knees. From there he looked down on the platform. The bright red painted circle in its center looked like a bullseye. Slowly Mount put his head down on the red, feeling where the spot was still warm from Gendron. Gendron led Chloe toward Mount so that she came to stand facing the top of his head, where he couldn't see her but could feel and smell her.

Mount heard Gendron start the commands, repeating them in the order they had come in before. The leg stretched forward and hung above him, and Mount could feel the potential coming out the bottom of the foot like heat from a fire, as though something was stored inside in such great quantities that it couldn't completely be contained in the space provided. Mount's ear began to heat up.

"Down!" said Gendron in his Chloe voice.

"Smile!" he said in his human voice.

But Mount let his mouth do whatever it would. The shadow came down, shortening sound and stilling the air until the very highest prominence of Mount's ear felt touched, its short hairs bending and tingling. And that was all. Chloe stopped. Mount smiled. The power went straight from Chloe's foot down into the hole of Mount's ear like water down a drain.

Vicksburg was the last stop on the river. From there the circus quit the barge and went overland, passing through towns with names like Dosta Verges and Dilly's Bottom and Ankle Wells, little towns where the people who came to the midway or sat in the bleachers hardly seemed to speak English or to live in any way similar to other people Mount had seen in the North—or in plenty of other places where, though life was peculiar enough, still it was familiar and recognizable and he knew some of the customs and the smells of the food cooking from one house or one town to the next. He knew some of the people, too, and understood the way they wore their clothes.

But in the center of Mississippi—heading toward Alabama and Florida—even Mother Danilecki's rock doves were harder to come by. And when he first set out with his bare hands and his burlap bag to catch them, he was frightened what might happen if he encountered some of these strange people or a species of animal native to that place alone that he had never seen or heard of.

So he stopped at Mother's wagon and asked if she would like to come along with him, she having been in Mississippi before and perhaps knowing the way things were done there. And she said yes, leaving

Mount to think how fine it was that the circus people looked after one another so well in the heart of dangerous and uncomfortable surroundings.

The name of this present town was Oakleigh Flats, the flats being a place where the river once had flowed until it left its banks and went elsewhere, leaving that wide, smooth place where the townspeople now came and dug clay and fingernail-sized shells that they used in making bricks and cements and a marly fertilizer for their crops. Before the river moved the name was just Oakleigh, after a man who had been hanged there before another man confessed, and that man was hanged too.

This much Mother Danilecki knew from another year when the circus had come to Oakleigh Flats and Semple had been bit by a bad mosquito or some other unknown insect, and had lain in his wagon sweating for three days until he threw up long and hard and was fine again. But owing to his illness, they fell behind schedule and stayed in Oakleigh Flats four days instead of two, giving (including one matinee) three half-price performances to lure back crowds that had already seen the show and seemed to like it no better as a bargain than they had at full price.

Mount had to walk slower to keep Mother Danilecki from falling behind. They went straight to the block of shabby buildings in the center of town, any building of two or more stories being the perfect place to capture rock doves. Mother Danilecki asked and received permission, and Mount climbed up the inside of the tallest building—the bank—and out to the roof where the sun had made it hot.

He heard the birds cooing over the edge. They were roosting in the cove beneath the overhanging cornice. This was where you always saw them when you looked up walking past on the street, no matter where you were—in Oakleigh Flats or Fort Wayne or Bolusburgh—and the sound they made was also always the same, a sweet, throaty happiness that drew Mount toward them across the hot roof.

When he reached the edge he crept his face over it until his eyes could see down. The birds didn't even know he was there. He counted five of them, purple-gray and shining even in the shade. A bead of his sweat dropped from his forehead straight down to the street, passing the birds in a flash. He waited, hoping they hadn't seen it. In his first few expeditions he had learned at least three things: never be too hurried to wait; breathe as slow as the birds must breathe, and always select the proper bird—the bird that in some quiet way signifies it wants to be, or is ready to be, the one that goes in the bag.

Mount watched a bird lean over and peck softly at the feathers of another bird, and that second bird jittered two steps sideways, away from the one that had pecked it and closer to where Mount's face was looking down. Mount decided that that was the very bird. It was four birds close together, and the one apart.

Beyond the birds in the street below, Mount could see and hear Mother Danilecki talking to the banker, who wore a white shirt and a straw hat under which none of his head was visible to Mount. But his arms kept moving wide apart as if he was describing the size of something big, and Mount saw Mother Danilecki's gray hair bobbing forward and back and heard her saying, "Oh, oh, oh," with her accent and in a cooing voice like that of the rock doves. Then her own arms went as wide as the banker's, and she threw her head back and laughed, her eyes looking right up into Mount's.

And, at just that moment, Mount flashed his right arm down, the hand closing around the neck and wings and upper breast of the bird that was perched apart from the others, while those others flew off astonished. His captive's heart beat wild under his fingers as he hauled it up and stuffed it in the bag. It fluttered in the dark, making the burlap come to life as he tied a cord around the opening.

And this was repeated three more times that afternoon. Mother Danilecki stayed down below and talked to people while Mount climbed up and went across the hot flat roofs, waiting and breathing and selecting the proper bird to catch at just the right moment. People came up to him in the street between times and asked him who he was and where he was from, and he watched their faces smiling goofylike while they waited for him to answer. And he felt the caught birds fluttering together at the end of his arm.

"A gypsy," Mother Danilecki answered for him thickly. "Like me, like my own son on earth." She put an arm across his shoulder and passed her fingers through his hair. Mount watched the people still smiling, some of whom were bold enough to come right up to Mother Danilecki and put their hard, creased hands on her heavy jewelry.

"Come to the circus tonight," said Mount, "and I'll put my head under an elephant."

* * *

141

One night after the show was over, the tent struck down and the wagons loaded for leaving in the morning, Semple Groves sat with his circus surrounding him and the yellow crock of sweet liquor circulating, and said that you could begin to smell Florida days before you got there.

"We'll be going down the western side, like always," he said. "I can just about smell it now, like sweet food cooling at your feet or a pile of coconut husks going bad on the beachfront." Mount could see he was trying to think of something else that Florida smelled like.

No one said anything. The show that night had gone poorly. Claire had tried and failed to do the one-footed thing on the white horse named Beau that was skittish and sometimes wouldn't let her do it, and this was one of those times. She spat out several manly curses that echoed around the canvas as she was bouncing in a circle on the horse's back. People sat in the seats like they were dead, waiting from one thing to the next for something exciting. Here was this pretty albino-skinned woman riding a horse standing up and swearing, and no one cared. Beau snorted and shook his head coming out of the ring. Claire reached down and slapped his ear as she was jumping off. Standing next to Mount, Chloe trumpeted, a piercing sound that might have billowed the walls of the tent with wind—Mount thought he saw them shiver, but the crowd was unmoved. With Gendron, Mount and Chloe went into the ring.

Mount put his head under Chloe's foot and couldn't even feel the power coming down out of it. He smiled at a particular person in the bleachers, and that person looked away. The foot came down and touched Mount's ear, and there was a perfect silence in the tent, the silence still unbroken when up he leapt and flung his arms out. Chloe banged her foot down sharp where his head had been, and some in the audience jumped in fright. That was the best thing all night.

So, later, when Semple started to talk about Florida, it was like he was promising everyone and himself that things were going to get better. And even just hearing his voice in that vein, Mount could feel the night's turmoil dying down like the dynamo shutting off at the Fort Wayne Isolated Edison Station. The moon was in and out, and the warm night smelled like something sweet, whether it was Florida or not. In a ready line near the circle of people the white circus wagons glowed. Mount heard his rock doves cooing somewhere in their cages. Gendron sat by Mount, not waiting to drink from the crock but drinking from his own private liquor and saying hard, disrespectful things about Semple under his breath, about what a fool he was to own such a bad circus that made no money and had no acts worth paying a quarter or even less to see.

"Shut up," said Mount, who liked Semple the way he liked the president. Gendron swung weakly at him with the hand that was holding the flask, and some liquor burst out and onto Mount's shirt, where it smelled sharp and wrecked the fragrance of the night, or of what Semple was saying was Florida.

"The water there is sweet and clean," he said, "rising up from an aquifer that is rich with minerals and deep in the ground and, so, cool even in the hottest time of the year, which this is not."

Chloe, on the far side of the wagons, jangled her chains, and the links jumbled together softly, as though there was a fog in amongst them cushioning the iron. Mount heard the air blow out of her trunk, the sound he had learned she made when she was falling asleep, which she often did in his presence, a thing that Gendron told him elephants never did unless they meant to flatter you with the fullness of their trust.

"There she goes," said Mount to Gendron. Gendron handed Mount his private liquor, and Mount unscrewed the cap and pretended to drink it but kept his thumb over the hole, hoping not to be made insensible.

"Thank you," he said, and passed it back. Gendron took the flask without looking at him.

Semple was like a show that went on without your knowing how long it would run. He would talk and then stop, and you would think he was done and had nothing further to state, and then he would come out with something else. People never replied to him, even if he asked them a straight question. After they waited a time, he would say yes and go on to some new ground or give the answer himself or hide it in the seemingly unrelated thing he had gone forward to. No reliable conclusion could be drawn from a silence into which he had entered. While he was talking, he was left by himself. The people around him listened as though he were a wire act unfolding from one balancing to the next.

Most of his time he spent alone in his wagon, doing no one but Mother Danilecki knew what. Just sitting, probably, or reading and writing. It was known to Mother Danilecki that he was writing a history of his own circus, but that no one had ever read a word. She had seen the papers on his desk with dates written large at the tops of the pages, and he had often asked her what she knew about what had happened that day or commanded her to describe a certain person from her own perspective and to give a judgment that was as true and complete as she could make.

She had revealed this much to Mount.

"He ask about you one day," she told him. Then she took a heavy necklace made from pieces of brass and looped it over his head, letting it fall into place on his breastbone so that the pieces clashed together with a sound like the rustling of Chloe's chains.

"I told him the total troot." She grinned. "Totally absolute honest, and you would tink so, too."

On the morning the circus crossed into Florida, passing a white-painted, black-lettered sign that marked the spot, Semple came out of his wagon onto the road and waved for the caravan to stop. He blinked in the sunlight and adjusted his hands in dozens of ways around his forehead for shade, spying in all directions as if to see how good things looked or how much they had changed compared with how he recalled them.

The horses, who were accustomed to moving along slow and steady without interruption, stood stamping their feet and shaking their heads from side to side. In the silence of waiting for Semple to speak, the circus people looked around at each other, raising their eyebrows or shrugging their shoulders. And Semple got down on his hands and knees and put his ear to the ground, keeping it there for a minute as though he was listening for a train.

Mount watched this from a distance, standing in the road beside Chloe at the rear of the procession. He was actually still in Alabama, unable to see much difference or improvement yet but looking forward to it. The white sign was just up ahead of him. From where he stood, Semple seemed a long way off, looking frail and slow with the sunlight beyond him winking around his limbs and thinning them brightly. Finally Semple smacked the road with the palms of his hands and jumped up along with the dust, hurrying down the line of wagons and telling everyone to get going while some of them hollered back at him that they would have been just as happy not stopping in the first place.

Slowly the wagons began to roll again, the horses first jerking them forward so they rocked on their springs like the movements of the fake

Balinese dancers who always kept their hair larded with bacon grease. Semple made it back as far as Mount and said something to him and slapped Chloe's flank with his dusty hands. Mount was so happy to be spoken to by Semple that he couldn't think of anything to say in reply and just stood there goshing inside himself and waiting for the moving of the long column to reach as far back as he and Chloe were. Semple had already turned around and was headed toward the front again, where a boy from Florida rushed forward to greet him like royalty that the boy had been assigned by the people of Florida to keep watch for and treat with the proper respect. Mount saw the boy dance around Semple and grab him by both hands as though a circus owner was the best thing that could come into anyone's empty life.

And Mount began thinking there might be something to this deep regard Semple had for Florida, because grown men and women soon followed the boy in greeting them, and this reminded Mount of the tales he had read about the way the native brownskins of the distant tropics would paddle out to the ships of England and America and let them know that anything they wanted they could have, including a party where pigs would be killed. It was like these Florida people had all been waiting with nothing better to do, as though they had known the circus was coming, perhaps smelling it three days early exactly as Semple had said that Florida itself could be sniffed that long before arrival.

The men, women and children walked along beside the wagons, and soon the first town of Florida presented itself. The town was Sippewissacola, where all these people who greeted the circus came from. They opened the doors of their homes and showed the circus people their parlours, which were uncommonly dim and damp on account of the houses being so closely girded by thick, shiny-leafed vegetation that, whenever the breezes stirred, brushed the outside walls like ghosts scratching to get inside.

Mount was in and out of several houses where cold drinks with chips of ice in them were offered. The ice was cloudy blue like the sky, and Mount, who remembered the yearly midwinter sawing of blocks of gray ice from the Bolusburgh Canal, wondered where ice might originate in an unfrozen climate. He asked a man, who told him the chips came from the ice machine in the center of town.

"An ice machine?" said Mount.

"That's the truth," said the man.

Mount stuck his finger down into the drink and pushed one of the small chips under like a drowning cat. Back up it popped.

"This comes from a *machine?*"

"It does," said the man.

"I'll *see* that machine," declared Mount. "My God, Semple Groves was right about this place."

The man just looked at him and shrugged.

"What's the name of your elephant?" he asked.

9

EDISON ON THE DOCK

*A*t the end of the long dock reach-
ing into the wide Caloosahatchee River, Edison, slouching, pretended
to fish. The pole arched out and the line hung down unbaited, and he
was alone, sunlight smacking off the pure white paint of the planking
and throwing up a dazzle onto his stern black linen coat and trousers.
It was just about at Edison's dock that the freshwater Caloosahatchee
met the saltwater Gulf of Mexico, and species of fish native to these two
waters were trading places back and forth beneath the dock, amongst
its hundred pilings, confused and turning and returning.

It was a perfect place to fish.

It was also a perfect place to be alone, with no room at all for a crowd,
and Edison went there often to get away from whomever would consult
with him on some business in the lab or the sundry matters requiring
his attention back up North, when all he wanted and needed was to sit
and think quietly about something for a while—that something on this
clear, dry April day being portland cement. And he had learned that no
one bothered a man who was fishing. Maybe daydreaming and thinking
were so idle appearing as to be fully interruptible, but fishing was *doing*
something—a combination of enterprise and prayer—and you would be
left alone while engaged in it.

So he would take the pole and bait bucket down, unfold his canvas
camp chair and let the live bait stew in warming brine while the
pole jiggled only from breeze. And he could sit there undisturbed
as people came and went, fretting, from the dock's landward end,
some of them even treading halfway out before thinking better of

it, unwilling to approach him, retreating from his black linen back.
He sat there more than half the morning, hunched forward. Sometimes he felt the planking tremble toward him like a wave, and hoped
it would tremble away again; and it did. Three or four fishing boats
chugged past, and he waved at their red-faced, stubble-chinned captains,
who held up stiff kingfish and tarpon and mullet instead of saying
anything—which was fine with Edison, who was deaf and couldn't have
heard them anyway. He watched their lips and knew they weren't
speaking. Fishermen, he thought, as though the word itself were a
perfect summary containing tides of meaning. Then he made himself
a pun about scales and the weighing of the day's catch. He laughed out
loud, a high-pitched snort repeated three times, and then resumed
thinking about portland cement.

There would be a valley full of factories unearthing glacial deposits
and kilning them into the finest construction medium ever devised, the
secret of its excellence lying in the smallness of the constituent particles
and the great heat of the kilns. Men would come to work in these
factories and would find themselves making the stuff of which their own
tidy homes would someday be built. He imagined a way of erecting
elaborate forms into which a whole house could be poured at one time
to harden so that even the kitchen cupboards were there for the people
to just come in and put food on after the three or four days' setting up
was completed. Take the forms away and there would be the family
home that no colony of bugs could consume. The workers would go all
the more eagerly to their jobs to make cement, knowing they were
building homes for themselves and their brother workers. Then the
factories could be dismantled and put on trains to go elsewhere, creating
a spreading zone of whole cities made up of poured structures as white
as limestone, shining by day and glowing by night.

Someday something would strike at his empty line. This possibility
unreasonably frightened him. He leaned over the edge of the dock and
watched it floating pointlessly. Farther out, the water was blue as the
sky, but below him the water was dull green and impenetrable. There
were things down in it, he knew. To think of them there unseen but
close half unsettled him, and so did the idea that he only had to hook
and bait his line for something in the water to want it and clamp down
upon it. Those fish below him were waiting, and it was as though there

were a natural development pending in the link between man and creation, and he was holding it up.

"That ain't like me," he said, his own words vibrating murkily through the bones of his head. Then he snorted his laugh, turning quickly to see whoever might have heard him. There was no one in sight.

Sometimes he wished he could hear. Other times he was just as glad to be free of the distraction. But when you wanted to know what was going on around you, hearing would be handy. As things stood, someone stealthy could come upon him—not here on the dock, but on dry land—and slap a strong cord around his throat and, zing!, that would be it. You wanted to know you could pretend not to hear and then turn around at the last instant and smack the assailant across the face.

He thought of a pair of glasses with a tiny mirror so the deaf could see what they couldn't hear. He'd call them "Seeing-Ear Spectacles."

Something hit the dock. He felt it, a soft thud. He looked over the side. There was a dull, yellow-gray shadow that the sunlight caught as it was moving under. He went to the other side, and there was the shadow again. Maybe a ray of some kind, but it was too deep, and stirring up too much trouble in the water to be seen clearly. And that was exactly like some of his ideas—like the cement pouring down into the enormous mold, into darkness. Would it fracture? Would it settle right? Would it flow? Would it need some kind of colloidal binder to keep the bigger constituents from descending and giving a structure too much strength down low and too little up high? He could ask himself these questions out in the clear, but the answers would lie somewhere down in the deep, like a yellow-gray shadow moving under the dock. Here he would reach the practical limits of contemplation: answers resided in the doing, not in his head. The only thing in his head was the dream, in this case the idea that it would be good to pour houses that could go up from scratch in under a week, leaving a residential block where before there was nothing but goldenrod and rocks. And people could live in these places and be as happy as Edison himself was at home in Florida or New Jersey, or spitting tobacco juice on the floor of the lab in West Orange.

The bait was dead. Just a few minutes earlier some of the things in the bucket had been moving, small shrimps twisting and spurting. But now they lay on their sides like the curlicues of Scottish paisley. Their shells, once blue as slate, were milking up like a cataracted eye. He said out loud that he was sorry. Again he looked around, and no one was there. He turned his face away from this senseless slaughter and gazed out across the Caloosahatchee. He bent forward and rested his elbows on his knees, his chin in his hands. He reached up with one hand and drew his straw hat lower, so the brim came down like a blade upon his line of sight. He sat there like that for a few minutes, thinking about nothing—the perfectly trivial stray cats of thought, what was for dinner or how long would the weather stay dry—and then he fell asleep.

On her walk Mina saw him out there sleeping. She worried that he might topple forward into the river and be wet for lunch. There was smoked fish and soda crackers and a fruit compote, and the Batchelors would be there, and Cora was baking a kind of cookie that used no flour, and that would be interesting. The ten kinds of tea in the pantry made it almost not like Florida at all—though you didn't want it *too* unlike Florida, for that would be confusing. Bad enough that in the North they had an Irish girl named Nora, and here in Fort Myers they had a Seminole girl named Cora, and that Nora had learned to do the things that Cora did well, and vice versa, so that life in the North and life in the South blended gently into one another. The truth was, Cora and Nora looked the slightest bit alike, after allowing for certain undeniable racial attributes, with slim figures and hair worn up the same way and being roughly the same age and both possessing an enviable briskness of movement, especially in their arms, while chopping something or carrying a dish from one counter to another or into the stove—as though their elbows had thick, strong springs inside.

Mina paid attention to these things, sitting in the kitchen planning the menu—an act that was done for herself alone, since Tom would eat, or not eat, anything set before him, depending on his temper. She would pretend to be fully absorbed but keep an eye on Cora or Nora, what each did and how she did it. And Mina found that both of them were accomplished in the same ways, smooth and dexterous and with a familiarity toward acts of service that Mina believed she had in common with them, owing to the happy guidance of her solid Methodist upbringing. Both Cora and Nora would take up the knife as though it was a friend—like a sixth finger or a third hand—and it would fit there perfectly and perform its task. Mina would take up her pen to write her correspondence, feeling the good cheer of her heart go flowing down her arm with an actual tingle that went straight into the nib of the pen as it scratched across the paper, leaving behind the vibrant ink of her generous thoughts . . . She could watch Cora take the scales from a fish and sense in Cora the same kind of pleasure in duty, as the sharp blade moved in swift, short strokes and the winking scales leapt into the sunlight angling through the window into the copper sink.

For all the differences between them that owed to their separate classes, their unity propelled house life forward just as surely as Tom propelled whatever it was he propelled, whatever the public was pleased to call it (for he was a public creature)—the life of the new, the life of improvement, of progress.

She arrived at the shaded bower at the threshold of the dock, which beyond gleamed cold and hot. She stepped onto it, letting go the shade, sending her white right shoe into blazing sunlight and following after in a white dress with a bold red belt that itself felt hot as soon as the sun fell fully upon her. Tom was out at the very tip, like a distant lump. It seemed such a long way to walk to reach that slouched black shape that was sleeping. She went slowly, putting her feet down toes first onto the planking so as not to catch a heel in the spaces between, through which the sound of the water came up menacing and dark, as though the water below were different from the water that flowed in brightness at the sides.

The dock was a long straight line, and Mina disliked it. So open and diminishing it was, and so unguarded with its lack of railings that an undisciplined soul might go careening left or right into the river. Even Mina's own regulated manner was threatened—loosened by her going out like this, away from the land and her houses and shrubs. She was uncomfortable, and grew uneasier with every step. She wanted a gazebo built—with a red roof and scrollwork decoration—out at the end, to give her the sense she was going somewhere, a civilized destination instead of a vanishing line of perspective that seemed to end nowhere. When she had asked him, Tom had said yes to her and sent up North for the pieces to be cut and tooled and shipped on down. That was more than a year ago. In the meantime, the planking had been painted, which worsened and sharpened its trick of perspective, and also made it shine like a slippery nougat or like the skin of a living creature, whose spine she was walking along.

When she was more than halfway to the end—with the south breeze blowing so that her blousy dress went tight against her side—she remembered she had news to tell him. Cora had passed it on to her, saying she'd heard it from her husband Owen, a white man who worked on the fish docks helping the incoming boats tie up and unload. A circus was coming. A man off a boat down from Bradenton said he'd seen it there, and it was headed this way and ought to be here soon—if it didn't turn back or go out of business first, which maybe it would.

Owen went and told someone and someone else, and that was how it started. The buzz spread fast along the docks, and soon there wasn't anyone in Fort Myers who didn't know there was a circus coming, whether in fact there was or not. There wasn't anyone who didn't know, said Cora, except poor Mr. and Mrs. Edison, who knew everything about what was going on in Europe or up North, but hardly anything about what was happening farther down McGregor Boulevard or out in Tice, where Cora's mother and father lived. So after Owen told Cora, Cora came out and told Mrs. Edison, who, she said, ought to know there was a circus coming even if she didn't want to go, not wanting to get so close to the animals and the way they smelled and what they did.

Mina had nodded and said what exciting news it was, and now she was on her way to tell Tom—who loved the circus above all other entertainments, mainly because of his being deaf, which was a handicap to appreciating the subtler musical or spoken arts of which Mina herself was fondest.

The closer she got to him, the stiller he seemed. A shiver passed in and out of her. It was a mysterious act to sneak up secretly on someone you loved, as though you were taking something through unfair advantage in an unshared and unrecoverable time. (Later, she would write about this in her diary, likening it to walking into an empty dining room where the table was set.) She stopped and stood there, ten yards away, and let the breezes flow past her, getting no closer to him, taking him in as if she were one of those houselike cameras on three slim legs and the light was willowing in through the tiny hole—focused beams, as Tom had once explained, touching the chemistry inside and changing it forever.

She imagined what he would look like in a gazebo. She put the red roof over him, and the shade drifted down like mist.

* * *

"Mother," he said. He felt her there even though she wasn't moving. His chin was sore, and his neck, too. "Mother." He took off his hat and ran his hands across his hair, which was damp and lay close to the scalp.

"You must have been asleep," said Mina, coming around to where he could see her and read the words from her lips. He saw the final two she spoke.

"I was dreaming," he said. There was a fishy taste in his mouth, as though the smell of the water, and of everything in it, had wafted up and infiltrated his head. The dream was indistinct. He saw someone walking away, letting wine spill out of a bottle carelessly held. But, otherwise, the dream went to white, like snowfall eradicating trees. "I can't remember," he said.

She bent forward and put her hands on top of his head.

"This will keep it from getting out," she said. "Close your eyes and try to think." Her father had taught her this one summer at Chautauqua, and she knew it didn't work.

"It's no use," he said. Her hands were heavy and hot on his head. Sitting while she was standing, newly awakened and mud brained while she was fresh and exercised, he was discomfited by her vigor, feeling himself weaker, smaller in her presence. And he imagined being quite old, sitting still, unable to remember, while the younger Mina bustled around him, in and out of the room to places where his eyes couldn't follow. By then his blood would be poisoned and tired inside him, flowing through old, sad channels like too-thick cement. He was already fifty-five. Mina was thirty-six.

"On the whole, it's a bad thing to dream in the daytime," he said. "Especially when you're asleep. A dream is only truly at home at night."

Mina lifted her hands from his head. He felt the restorative breezes rush across his scalp, cooling it. In the mixing waters beneath the dock, manta rays and manatees brushed against the pilings with a sound like that of snowballs falling into deep, wet snow. He couldn't hear them, but he could feel them down there, gray things gliding at a certain unaltering speed through light and shadow, unsusceptible to reason, indifferent to the presence of the dock and to everything else he had put on the face of the earth in his fruitful lifetime.

But they're only fish, he thought.

Mina heard the whooshing sounds and wondered what they were, but she didn't ask Tom because she knew he couldn't hear them. Instead she told him about the circus that was coming and watched the impersonation of juvenile glee spread across his face, his eyelids sliding up into the low bones beneath the brows, their eaves.

"No fooling?" he said. She nodded. Then she took him in to lunch.

Lunch with the Batchelors was desultory. Edison's fork pushed things this way and that. Each of the several foods on his plate had a quality of littleness to it, the total dosage consisting of small flashes of delicate flavor when what would much better have suited his mood was a single, full-sized, overpowering taste—something like a stew, spreading from rim to rim of the plate like a tide full of rough-and-tumble boulders and kelps, something bracing to wake him up, not something that plainly needed as much refined appreciation as did what lay before him like knots of sensitive children.

At the ten o'clock position there was sugared fruit with almonds; at one o'clock was a mound of flaked smoked fish; at five there were slivers of avocado in lime juice; and at eight there were bland white crackers to be used, he guessed, in dredging up the mound of smoked fish. By dint of his restless manipulations, the tastes had been moved here and there, making one another's acquaintance without being much diminished. Whenever Cora came into the room, she sized up his plate and scowled, pretending, as he believed, to care what he ate, how much and how fast, thereby forcing him to pretend to eat lustily. He drove his fork toward a pile of food like a shovel into coal, bringing it up to his mouth and his mouth down to it as though neither end of the deal could wait.

To eat this way was tiresome, having first to figure out what was on your plate and how to eat it, then why—since the food gave off no tantalizing aromas to make your mouth dampen up; and then having to worry over the feelings of the woman who thought it up (Mina) and the woman who prepared it (Cora) . . . You had to be on your toes to have lunch under these circumstances. Easier by far was to chew a few inches of beef jerky in the lab, and a glass of milk, or simply to stay where he'd been on the dock, letting his stomach's intemperate rumblings scare the fish up to Tallahassee and down to Naples.

He looked at his plate, closed his eyes and wished that it would turn to stew. When he opened them up again he saw that everything was just the same, except that Batch and Mrs. Batch had cleaned their plates.

"Good boy, Batch," he said. "You ate it all."

Batchelor looked at him strangely. Edison recognized the look. A deaf man simply said whatever he wanted to say, whatever popped into his head, without anchoring it anywhere in the flow of conversation. Strange looks were familiar stuff. On their heels, talk would either turn in his direction or wouldn't, instead going back to where it had been before he opened his mouth or taking some new path altogether.

"It was very good," said Batchelor.

"Delicious, Mina," said Mrs. Batch.

And the conversation that he had interrupted began again. He watched the mouths move faster and faster, the effort of keeping up outstripping his interest. It was like chasing a train that he really didn't need to catch; so he let it leave him behind. On this account he was sometimes quietly aggrieved, watching all the talk that swirled on at what seemed like a very great distance from himself, taking little heed of who he was.

For this reason total strangers were a comfort to him. In crowds people pressed near him, smiling, reaching out to touch him as though he were their only object, their hub. If schoolchildren came to see him, he received them all and showed them something—lighted a light with a battery or made a blue spark crack in the open air. Their awe was a week's reward in place of whatever else was missing or unsatisfactory in life. He imagined that the eagerness of children was like his own un-spoiled eagerness that refused to die in maturity. Bless the children, he thought, visualizing generic editions not necessarily much like his own offspring.

Mina reached to the center of the table and rang the little bell. He watched the brass go back and forth briskly, a blur. Cora appeared instantly and cleared the plates away, leaving his to last, as he thought, to call attention to his not finishing. He cast a sharp expression at her, thinking that she would be ashamed to be caught at trying to shame him. But she lowered her eyes and pretended not to see it.

"We're going to the circus, Cora," he told her.

"That's nice, Mr. E.," she replied. She had his plate in her hand and held it up near his shoulder. His eyes fell upon its mish-mash of unfin-ished business.

"The lunch was very good," he said, "but the damn gullet is an awful crybaby today." He patted his shirt on top of where some fallen bit of peach had stained it faint yellow. Cora said she was sorry and then went back to the pantry, where she would sit on a low stool reading a book as meals progressed, always near enough to hear the bell and come quickly.

After a few minutes she returned and set a plate of flat chocolate cookies on the table. The cookies were arrayed in a circle around the rim of the plate. Inside the circle were orange sections that went on jiggling after the plate had been set down. The arrangement of colors was pretty, and the jiggling was like a trick done by animals, which put him in mind of the circus again.

He saw himself sitting in the audience, wearing his white suit and white bow tie. Other people attending constantly watched him to see how he was enjoying it. In this way he was their bellwether. He smiled, imagining himself smiling at something especially entertaining and clever done by the circus—such as the whimsical jittering of orange sections—and at how those others who were watching him smiled, too, and how much that pleased him.

He reached out and took a cookie, breaking the circle.

"Is something funny?" Mina asked him. The orange sections kept on moving. Outside the windows, the fronds of potted palmettos scraped against the screens.

On the day the circus came he was also out fishing on the dock—pretending to fish. The strains of steam organ and drum reached down the river from the center of town, music fractured into small bits carried, as crumbs are carried by ants, on smaller dashes of breeze—a drumbeat, two or three notes, the trill of a whistle. Edison sat there, hunched. The music floated above him, past him, swirled around him unheard. The fishing pole arched out, the line hung down unbaited, and the live shrimps stewed in their bucket of brine.

About ten fifteen by his pocket watch, a boy crept out to see him, one of those local Fort Myers boys who sported bright red hair and short, squarish teeth that Edison could see right off were no good for biting anything straight through. There was a rash of red hair and bad teeth in Fort Myers, as though the constant heat and damp had both scorched and warped everyone's heredity.

Edison saw the red hair first, then the form of the boy, who just suddenly appeared in his peripheral vision like an idea, startling him out of a reverie about how to keep the potash electrolyte in his nickel anode battery from leaking out into the world; over time the potash would eat the solder that held together the seams of the battery case. The trick was to stop the potash from interacting as successfully with the lead-based solder as it did with the anode and cathode. And since he didn't want to diminish the alkalinity of the potash, the answer was in the design, not the chemistry.

"Crimp the seams to the outside instead of the inside to keep the solder out of contact," he said to the boy. He pulled out his watch and saw it was ten fifteen. Then he reached down and jerked the fishing pole so as to seem to the boy to be tending it. The empty line whipped up into the air, snapping at the tip and flinging off droplets of water before it drifted down out of sight again.

"Hello," said the boy.

"You sneak up pretty good," said Edison. The boy was one he'd never seen before. He was dressed in poor, worn clothes, a boy whose mother didn't care what he put on in the morning.

"Fair enough," said the boy, meaning, yes, he snuck up pretty good. Edison saw the words as though the boy had said "Friar Tuck," except he knew that couldn't have been it.

"Try to speak as loud as you can, okay?" he told the boy. "And look straight at me when you do so's I can watch your mouth to see what you're saying. Talk slow, too. I'm a little deaf."

"Okay," said the boy. Edison saw the O and the K snap off the boy's mouth clean and true.

"Okay," he said back. A boat was chugging by. He waved. The fisherman at the helm waved in return and took off his hat. He had red hair like the boy, but the boy didn't wave at the fisherman and the fisherman didn't show any sign of knowing the boy.

They stood there and watched the boat go upriver. Edison felt a fish bump against the dock. He looked over the side and saw nothing there.

"Do you know who I am?" he asked the boy. The boy nodded.

"Then tell me who," said Edison.

"Everyone knows," said the boy, but he wouldn't say the name.

"You're shy," said Edison.

The boy shrugged. "I came out here," he said.

"That's true," said Edison. "But shouldn't you be in school?"

"Not since the circus just came to town. We got let out to see it."

"The circus?" Edison said. "It's here already?"

The boy nodded. "Believe me, it ain't much. They only got but the one elephant. I seen a circus with five or ten. And I'm only eleven years old."

Edison nodded. He decided he didn't like the boy, and thought of him filled with potash, the potash squirming around looking for seams. The boy just stood there listless and dull, scratching at his nose. There was something about him that was altogether unlike a stranger. In fact, he acted as though he'd known Edison all his life. Edison, in turn, began to look at him the way he might look at one of his own sons—with a keen disappointment that he wasn't turning out better and the wish that he would go find someone more nearly his age to play with. He imagined how, if the boy had been more like a stranger, the two of them might have gone into town to watch the circus setting up its tent, and so forth, the boy so pleased to be taken around by Edison, Edison buying him a ginger ale and walking him home finally, greeting the father and mother, who would both recognize him right off.

"So, what are you here for?" he asked the boy.

The boy had half a finger up his nose. Edison caught him at it and was about to look away, except that the boy didn't seem to mind he'd been caught. Potash for brains, thought Edison.

"I dunno," said the boy. "My sister said you sat out here. We crawl all over this place for fun, she and me and others. I been in most of the buildings here, and I been out on this dock at night and in the early morning, and I seen you and the lady eat your supper, me being out on the porch there, with the skeeters. I just come and go with everyone else. You're here sometimes, sometimes you're not. It don't matter."

"That's trespass," Edison said. The boy shrugged. The law just rolled off his back. Edison now had to think that any evening when he and Mina were inside, playing gin or cribbage or reading a book, there might be a dozen children all over the place outside, hiding and watching. And he wouldn't hear them at all, while Mina would think they were just the wind blowing through the potted palms on the veranda. He imagined how the future might come to include the sudden standing up and going outside to stare into the darkness, wondering, trying to catch them with their eyes alight like cats.

He looked at the boy in a brand new way, as part of a hidden process that had been going on under his nose. It worried him that the world was now revealed to him to have been working in this way, possibly for many years, without his knowing or suspecting. And this boy had come along and told him so, and it made the boy seem awesome and powerful to him—that he had possessed and then so casually revealed this long-held secret about the world. Edison wondered whether, on account of telling, the boy would be in trouble with the unnamed others who had joined him and the sister in watching everything. More like wolves than cats, he supposed.

"Did you watch everything?" Edison asked the boy.

The boy shrugged. "My favorite place," he said, "is in the bamboo patches, lying down in the middle looking up and watching how it sways and clacks together . . . and the other sounds it makes, down at the bottom, squeaking like an old door swinging slowly. I been in the middle there one time a week ago when you walked by. I'd rather be here than any circus. I don't need to sit so still."

Or Mina might mistake the children for the clacking of the bamboo, whatever the bamboo sounded like. Edison had sometimes stood and watched it, stiff and still at the base of the stalks but moving in wide arcs at the top. He had seen the frequent collisions but had never thought what sounds were produced. Clack, he thought. Using the word, he tried to hear the bamboo the way the boy could hear it. The sound was all hollowness, like a dull bell. He imagined there was no richness in it.

The boy rubbed his nose.

"What's the matter," Edison said, "you got an insect up there?" The boy laughed.

"Do you do this creeping around at other places, or only here?"

"Just here," the boy said.

"When you go inside the buildings, what do you do?"

"I see how the rooms are and what they're for," said the boy. "I pick a thing up and put it back down the same way I found it. I turn it over and look on the bottom to see if it has a name or, if it's a statue, if there's a hole in the bottom to let the air in and out. I go to the windows to watch and see if I can see other people out there, you or the lady or anyone."

"Are you ever in here when we're in here?" asked Edison.

"No."

"Why not? How can you help it sometimes?"

The boy shrugged. "The Seminole lady saw me once."

159

"That's Cora," Edison said.

"Cora," the boy repeated. "She just stood there and looked at me. She was holding a broom. I stayed as still as a lamp. My clothes didn't even move when a breeze came in the room."

Edison looked back to the landward end of the dock. He was surprised to see a girl standing there, redhaired. The sister.

"Is that your sister?" He pointed, but she was gone.

The boy didn't even look. "She's back there, yup," he said.

A fish bumped the dock, a heavy fish. Edison and the boy both looked over the side and saw a yellowish thing, a shark with a curve in its body, turning, leaving the river water and going back to the water of the gulf. The shark was long as a skiff.

"Look at that," said Edison.

"Yup," said the boy. The yup was lifeless.

"He could eat us both," said Edison.

"But he'd spat me out," said the boy. "I'd be okay."

Edison looked carefully at the boy for signs of a feral nature. He looked especially at the eyes, but they struck him as soft and unintelligent, the eyes of someone falling asleep.

"Do me a favor, eh?" said Edison. "Sometime I want to see you all, you and your sister and the others. You come and get me and take me with you, and show me what you do here, step by step, where you go and hide, and so forth. That's what I'd like. I'm curious about this business. Okay?"

The boy seemed to think it over, narrowing his eyes to where they looked worried.

"I'll have to see," he said.

Mina saw the boy at the end of the dock with Tom. She had heard the looping, up-and-down circus music, had changed her clothes and now was running to get him to walk with her into town to see it—the circus—whatever it was doing there. She didn't expect to find him with a boy, but she thought they might take the boy along, too, as long as no one thought the boy was one of theirs (he looked to be about Charles's age). She saw the terrible red hair and wondered if it might be the sign of some disease that you got from not eating properly, or from the mother's not having eaten properly when carrying the boy. Mina set great store in good nutrition; to flout it was to court some inner tragedy—the disintegration of heart and mind and gut, the draining away of the organism's vitality and the consequent loss of its deepest connection to an inclination toward righteousness: the enjoyment of a vigorous life. She was fully persuaded that many examples of crime and degradation were the certain result of poor nutrition—a lump of lard in the place of an apple. Sometimes when she watched Tom eat she shivered inside and wondered if his diet was all of a piece with his agnosticism. Red hair was only one kind of peril, the kind you wore on the outside instead of in.

She arrived at the beginning of the dock, the stillness of the shaded bower. The bright planks stretched ahead of her, and she felt the familiar dread and longed again for the red-roofed gazebo out at the end of the dock. She wished that she could have called to Tom instead of having to walk that distance. But there was no defeating his deafness— which not only left many things unsaid but some also unshouted.

Still she hesitated, hoping he might look in her direction so she could wave him in. She counted to ten, then a second ten. In her third ten she heard a rustling in the bush beside her. She saw a broad leaf trembling there like a huge hand saying stop. She imagined a bird was in the bush, and reached down to see what kind it was, parting the cover of leaves. She saw a flash of red that became red hair surrounding the face of a girl.

"Here! Come out here," said Mina. "Come on, now." The girl came out of the bush like a captive.

"It's all right," Mina said. "Don't be so frightened, dear, whoever you are. I only want you to do me a favor. Very easy."

"Okay," said the girl.

"Go get that man and bring him here," said Mina. "There's a good girl."

The girl ran off down the dock so easily it made Mina ashamed of her own timidity. She watched the red hair bounce. She heard the bold smack of the girl's feet on the planks and imagined that the very nails were shaking. The girl ran as though she was on the firmest ground and there was no danger of veering off to either side. Mina worried. Tom and the redhaired boy turned around right away. Mina waved. The boy waved at the girl. Tom waved at Mina. The boy took the bucket of bait, and Tom took the pole and chair. The girl spun and began running back, her toes turned out exactly the way Madeleine's did when she ran (the girl seeming to be about the same age as Madeleine) and her dirty soles winking above the white planks.

Mina had the overwhelming feeling of a family approaching, even though the children were unknown to her. The three people coming toward her had the appearance of being unified, as if they shared some long-accumulating knowledge of one another and the gift of having fun together. Mina smiled like someone remembering all the fun they'd had together. She wondered who the mother of the redhaired children was. She fancied she saw the children smiling back. She fancied she saw Tom run a step or two, the space growing between his shoes and the planks, which clamored under three sets of feet. They were almost there.

The girl reached her first. Mina expected that the girl would stop and be breathless and giggle like a girl, but instead she kept on running, past Mina, as though a second mother waited some distance behind. Mina felt the breeze of her wake and turned to watch as the girl went faster, leaping bushes and skirting the bamboo patch until she was gone from sight, without any sign of why she was running or where she was running to.

By then, Tom and the boy were there.

"That was his sister," said Tom, pointing at the boy.

"These here shrimps are dead," said the boy. But Tom didn't hear him. The boy sloshed the water around, trying to rouse the shrimps. "See?" he said. "Look at them." Mina looked down at the floating curls. She wondered if Cora could do something with them.

"The circus is here, Tom," she said to her husband.

He nodded. "I know," he said.

"I told him that already," said the boy.

Mina looked at Tom and saw he was red from the sun. She touched his hat as though it was part of his head. She felt the affection going out of her hand to the woven straw. The hat was warm.

"You're red," she said. He smiled. "Who is this boy?" she asked, the question being directed at both of them, whichever would answer.

"His name?" said Tom.

"I'm Terry," said the boy.

"Do you want to go with us and see the circus?" asked Mina, bending down from the waist the way children are sometimes bent down to.

"No ma'am," said Terry. "I gotta go home now and see to things as if I was coming home from school. My sister'll already be there telling my mother this and that. Okay?"

He turned and ran the way his sister ran, except with his feet falling straight ahead and not outward. His hair bounced, too, and he took the same direction as she had, over the bushes and around the bamboo, picking up speed until he was gone.

"What was all that about?" asked Mina. Tom shook his head and shrugged.

"Just children," he said. "Like Charley and Mad."

They walked into town and bought squid for lunch from a vendor who held a black pan over fire and twirled the cut pieces in butter and a sauce. There was shrimp prepared the same way and other kinds of fish to get from other vendors, who were friends or family of fishermen, or the fishermen themselves, first catching the fish and bringing it in, then selling it cooked before going out to catch more. With so much fish waiting to be caught, there was never a question of running out and seldom a question of bad luck. The boats that went past Edison's dock had captains who always smiled and held up a fish. The holds were always full. The people of Fort Myers had to stop and eat on the street—whether they were hungry or not—just to keep the fishermen going back out.

Tom and Mina stood and ate from tin plates with tin forks. The vendor watched them eat, knowing who they were and happy to have them eating there since they weren't often seen downtown and to have them standing there appearing to enjoy it was bound to promote his business.

"Have some nice shrimps," he offered. But all Edison could hear was his jaw muscles working.

Other people walked past and said hello to him. He ate and waved or, if his mouth was empty, said hello back. Mina smiled. She wanted to sit down somewhere, but there was nowhere to sit. Her bonnet cast a shadow down her dress, and she contented herself while eating by imagining that the shadow was all the privacy and peace a person could either have or want on earth and that the taste of garlic squid was the best taste a person could savor. Tom ate loudly and happily, and Mina imagined that the sounds of his eating were stopped just outside the shadow of her bonnet, as though it was a barrier. She turned her head and looked at him with fondness as his smile spread and he waved at people who knew him as a public person—the bringer of light, the eater of squid.

"Hello," he said to a redhaired, green-eyed stranger.

Later they followed the route the circus had taken on its parade through town. Spore of its passing remained. There was horse and elephant dung still fresh in the street and the sour-milk smell of animals in the air. There was also a human turbulence lingering, as though the excitement of people who were no longer there still swirled. Windows were open, and curtains blew outward. Small knots of men stood talking like conspirators. In one of the buildings some dishes were dropped and broke. Three boys chased a dog that got away. Then they veered and chased a fourth boy, who didn't get away. The victim boy's squeal pierced Edison's deafness.

"Here, here!" said Edison, scolding the boys.

Mina held his hand. She tapped a message in Morse on his palm, a method they had of communicating privately.

"How are you?" went the message. He tapped back, "Fine."

At Poinciana Park they found the circus. Local boys had been set to work clearing scrubby growth from the place where the tent would stand. Roustabouts were dragging the canvas from a wagon. The canvas was yellowish, probably stained by the sun, though it must have been pure white once.

Edison said he wanted to go in close, and Mina replied that she wanted to stay far away—exactly where they were was fine. A minute later she relented and told him she'd move closer, but he said he'd gotten used to where they were and was determined to stay.

A stockade fence was set up for the horses. A wagon from the local feed store arrived with bales of hay. A man about Edison's age walked the only elephant to a spot far from everything else and drove an iron stake into the ground. The stake was three feet long at least and had a thick chain attached. The man ran the chain to the elephant's left front leg and joined it to a heavy iron cuff. Then he drove a second stake and ran a second chain to a second cuff on the elephant's right hind leg. This gave the creature an effective grazing range of about three feet. Then the man drove shorter stakes in a circle around the elephant and strung a rope from stake to stake, creating a barrier that the public was to stay outside of. All this imprisoning paraphernalia had been carried to the spot in the grasp of the elephant's trunk. Edison saw the man post two signs on opposite sides of the circle. He decided the signs must carry a warning.

He asked Mina to guess what they said. She answered with total certainty that they gave the elephant's name and age and weight, whether it came from Africa or Asia, and related the kinds of foods it liked to eat.

"Do you think it gives a warning, too?" Edison asked her.

"A warning of what?" she said.

That night at dinner they reminisced about the canvas going up, how it rose as swiftly and suddenly as a giant creature awakening, air and space filling it with life. Mina declared it was delicate; Tom said the surprise was how fast it went from being flat as a pattern to being a fully pitched tent. The way it leapt up, he said, he had thought the process had gotten out of control of the men and the canvas would go on rising until it became a cloud and floated out over the gulf. But then it stopped and quivered, and the sides puffed out, letting some of the air escape.

"Like a cloud?" said Mina.

"Almost," he said. "Almost like a cloud."

In his mind's eye he saw it rise again, with a whoosh, from nothing to something, becoming a place. Sometimes he had the urge to write a book. In such a book as he might one day write he would place this tent going up, and inside the tent there would be a circus of lights behaving colorfully and spelling out world-famous quotations that the audience could try to recognize before they had been completely spelled out. There would be other marvels. A circus was best that featured one part education to two parts entertainment. A person in the stands on one side of the tent could place a telephone call to someone in the stands opposite. There would also be a way for people to record their voices as messages to loved ones in other cities, the messages to be sent by mail and then answered in like fashion when the circus reached the loved one's city. Animals would be shown off operating modern appliances with ease.

His book would be about the future, as though it were springing up as swiftly and powerfully as the tent itself.

Mina ate her fillet of bonita slowly. Tom's was already gone. He had burnt the roof of his mouth. Mina held small bites at the end of her fork and let them cool in the air before her nose, looking along the fork with a disciplined fondness. Tom had nothing to do but watch her, licking the tips of his fingers and stabbing them down upon crisp shards of bread crust that remained on his plate totally alone. They stuck to his moistened fingertips, and he brought them up to his mouth.

While Mina ate he recounted to her the differences between erecting a tent and bringing an invention to birth. They were the differences between task and adventure. The one thing was certain; the other was not. The tent happened suddenly; the invention happened slowly, progress being often imperceptible (or disguised as a setback) and discouragement being a common infection among all the staff, even including himself. There was always more missed than hit, and sometimes the object disappeared altogether or, worse, came to seem so small as to be not worth the trouble.

"But when you set out to put up the tent," he said, "there's a fair assurance it will be up in half an hour or so. Your effort is rewarded right away. Think how it would be if the tent had to be invented each time."

Whenever he stopped talking it was as though a dense, murky pressure drained from his head. He had always been able to hear himself talk. The words blurred together inside his skull and vibrated. Experience had shown him that the sounds he made got out into the world as surely as the fruits of his labor did, but sometimes he thought of them as trapped—oceanic murmurs confined in a thimble. The sound of his thoughts was more soothing to him than the sound of his voice, even if his thoughts were troubled. Mina looked at him and smiled.

"I can't imagine," she said. "A tent is a tent."

"Sure. But what if it never existed before? What if it was just an unknown answer to a present need?"

She knit her brow. It stayed that way for a moment and then went smooth. "I just don't know," she said. "I really can't think that way, dear. As far as I'm concerned, everything that is, is, and I don't see anything missing. That's your business—finding the things that are missing." She ate a bite of fish.

Some days in the laboratory were gossamer with silence. His people worked, his engine. He walked the shop floor and watched them, his cheek stuck full of tobacco and his hands behind his back like a professor. His walk matched the rhythm of the work; he was the lubricant. He looked at each man's eyes. Their concentration was a tonic to him. He was energized by the countless productive squints. Sometimes the hard ring of a tool slipped through his deafness like a small surprise, like a bird flying in and out of a cloak of ivy.

Back inside his private office he closed the door and drew the shades. He put his elbows on the oaken desk and rested his chin in his hands. When he shut his eyes, his ideas floated in the middle distance as bright as sharp-edged clouds. While thinking, he spoke to himself as clear as a bell, in a voice unobstructed by his deafness. Alone in the darkened office he gave shape to many plans and took hold thereby of the pleasure of being himself—the tamer and user of accidental nature. Throughout his domain the process flowed on like a river. Along its banks tent after tent flew skyward, filling with life. It was only later, when the newspapers came around and asked why he did what he did, that he uncorked the usual bunkum about wanting to do good and useful deeds for the people of the world. The truth was many times simpler: It was just the way he lived his life.

Mina rang the small brass bell, and Cora came and cleared the plates away.

Because he hated the sharpness and constancy of cooking odors, Edison had had two houses built side by side in Florida: one for cooking and eating, the other for living and sleeping.

After dinner he and Mina adjourned to the parlour of the second house and played cribbage on a double-length board with tiny black and white ivory pegs in the shape of lightbulbs. Mina won the first game, Tom the second. He was cutting her a crib card to begin the rubber game when he saw her look away and listen attentively.

"What?" he asked her. She turned back and took the card, a jack, and pegged herself two points.

"I don't know. A noise. I thought I heard something. Maybe it's only the wind in the bamboo."

But Tom stood up quickly, stunned with anger at the thought of the dozen unseen children hiding outside and spying on them. Mina hadn't seen him move so fast in years. He was out through the hallway and onto the veranda in seconds. She heard the screen door bang back and got up to see what was happening, leaving a twelve-point hand behind.

When Edison burst through the door he found the redhaired boy waiting at the edge of the light thrown out from inside.

"Hello," said the boy, his mouth remembering to form the sounds fully, as though he were just then learning them for the first time.

"It's you," said Edison foolishly. He looked out beyond the veranda steps and tried to see the others, but they were either not there or well concealed, because all he saw was darkness.

Mina came to the door in time to hear the same redheaded boy she had first seen earlier in the day say "Yup" to Tom.

"I've thought it over and checked with them others," said the boy, "and I guess it's okay." It was no trouble hearing the boy because he talked so loud. Mina wondered what was okay.

"We can do it right now, if you like," said the boy.

Tom looked behind him. Mina was in the doorway watching.

"I'll be back in a little while," he told her.

She saw the boy reach out his hand to Tom and Tom take it, and the two of them went off in the darkness. She heard others out there, too.

"Be careful," she said, but she knew he couldn't hear.

"We'll start with the dock," she heard the boy say loudly.

10
PERFORMING

The people had been so nice it scared him; but he supposed the scare was a small thing compared to how nice they were.

Before Florida, Mount could have counted the smiles on one hand. But here they were never-ending. People came up and treated you like their brother. They asked your name in a way that didn't set your teeth on edge. And five out of ten of them offered you something—a piece of food or a cold drink or a cigarette.

In fact, Mount had never had a cigarette before Florida, but he finally took one after people had offered so often. Even though he thought he knew from observation, he acted shy and said, "Well, how do you do this? How do you smoke?"

And the other fellow said, "You do it like this . . ." And he struck the match and touched it to the tip and drew in the smoke. Mount could hardly wait. This looked so easy and pleasurable. He watched the smoke disappear backward with a hiss and then return up again, real quick, in and out like that. It came from the fellow's nose and mouth at the same time, as if some had been in the brain and the rest in the stomach.

"That's all?" Mount asked. "Just drag it back and let it out?"

"That's right," the fellow said.

So Mount took the cigarette and did it. Right away he liked the bright orange blooming of the ash. Then he dragged down the smoke and began to cough the second it hit his pipes. The sensation was like being scratched inside. There was a ringing in his ears as he sailed to what seemed like another land, from where he heard the other fellow laughing

169

and felt him pounding on his back. Mount was doubled over and looking at his own knees. His eyes stung.

All through that first cigarette he was dizzy. The ringing echoed louder with each succeeding puff. But after that smoking got better, and he knew he could learn to do it well because he had an ambition for it. He controlled himself by taking in smaller volumes of smoke, and, so, the coughing soon went away and the smoke felt more and more like regular air and didn't scratch him inside so much.

In Sarasota he went to a tobacconist's and bought a tin of Diamondbacks with a rattler painted on the lid and the slogan, "Twenty Hard White Fangs," written beneath where the snake was coiled. There was smoke coming out of the rattler's mouth.

Mount kept the tin on a shelf in Gendron's wagon, between a picture of Gendron's mother and father, who were old even in the picture, and a book of drawings of a man and a woman standing up naked or lying down together on the ground as if they were alone and not being watched by whoever had the book. The woman looked nothing like Malvina T., but the man bore some resemblance to Mount's own father, especially in the wideness of the eyes and the fact that the lower teeth showed but not the uppers. Whenever Gendron took up the book to taunt Mount with it, he smiled and waggled the pages back and forth as if to see if he could make the man and woman move. But Gendron's smile was of a totally different order than the smiles Mount conjured up when he thought about what made the people of Florida so nice. There was always something hiding in Gendron's heart that crept into his voice and smile and made them mean. The Florida people were better than Gendron.

But Mount was scared by their niceness because he had no reason to think it was true or lasting or had much to do with him. Niceness just flowed out like a river, suddenly, from people who didn't even know him. And the next day it might be gone, like a dog that followed you home one evening and slept on the rug beside your bed, but then you let it out in the morning and never saw it again. The same person here in Florida who smiled at you the day before, was there any reason he couldn't come up to you tomorrow and do something else—Mount didn't know what—that also just flowed out like a river, suddenly, but wasn't nice a bit? His fear was based on the unknown—a new town, a new face, strangers approaching.

"There's a word for this world," said Gendron, taking a cigarette out of Mount's Diamondback tin. "It's careless," said Gendron. "Just look at that stupid man."

Mount looked where Gendron was pointing. They were sitting outside of Gendron's wagon where the circus was camped in a park in the town of Fort Myers. Gendron was in the one chair and Mount was on the ground. They were taking a break.

"Got a match?" asked Gendron. Mount gave him one. Mount loved the sound and smell of a striking match. Sometimes after the match was blown out he would hover his nose near it to draw up the lingering wisps drifting slowly. But he didn't do it this time, fearing what Gendron—who he was afraid of—might say. The man Gendron had pointed at was over near Chloe trying to get nearer. His one leg was inside the rope circle while the other was on the outside. He was stretching far into the center to offer her something.

"He's giving her stones," said Gendron. "He come over and got nothing to give her, but yet he wants her to come over close. So he picks up them stones to give her. Hah!"

Mount watched Chloe's trunk reach out to take what was offered. The trunk coiled back and held the offering briefly, then uncoiled like a whip and flung it away. One of the stones hit the man in the cheek. He staggered back, clapping his hand to his face, caught his heel on the rope and fell.

"You stupid!" Gendron shouted. Chloe shook her head and shrieked.

That was exactly the kind of thing Mount meant to be scared of when he considered the smiling kindnesses of the people of Florida. Instead of a piece of food or a cold drink or a cigarette, there was the chance of getting stones. And the approach would be just the same—the smile and the hand held out, and so forth, so that you wanted it. He confided this to Gendron, but Gendron had nothing to say about it.

The circus had been in this spot just half a day. The first performance was scheduled for that evening. The afternoon heat was ponderous, and people were going about their business slowly and walking as if their clothes were heavy and stiff. With the tent pitched, business consisted mostly of seeing to the animals, practicing acts or wandering through town to post and pass out handbills. Gendron and Mount were resting, and Gendron had let Mount have a bite to eat.

"Here's some of this," he said, handing Mount a sack of raisins, which were all stuck together like a fist and had to be crumbled apart to be eaten.

Mount watched the stupid man pick himself up and walk away, looking to see who had called him stupid. A red welt was rising on his cheek. Mount was glad to see it. He got up off the ground and followed the man until he caught him.

"I'm sorry that happened," he said.

"That's all right. It wasn't your fault," said the man, who was still rubbing his cheek.

"Come back tonight and see her," said Mount. "She'll do a trick, and you can say to your friends you know her."

The man smiled that familiar Florida smile and offered Mount a piece of chewing gum.

"No thanks," said Mount. "I'm a smoker myself."

"Then keep it for later. Was it you that called me stupid?"

"Nope," said Mount. "It was him." And he pointed at Gendron. "He knows the heck out of that elephant. I'm his assistant."

"I shoulda read that damn sign better," said the man. He rubbed his cheek some more.

"Does it hurt much?" Mount asked.

"Stings like the bumpus, mister."

"Well, I'll see you tonight," said Mount. "I'll put my head right under her foot and she won't even hurt me."

"Okay," said the man. "Good luck."

Mount turned away and walked back to Gendron.

"It hurt him pretty bad," he said. He reached for the rattlesnake.

Later in the afternoon he got Gendron's permission to go with Mother Danilecki to greet the citizens and pass out bills.

The day was so hot, they took a swim first. Mount hadn't been in any river water since the circus fished him out, so he wasn't sure about going back in. But they found a good place along the palmy bank of this Fort Myers river—whatever its name was—with white sand as fine as damp dust. Mother Danilecki kept all her clothes on, but she lifted her skirts up high, and there were her legs. Mount was surprised to see they weren't old and bumpy and yellow like her face, but were slim, muscled and smooth, as though in the stillness under her skirts, away from air and light and other commotions, they

had somehow kept their youth, coming to look like the legs of someone else.

She waded in. Mount watched her go ahead and saw the water climb
just to her knees. He took his clothes off, except for the last garment,
which hung there foolishly in the heat. So he took that one off too.
Mother Danilecki turned and saw him naked, but he figured she was
only Mother Danilecki and not a normal woman—though, suddenly,
she smiled in a certain way, and he saw some of the yellow drain out
of her face as she just kept looking at him. He stood there wondering
what to do but also feeling like a statue that was enjoying all the
attention. So he didn't budge. He let the hot air settle around him and
find its place like water calming in a pond, and he just looked straight
ahead at nothing—some small green spot far across on the opposite
bank. And he let this old woman stare at him, believing it wouldn't harm
either one of them and that his own true self—the one that would have
been ashamed—was floating up in the heat and thinking about having
another cigarette sometime and a glass of beer.

When she finally looked away he waded in.

At first the water felt almost as warm as the air, warmer and stiller
than the Mississippi. He went in past where Mother Danilecki had
stopped. He kept going until the water covered his parts and tingled at
his waist as if it wanted even more of him. The river got colder by layers;
slices of it were a temperature unto themselves and did not mingle with
the higher and lower slices. These different temperatures cut right
through him, conveying one sensation to his bowels, another to his knees
and another to his ankles. Under his feet, the bottom was smooth. He
felt there was so much to notice.

Mother Danilecki taunted him. "You getting in water like some old
dog, boy," she cried.

So Mount dove forward. He felt his back rise up and the lower parts
follow into the air from where they'd been submerged; then he was
falling, and his hair hit the water, and his forehead, and everything else
followed downward and he knew he was under—except the last bit of
his feet, which he kicked with until they were under too. He stayed
there, sliding through the river, until he stopped. He heard his own
bubbles. Then he came to the top to see where he'd gotten to.

Mother Danilecki's voice was going the instant he could hear again.
The water ran off his head along with her words.

"What?" he hollered. She was behind him. He turned in the water, and there she was, beckoning. He reached for the bottom with his feet, but it was too far down, and his feet just stopped, suspended there foolishly. So he pulled forward with his cupped hands and danced with his feet like a bicyclist, and he was moving, up and down like a cork until his feet touched something—at first with just the toes—and he could walk on the bottom that got shallower until he was almost completely out. Mother Danilecki watched him, still with her skirts held high even though she was no longer in the water. Her shins were white as bread.

"Now, shake like that old dog," she said, and she bent over laughing, letting go of her skirts so they dropped with a heavy sound. Mount kicked at the water with the blade of his foot.

He came out of the river and crouched on the sand. For a few minutes he dried there. The day was so hot that he could see the water drops getting smaller by the second on his skin and the nails of his toes.

"Don't move," said Mother Danilecki, and Mount thought he must have had a bug on his back that she was going to swat. But instead she got a stick and scratched a circle in the sand around where he was crouching. The stick came close to his heels and toes. Then she drew an outline of where his shadow fell, and after all the lines were joined she told him he could move away.

"What's that for?" he asked.

She shrugged. She stared down at the lines and shrugged again. "Just wait," she said. Mount waited. He watched her shut her eyes, and he wanted to sneak away like Freddie Blackhage had, and surprise her by being gone.

Still waiting, he put on his first garment and then his pants. The pants were dirty and squeaked against the wetness of his hips.

"Sssshhh!" hissed Mother Danilecki.

Even after being completely immersed in the river, Mount was hot again. He gazed up into the sky the way he remembered his father doing on a hot day, seeming to be looking for the heat itself. But instead of the heat, Mount saw a bird, a dark form soaring. It winked across the sun and got bigger, coming lower. He watched it all the way down, the bird growing, descending in circles with its big wings hardly moving. It landed in the middle of the outline of Mount's shadow, and Mother Danilecki turned to him, smiling, spreading her arms like the bird's big wings and saying, "You see?"

"I guess so," Mount said. "Can you make it catch on fire?"
After that they walked into town.

As they were going down something called Tice Street, Mother Danilecki reached up and put her hand through his hair and mussed it. The
hair had dried stiff and close to the scalp, and he looked "like dead,"
she told him.

"There," she said. "Now it much much nicer." After the hand was
gone he felt the hair floating strangely, tingling as if there were thou-
sands of insects in it holding each strand above their heads while standing on other strands.

"I don't know," said Mount about its being nicer. "I really don't
know."

It was three o'clock or so. There were maybe a dozen people in sight
on Tice Street, some on one side and some on the other. Most were
alone, but a few were together like Mount and Mother Danilecki.

"You go over there, and I'll stay over here," she said. She reached in
her pouch and gave him some bills, which were the usual thing, white
with blue printing and a drawing of Semple Groves's head with blue
words coming out of his mouth in a white balloon, saying, "This is the
Show you should See!"

Mount went across the street to a man tending a four-wheeled stand
that had a cook fire blazing in its center. The man was cooking fish to
be eaten on thick slabs of white bread with a dark brown crust. But the
day was too hot for that.

"Come to the circus tonight," Mount told the man. He handed him
one of the bills. "How's about you can put this on your stand here so
the people that buy your fish might see it and know to come to the circus
too?"

"I'll do that," said the man. "But it's too hot today, and no one's
buying anything. So I doubt my putting it up here'll do any good."

The man took one of the bills and read it. " 'This is the Show you
should See!' " he said, quoting Semple Groves. Then he brushed the
back of the bill with butter and slapped it against the front of the stand,
where it stuck like something glued. Mount noticed the shadowy smears
of butter showing through the paper.

"I'll take a piece of fish," he told the man. The pan was smoking, and
the man dropped in a diamond-shaped slice of milky pink flesh, where

it blackened suddenly and was flipped in the air by the man so it could blacken on the other side. Then he put the bread in too, where it sopped up the rest of the black that couldn't fit on the piece of fish. Soon he slid out the bread and the fish together onto a tin plate for Mount to eat.

"How much?" said Mount.

"You can have it free," said the man, which made Mount scared again on account of all this niceness cropping up in Florida for no good reason. But the man said, "It's such a bad day, all these pieces'll only go begging anyhow. Just tell me how you like it."

So Mount stood and ate the fish, smiling so the man could see how much he liked it. Sweat collected on his forehead.

"You think it's good?" the man asked him.

"I surely do," said Mount. The bread's dark crust was cutting the roof of his mouth, and the hot fish was burning it. But the flavor was good.

"How does it get so black?" Mount asked.

"That's a secret," said the man. "But it has something to do with an ingredient I add that works in combination with a certain gland in the fish itself. Some days I go out and catch the fish, and other days I stay here and sell it cooked up black like this so I can go out and catch some more."

"That sounds like a pretty good life," said Mount. "Catching and cooking. You get to see both sides of the work and the people that enjoy it, all the way down to me, who you gave it to free."

"Not like a circus, though," said the man, shaking his head in wonder. But Mount didn't understand what the man was talking about, except to hear the admiration in his voice that was common all over Florida where circuses were concerned. For some unaccountable reason, Florida people would as soon go see a circus as pat their dog or go to church or eat a piece of good pan-blackened fish.

Mount stood back from the stand and admired the bill that the man had stuck there at his suggestion.

"Then you'll be coming tonight?" he said.

"Oh, yes." It was like the man was helpless. Everyone in town was coming, and this handing out of bills was a waste of time. Mount imagined the crowd overflowing the flaps of the tent and the massive hush that spread at just the moment Chloe lowered her foot to his ear when all he could hear was her slow-thudding heartbeat coming down through that flatness.

"I'll be there certainly," the man said.

"Then I won't say goodbye to you," replied Mount, repeating something he had often heard Semple Groves say to ladies while bowing: "I'll only say until we meet again in the shadows of the midway."

"Okay," said the man. He had dropped another piece of fish in the pan, and it was blackening fast.

Mount looked down Tice Street and saw that Mother Danilecki was almost done greeting the citizens on her side and was about to turn the corner out of sight.

"Goodbye," he said, and hurried off toward two redheaded boys who were trying to spit over a wall that a dog was barking on the other side of.

Some tragedies a person sees don't mean that much to that person, but still he has to be there and experience them somehow. This was the way it was with Mount when he and Mother Danilecki got back from passing out bills and saw a circle of people gathered in the middle of the grounds.

When they got closer, Gendron turned and whispered that Hiram the horse was dying. To hear Gendron whispering shocked Mount so much that he understood right away how serious a thing this was.

Mother Danilecki hurried straight into the center of the circle and knelt beside Hiram, who—as far as Mount knew—was just an old ginger-colored dobbin that Semple sometimes got on top of and sat there not going anywhere. Mount didn't know how old Hiram was or about all that he used to be able to do. But in the sad days and weeks after—after the circus left Florida and started north again in anticipation of summer—someone would mention the faded red hat Hiram used to wear or the way he liked cheddar cheese so much and grape leaves picked wild and handed to him one by one, and so forth, always including the time he saved Claire, the albino lady, by galloping under her while she was falling. And Mount, around to hear these recollections at a time when the tragedy itself was past, was connected back to that day and felt the sorrow of it sharply, growing into the love and knowledge and loss that he hadn't possessed before, to the point that he could think wistfully, Good old Hiram.

177

But now, while the tragedy was actually going on, when a man like Gendron was struck down to a whisper, Mount felt like someone who had wandered up at the wrong moment to ask directions to another place. And he looked at the mound of ginger-colored Hiram showing through the encircling legs, and he just thought, That's an old horse there.

In fact, Hiram died not long after Mount and Mother Danilecki returned, sighing a long last breath that emptied him out without filling him up again. (Later that night, before falling asleep, Mount tried this himself, letting the air completely out and then stopping, not drawing any back in; the sensation terrified him so that he hardly slept at all.) After this long last breath, the circle of men and women and freaks surrounding the horse was silent for an instant before breaking outward in grief, leaving Mother Danilecki and Semple kneeling on the inside, nearest to the death itself.

Mount, thinking, It's only a horse, remained still as the others swirled and worried and cried around him, making the heat feel harsher by filling the air with the heat of their feelings, the heat in their stricken lungs. As the grief spread, some of the people crept back toward the horse and then shot away again; others did not return but kept on circling farther from the center until they were only walking, almost normally, with their heads down, toward the tent or to the wagons where they lived. Mount marveled how fast they went away and how the sharp sounds died in their throats as they got farther from the horse and from each other, as though the quickest comfort would be to find silence somewhere by themselves while thinking about the horse and what it felt like to be together where he died.

After just a few minutes, Mount and Mother Danilecki and Semple Groves were the only ones left. It was Mount who buried the horse.

"I'll dig the hole," he said.

Semple and Mother Danilecki looked at him in a noticing kind of way.

"All right," said Semple. Mount saw he was crying. First, Semple sent Mother Danilecki to get permission to dig from the people who ran the town. "She's good at this," he told Mount. "No one ever says no to her." Then he got the idea that while the hole should be dug right away, the burying itself should wait until the performance that evening.

"Pick a spot where people can gather around. Have it close to the tent and put torches on poles. I'll see if I can get a stone carved."

Mount picked the spot and got the shovel and started to dig. After a while people began to reappear. Claire came out of her wagon and sat on the ground near where he was digging. She had on a white dress with blue flowers. She didn't say anything but just watched him dig.

"This is the place," Mount told her. She only watched, though. In an hour or so Semple showed up with the stonecutter. They stood and watched Mount digging.

"H-I-R-A-M," Semple told the man, who nodded and repeated the letters.

"Any dates?" the stonecutter asked.

"Can you do it in time with dates? It's just five letters, no last name."

"No," the stonecutter said.

"Then, no dates," said Semple.

"Course, I could do just years in time," the stonecutter said. "No months and days, just years."

"Okay," said Semple. "1880 to 1902."

"Is that right?" Claire asked him.

"I think so," said Semple.

"I got one carved already that says 1882 to 1902," the stonecutter said. "I got a few like that with no names yet that my son carved just for practicing. But no 1880. My son was born in '82. Is that old for a horse?"

"I don't know," said Semple, looking at Claire. "Maybe it was 1882."

"It might have been," said Claire. She started crying. Mount thought she looked so pretty. Hiram was still on the ground fifty yards away. Mount was down in the hole now, better than three feet deep. When he looked up he saw the mosquitoes and other bugs floating around the horse, rippling in the warm air like a blown shroud.

"Make it wider," Semple ordered him.

Mount thought, but did not say out loud, I've buried before, and I know what I'm doing. He whacked at the sides with the flat of the shovel; sandy dirt slid down into the hole, and the hole widened. Then Mother Danilecki returned with permission to dig and with a man named Fleming who said he ran the town.

"You seem to have started without me," this Fleming said sternly. But when Claire sobbed softly, Fleming noticed her and became quiet, and all that could be heard besides Claire was the soft, ringing slice of the shovel deepening the hole, and the flung dirt falling like rain.

Before beginning his funeral speech Semple stared around the circle, from torch to torch and face to face, turning like a beacon, shushing everything, even the children. The crowd was four and five deep in places—maybe more—as deep as a cockfight crowd, but quieter. Almost as quiet as a church. Mount heard the quiet spread as Semple turned. He watched the blankness come like cold across the faces of children who didn't know what was going to happen and were scared by the sight of Semple turning solemnly, his feet hardly moving. The yellow torch-light danced in everyone's eyes, and in the shiny brown, unblinking eye of Hiram.

The horse was ready; everything was ready. All through the late afternoon and the sunset Mount had worked hard, giving himself to the tragedy that wasn't his. He finished digging the hole, cordoned off the circle, set the torches and recruited three other roustabouts to help him drag the horse to the spot. All the while he hated the flies and other bugs that buzzed around and landed on the horse's various openings, some of the insects then buzzing over to Mount, nearing his mouth and eyes and ears in a state of excitement over the lifelessness of the horse. Mount twitched as he had seen horses twitch, trying to make his skin ripple and snap to shoo the insects. When the townspeople started arriving he was still at work, tying ropes around Hiram, trussing the legs up close to the barrellike body so they wouldn't get in the way or snap when it came time to commit him downward. He made the knots along the spine, leaving generous portions of excess rope in loops to be used as handles for dragging the body the last few feet to the hole.

Even after everything was ready, Mount continued working, doing things twice and checking on things he had already done twice and checked once. He bent down and checked the knots, tugging sharply and causing the flesh of Hiram to quiver, surprising the bugs. Mount kept moving in the deepening dusk as the crowd thickened. He was waiting for the rest of the circus to come out of their wagons and take the tragedy back from him, since he was only watching over it, like a custodian, in their absence and with no entitlement of his own.

It was Semple who came first, alone, working the crowd like a minister, from the outside in, moving from handshake to handshake as though crossing a stream on stones. With his face and the sound of his voice he spread sadness, reaching up to pat the heads of children sitting on their fathers' shoulders. Mount heard some of the things he said; he got people to admit how sorry they were the horse was dead, and these people didn't even know the horse as well as Mount did.

"Who was your favorite horse?" he asked a girl.

"That one," the girl said, pointing through a lot of other people in the direction of Hiram.

"I know," said Semple, his voice falling slowly like a shot bird.

Finally he came into the circle where Mount could see his full black-ness—the black silk clothing shining in the torchlight. He made his way around the inside perimeter, greeting people and performing grief. Mount stopped working, knowing what was happening. People in the crowd kept saying, "I'm sorry," or "We're sorry," or "What was his name?" or "How old was he?"

Once, while passing from one person to the next, Semple glanced at Mount as though trying to order him to go away; he glanced again, and Mount crouched down where he stood near the horse, feeling this happen so suddenly—the tragedy being taken back. Mount was just as happy. It left him time to think.

He looked in the horse's eye, believing he might find the horse's last sight trapped there—a hazy sky above Semple's and Mother Danilecki's heads, caught and kept forever, or until it decayed into bones. The eye was big enough to hold an entire last sight, but Mount couldn't see deep enough inside, only the leaping of the torches flashing across the surface like curtains flapping in a window. He looked at the horse's whole head and thought, What a kind expression he has, as though this was as much as he knew about horses and death.

Then he heard the rest of the circus coming and the people in the crowd drawing in their breath. The circus members were singing, a slow song in a foreign tongue that, by its tempo and sorrowfulness, greatly reminded Mount of the pig-butchery song the Old Musicians sang each spring in Bolusburgh. Mount crept to the break in the circle where the crowd was letting the circus enter. He saw that they all held candles and were dressed in sheets like a holy choir, with the smallest people first and the tallest last. The flames of the candles lay back sleekly owing to everyone's forward movement, but did not go out.

What glory, thought Mount. The faces of the circus members winked in light; they came two by two, dividing into clockwise and counter-clockwise as they entered the circle, still singing, not in a foreign tongue at all, but—now that Mount could hear it up close—in perfect English with their mouths wide open to sing each syllable distinctly:

He is gone away,
He is gone away.
Listen to our prayers,
Listen to our prayers.

He was ours one day,
He was ours one day.
Now he's always theirs,
Now he's always theirs.

And so forth, the two verses chanted over and over again.

Mount was much impressed with this entrance and thought how proud he was to be playing a part in their performance, and that it was just as good to prepare the way by digging and setting the torches and all the rest, so that the others only needed to worry about what to sing and what to wear and how slow or fast to walk, and anything else that would add to their dignity.

After the two smallest people were reunited opposite the point on the circle where they had entered and separated, everyone stood still and sang the two verses one more time before stopping and blowing out the candles. Mount crept back near the horse and knelt there; the day's stored heat seeped up from the dirt and into his tired knees. He waited.

Semple then came forward in this darker silence to start his funeral speech, first turning solemnly and shushing everything, his feet hardly moving.

"When we come here," he said, beginning quietly, "when we come into any town along the way, we're strangers to you—just like the gypsies who most people only ever see the backs of on their way to somewhere else. But the difference with us is that we show you something, which it is our job and life to do. And you come see it and spend the few coins that pay our humble way in life. And, even though we're total strangers, one to the other, still you know who we are and we know who you are—we all have our parts to play.

"But sometimes . . ." He raised his voice and waited. "Sometimes, something unusual happens that shakes half the strangeness out of us, so that we reveal more of ourselves—the softness inside us—than we would ever have showed you otherwise. That we didn't show in the last town and won't in the next, and yet here it is for you to see . . ." He gestured around the circle at the sheets and candles, the trussed-up horse.

"One such singular event occurred today: this good horse, Hiram, died here this afternoon, a horse some of us have known his whole life long, and that all of us have known for part of it. He died without fear, and knowing what was coming—gazing around the circle of all who knew him and loved him before he breathed his last.

"And we shall miss him."

Mount heard some weeping begin and knew it would only grow sharper the longer Semple went on. He thought back over all the buryings he had known—from the two dogs, Phantom and Canasta, to Freddie Blackhage, to that pigeon killed by Mrs. Collamer in Fort Wayne the year before—and he knew he'd never seen better than this. He imagined that every word Semple uttered was going deep into the horse's ginger-colored head and sticking there like those tiny sacks of herbs and spices that old women put in their drawers to keep the linens fresh. And he thought how having such things said about him would be nice on any occasion, even if his was the body waiting to be committed downward. He patted the horse's hard jaw and realized how much he wanted to have a cigarette.

"We shall miss him two days hence," said Semple, "when we strike the tent and load the wagons, and leave this plot of earth behind. But yet we take great comfort knowing he resides here, among these good people, the grass kept short around his stone as though he himself were grazing it . . ." Mount heard a tiny moan from behind. A little girl ducked under the cordon, between two circus people, and came to kneel beside Mount, crying, bending down to kiss the horse's head and then retreating, back to where a mother and father snatched her close to them.

"We shall miss him two days hence, and two weeks and two months and two years hence, always straining more to remember him, but losing him as though he were galloping away, raising thick dust along the trail of time . . ."

Mount felt all the spirit inside him moving like earth sliding down a steep hill, and he wanted the little girl to come back and kneel again that close to him and the horse, where he could notice her feelings and offer her something sturdy and honest—his warm arm of comfort wrapping across her soft shoulders like a friend. Something unbending in Semple's voice compelled the spirit to move in him, and he was helpless to prevent it—he was its victim. To the pit of his stomach he trembled as the tragedy that wasn't his was given to him relentlessly, like a religious opportunity he couldn't dare say no to, especially not while everyone around him was saying yes.

Finally, he felt the tears coming into his eyes. They burned like vinegar and fire, and he wished the horse could just leap up and stop pretending to be so dead. Maybe then the earth would stop sliding inside him.

Later Mount lay his head on the drum-shaped wooden platform and waited for Chloe's foot to descend.

His eyes still stung from mourning, and his arms and shoulders ached from helping to drag the horse over the edge of the hole and then shoveling the dirt in upon him, and from helping the stonecutter set the stone deep enough to stand by itself while supporting the weight of a man leaning against it. Mount was that man.

"Come and watch the rest of the show," Mount had told the stonecutter when they were finished.

"No, son, I'm tired," the stonecutter said, and reached out to shake Mount's hand. Mount took the hand and felt the rubbing of sandy dirt meeting between the two palms. He grinned in the torchlight.

"Good work," the stonecutter said. Mount looked at the loaflike mound of tamped-down dirt and the stone rising out of it.

"Yes," he said, "it takes a lot of work to make a tragedy."

"You're right about that," the stonecutter said. "I see it every day."

Then they parted, Mount going toward the waxy light of the tent, the stonecutter off toward the center of town. Mount heard the steam-organ music drawing nearer and nearer the composition that signaled the start of Chloe's act. After he ducked inside the canvas there was hardly time enough to slip into his blue silk costume and go pay his respects to Chloe herself, which Gendron had instructed him always to do on occasions when he was about to put his head beneath her foot. She had seemed pleased enough to see him, draping her trunk across his shoulder and allowing him to scratch her neck and the softer underside of her mouth.

"That ginger-colored horse is dead," Mount whispered up toward her ear. He liked the matter-of-fact sound of his voice. Chloe did nothing that indicated she understood or cared about this news.

"We'll have a good performance tonight," he told her. Then he left and had half a cigarette while he waited for the music to change.

Now he was down on his knees with his head lying flat on the warm wood. Heat stored in his hair drifted down around the one ear and made it sweat. He gazed sideways into the audience, noting the usual, ever-present yellow light within the tent, a yellow that gave the faces a taint of ill health that was often contradicted by their lively, amused expressions. When he saw them sideways, Mount would slowly let his eyes unfocus and look right through them to the ends of the earth as he felt Chloe's foot coming down. He would wait for the tiny hairs on the rim of his ear to feel the touch of delicate contact being made.

He would smile.

This night he did all the things he always did: he waited, looking sideways into the crowd and letting his eyes drift loose until the faces blurred. And as the blur deepened he sensed what he always sensed: the foot descending, descending, the sounds beginning to change as the flat immensity came closer . . .

But then something different happened. His eyes snapped back into focus, and he was suddenly seeing one single face among the sea of faces—a heavy forehead sloping to heavy brows and sharp black eyes. He tried to lift his head to see it straight instead of sideways, but Chloe's foot was there like a ceiling, and he bumped against it.

"Uff," he said, and tried again. He heard a first, tender breath from Gendron's whistle. The foot was pushing him slowly down. His lower ear was pressed against the wooden platform while the pad of Chloe's foot weighed down on the upper ear. Mount heard Gendron's whistle again—first shrill, then muted as his ear was sealed shut by Chloe's foot.

"Chloe," he said. He heard the word murkily, as though it was trapped inside him. "Chloe!" The whistle blew again, distantly. Faces in the crowd began to lean in toward the ring, including the single face—the one he recognized—with its eyes like railroad lamps. Mount waited. The pressure grew.

It was Edison. It was that same damn man whose portrait hung in the Fort Wayne power station. Mount's cheeks tingled as though the blood was either rushing in or rushing out. The tingling spread to his eyes.

"Chloe!" he cried. He saw Gendron dancing around very close, whapping Chloe's leg with a stick. Mount thought he could feel his skull flexing. For the first time he thought: What if she doesn't stop?

He focused on Edison. Beneath his bottom ear he could hear the wood giving way by the smallest degrees, and he knew it would never give way enough to save him—it was stronger than his skull.

Oh, break, he thought, meaning the wood. Please break.

Edison was interested in what he was seeing. Mount saw him scrunching down in his seat to see as much of Mount's face beneath the foot as he could. In fact, he even turned his head sideways, and Mount could suddenly see straight on: it was just who he thought—Thomas Edison.

"Help!" Mount cried. Edison kept looking at him. Mount imagined Semple having to fetch the stonecutter again. "Mount—M-O-U-N-T." No dates. A second hole next to the horse's hole. More candles, sheets and singing.

Suddenly Semple's face was inches from Mount's.

"How are you?" he asked.

"This is terrible," Mount answered. The blood was growling in his head, maybe turning black under the force of the elephant's foot.

"We're trying something," said Semple. "Hold still." But, of course, there was nothing he could do but hold still.

Gendron started chopping the wooden platform with an axe. Each blow sent a buzzing sting deep into Mount's ear. Wood splintered near his head.

"Don't hit me!" he cried.

Gendron brought the axe down again and again. But the platform was a sturdy object. Mount opened and closed his eyes indecisively, in fear and discomfort, never knowing when he might see the very last sight of his life. He looked at Edison and wished himself back in Fort Wayne at the power station, looking at the painted edition of Edison. The pressure from Chloe's foot was growing steadily, bit by bit, long after he thought his skull would have burst.

"When it give way . . ." Gendron shouted, "roll to the side real fast!" But it wasn't giving way.

She'll get tired of this, Mount thought. Then he repeated out loud: "She'll get tired of this."

"What?" said Semple. "What did you say? Hold on. We'll get you out of this."

The axe head crunched into the wood, no telling how close to his skull. Mount flinched. He saw Edison and others applauding and cheering on the rescue efforts, first shyly, then harder and harder.

"Don't hit me," Mount said again. His lips were so puffed up with blood it hurt to move them at all, and he believed his eyes might squirt out across the ring like seeds at any moment.

She can do this if she wants, he thought—meaning that her wanting or not wanting was the difference between living and dying, and the business was out of his hands completely.

The axe came down, and the gay red-paint bullseye buzzed under his cheekbone. But the wood stayed solid, and Mount began to drift, Edison's yellow face going grainy and prickly, then gray, and then not there at all, Mount's neck feeling cold and numb until he ceased to exist as himself and was absorbed into Chloe's blood and thoughts, from the pad of her foot on upward.

This is it, he later remembered thinking.

Then Chloe simply took her foot away. One second the pressure was there, the next it was gone. The sound of cheering filled Mount's ear like honey, and the yellow light trickled back into his eyes.

He was still there.

11
NORTH

For the first part of the trip north Mount wore a bandage around his head. He asked Mother Danilecki, who had wrapped him in it, why she wanted it there when nothing was broken or bruised or cut, except for the tingling rawness of his ears, which she left unbandaged so they could get at the air. She told him the white gauze wrap would heal the hurt inside and be a sign to Chloe of what she had done to him and a sign to others in the circus of what could happen in a flash and without any warning.

There were headaches, though, for days on end. They came and went, settled down and flared up, made him shut one eye or the other, or both, to keep the light from making the pain worse. The morning they left Fort Myers was the worst of all, and he wanted most deeply to curl down in a ball and be soothed by Mother Mount—anyone else would do, but no one was offering to help.

The wagons were loaded and the horses all rattling in harness, ready to go. Mount sat with Gendron and two other roustabouts—Harold and Tiff—atop piles of folded canvas in one of the open buckboards. He felt the ache wander the sides of his head and into his shoulders and back, down then up, down then up. And when they had all finished going to Hiram's stone for one last look and a prayer and were back in their places, waiting to roll, and when the wagons in fact did roll, the ache flared up unendurably, and Gendron had to turn away, disgusted at the sound of Mount's woeful moaning, saying, "Shit and potatoes." Mount put his hands on the bandages trying to draw out some of the ache, or

188

at least to distract it the way you might quiet the squirrels that lived in the walls by scratching your nails across the plaster.

"Oh, me," said Mount. He looked over at Harold and Tiff, who were friends and shared a resemblance, but were not brothers. The two of them just looked back at Mount because this was none of their business.

Some of the Fort Myers people who had grown fondest of the circus tagged alongside for a while, saying, "Can I come with you?" and "Will you remember me?" A thin girl in pantaloons did cartwheels for almost a mile trying to show she was ready to be in an act of some kind. But Harold and Tiff, on whose side of the wagon the girl was, didn't even turn around. And in the state Mount was in, he didn't care a bit if all of them who were lingering along just toppled down in the dust and were left behind like tired dogs.

Soon enough that's about what happened, and the circus was finally on its own between two places, the way it always liked to be. Gendron sang a song about how bad rats smelled, and Harold and Tiff took out a set of various-sized steel thimbles and put them on their fingers and had a little fight—the fingers of one against the fingers of the other, like cats, banging together with a funny kind of clacking sound that Mount fell asleep to.

He slept a nauseated sleep that the ache declined to take part in and from which he was stirred by Gendron nudging him and asking for a cigarette. Harold and Tiff said they wanted one too. Mount said no, but Gendron just made himself free and took the rattlesnake tin out of Mount's back pocket, striking a match on his brass belt buckle that was in the likeness of an elephant. Then he passed the tin to Harold and Tiff. Mount sat up and had one himself, lighting it off Harold's match and sniffing the sulfur after he'd blown it out. The ache sagged down into the back of his neck, bulging larger and smaller as his heart beat.

"This is a good cigarette," said Mount.

"Uh-huh," said Harold, and Tiff also nodded.

The rest of the day was a terror as the wagon bounced along mile after mile. The ache was buffeted around in Mount's skull like an angry tenant stalking back and forth in a tiny room.

There were many tedious days like this, moving not much faster than a healthy man might walk. Mount kept the bandage on, and every morning at breakfast Mother Danilecki came and looked at him, asking various questions to test his mental sharpness, some of which were easy while others were real puzzlers that he would get wrong, eliciting a hiss from between Mother Danilecki's tongue and the roof of her mouth.

The first bandage had to be replaced after only three days because of the dust that collected in the pores of the gauze and turned it as brown as the road itself. Mother Danilecki unrolled new gauze and measured it against the old.

"This perfect," she said, exactly what she always said of everything she did—in the light of which making a bandage was only the smallest of challenges. "This perfect."

Gendron was watching and told her, "Make it tighter this time to keep that gourd from falling open and spilling everything out." But Mount kept quiet. He felt her old fingers brush against his ear and bet that Gendron would have wanted to feel such a nice sensation himself if he knew how good it could be.

"You know why she do that?" Mother Danilecki asked him one morning, and right away he knew she meant Chloe pushing down on his head.

"No," said Mount, though he thought he knew more than he knew how to say. And Gendron pushed in with, "You can't never tell with a pachy sometimes. They just does whatever it is."

But Mother Danilecki ignored him and gave her own opinion, which was that something got into the air between Chloe's foot and Mount's head that was like an invitation to the foot to do something different than usual, and that Chloe was no more responsible for what had happened than Mount, but that the something that got into the air had a life of its own and would stay among the circus people doing interfering kinds of things until it could be caught—probably in a trap of some kind—and tamed like any other animal.

Mount nodded. He liked Mother Danilecki's answer better than his own—which, as best he understood, declared there was more of a trick to putting his head beneath Chloe's foot than he had thought, and it was his act as much as hers, needing more concentration on his part than just getting down and kneeling there like a bump. But if that was true, then there was a skill he hadn't mastered yet, and it was just dumb luck she hadn't gone and squashed him a long time before. And he was nervous on account of having to keep going out there and doing the trick without knowing if he finally had the skill or not. Under circumstances like those, every extra day of life was bound to be a surprise.

So he told Mother Danilecki, "I think you're right," and left it at that, with a strange secret something loose in the air causing unpredictable mischief whenever it wanted.

"Malarky!" said Gendron. "Malarky and poison." And he flung a spray of black coffee out of his tin cup onto the ground and walked away, which Mount knew was because of a woman having her own opinion on anything any elephant did, even though she didn't hold Chloe to blame.

"How do you catch it?" asked Mount. He imagined this force was something invisible, like e-lec-tri-city, that you wouldn't know was there unless it came in contact with you. It was sure to take a special kind of trap.

"Well," said Mother Danilecki, "it peripatate from person to person, like bad ache in muscle, and person dun suspeck nothin' unless it leave away quiet or else come out in open and do bad troubles fast as hell. So, only best kinda trap to use is you be the trap yourself."

"*I* should be the trap?"

Mother Danilecki shrugged. "I dunno," she said. "But one ting: whatever it is, already it know you good, huh?" She slapped his shoulder.

"Never mind," said Mount. "Never mind." He stood up to leave and tossed coffee from his own tin cup on top of the coffee Gendron had tossed, seeming as mad as Gendron and hoping Mother Danilecki was watching.

"Next time I'll be dead!" he cried, whirling around to face her. But she was already going in her own direction with her skirts swaying behind her and her bracelets jangling loose.

So there wasn't much to choose among the various outlooks on how Chloe happened to almost crush his head: it was either the plain un-knowability of an elephant, or Mount himself not concentrating hard enough on mastering all the skills, or else something that just got out into the air.

Maybe, Mount thought, it's still floating free somewheres, and not in me at all.

After two bandage changes they still hadn't made the train. Semple supposedly had one waiting somewhere, in a town near the Georgia line, wherever that might be, or maybe across on the other side. And supposedly the train had special cars that could carry four entire wagons loaded crosswise, and the circus people could go inside the train proper—not like the deck of the river barge—and sit in seats by clear glass windows watching the terrain go by and not have to lift a finger between towns. A pretty good train.

Earlier, Semple had held a meeting to discuss the trip, having heard some grumbling about the fatigue of the road working into people's bones to the point they weren't moving their bowels properly or sleeping steadily through the night.

"We need to perform," he told everyone, "in every aspect of life. We need the strictest discipline in even the smallest things, including eating and sleeping and evacuating our daily wastes."

Gendron leaned over and whispered to Mount, "Oh, here we're gonna get some damn lecture on shitting." But Semple didn't add much to that—the part about discipline—though the circus sat quiet and watched him, waiting for more because they could see he wasn't the least bit shy about it. The meeting was in a farmer's field, and the farmer at first came up to Semple and asked if there was any boys that wanted to pick some ripe cabbages for an extra something in their pockets.

"Sir," said Semple so everyone could hear, "these people are circus performers, not stoopers, and they all belong on the road and not down to the side of it grubbing in the dirt." So the farmer just stepped back meekly and monitored the rest of the meeting with a shamefaced look like he should have known better than to ask. And he didn't even laugh when Semple got to the part on keeping disciplined right down to the bowels, but just stood there nodding as if he agreed and knew what that was all about.

"We also need to perform in the usual ways," Semple said after letting the business about the rest of life sink in. "And, so, I'm looking up and down the map here for sites where we might do some abbreviated tricks and such in the streets, without we have to set up the tent." There was some murmuring all in favor of that. People started volunteering what they would do and how they could make good use of buildings along the main street of wherever they were to save a clown-baby from a ledge or have the clown cop-and-robber battle in and out of doorways.

"And, that way we can keep on going and make the train all the sooner," said Semple. This was the first anyone had heard mention of the train.

"What train?" asked Darien Whitesides, the man who did tricks on horseback dressed as a Confederate soldier in the South and as Abraham Lincoln in the North, standing backward on the rump of a horse pounding hard around the ring, all the while singing favorite regional songs in a fine tenor voice that Mount believed could have earned him the famous tear-jerk spot in the Old Musicians' troupe.

Then Semple explained how the train was being kept waiting by an old friend of his who ran the whole railroad. And that was when the business about how good a train this was began to get settled in people's imaginations, so that getting up in the morning and persevering on the road were less of a burden with something so grand to look forward to—even though the joke amongst the people coming and going between the wagons and the portable men's and women's so-called sugar sheds was that discipline was still lax and needed work.

As far as sleeping went, Mount could only account for himself and Gendron, who still shared the same wagon, Mount on a patch of floor and Gendron in the bunk. Gendron slept like he always slept—drunk and snoring, and sometimes shouting at people Mount couldn't make out the names of. And Mount slept in short bursts, like a dog, waking when the ache in his temples rattled and made him want to spit at the ceiling, just to get something out.

But performing in all the unknown towns was nice. The circus came in unannounced, morning, noon or evening, taking people by surprise on their red clay streets or drawing them out of their houses, napkins sometimes still stuck in their collars, mouths still chewing slow. The clowns poured out of their dressing-up wagon and ran a series of stunts that were half improvised, half planned, taking a child or two captive for a few moments, and then going to prison for it, which always pained Mount, even though he knew this was just a performance, because they looked so sad and innocent, and he knew what prison was going to be like and wished they could be forgiven.

They did only the least amount of scouting for these forays, Semple riding a horse up into each town alone, then back to where the circus was waiting to hear his ideas of what to try. He described the main street and how the houses were situated, if they were big or small, and if there were dogs about. He rattled off the names he'd seen on shingles and in the windows of stores—if stores there were. If he'd had a conversation he recounted it and described the person right down to the shoes—

buttoned or tied, or if he even had any shoes at all. And he always gave an estimate of what the mood was like in the town—if it felt like people were happy or not, prospering or failing, or if someone had died in recent times, which would mean there wasn't any point in doing the stunt known as "Mother's Last Hours," where the clowns split up and played good and bad angels.

Once when Semple was giving his estimate Gendron leaned over and told Mount, "Ask him if these people's bowels is okay." But Mount just sat with his back against a wagon wheel and his eyes closed and imagined what the unknown town looked like—whether the houses had dim parlours with lamps under brown damask shades with things that dangled down and moved gently from the heat of the yellow flames.

"Ask him how much farther this train of his is," said Gendron.

Sometimes in these small towns peaceful citizens minding their own business were flat put out by the sudden invasion, the noise of it springing up so loud. But they almost always got over it when they saw that nothing was in earnest and their neighbors were enjoying themselves, and no harm was being done. Still, now and then there was a touchy second with some of them, and the blood rushed in and clouded their faces until the situation made itself clear and they subsided. But Gendron always said that was his favorite time, when a stunt hung there, in the mind of some rube, on the cusp between serious and just fooling, and could go in any direction, no telling which in advance—and the rube might pop off in total anger so that someone like Gendron could leap in and set him straight.

"Ain't nothing that pleases me so," he told Mount during a kind of confession where he owned up that a tiny part of him hadn't been completely sure what it wanted Chloe to do with her foot on top of Mount's head.

"I was all over fascination about it," he said. "Even as hard as I was tryin' to get her to let up. It's true. Anything could of happened then, and that's the only exciting thing there is for a body that's seen this life for all these years."

But Mount didn't mind. He knew it was all just between himself and Chloe, or else that force that was loose in the air.

"If it'd been you," he told Gendron, "well, I don't know either."

And Gendron looked him back and said, "I bet."

* * *

The eleventh day on the road, Semple called a meeting by a small lake teeming with enormous skimming birds with scissorlike wings. He announced that the train was only three towns off, four at the most, and that he'd been to the Western Union office and sent a message with their present position up to his friend who was so thoughtfully keeping things waiting.

"The names of the towns are these," Semple said. And he named them, including the fourth. Mount watched the lake and saw alligators lying as still as death and the low-flying birds snagging insects an inch off the top of the water. There were meetings every day now—sometimes twice a day—and it got to be more like a church than a circus, with long ponderous silences between the speeches, and questions asked that either had no proper answers or else answers so obvious it seemed like they couldn't be right, and instead you had to search deeper while the silences stretched on and on. And usually no one gave the answers anyway, and you could hardly figure out the point of much that was said, except about the train, which became better and better, closer and closer.

But Mount found the meetings a way to breathe easy. Everyone sat quietly and kept his head down or looked off into the swamp or across the field or into the woods—wherever the group happened to be. And Mount would sort of let his mind go still, like the deathly still of the alligators, so that he took up no more space than what there was around him, and let no more thoughts get out nor had any more feelings than if he were a cabbage lying in the rain.

In fact, it was in the middle of such a meeting that he noticed the ache in his head was gone. If it had been a tent church, up he'd have marched to the preacher crying about the cure and going down on his knees in thanks. But as it was he just kept quiet, except for shaking his head to see if he could summon up any ache at all, which he couldn't.

This is pretty good, he thought, suddenly left alone like this by a pain that had been so constant. He couldn't wait to tell Mother Danilecki so she could take the bandage off and leave it off.

But she refused. She unrolled a fresh length of gauze and told him not to be deceived by what he felt or didn't feel, she could see the injury still in his eyes, the tiny black dots of which had been stunned from the inside out and had a ways to go yet. And it was into them that she looked each morning to figure out when to take the bandage off for good.

Anyhow, the ache was gone, and bandaged or not his head was left in a better frame of mind. He even went back and had a reunion with Chloe in which he forgave her and rubbed her skin with a brush, watching her hide stretch and shrink and the hairs stand up and decline as the bristles passed over. Exotic rumblings came from deep inside her, long arpeggios of hunger or pleasure, or of something building to an unknown finish. Mount thought of the mysterious force let loose in the air, and Chloe scared him for the first few minutes as her trunk sniffed slow around his head and shoulders, specializing mostly in the bandage.

Gendron stayed close and watched the reunion, fearing something might flare up anew. He kept a cautious eye for signs of vengeance lingering, and circled Chloe three whole times examining every part of her body, especially her eyes and mouth—which was one of the first and most expressive places where her fury showed itself.

"I think it's okay," said Gendron. But Mount said nothing in reply. He only turned around and nodded since Gendron still insisted on the old rule that Mount mustn't talk directly to Chloe or even let her hear the sound of his voice too near. What Gendron didn't know wouldn't hurt, so Mount still honored the rule for appearance's sake and held his conversations with Chloe in secret.

"Yep, I think it's okay," Gendron repeated. "We'll have you back in the ring by Valdosta," which was the first time Mount had heard of this.

When they reached the town of Creosote, Florida, where the train was supposed to be, it wasn't there. Semple stalked off apart from the rest and stared at the empty tracks as though he could conjure the train upon them if only he concentrated hard enough. Finally he came back and said, "It isn't here," and the muttering went up and down. Then he told everyone to wait and went away looking for a telegraph to send a cry off into the wilderness and see where this train had gotten to.

While Semple was gone there was a lot of debate over whether or not the train had been just a lie to keep them going. The pro and con sides argued heatedly, and angry fights had begun to break out by the time a whistle sounded in the distance, and everyone became quiet and hopeful. The whistle sounded again, and debate shifted to the question of whether the whistle was getting farther away or coming closer—both positions also being represented hotly during a long, whistleless stretch that finally ended with a clearly closer blast that set everyone to waiting quietly and looking in both directions along the tracks, unsure which way the train would come.

Then someone said, "But it probably ain't ours," and the squabbles began again. People backed away from the tracks and stopped looking, forming small clusters of argument that would break apart angrily—almost acrobatically—and reconvene, though slightly altered as to the people involved.

When Semple returned after having been out of sight for fifteen or twenty minutes—no one knew where exactly, but many said hiding or waiting or thinking up some excuse—when he returned the whistle was close indeed, and in one direction dark smudges of smoke were rising above the treetops. The tension built up mightily before the train finally curved into view—just an indistinct black blot jittering on the tracks, still a long ways off and no telling if it was their train or not, nor how good a train compared to everyone's imaginings.

But it did turn out to be the right train, and nearly as good a one as anybody had hoped. The so-called friend of Semple came off first as it rolled in clanging, a smiling man with half an arm missing and his cuff stitched shut on account of it. He ran up to Semple, calling him something else that Mount heard either as Jeff or as Seth, and Mount thought he saw Semple hug the man as though he, Semple, also had something missing, letting his left arm operate at only the sudden fraction of the total capability of an arm. And the two of them then walked up and back alongside of the train, probably figuring how to put everything on board.

This man turned out to be Semple's new partner, and the train itself the equity the man brought to the new partnership. Once all the wagons and animals had been loaded and the train stood ready, hissing, there was a meeting held by the side of the tracks to explain all this.

"This here is Jack Berlin," Semple told everyone, "and he owns everything of half we've got, or half of everything we've got, whichever you please." And Jack Berlin waved his good arm and smiled, and said howdy and pleased to meet and so forth, looking out at the circus people and back at Semple, and beyond at the knots of Creosoters watching it happen, pointing and nodding.

Semple went on to explain how the circus was getting ready to grow up bigger and stronger, like any healthy adolescent youth, and there would be new acts and bigger towns to play in—sometimes even indoors—and the reason everyone had been put through this awful, tedious march to meet the train was because Jack Berlin had made significant new bookings in Atlanta, Richmond, Washington, Baltimore, Philadelphia and New York, as well as some of the same old lesser towns in between. "But where Valdosta and Macon and Raleigh and such have been the biggest time we did, from here on in those towns are just second-rank stops to give us a warmup for the big bookings," said Semple.

And another reason they had to get cracking was that two new acts were waiting in Atlanta—one of them a man with talented apes, the other four Swiss sisters who did headstands on each other's heads whilst having a violent argument about whose husband is the handsomest, and a bunch of clowns played the husbands.

"So, things are really changing," said Semple, and Jack Berlin nodded and smiled, and was obviously proud of his part in these new things.

"And that's why we're cutting out Macon this year," Semple added, "though we'll still play Valdosta."

For the first few hours after the train pulled out the circus members coursed through the cars that were now not just waiting for them but theirs exclusively, to take them wherever the rails went. Although no window was better than any other, people would alight at one, weary of it after a while and get up to find another—intoxicated by the freedom of movement and the freedom of having more windows than people to look out of them. So there was a flurry of adjustments to make, and Gendron told Mount this was all just a pack of selfish shits trying to find new ways to be selfish when a lot of the old ways had been temporarily spoiled. That was the reason for all the flying around and taking up new space—because they had an unfamiliar world to conquer and bring the old regime of privileges to.

"I'm doing it myself," said Gendron. "Don't I gotta get something that's better than what you got?"

So Mount pitched in and took part as best he could, going from one end of the train to the other, except for the car at the very end that was Semple's and Jack Berlin's alone. There were also two sleeping cars, a men's and a women's, which was not altogether agreeable to some of the performers who were married to each other and had, under the old system, been able to bunk together in a wagon of their own. Some of these people went complaining to Semple but were met at the door of the private car by Jack Berlin and told that this was a new system that was all for the best in the changed professional climate of the growing circus, but that he, Jack, would think about it and try to come up with an acceptable compromise before they reached Atlanta.

The circus members talked about all this new business right away, and the fact of having things to talk about gradually slowed the scurrying around and the exploration of the train until people collected in one of the cars and sat together in a tight knot, not even bothering with the windows or the terrain flowing by outside. Some of the married couples said boldly that they were going straight back to their wagons, although they admitted they didn't know how they could get to the special flat cars where the wagons were stowed as long as the train was in motion.

Mount thought you could probably walk along the roof and then climb down, but he didn't suggest it because he wouldn't have wanted to do it himself.

When the grumbling died down and people were just sitting there, the car got terribly quiet and sad, and Mount could see a general attitude of bewilderment and caution replacing the earlier eagerness that was now laid flat and left behind.

"What a lot of changes," said Mother Danilecki, who had always been thought of as close to Semple and in on everything he did—and yet here she was with the rest of them and not with Semple in the private car.

Then slowly people moved away from each other and spread through the car and turned to the windows, where whatever was left of Florida was speeding by—the woods and the backs of houses and towns, all of it taking no notice of the train. The sound of the tracks underneath was dull and stupefying, making Mount's head feel heavy on top of his neck until he leaned back and fell asleep. The last of Florida slipped by without him, a slim boy with a pig at his side waving from beneath a tree as the empty window went past.

Atlanta came up as promised, and the new people joined the circus. The talented apes were a caution. Jack Berlin introduced the man whose apes they were and then stood aside and laughed and held his belt as the man led the apes through a series of activities any human could do without thinking, and yet to see apes do them was funny. Mount watched and was amazed to see the high degree of emotion the apes exhibited, rubbing their eyes and moaning when a thing they loved was taken away, then jumping up and down and whooping when the thing was given back.

"That's good," said Mount.

They were in an indoor hippodrome where the new people had already been waiting by the time the circus arrived from the train station. The roustabouts looked around them and wondered what to do since there wasn't any tent or grandstand to put up. Everything was fully prepared. The seats were permanent, and the hippodrome's open center, down upon which the seats were aimed, had been adapted with sawdust and wooden curbing for the circus's performance.

When the apes were through and the man went around and shook some hands and got people to shake hands with some of the humanlike apes, Jack Berlin introduced the four Swiss sisters one by one, who nodded their heads at the sound of their names—the complicated likes of which Mount had never heard before and couldn't have repeated without first practicing. But instead of going through their act as the apes had done, the Swiss sisters only walked around and met their new circus acquaintances, bowing from the waist and smiling hello in what Mount could tell was a strange language (that Gendron later told him was known as cheese talk, because of all the smiling that went along with the words).

Then Semple and Jack Berlin went off and discussed where to put the two new acts in the timing of things and how high to bill them on the advertising placards. Bits of this could be overheard, and Mount and others glanced over to see how the two men's tempers were holding, wondering whether they would or wouldn't hold at all. But there wasn't a sign of anything but the happiest collegiality and politeness and deference, as though each was the servant of the other and wanted nothing more than to please him and ease his way through the best, most perfect life until heaven. Mount could see this dismayed a lot of the people who were partial to Semple and displeased with the changes brought by Jack Berlin, but there was nothing to do but keep on, playing the new dates in the big towns on the way up north and welcoming the apes and the sisters and making the best of it and them.

Everything had been okay so far, at least where Mount was concerned.

They had made Valdosta, and Gendron had put Mount back in the ring that night, and Mount had gone to Chloe first and whispered, "Please don't hurt me again," and she hadn't. He had allowed his eyes to go loose and let her foot come down just so, gently and carefully, not moving until it was over and the foot gone. It was a triumphal return to business, and Gendron shook his hand and told him he could start to put the memory behind, which he began to do that very night.

Later he was standing outside the tent, smoking on a cigarette and looking up into the deep Valdosta sky, and a girl came up to him and said her name was Tiffany and what was his.

She told him how much she admired the way he put his head down there and endured the profound risk of the elephant's great weight. And he replied it was nothing but discipline and concentration, to go along with character development and a strong upbringing in a Normal School in Ohio. Then he smiled in exactly the way he later discovered the Swiss sisters smiled. The girl Tiffany smiled back, and Mount blew smoke up above her head to where it disappeared into the rest of Valdosta.

"You want to come with me for a walk?" she asked him. She turned up her face and got close enough for him to smell her, a warm smell that he liked.

So he went along with her in a direction where it turned pitch dark and there weren't even any houses showing lights. Tiffany's white dress showed a little light, but other than that he wouldn't have been able to tell where she was until she reached her hand into his and left it there like a small warm fish.

"Take this here turn," she told him, and he did even though he didn't see any proper turning such as a walk or a road. "That's right," she said. He found himself suddenly headed downhill and could feel bushes close on either side, though they didn't quite touch him or his clothes. And she was right behind him, he was sure, hearing the rustle of her white dress—though it could have been light blue or pink—until he reached a kind of bottom where the downhill business tapered off and he ran himself up against a tree, his cheek half smarting on the bark.

"Okay," he said, and turned around. "Okay, Tiffany." But he didn't hear anything, and another five minutes passed before he was completely sure she wasn't there, and no one else was either—no one like Gendron, who might have leapt out of a bush whooping as the end of a long joke arranged between himself and this Tiffany. But nothing else happened.

Then he walked back slowly, aiming for the lights of the tent and thinking he might see the girl along the path in her dress, waiting for a laugh. But the route was empty and dark all the way back, and he didn't know what to make of it.

Still, other than that one episode, things had been all right. In three nights in Valdosta, Chloe's foot came down lighter and lighter on each successive try until he scarcely felt the touch at all and began to believe he was learning how to control it, turning the act into something that was his as well as hers. And after he was finished he always went outside the tent and smoked a cigarette, leaning up against one of the slanting tethering ropes and waiting for something to happen the way it had that first night with Tiffany. But it never did, and all he could do was finish the cigarette and stare off into the deep Valdosta night by himself, wondering what lay in store in future towns.

In Atlanta Gendron got into a fight with the man who owned the apes over a sack of feed that Gendron said was Chloe's and the ape man said was his—or that he had a right to use for the apes, never mind whose sack it had started out as, since they were all in the circus together. Mount saw Gendron throw the first punch, and the second and the third, until Jack Berlin rushed up with Semple, each taking one of the two men fighting and shouting at both to stop. Then the story of how the fight began was related, and Semple told Gendron that because he and Jack Berlin were paying for the feed, it belonged to the circus and not to one animal or another or one trainer or another. And so, Jack Berlin took up where Semple left off, if the apes needed feeding, the man who owned them could pick up any sack of feed he wanted, and the same was true of Gendron and Chloe (even though Gendron didn't own her). It was first come, first served, as the need arose.

"And as far as fighting goes," said Semple, the next time Gendron resorted to it would be on the last day he worked for the circus. "Got it?" Semple said.

Gendron said he did, though Mount could see he was none too happy about getting it. So the two of them sat down together on a couple of buckets and watched the feed sack be taken away and the crowd that had gathered to see the fight thin out. And Gendron said nothing while Mount respectfully joined in the silence, just the two of them. Finally, when everyone was gone, Gendron said, "Did I get him good?" And Mount answered that it was three to nothing and getting better before the fight was broken up, which put a smile on Gendron's face. So Mount sat there on the bucket smoking with Gendron and keeping company until it was time to get up and go through the hippodrome with the other roustabouts in preparation for the show—dusting the seats, raking the sawdust and tightening the turnbuckles that secured all the rigging up over the ring. Then they rolled out the calliope and filled its boiler with water and started a fire in the firebox, waiting around until the steam began to hiss and the whole thing seemed alive.

They played Atlanta for five nights, which was the longest the circus had stayed anywhere since Mount had joined. Mother Danilecki still came to check his eyes each morning, bringing her sour breath and black dots close to his until she was a warm yellow blur and he wanted to look away. She gave him grudging permission to take off the bandage during performances, but she said she'd rather he wear it and stick some gleeful decoration on instead, because it was doing all that good, both inside and out, and his black dots were shrinking up to the light almost the way they ought to, and a few more days wouldn't hurt. So he agreed, and she brought him a giant ruby stuck to a pin, though she said it was only nice cut glass, and pinned this to the front of the bandage so the gauze looked like an Arab turban.

"This perfect," she said. She opened one of the large bangles around her neck and held up its mirrored insides for him to see himself. But her hand was shaking, so all he could see were flashes of his forehead and the shine of red glass and the blur of gauze, and he kept on moving his head in front of her hand, trying to catch himself at some angle, but it didn't work.

"Okay," he said. "That's okay."

Before the first Atlanta performance Jack Berlin called a meeting. He asked everyone to go around the circle and say who they were and where they were from and why they got involved in the circus in the first place. Semple stood off to one side with a sour expression, but he didn't interfere. People spoke slow and dull, and like they didn't understand what was happening and why. But Jack Berlin seemed pleased to hear it all, and nodded and smiled at each person speaking to draw out as much as he could, leaning toward them and winkling up his eyes. When Gendron's turn came, Gendron stood up and said he was really named Reinhorn Roosevelt, and he was a cousin of the president from the

French side of the genealogy and had got to know elephants whilst in the African army, when he had been a general in command of three hundred almost-naked children who could speak no languages at all but got along solely by using hand signals.

"They was the greatest little fighters," he said. Then he sat down.

People laughed, and a cloud of displeasure passed across Jack Berlin's face. And then it was Mount's turn, he being seated next to Gendron. He got out his whole name okay, but Jack Berlin's patience suddenly wore out and he interrupted and said it was time to move on to other business, which turned out to be the announcement of a compromise concerning what to do about the married people who were kept apart on the train.

"From now on," Jack Berlin said, "married couples can live in their same old wagons while the circus is in a town somewhere. But they have to observe the new segregation when the circus is in transit on the train. You'll find it's the best for hygiene and the consideration of other people, as well as the good order of the institution." The affected people looked at each other and shrugged, since the compromise was no different than what was presently being done. Gendron raised the question of the hermaphrodite man/woman beast—where did he or she bunk? And Semple jumped in on this right away and volunteered Mother Danilecki to do a close examination and figure out what was best, taking into account, of course, the wishes of the hermaphrodite. The hermaphrodite, who had been born as George Flaxman but was now known and billed as George/Georgette, stood up abruptly and gave a sincere demonstration of simultaneous weeping and gnashing of teeth to show how hurt and angry he or she was over being debated about in this way—"As though I wasn't even here," which was flung out in a voice that Mount thought sounded both stern and fragile, and full of justice and music and the flapping of wings, as if it wanted to accomplish too much in too short a time.

Then Jack Berlin hurriedly adjourned the meeting, looking somewhat confused but wishing good luck and Godspeed and a snappy performance to all, and bowing deeply from the waist so the gold ringmaster's whistle accidentally fell from his jacket pocket onto the sawdust, where everyone stared at it for an instant. This was the first sign that Jack Berlin planned to take over Semple's ringmaster chores, and the incident fueled the rumor—that had started the day before—that Semple was

204

dying of an awful disease that would claim him before the show got completely north.

When someone is dying, that changes everything, and they can't be blamed anymore or have the same power. Between Atlanta and Richmond Semple stayed on the train in his private car. Whenever anyone came to see him, Jack Berlin answered the door and smiled and nodded and said, no, Semple wasn't seeing anyone and no one was seeing him, but, yes, he was feeling just fine. Mount sat and listened as people recounted these stories of trying to see Semple, and he figured Semple was murdered by Jack Berlin and stuffed out the door at the very end of the train and bounced along the tracks and left for whatever found him there. Gendron vowed he didn't care one way or the other if things were run by Semple Groves or Jack Berlin, one king was as bad as the next, or else if one was better in some small ways, then those were evened out in others. And too bad for Semple if he was murdered or only dying, but they still had to keep Chloe fed and happy and going out there into the ring night after night. And they did, in one town after another up through Georgia and the Carolinas—Greenville, Charlotte, High Point, Durham—finally hitting the coast in southern Virginia, where Mount got his first look at the ocean and didn't like the smell or the things that washed up when the ocean rolled back and were left there lying on the sand like something out of your nose.

Mount asked Mother Danilecki if Semple was murdered, and she told him yes. Then he asked her how it was done, and she told him, "Money."

The bandage was gone now, and Mount's hair was finally lifting away from the scalp, where it had been pinned for near to a month. Mother Danilecki had promised him a trimming when the hair recovered, and each day she came and looked to see if he was ready. By Richmond she decided she could do something with it. She sat him down in her wagon in a chair in the middle of the floor. She shut the door and blew out the lamp so they were left in total darkness. Then Mount heard the scissors clacking, warming up.

"How can you cut it in the dark?" he asked. The scissors came closer.

"I feel wit my hands. Dun need to see." The scissors closed carefully and rhythmically, and Mount felt the cut hairs falling in the dark, glancing down his eyebrows and cheeks and against his neck. He smelled the smoke from the snuffed wick and the breath of Mother Danilecki bending close.

"There," she said. "That perfect." She went and opened the door and then to the lamp, striking a match. She held a mirror up to him. He looked small and sad and frightened in the light that washed through the door and onto his face. He squinted. The more he squinted, the less he could see himself. He squeezed his eyes until they shut.

"Pretty good," he said.

"That perfect," said Mother Danilecki.

Mount wanted to find some evidence of Semple Groves's murder. He talked about this with a boy named Teddy who hung around the circus in Richmond. Teddy came with his older sister Grace, who commented on Mount's haircut.

"The front looks like a staircase," she said.

Teddy was ten or so. He said he wanted to be a detective.

"What are you gonna detect?" Mount asked, adopting the voice of someone older talking to a boy, and throwing in a little bit of Gendron.

"Crimes that ain't been discovered yet. Say someone put a bomb inside your elephant. I get there first even though there's no good reason to think it's in there, and the police are all off drinking coffee and playing cards."

"Why would they do that, Ted?" Grace asked. "Put a bomb in an elephant?"

"How would they get it in there?" Mount asked.

"Down the mouth or through the ay-nus," Teddy said.

"Oh, Teddy . . ." said Grace.

"It'd just be a small bomb. I'd say you can mostly never tell why a villain does a thing, but they'd do it to show me up, I think, to see if I could find it even if it was so well hid."

"Well, we're all looking for a body," said Mount. "Our owner was murdered, and not a soul's seen the body for over three weeks, since Atlanta."

"Did you ever see him dead?" asked Teddy.

"Nope," said Mount. "But he just disappeared one day into his railroad car, and everything he used to do got taken over, and now he's completely gone."

"So, as far as anybody knows, there ain't even been a crime," said Teddy. "That's exactly the situation I favor most."

"Then you'll help me?" asked Mount.

"I'll do it," said Teddy. Grace smiled and patted her brother's head. She seemed to be about fifteen or sixteen, and Mount reached over and likewise patted her head.

The three of them planned to meet up again later, two hours after the show, which was being held in the traditional tent because the local Richmond hippodrome was occupied by the U.S. Cavalry for horse-training exercises and a bivouac. Mount crept out of Gendron's wagon, moving slow so nothing would creak. He wanted to get to the bottom of Semple's murder mostly to catch the notice of everyone and be renowned as a man who could get the answers even if no one expected him to.

"Hello?" he whispered when he got to the place where they had said they would meet. "Hello?" There was still a ways to walk to reach the siding where the train was kept, so Mount didn't want to waste any time. He wished there was a moon to make the going easier and show his features clearly to Grace and Teddy so they wouldn't be afraid of him in the dark.

"Hello?" a voice came back.

It turned out to be Grace. She emerged from concealment and told Mount how Teddy had unfortunately fallen asleep straightaway when they returned home from the circus, and no amount of persuasion could get him fully awake again.

"Besides," she said, "Teddy says the dead man'll still be dead in the morning."

"That's true," said Mount. He could hardly see her face in the dark, just sometimes a gleam of light from who knew where that shone off one of her teeth as she talked.

"Anyway," she said, "I just came to tell you and then to go straight home. Teddy says we can meet up tomorrow and get this thing figured out right proper, and once we do we can call the police."

"Okay," said Mount. "Sure thing." Then the girl was going away, and he stood there and watched until she was out of sight and he couldn't hear the rustling of her clothes. But instead of going back to Gendron's wagon just to lie there and hear Gendron's mouth fall open spookily and

207

the sounds—words mixed with snorts and coughs—pour up to the ceiling, he went where the three of them had planned to go in the first place: the railroad car where Jack Berlin and the disappeared Semple supposedly lived.

Under the new routine that had been established, when the circus got to a town the wagons were first loaded off the train and then the animals and other assorted equipment. All this became the circus parade, as usual, and the parade went through town to wherever the hippodrome was or the tent would be, just like in the old days, with people resuming what they recalled from that former life. Which meant that whatever new order had been set forth on the train would be suddenly and regularly suspended and the old order reinstated, and this was uncomfortable and confusing—though people seemed to do their best to enjoy the familiarity, except for Mount, who hadn't really been at it long enough before the changes arrived and liked his little berth on the train and the black damask curtain that dropped down beside him for privacy whenever he wanted.

But while everyone else was making these transitions back and forth between old and new, Jack Berlin stayed in the railroad car, where, according to Jack Berlin's version, Semple was staying too, immersed deep in important business matters and sensitive correspondence and eating nothing but grapefruits and Chinese tea and biscuits and making extraordinary plans that would affect the next three years of circus life.

"He's such a brilliant man," Jack Berlin reportedly told Claire, the albino lady, who told the knife thrower, Renzo Kovacks, adding that Jack Berlin's honest opinion was that Semple shouldn't waste his time doing anything but thinking, and that his thoughts alone could save weeks of labor every year and create ideas enough to start dozens of new subsidiary ventures with his and Jack Berlin's names on them.

"And Jack Berlin said Semple agrees," Claire told Renzo, who told Mother Danilecki, who told Mount—on condition that he'd let her shut the door and blow out the lamp and cut his hair some more, until it was "even better perfect."

But none of this changed the fact that no one had laid eyes on Semple since the train left Atlanta.

"He's murdered," said Mount. "Don't forget."

"I know," said Mother Danilecki. "But you dun forget neither—still he could be tinking."

*   *   *

By the time Mount reached the train he had taken three full tumbles and stubbed his feet over stumps or roots or other unseen changes in the lay of the land. The train was dark and cold except for the last car, which was the home of Jack Berlin that Semple was said to share. Lamplight came from the car, amber and sweet and parlourlike behind wheat-colored curtains that gave the flame a halo. Mount went toward it through grass that ripped at his ankles. Finally he arrived.

He put his hands on the side of the car and tried to feel what was happening inside, the way he might put his hands on Chloe's hide and take the deep rumblings up through his palms. The impression he got of the car was peaceful, like a sleeping house with a light left on just in case someone came home in the middle of the night from England. But when he put his ear to the varnish he heard people moving and a voice or two, soft and indistinct. The sounds faded away from the spot where he was listening until he heard a door open and close at the nether end of the car. He crept along on all fours in that direction, going from one tie-end to the next so as not to make a commotion in the surrounding gravel.

When he reached the corner of the car he peered around and up at the platform there, with the iron railing boxing it in. He could see two men just standing on it, facing off down the tracks and saying nothing. It was Semple Groves and Jack Berlin, and Mount could see by the light escaping from inside the car that the two of them hadn't a stitch of clothing on, their pale backsides ambered up by the light and their fronts hardly showing at all.

Mount stayed there as quiet as could be and watched them stand like statues for the longest time—speechless as statues, too—and wondered what was going on, and why they'd risen from their beds and come out like this just to stare down the empty tracks, unless some frightening noise had disturbed them at the same time and they were out here investigating it. Then slowly it dawned on Mount that they were probably looking for him—some skulking prowler invading their peaceful night—and this made him feel ashamed. So gradually he withdrew his head out of sight around the edge of the car and crouched there breathing softly until he heard the door open and close again, after which he waited even longer to make sure he could get away clean and be no more a disturbance to those two.

But, as bad as he felt about upsetting their sleep, Mount was satisfied on account of having learned conclusively that Semple was alive and not murdered at all—though it was still probably true he was dying slowly.

In Richmond Chloe caught cold and simply lay down. Gendron got in close and felt her ears, which were burning. He said she had a fever. All the muscle seemed to have gone out of her trunk, and her eyes were slow and dim. The U.S. Cavalry veterinary officer was sent for from the hippodrome, and he came on the double, galloping in on a chestnut mare that snorted from the exertion. The officer began to swing himself down while the horse was still in full gallop. Mount thought it was stirring.

"This is pretty good," he said. Gendron took one look at the cavalry vet and blew out a hot blast of hatred through his nose. Jack Berlin had ordered the vet brought in. Gendron had wanted to see the fever through by himself, but Jack Berlin reminded him the elephant was circus property no matter what Gendron might think, and it was damn well circus business to do the best for it and see it survived at least until Baltimore, where four new elephants would join the circus—two from Asia and two from Africa. This was the first mention Gendron had heard about any new elephants, and it made him mad.

"I got a goddamn fever, too," he whispered to Mount while the vet was holding a match up to Chloe's eye and she didn't even swat him.

To everything the vet said, Gendron replied, "That's right," letting him know he knew it too, and maybe better. Mount watched Chloe stay so still and let all kinds of things be done to her that she never would have allowed if she hadn't been sick. He moved back and forth across the front of her trying to get her eyes to follow instead of lolling so hard in one place. Finally, when nothing was happening, he decided she would die like Hiram, like Semple Groves was doing—like anyone ill just drifting away with no interest in struggling on to gain whatever extra might be gained.

"Make sure she don't slouch over on her side," the vet told Gendron. "Otherwise she'll squash her own insides with all her weight."

"That's right," said Gendron coldly. Mount knew for a fact that Gendron already knew that, too, because he'd heard him say it a dozen times—for one thing, the lungs collapse, and that's that, after just a few minutes.

Mount watched and listened, and Gendron nodded angrily and said,

"That's right" over and over until the cavalry vet finally finished and said what he thought should be done—which was let her rest and ride it out, and give her plenty of water but no food until she gets to her feet, and then all she can eat. And after he said this he went to his mare and swung himself up, spurring her hard so she was off like a rabbit, springing into her gallop. He hadn't even once said his name.

For a minute Mount just stood there and listened to the air settle down again, while Gendron went over to Chloe and knelt beside her hot ear, whispering things up close to her and running his hands across her hide.

Then Mount went to get her more water.

Teddy and Grace came looking for him later that afternoon, and he was able to astonish them with the story of finding the murdered man alive. Teddy was the most disappointed, saying, "Sometimes a crime just don't quite fully mature to the point that it can be detected," and suggesting maybe there was something deeper to the business of the two men being naked out there on the back of the train. But Grace shook her head and said she doubted it, and Teddy looked up at her bitterly because she'd contradicted him.

Mount went and snuck them some tickets for the show that night and explained how he had to go look after the sick elephant and couldn't spend time with them, much as he wanted to. Teddy didn't seem to care. He announced he was closing in on something big right in his very own family, which made Grace look uneasy, as though she had warned him not to do it. Grace took Mount's hand and shook it firmly, wishing both him and the elephant well.

"Teddy . . ." she said, urging him on to something. And the boy stepped up and also took Mount's hand and shook it.

"That's right," she said.

"Thank you for the tickets, sir," said Teddy. Then the two of them turned and ran off like children, which surprised Mount, since he thought of them both as old and serious.

That night Chloe's act was replaced by the four Swiss sisters and two clowns. The clowns took the roles of Mount and Gendron, and the Swiss sisters dressed in a heap of gray-painted canvas with eye holes and pretended to be Chloe, slumping around the ring colliding with things, falling down and squealing shrilly.

The clowns didn't seem to know what to do, so they mostly chased around behind the heap and pretended to try and control it, which they plainly could not. Sometimes the smooth pink legs of one or more of the sisters peeked out from under the canvas, and one of the clowns would creep over to look close at them and touch them, which pleased the crowd so much it started happening almost all the time. Then one of the sisters stuck her long pink tongue out of one of the eye holes, and the clowns made as much as they could of that, getting up close to the eye hole and staring at the tongue.

Mount stood at the tent perimeter and watched the act, thinking it was pretty funny and bold. Jack Berlin came over and said, "So, what do I need an elephant for, eh? Tell me that, eh?" Then he went off laughing. Mount laughed too, wishing Gendron was there to see the act instead of back in the wagon stringing together a garland of myrtle leaves that Mother Danilecki had given him to hang around Chloe's neck.

Then one of the clowns put his head on the wooden platform the way Mount would have done, and the four Swiss sisters came and made the elephant sit on the head of the clown. And Mount thought that was funny too. The clown kicked and screamed, and the second clown ran over and nudged at the Swiss sisters until they all fell down in a heap, under and on top of the canvas, finally leaping up together to take their bows, all six.

The steam organ played a string of loud chords, and the audience gave a fine long ovation. Then the Swiss sisters quieted them with their hands and sang a song in a foreign language that had a lot of people nearly in tears—without even knowing what the words meant. Each sister took a verse of her own, and each had a beautiful voice that was different from the other three and yet went together with them perfectly. Mount had never heard such a solemn quiet follow so close on the heels of such commotion. But it made a lot of sense to him somehow, and he felt his heart go slower and slower.

When the sisters had finished they hung their heads and walked out ponderously, like they had all just had a great experience that they would recall for the rest of their lives. Everyone was so moved they didn't even clap. It was churchlike, with all the clowning around forgotten.

"How about that," said Mount when the sisters went past.

"Fuck you," said the last sister in line.

*　*　*

On the circus's final morning in Richmond Chloe stood up and was better. Her eyes were suddenly clear, and some of the dusty, disused appearance of her hide evaporated. Mount and Gendron stood there excited, watching her rise unsteadily like a newborn calf, and Mount shook his head to think he had believed she would lay down forever and die like Hiram, and need a pit to be dug.

But Mount patted Gendron's shoulder like a friend, and Gendron lowered his head happily and said, "Well, Jesus, what do you know," and blew out a long stream of amazed air from deep inside himself. "I thought she might be a goner."

Eventually people came by and congratulated Gendron on having Chloe up and well again. Gendron took it all in and didn't say much, especially when Jack Berlin had his turn and stood there looking Chloe up and down like he was considering buying her all over again.

"She's better?" he asked Gendron.

"That's right," Gendron answered, exactly as he had done with the cavalry vet.

"I had half a thought we'd have to shoot her," said Jack Berlin. "But this *is* good news." Then he walked away with his short arm swinging strangely inside a full, unaltered sleeve that blew and billowed.

By noon everything was packed and loaded on the train, and the circus was on its way farther north, to Washington and Baltimore. Gendron decided to ride back in the boxcar with Chloe to see that she ate and drank enough and continued regaining her usual vigor. So Mount sat by himself on the train with his face near the window glass and felt his breath rebound from it warmly while the outside went by too fast to be properly understood or thought about. Now and then black-orange cinders from the locomotive floated across the frame like insects, reminding Mount of e-lec-tri-city and then of Mother Dani-lecki's invisible force that was loose in the air just biding its time before making more trouble.

"I wonder who it's near," Mount thought. Then he took out his tin of cigarettes and examined each one before choosing the firmest, most fragrant one to smoke. It was like picking which chicken in the yard to kill, except that his mother wasn't there to say, "Oh, yes, that's the one, Jay."

12
TRUE NORTH

Gendron fretted about the new elephants Jack Berlin said the circus was getting in Baltimore.

"I feel them coming," he said. "Like a wave." He wondered out loud about their gender, and whether they came with their own trainer, or two trainers, or three or four? Or else none. And were these elephants known to each other?

"An elephant needs to get used to them others," said Gendron. "Sometimes pachys and pachys don't mix so good."

But Mount just shook his head slow, not knowing any of the answers, and deepened his eyes to a certain degree of woefulness until he felt them weighed down almost to the tops of his cheeks.

"I know," he said.

Then Gendron went on mystically about the identities of these new elephants, what their inner characters were like and what kind of voice he would have to use to talk to them.

"I wonder if they can imagine me just like I'm imagining them," Gendron said. Mount closed his eyes and saw them too, four new Chloes lumbering stately down imaginary streets in a direction labeled "Gendron," as if this was a town they knew they were going to.

"You think they think about the future?" Gendron asked. Mount shrugged.

Gendron had begun to talk all the time about the future. This was a new thing. Mount's first thought on suddenly noticing it was: death. He didn't know why, but the two words, death and future, just got close to each other in his head, and both of them then joined up with

214

Gendron. When Mount first knew Gendron all the man talked about was the past, about things that were much too good to have happened in the present ("These days hasn't half got what it takes," he might have said). Or if he wasn't talking about the past, it was about something going on right then, even as he was speaking, so that Mount couldn't tell which would finish first—the thing that was happening or what Gendron was saying about it.

But while Mount had grown up believing what a fruitful thing it was to look forward to the future hopefully, Gendron gave a strong example of just the opposite. When Gendron looked ahead his mood would darken, shoulders hunching up around his neck, and Mount would stand by ready to agree with anything he said just to keep from getting in the path of all those black thoughts that could shoot out in any direction like a gun.

"Well, he's like that again," Mount would answer whenever Mother Danilecki came asking—which she was doing more often now since Gendron's moods were creeping into plain sight.

"It's a frog in his brain," said Mother Danilecki, explaining that the tiniest frog was small enough to enter through the ear and lodge inside, maturing until it was large enough to change a man's whole being. Mount thought Mother Danilecki ought to wrap white gauze around Gendron's head to see if that did as much good for him as it had for Mount, who was fully recovered.

One day Gendron kicked over a bucket of water for no good reason just as Jack Berlin was bringing some stranger by to look at Chloe. Mount laughed when the bucket went over. "You kicked the bucket!" he yelped. But that was before he saw the legs of Jack Berlin and the stranger on the other side of Chloe.

Mount figured Gendron had done this on purpose, wanting Jack Berlin to be embarrassed in front of a guest. But what Mount saw afterward on Gendron's face was pitiable and confused, as though his foot had done something strange.

The circus was spending a week in Washington. The indoor exposition hall had an arched, milky-glass roof that let in the light all day and made the air hot and dry to breathe. Chloe needed twice the normal amount of water to spray herself so she would stay cool in the strange, unmoving climate. Mount kept busy fetching it for her, wishing he could set up a sluice from the distant spigot to Chloe's pen, where the

215

straw became fully saturated at least twice a day and had to be changed three times.

Important members of the government came by unexpectedly and said their names as though they ought to be recognized. One man asked Mount to drop what he was doing to demonstrate the steam organ for him, but Mount pretended to be a mute and just smiled and widened his eyes until they hurt and the man became nervous and left. In a circus you could do that easily without arousing suspicions. When animals made up half of everything in sight, people's expectations were upended.

"I could take off all my clothes and sit in there with the talented apes," Mount told Mother Danilecki, "and no one would care."

"Go ahead," she told him.

Semple Groves remained invisible, but Jack Berlin was in evidence everywhere. He came up quietly, wearing a special kind of shoe that gave no warning. Mount thought the missing lower arm might also add to his stealth, throwing the balance off so that extra care had to be taken. If every move was deliberate, you could set out to add quiet to it.

What Jack Berlin did after stealing up somewhere was stand still until he was noticed, almost as if the sole point was to be seen there, and only after he was greeted with a nod or a wave could he go on and be seen somewhere else. Sometimes when Mount had nothing to do he would hide and wait until Jack Berlin came by. Watching someone who didn't know he was being watched was always an education. You got to see the face compose and uncompose on a schedule that was based upon who the person believed was seeing it.

One morning in Washington Mount went four places with Jack Berlin inside the exposition hall, sneaking after him and verifying that his stealth was done carefully and deliberately. Then, at the fourth place, Jack Berlin turned around and caught Mount following, whereupon Mount pretended to sprain his ankle, letting out a gruesome cry that brought Mother Danilecki and others running and led to a series of test manipulations of the weak joint, Jack Berlin standing over and saying, "If it's broke we'll have to shoot him," and trying to get people to laugh at that, which they did. A couple of times Mount said, "I think I'm okay."

But before Jack Berlin caught him Mount had already decided that what he was seeing was a man who didn't have enough work to do going around trying to find it. If Jack Berlin had worked at the asphalt shingle factory in North Fort Wayne and the manager there had seen him walking around with nothing to do, he soon would have found himself cleaning the mixing tanks with a steel brush, a scraper and solvent, and falling down dizzy from the fumes. There, any display of aimlessness was a dangerous thing that could get you doing a task you didn't want.

Mount deliberately didn't look at Jack Berlin when he was getting up off the ground, but Jack Berlin found him with his voice.

"You be careful, there, young man. What's your name . . . ?"

"Mount, sir."

"Well, you be careful, Mount." And Mount knew it wasn't his ankle Jack Berlin was talking about; what he knew was that he had just become part of the work Jack Berlin had been walking around trying to find.

"Yes, sir," he said. "I will."

Being caught by Jack Berlin was haunting Mount, so he told the story to Gendron, whose reaction was to admire Mount more than he ever had before.

"You followed Jack Berlin around?" Gendron asked.

"I did," said Mount, his voice full of shame and bewilderment, as though he didn't fully understand why. But Gendron just smiled and bobbed his head from side to side in wonder.

"That's great," he said. "That's great."

Even though this wasn't what he had wanted from Gendron, Mount slowly got rid of his shame and began to smile himself.

"Yeah, it was pretty good," he said. "I guess it was." He started explaining all the places he'd hid in before Jack Berlin caught him out in the open near the curtained changing booths set up for the clowns to dress and put their paint on.

"How did his face look?" Gendron asked.

"Surprised," said Mount. "Just surprised, that's all." It was good to talk about being caught. With every word that passed between them the haunting grew lighter to bear. By the end Mount was even joining Gendron in imitating the uselessness of Jack Berlin's second arm, swinging it stiff and birdlike, which then led to the two of them bending down and imitating Chloe, trying to capture with their bony arms the suppleness of her trunk, which they could not do.

It was about that time that they noticed the four Swiss sisters standing

217

in an orderly row watching them fool around. The sisters had no expressions on their blank Swiss faces. "Empty, like the holes in cheese," Gendron said later. He told Mount he was sure they'd gone off and told Jack Berlin everything they'd witnessed, and he called them "cheese eaters," which Mount didn't understand and asked the meaning of.

"It means they're foreign enough to tell tales for their own devices, and don't you bet they ain't got that profit motive locked hard in them Swiss hearts."

But two days later Mount found out from Mother Danilecki that they weren't Swiss at all. She revealed they came from Savannah, Georgia, and that there was no language they couldn't pretend to speak and they had spent their whole careers being sisters of one nationality or another when in fact they weren't sisters at all and had grown up on the same street in Savannah and concocted this fraud with the help of their four mothers. The mothers continued to advise them by letter—each taking her turn writing to the four together as though it was all one grand sorority, one mother to all the daughters and one daughter to all the mothers. And now the sisters had taken Mother Danilecki on in a sort of honorary capacity—the fifth mother—and were telling her everything, even doing her the honor of telling it in the accent of Mother Danilecki's native Poland.

"Well, how about that?" said Mount.

The Swiss sisters probably wouldn't have told Mother Danilecki anything or made her an honorary mother if they had known she would tell their story to someone like Mount. But the brilliant thing about Mother Danilecki was that she knew intuitively that she could tell Mount anything she wanted and he would make no use of it whatsoever aside from being momentarily astonished or entertained or struck with grief or happiness. This was just something Mother Danilecki knew about Mount without being told and that the Swiss sisters were better off not having to think about at all, since they didn't trust anyone. They didn't even trust Jack Berlin, who had also come from the same Savannah neighborhood and had known one of their mothers well and, through that connection, had hired the four daughters to be Swiss sisters in his circus, half of which of course still belonged to Semple Groves.

Mount didn't know what to think. He was more amazed that they weren't sisters than he was that they weren't Swiss. They looked so much alike. They would be standing together not doing a thing, and somehow it would come across how much they shared with each other but didn't share with anyone else, as though the same thoughts whispered through all of their heads at the same time. One mouth would move, and the other three would seem to follow along exactly alike. And suddenly there would be singing, and the epitome of unison.

"It must be the result of training," Mount told Mother Danilecki. She shrugged.

This was the final day of their stay in Washington, and an exciting rumor was circulating that the president himself was coming to the show that night and would consent to ride a horse, provided his own saddle could be used. In fact, the actual rumor was that the president's saddle had already been delivered to the exposition hall and was being kept in a locked office, and if anyone wanted to go and check they could see members of the president's personal guard stationed outside that office door, protecting the saddle.

That was how solid the rumor was.

Semple Groves himself came out of nowhere and walked around with Jack Berlin. Mount saw them together and thought Semple Groves looked shorter than usual and that the smile on his face was thin and pathetic, all perfectly of a piece with the notion of death making steady progress. With his good right arm Jack Berlin held Semple's shoulder. Semple turned his head this way and that as though it hurt his neck. Mount nodded as they passed him.

He confided his impression to Gendron, about the death coming closer.

"You pay a pile of attention to what ain't got nothin' to do with you," said Gendron. "You'd think that skinny old man was kin to you."

"Well, he's not," said Mount.

Mother Danilecki turned out to be right about Mount not carrying tales. When he thought of the startling news she had told him concerning the four Swiss sisters, he decided to keep this to himself—as if it was a precious photograph of Mother and Father Mount standing in front of the house on Erie Street squinting out at nothing for the moment the picture froze them there. That's mine, Mount thought about his mother and father and the four Swiss sisters. That's family. Even though there wasn't any such photograph.

Gendron immediately began to talk about the president since he had heard all the rumors. He even described the saddle. It was nut-brown leather polished almost to the point that you could see your reflection. And the pommel had a silver cap with Spanish scrolling engraved to give it friction when the president grabbed it.

"That's good," said Mount, who—being the son of a mechanical-minded man—could appreciate any detail that had a deeper purpose.

When Gendron was through describing the saddle Mount asked him if he'd seen it.

"Yes I have," Gendron told him, and went on nodding his head in a way that told Mount there was more to this than simple honesty.

"And I done something to it, too," Gendron added. He wrapped his arms around his own shoulders, hugging as if to hold himself in a single piece, and began to laugh in rich, dark, Gendron-style bursts so that Mount knew well not to ask what Gendron had done nor to think about it again, which he tried not to do.

"You'll see, all right," Gendron teased, but Mount just tightened his lips and thought about the four Swiss sisters spending their youths pretending to speak foreign languages and to be related to one another.

Finally, after Gendron's tease had subsided to just a little bit of smiling and nodding his head, Mount relaxed and allowed the day to go forward effortlessly, seeing to the normal round of preparations and bringing Chloe twice the usual amount of water so she could spray herself down in the motionless, drying heat of the exposition hall. In the late afternoon, when Mount was on his knees taking the rasp to Chloe's blue-gray nails and feeling the air around him flutter with her pleasure, Gendron came and invited him to go for a walk.

"I guess you could say this was the North," said Gendron a few minutes after they had left the grounds of the exposition hall and turned right and then left and walked on in uncertain silence along a flat, treeless esplanade where the other people out walking looked small and unhappy, smitten and squinting in the sun.

"But it sure ain't the true North," Gendron continued. "And it ain't the true South neither. In fact, it ain't much of anyplace else since all it's really got is the seat of government. But I'd say it's surely more South than North, partly because of the food and the weather. And Baltimore's even more South than this is, despite it being up farther in that direction." Gendron aided Baltimore's Northness by pointing ahead of where

220

they were walking, whichever way that was. But Mount got the idea, and sure enough Gendron began to speculate about the four new elephants the circus was acquiring in Baltimore, though he didn't do so out loud—he just took on a kind of resignation that fell short of the usual belligerency that Mount had learned to adjust to.

"And after Baltimore we get to the true North, where you can say exactly what you want and people just accept it without feeling they ought to like it."

Gendron stopped walking and fell into a silence. Mount stopped and fell silent too, and the two of them stepped aside on the paving stones to let two knots of squinting people pass, all of whom looked to Mount as though they ought to be able to say anything they wanted and not care whether anyone liked it or not. They just brushed past.

Mount had learned to recognize certain behavior in Gendron, and it now struck him that he had figured out Gendron in much the same way as he had figured out Chloe—just by watching and comparing this thing to that. Which was the way his own father had mastered the arts of mechanical repair—by putting the thing in question on the dreary workbench and staring at it as if the thing was a tired or scared trapped animal that any second now was going to behave in a characteristic manner.

"Everything teaches you what it wants, young Jay," Father Mount would say, and the secret was to become good at watching, for which Father Mount had an inexhaustible patience, so that a machine could sit on his workbench for half the day without his doing a thing to it except moving his head around it this way and that until he had taken almost everything the machine had to surrender in the way of an understanding. And Mount would watch his father watch, thinking, What's he doing there?

That experience came in handy with a man like Gendron, or with an elephant, neither of whom said what was on their minds. So when Gendron stopped walking and fell silent, Mount had seen this before and had grown to understand it had something to do with acquiring those four new elephants in Baltimore, the Southerliness of which Mount took to be a riddle for Gendron's terrible dread of the future, which was indissolubly linked with death.

"That's too bad, Gendron," Mount said, shaking his head. Gendron just looked over at Mount and stared.

"What's too bad?" he said.

It wasn't like Gendron to want anybody's sympathy for long, so Mount let the feeling die in the air like the warm spring breeze that drifted along the esplanade like a slow old bitch looking for a place to squat.

"Never mind," Mount answered.

"Well, anyhow," said Gendron, "after Baltimore is where the true North begins, and don't nobody mistake it for anyplace else."

That night Teddy Roosevelt came to the circus and shook Jack Berlin's and Semple Groves's hands. Then he climbed aboard Nick, the palomino horse that his own saddle had been put on top of. He took three gallops around the big ring, and each trip the cheering grew louder until the inside stirrup snapped and the president fell off and sprained his wrist and his hip.

Mount felt Gendron's elbow in his ribs as they were standing off at the edge of the runway. Gendron laughed a hot raspy burst of secret laughter no one but Mount was supposed to hear. Members of the president's personal guard raced into the ring and picked him up off the sawdust as Nick kept on going around and around, slowing until, finally, he went down the runway by himself. Mount reached out and touched the shiny nut-brown leather and saw for himself the clean line where the stirrup had snapped.

"That was me," whispered Gendron. "I cut that halfway through from the back and made that bastard tumble."

Soon the president was led off down the runway too, looking shaken. He was holding his glasses in his hand and was limping.

"Are you all right, sir?" Gendron asked Teddy Roosevelt. But one of the president's personal guards elbowed him out of the way.

The next day was just a short ride up the tracks to Baltimore. The four new elephants were waiting there in a lot down on Howard Street, at the edge of the inner harbor and in the very shadow of the ship that had brought them from Europe. The ship was called the *Lucy Baggsby*.

Jack Berlin rousted the shipping agent from a tin shed. He had insisted that Gendron accompany him on this errand to collect the elephants, and Gendron had in turn insisted on Mount's coming. So the three of them were there together to get the four new animals and—as it turned out—one new trainer who the shipping agent, winking, sent a boy to fetch.

In the meantime Gendron performed the ritual he called first love, in which he approached the new creatures using a specific sequence of gestures that were guaranteed to demonstrate good will as well as a profound understanding of the varied and complex natures of the creatures being approached. These were gestures Gendron himself had devised and had not learned from anyone else, but they looked to Mount much like the dance that Whit Henning, the phony Navaho brave, always did to begin his sideshow, peering down off the stage with a scowl and his hand held out in the air in front of his forehead, chanting HYAhyahyahya-HYAhyahyahya. Still, Mount admired what Gendron was doing—creeping, crouching, spreading his arms out wide and turning himself in a circle, but doing everything slow and careful and making elaborate, generous stroking motions against the air between him and the elephants as though he was pushing it gently out of the way. Mount could tell the elephants liked it.

But he turned and saw that Jack Berlin wasn't watching at all. Instead he was looking in exactly the opposite direction, at the boy who had been sent to fetch the trainer returning with a very small woman in a shiny white helmet. This woman turned out to be the four elephants' trainer. Her name turned out to be Claudia Cruikshank-West, and she was from England.

Jack Berlin started smiling at her and striding forward before the boy had quite delivered her to him. Mount looked at Gendron, but Gendron was still going on with his ritual, crouching low with his feet spread wide, his hands on his knees and his back to this woman arriving.

"Claudia!" cried Jack Berlin, greeting her as warmly as if he had always known her. The sound of this stopped Gendron in the middle of slowly lifting one of his feet the way Genji, the Nipponese wrestler, might have done. The foot came down much faster than it had gone up, and Gendron backed away from the elephants, who were shifting this way and that in a clump and lifting and lowering their own feet slowly, as Gendron had seemed to be doing.

Mount saw Gendron see the woman trainer, and he looked like he'd been struck a blow. All the color went out of his face.

"Come over here, Gendron," ordered Jack Berlin, "and meet Miss Claudia Cruikshank-West, the premiere elephant trainer of all England."

Then Mount too got dragged into this business of shaking hands and smiling, though what he wanted instead was to go over and see what good had been wrought upon the four elephants by Gendron's special gestures. All the while he would glance at the elephants over his shoulder and think he could see a change that had come to them suddenly, as though Gendron had gone right up and rubbed their temples softly, letting them know he knew what they liked and knew how to get them to love him instantly.

"I can do this with women too," Gendron had told Mount more than once. But Mount looked at Claudia Cruikshank-West and was sure there was more to her than five minutes of Gendron's ritual could undo.

In fact, she sized up Gendron right away and told him her father Basil was the greatest elephant man in all the U.K. and that he had used these very elephants to help in the building of his private estate in Northumbria, which he had done in the Greek revival style with white stone pillars that a certain kind of vine would be trained to wrap itself around and, over time, to cover completely.

"Basil taught me the *awwlll* of it," she announced, stretching out the word to convey a fair suggestion of everything under the sun worth knowing. Then she took off her helmet and gave her head a shake, letting loose a fall of honey-colored hair that bounced three times after falling. "Didn't he, Jack?"

But without waiting for an answer she went straight to her elephants and made them lie down and stand up, assemble themselves in a row and mount each other's backsides; made them raise their trunks and trumpet, lower their heads and swing their trunks from side to side; made them link trunks and tails and go in a circle until she clapped her hands, which made them stop and circle backwards. She made them do a dozen other things that Mount thought rivaled the humanlike activities of the talented apes and made the few simple tricks of Chloe seem like nothing—foolish, tired and unskilled. And the woman did it all without a hook or a crop, using only her voice and her hands.

Jack Berlin was grinning from ear to ear. Mount knew this was the saddest day of Gendron's life.

"That's damn wonderful," Gendron said when Claudia Cruikshank-

West came back to them leaving her elephants up on their haunches like begging dogs. "And I mean that, too." She looked up at Gendron and smiled a smile that won Mount's heart. After that the rest of Baltimore was a blur—except that Mount noticed it was a town that admired and praised itself more than any other he'd been in.

Gendron always warned Mount to stay away from the freaks, but the warning wasn't necessary: Mount surely would have stayed away on his own. But in the North, the need to keep away was greater.

"They're much more ashamed up here," said Gendron. "That's because the audience don't seem to enjoy it as much and is quieter when they file on past and just sort of stare and then look away. Suppose it was you."

Suddenly Gendron had fallen in love with Claudia Cruikshank-West. Mount couldn't figure it. They spent all their time together sitting on a bale of hay trading secrets about the business, and what this meant was that Mount was working for five elephants, not just one, and had to learn what each was like and how to approach it. In the meantime Gendron and Claudia talked about Basil in England or Gendron's dead daughter or whether it was really true about mice crawling up the trunk into the brain. Otherwise they just sat there and watched Mount work, Claudia correcting him if he did something wrong with one of her pachys. On top of that, Chloe had turned strange and unpredictable now that there were four others around. Their names were Belle, Victoria, Tiny and Sarah, all females.

"Be careful," was all Gendron said to him about anything. He looked happy sitting still as long as Claudia was around. When they sat on the hay bale her feet didn't touch the ground and she looked like a child. Gendron sometimes asked Mount to get things for her that she didn't ask for herself. Mount thought Gendron had surrendered everything to her, and that she had got this by being nice.

But Mount didn't mind. He loved her too. She sat quietly and listened to Gendron warning Mount again about the freaks, and Mount got the feeling this was meant more for Claudia than for him, and he was jealous.

"Go on. Suppose it *was* you," Gendron said. "How would you like it if them people looked at you and then turned away their heads?"

"No, I wouldn't," said Mount.

"Well, see, that's it. In the South the people don't look away. They yell and heckle and talk, and them freaks do it back. So down there it's more like they're entertainers than freaks. And, all in all, that's a comfortable thing to bear, compared to here."

The circus had got all the way to Philadelphia, which was definitely in the true North, and when Mount thought about what everything had been like when he joined, the idea of the circus coming so far in so short a time was like a dream.

"I started out in Fort Wayne," he said, reflecting that he had come even farther than the circus. Claudia asked him what his name had been there, as if people changed them wherever they went.

"It was just the same, ma'am," he said.

"That's right," said Gendron, taking back the talk. "My name's been Gendron as long as I can think."

"And how about you?" Mount asked her.

"Well, not always," she said. "Basil and Mum called me Clara when I was born in India. Then Mum died of fever and Basil called me Dearie, after Mum. And then I was sent to school, where they called me Tina—because I was small and it sounded a dead small thing to call a girl Tina. And later I joined a show in Paris where I was put on the bill as Violette, though I answered to Letty and Vi both. That was shortly before I met Jack, who knew me as Claudia on two occasions—once when he was in London seeing Basil about selling the U.K. rights to some locomotive brake improvements he'd made, and again on an elephant-getting expedition to Madagascar that Basil invited him on."

Mount had never known such a small woman who wasn't a freak. When he said this once to Gendron he thought Gendron might be mad. But Gendron just seemed to think about this for a moment and then started laughing in a way that reminded Mount of the old Gendron, the one who didn't care what people thought about what he said and who didn't think about the future more than once or twice a year.

"You just stay away from *all* them freaks," he said, still laughing.

Then, late one night when Mount was almost asleep on the floor of Gendron's wagon, Gendron yanked him back from the brink by saying, "I'm gonna tell you what I'm doing so's you know it when you see it happen."

Gendron was propped up on his bunk with a silvery flask of whiskey resting on his breast like a baby. When he spoke his voice moved the air nearby and made the lamp flame leap and dive.

"What's that?" said Mount.

"Just you listen," Gendron said. Then Gendron revealed to Mount how he planned to take control of five elephants instead of losing control of one. And that explained his peacefulness in doting on Claudia Cruikshank-West and letting her have her goddamn way all the time and complimenting her.

"You'll see," said Gendron. "I just thought you ought to know in case of you didn't like the sight of the new me."

But Mount only wanted to go to sleep and cared nothing for the sight of the new Gendron. He could hear his breathing change even as Gendron was still talking, and he underwent one of those miniature presleep dreams: a wagon wheel was rolling along a dark floor all by itself, and a voice was saying, "It's a shame to fool something so little so bad." Mount figured the voice was a woman complaining about what Gendron was doing, even though she didn't know what it was yet. The wagon wheel was what her voice was coming from, and Mount found it pretty to look at rolling.

"Wake up!" said Gendron. But Mount pretended he couldn't until it was actually true.

Jack Berlin came to him one day and said, "I know what your chum is up to," and pointed his good index finger at Mount's nose and smiled. Then he took two steps back and turned and walked away. Mount wished this would happen again exactly the same so he could figure out what it meant. But he didn't tell Gendron, who went on seeming to love everything in life.

There was a river in Philadelphia with a stupid name, and Mount and others kept on trying to say it the way they would hear it said, imagining how it must have been spelled to account for being said that way. A session of joking around such as that made the day lighter, after all the buckets of water and bales of straw that he was hauling for the five big elephant ladies—Chloe and Belle and Tiny and Sarah and Victoria—though he meant to keep thinking he didn't really mind all the work.

One of the things that happened in Philadelphia, aside from the confounding name of the river, was that Chloe began to learn new acts and Mount spent more time with Claudia, who would sometimes lean over where he was working so that the fabric of her blouse billowed down and touched his shoulder, which he never failed to notice.

She always said something nice at that point, putting the cool British twist on regular American words so that Mount heard a freshness in them that probably wasn't really there.

"Yes, ma'am," he would say, and try to turn his head just enough to take in the smell of woman's work that was coming off her. Even when he was kneeling and she was standing, they weren't that different in height. Gendron would joke at night about doing things to her small body, and this made Mount feel the purity within himself flow stronger than at any other time. He always tried to find something useful in Gendron's meanness and bitterness, which was the only way to like him and go on living on the floor of the wagon as a friend.

On the third day in Philadelphia Gendron took Mount aside and complained that he was spending too much time with Claudia, and what was the meaning of it?

"There ain't no need for it," he said. "And besides, I want her close to me so to keep the plan in motion." He raised his eyebrows.

Mount tried to tell Claudia this without telling about the plan itself, but she put a cool hand up around the back of his neck and said she preferred his company on a steady basis to Gendron's, and she didn't like sitting on the straw all day and not keeping touch with her herd, as she called it.

"Well, you ought to talk to him, then," Mount said, "because he'll take it right out of me if this goes on like this."

"Are you telling me to go away, then?" she asked him, frowning.

He didn't answer. She had a way of putting her hands on him that made his head buzz hot, and she took the one from off his neck and moved it down to the pit of his back and pressed upon him with the heel of it, saying, "Don't worry about Mr. Gendron, Mount. Don't you see how Chloe's coming around?"

It was true. Chloe was doing new things, and her unpredictable moods gave way to what looked to Mount like eagerness, which he recognized from the recollection of certain schoolmates in Bolusburgh who were proud to turn everything they didn't know into everything they did. And Chloe grew abler and abler to repeat things until they were perfect, as if she herself had grasped what perfection was in these things and wanted it just as badly as Claudia did when she clapped her hands or shouted out a command.

Sometimes when Mount was working in the ring with Claudia the five elephants would seem to come together in the style of a single machine, fulfilling a single purpose with their joined obediences, until the noises they made were only one noise and the trail they stamped through the sawdust was only one trail, and they'd become blended. Mount could sometimes close his eyes and feel it, the single blood, as though this flowed through them all electrically—from trunks to tails in a circle, endlessly. He saw them as so much a part of each other that it filled him with envy. And he wondered what chance there was for an ordinary person to have such a unity.

"After that," he asked Claudia, "how can they stand to be by themselves?"

She threw back her head and laughed like Gendron. Because Mount was so much taller, he could look all the way down her throat to where it got dark. He sniffed at the small wind rising up from her laughter and was surprised at its sweetness.

"They can stand it," she said. "Oh, yes, they can."

For a day longer Gendron sat back watching. In an uplifting voice he called out to Claudia now and then to ask if she wanted anything, a lemonade or a soda biscuit, or a shawl if there was a chill in the air. She always shook her head.

"No thank you, Mr. Gendron," she would say. "So kind, though." More than once Mount looked over and saw the smile turn damp on Gendron's face, as if he was trying to swallow it from the inside out.

That night he got Mount in a hold when Mount stepped into the wagon. The forearm flew across his throat and banged there smartly.

"Now, look," said Gendron, forcing Mount's wrist up behind his back, "you better watch out what you're doing with her." The whiskey-smelling words were hot and sour around his head.

"Doing what?" rasped Mount.

It was then that Gendron, trying to trip Mount, slipped and fell himself, dragging Mount down, and was rendered unconscious from hitting his head on the edge of the bunk, so Mount had to postpone temporarily learning what he was doing wrong. The wagon rocked and settled on its springs, and Mount found himself sprawled on the floor with Gendron's arm still clenched around his neck.

"Gendron?" Mount said. "Gendron?" But there wasn't any answer. Mount picked himself up and looked at the man and thought at first, "He's dead," but then saw the chest breathing in and out steadily and the eyelids fluttering like the tiny legs of a just-crushed insect.

Mount waited until Gendron was restored to his old self again and sat up half the night with him hearing him go on about the bygone days of the circus and what they had meant, and about all the people who were gone now and how much better they had been than the ones who replaced them, both in the way of what they could do and in the fine qualities they possessed. When the night fell silent around and through the wagon, Gendron would call out one of these old names in a preacher-like way and shake his head at the magic of it, sometimes even starting to weep, whereupon Mount would suddenly pretend to be absorbed in an itch on the side of his body farthest from Gendron, scratching until a decent time had passed.

They also talked about the future and how it should allow a man to go on doing the same thing year in and year out and not be cut off uselessly like Jack Berlin's bad arm just because there was somebody come along who could do it different.

"That's it, see?" Gendron said. "I got no damn interest in doing anything new. My wants is just to carry on with the usual bits and pieces and to stick with the same old hoi-polloi that I'm used to. And not to have to think about it or worry about it that here's this goddamn lady dwarf in a pit helmet getting set to watch Jack Berlin scuttle my butt in Philadelphia. No, sir. No thank you at all."

Then he drank from the silver flask and wept some more and, eventually, went back through the Claudia plan again, detailing how he thought he could turn her head and body around using simple kindness, peaceability and charm, it constituting a known fact that any woman that small had a lower resistance to flattery on account of being unsure of herself among taller men and needing to combine with one to keep from seeming too unusual and losing her power because of that.

"And where's this goddamn Basil *now?*" sneered Gendron, meaning Claudia at the present time was lacking in an important connection that he had nominated himself to provide.

"You mark me, Mount. She ain't long able to withstand. Otherwise, it becomes like you said, and all she is is a little freak lady."

But then silence fell in the wagon and Mount saw the fear creep over Gendron's face.

"The thing of it is," he said, "I just figured it'd work by now. And it ain't." And then he was weeping again.

It didn't work the next day either.

By then the transformation was finished and Chloe was as thoroughly blended with the other four elephants as if they'd all been whelped together on the African savannah.

"Look at our ladies!" said Claudia, slapping Mount on the back. Mount was tired out from being with Gendron, and Gendron was sitting listlessly on his bale of straw, pretending to smile and spewing forth corny compliments, sometimes getting up to adjust his trousers before sitting down again.

Jack Berlin came by around noon and asked to see Gendron in his office, which, in Philadelphia as elsewhere, was a joke for wherever convenience said the office was. So he just led Gendron away to a quieter corner of the public auditorium and gave him what Mother Danilecki later told Mount was a mean and unconditional ultimatum of farewell and goodbye. Witnesses saw Gendron smack Jack Berlin in the face with an open palm, and saw Jack Berlin strike back, hitting Gendron on the side of the head with his walking stick and leaving a bright red mark that crept down out of the hairline to the cheek, where it ended in a spreading purple bruise.

Later Mount watched him get ready to go. The door to the wagon was open, and Mount stood outside as Gendron moved around within, causing the space to dip and tilt and groan. Gendron pretended Mount wasn't there. When Mount asked him a question, Gendron wouldn't answer.

"Where are you going?" Silence.

"What happened with Jack Berlin?" No reply.

"How did you get that bruise?" More silence. The wagon rocked angrily.

Finally Gendron came out with a bag and stood in the doorway hunched, squinting in the sun.

"It's all yours, and whatever's left inside," said Gendron. "You worked your way up to the goddamn bunk. Good luck with Chloe and them others."

Then he went to say goodbye to Chloe and Mother Danilecki and a few more. And after that he was gone. Mount saw him go from Chloe's pen but didn't see him go for good. The story was that Semple came out of somewhere, looking agitated, and pressed some money in Gendron's hand. Then the two of them went their separate ways out of sight. Semple was like a ghost, and Gendron just disappeared into Pennsylvania.

That evening Mount sat in the wagon alone and looked over what was left. It was just the Bible and that other book, the one with the man and the woman naked on one page after another, standing and sitting and lying together—and smiling as though they believed it was fine to do it.

After the show that night Mount was ready to try the bunk for the first time. He was tucking the blanket at one end when he heard a knock. Before he could say, "What is it?" The door opened behind him and he turned and saw Claudia letting herself in and smiling.

13
UNLUCKY

It turned out Chloe missed Gendron.

No sooner was he gone than she seemed to know. Mother Danilecki stood there, watched him turn the corner and marked the change in Chloe, the next day describing it full of hocus-pocus, telling Mount it was as if a storm had come down out of the sky invisibly, had crept in Chloe's ear and then expanded through her interior like anger, dulling her hide.

"In the eyes was where it most showed," Mother Danilecki said.

Right away Mount had to go and look at the eyes. The circus was just then getting ready to load up and leave Philadelphia, so taking the time to consider the thing properly was hard, but Mount thought the eyes looked the same as always—too smart for a thing that big. He offered her a treat of acacia leaves, which she took from him in the usual eager way, the tip of her trunk curling back to her mouth, the mouth chewing slowly as the eyes drifted shut and the big gray bulk swayed from side to side.

"You're still happy," said Mount, and he walked away not bothered by a thing.

But later, while he and Claudia were marching the five elephants down to the train, Chloe's shoulder strayed into the side of a wagon and tipped it over, spilling out coils of rope and canvas bags full of spikes and turnbuckles, brass eyelets and other rigging materials.

"Chloe!" Mount shouted, and she suddenly turned her changed eyes upon him and showed what Mother Danilecki had described—a storm

233

inside that hadn't been there before. Two of the wheels kept winking around as roustabouts and riggers came running to fetch the wagon back upright. They hollered at Chloe and Mount, and tried this way and that to lift the thing off its side, but without success. Then Chloe reached out her trunk and helped, and the wagon came up slow, and she was all right again, standing still and seeming peaceful.

"Damn!" said Claudia, squeezing Mount's elbow hard. "Damn! I didn't ask her to do that."

From then on Chloe was hard to work with. She did only what she wanted to do and not what she didn't, and Mount thought maybe she needed a taste of the old familiar by getting a chance to put her foot on his head again—which she hadn't done in two towns and nearly three weeks. But Claudia looked at him and scoffed.

"It's a blessed miracle that beast didn't turn you to a pudding, Mount," she said. "Never tempt a thing to hurt you. Because, don't you worry, it'll go ahead and do it."

There were three days to play in Newark as a warm-up for New York. The tent came out and was raised on a good spring afternoon in a fragrant fairgrounds where the grass was high and the horses were set loose to graze. The wagons made a town-like camp, and people kept their doors wide open and went from wagon to wagon socializing like neighbors. Two of the dwarfs appeared and rolled in the grass like dogs, wrestling each other and kicking and laughing. Boys from Newark who had traveled out to see the setting up wandered around gawking and looking to find some opportunity for themselves.

"We're only going across to New York," Mount told one boy who stood there looking eager. "That's where it all ends for the season. Then in the fall we'll start going south again."

The boy nodded, but then he turned out to be deaf and a friend had to come lead him away to see something else that he himself wasn't making the decisions about. He just smiled and let himself be led, and Mount watched him go in a hurry and heard his voice making sounds like a baby.

Claudia picked out a spot where a large enclosure could be set up and strung with picket wire to keep the elephants chained and hobbled inside of. Mount drove the stakes while Claudia paced off the distance to the next one and stood waiting at each like a destination. In this way slowly a circle grew and closed.

They led the elephants in and waited until they were settled where they wanted to be. Then Mount went from one to the other and drove the iron spikes that anchored the chains attached to the cuffs encircling the elephants' forelegs. As he hammered Chloe's spike, Mount felt her trunk sail back and forth over his hunched back like a sword, whispering through the air with a will of its own.

"Will you look at that," said Claudia. "Will you look at that." Chloe raised up her head and trumpeted sharply. Mount thought it might be best to crawl out fast, and he scraped his back scrambling out under the picket wire.

Then he hung the sign that said KEEP OUT.

When things were quieter later and a knot of people had formed up around the cook wagon, Mount went back to the enclosure and crept inside and wandered among the five elephants, some of whom were sleeping. They were all apart from each other, and reminded him of a certain clump of quiet houses down on Erie Point in Bolusburgh. No one lived in any of the houses, and children in his youth had gone there sometimes after school and had stood around wondering why they were empty, peering in at the bare floors beyond window sashes where dried-out bugs that had lost their shapes were stranded in tattered webbing just inches from the children's faces. No matter how long a boy imagined someone would suddenly walk through one of these empty rooms, it never happened. At the most a bird might have come down the chimney or flown in through a broken window—a crow going busily across the floor as though looking for another crow or the way back out. Maybe sometimes it was a squirrel. But there were never any people, and none of the boys he knew who stood outside was willing to find a way in.

To Jay it was better like that. Each house was exactly what it was, unbothered by people, and he liked to think that no one was ever inside and that all the small changes he noticed from one time to the next were caused mysteriously, either by the houses themselves or by the wind seeping through and moving something by inches every day for a week, then the next week back in the other direction towards a door that, by itself, was opening wider and wider as another Friday neared. A single shoe glimpsed in a shadowy closet was like something swallowed up lifetimes ago, and was no more connected to the foot that once had fit it than the lost bronze bust of Tyrus Portman Bolus, Sr.—now probably burrowed deep in the mud beneath five feet of Mississippi River—was still connected to J. Fielding Mount. The shoe belonged to the house just as the bust belonged to the river.

Except for those houses in Bolusburgh, an elephant was the only thing Mount had ever known that was so exactly itself. And when he stood near Chloe he felt about as close as he had felt to anything in his life. The word he used to describe it was *love*.

"Hello," he said to her. She opened her eyes, light sleeper that she was. In the distance, from the vicinity of the cook wagon, Mount heard the clash of tin forks and tin plates and the sounds of people talking and laughing. Chloe's trunk snaked over and ran itself up and down Mount's body.

"That's right," he said. "It's me." Then Chloe turned away from him and suddenly swung back sharply so that her trunk struck the side of his head and knocked him sprawling, his elbow sinking into a warm loaf of fresh manure just astern of Sarah. All of the elephants rustled their chains and swished their tails.

"Goddamn!" said Mount. "Goddamn you, Chloe!" He picked himself up and stood there angry. "No house would ever have done this to me," he said. Then he walked back toward the cook wagon.

Something in the manure made his elbow itch for the next three days.

On the nights it could be arranged, an attachment was formed between Claudia and Mount. The attachment had started that night after Gendron was gone, when Claudia came in and said she had had it burning in her mind for so long. She took off her helmet and shook loose her hair. Then she spun the helmet down to the floor where it clattered like a bowl. She was so small that Mount thought of her as a child and backed away at first, trying to feel the purity flowing within himself just as Dr. Milan Mastergeorge, of Bolusburgh, had told him life intended it should.

But Claudia said, "It isn't *bad*. Truly not." She came a step closer, stopping first to take up Gendron's book with the pictures of the man and woman, and held it open to show him. "See?" she said. "It's only two people enjoying a well-known fact together. If it was bad it wouldn't be here in this book."

She took another step. Mount's head started ringing, and the ringing grew so fast that it soon spread down through the rest of him until it was much too powerful to stop and was organizing events on its own. Mount knew then that he'd been invaded by that restless, invisible force that Mother Danilecki theorized floated loose in the air in search of mischief to do. In any instance of choosing between two things, that force could make the difference, and when the ringing reached its fullest pitch Mount knew there was nothing to do—it had come and taken its opportunity.

He and Claudia tried it twice that first night, once with the lamp blown out and once with it lit. She was small and active, seeming to spin and crawl without going anywhere, ending up like an overturned turtle—arms and legs moving slow, eyes squeezed shut, teeth bared, and a thumping sound down deep in her throat as if an even smaller person than she was in there banging to be let out.

"This is pretty good," said Mount in the quiet afterward. He blew out the lamp, then lay there fearing this could happen again and again and that he might never give it up and would be caught at it sooner or later and punished severely and not have the purity flow within him again, it having been repulsed and set in flight like someone good who had witnessed a murder on the way home from church. He was dismayed.

"Chloe'll know," he said.

"She'll know what?" asked Claudia.

"About this between us."

"What rubbish," she said, and laughed. Then she put her hands upon him and tried to get the ringing going again, which was easy enough and successful. And all Mount could think was, "Now I'm trapped." He imagined it could last forever, the invisible force setting up inside him permanently and bringing mischief to bear on one moment of choosing after another, never leaving until it had done the one final great mischief that cost him everything he had.

"This is pretty good," he heard himself saying again as the ringing inside him spread like an overflowing river. The rich, deep pachyderm smell filled the wagon that night like a cloud. Below them the wagon's iron leaf springs moaned as the room sagged and swayed.

* * *

"Now that we've become the very best of friends," Claudia told Mount, "we'll have to be partners too." She said she planned to go to Jack Berlin and ask to have Mount's name put next to hers on the billing.

"It's as good as marriage, ducks," she said. "In fact better." And Mount answered, "Thank you," imagining the *J* and the *F* and the *Mount* plastered up in a place where anyone might see them—even on a low wall in Bolusburgh where Father and Mother Mount might pass and think, "I wonder if that's our Jay?"

Slowly she began to take his arm in public, and he would want to snatch it away since her gait and his were different, and to hitch the one to the other was a complication she seemed not to mind, but he did.

He asked her if she thought they ought to be married in actuality, and she replied simply that she already was—in England, though under a different name and to a man that she said would never come looking because he was "too bloody stupid to cross the road, never mind the sea."

Mount still thought of the wagon as Gendron's, but Claudia told him it was his. "You deserve it, too," she said. If he ever said he missed Gendron she would shake her head and snort. When she came around at night she didn't knock at the door, she scratched. She always had her helmet on, and she always took it off and spun it down to the floor, and smiled as it clattered while she was shaking loose her hair. Then she would pull him this way and that around the wagon, pretending to teach him dancing and getting down on her hands and knees to position his feet through a series of steps, but then finally reaching up to undo his belt to set off the ringing and heat inside him.

"I've made it happen," she said one night in the dark. "Everything in my life. I've done what I wanted and made it come true. I have the will of iron, and nothing can shake my wishes out of me. That is the very minimum required to become a trainer of any species. Size is not important, as you have certainly learned."

On the second day in Newark Chloe refused to do anything. She refused to stand and refused to eat, and Mount lost his temper with her, poking a handler's hook into her hide to try to get a single muscle to perform some work. But she didn't budge. The other four elephants, out in the middle of the fairground demonstrating remarkable abilities, would now and then glance over at Chloe and look away quickly, as

238

though they knew she was failing at something fundamentally easy. Mount felt their rebuke.

"No food," he said. And though she showed no inclination to want it, he bent down and gathered up her hay like laundry and carried it away. Then he went and sat on a bale of straw as Gendron had used to do and smoked a cigarette, wishing Claudia was sitting there beside him so he could put his hand on her knee and feel it squirming inside the pants leg. Instead, she was dashing around in the sunlight like a small swift collie, putting the four through their paces. Mount watched them rise on their hind legs and paw the air with their forelegs.

He thought, "They look so stupid."

But then he remembered what Claudia had told him one day in the ring: "What a damn fine thing it is to make a beast do something so unnatural. It has nothing at all to do with them—it's us! It's a demonstration of what *we* can do. For their part, *they* are just stupid, too stupid to keep from doing what they so plainly hate to do."

And yet here was Chloe showing this theory wrong by doing nothing at all. Mount smoked his cigarette and tried not to look at her, so angry was he over everything she refused.

"You'll see," said Claudia later on. "We'll have her dancing on a ball before too long. She's only just moping over Gendron."

But Chloe worsened in a terrible way—not by getting steadily worse to the point where she just stopped living, but by getting better for half a day and then deteriorating for the rest, or going up and down like that from moment to moment unpredictably. She could by turns be bright and affectionate, then surly and unresponsive; and there was no pattern to it. She may as well have been weather. If she was halfway into something—say, spinning a baton in her trunk—she might suddenly let it clatter, walking off like the spirit had just sagged out of her and left her vast interior empty and dead.

Mount thought this was eerie, but Claudia said it wasn't, it was only a dose of trouble. "The longer one spends among elephants, the less the vicissitudes shock one. Here is a perfect case of elephantine dementia. It will pass, or else it won't. If there was a pachy Bedlam handy, we'd lock her up for a time, eh? But the truth is, Jack Berlin ought to sell her posthaste. Too much trouble is too much trouble, no matter what."

Mount looked at Chloe lying on the ground in a heap, her trunk stretched flat like a culvert where the soil has washed away. He thought: She's too much trouble, all right, and he wondered what it would cost to buy her.

"Less than the cost of her keep for a year," said Claudia, reading his mind as clearly as Esau the Human Oracle could. "But more than you might scare up at one time, I'm sure." Then she looked up at the sky and clapped her hands twice, making all her four elephants come to her and kneel so she could choose the one to ride on back to the enclosure where they would be left until the final Newark show that night.

Mount waited another hour with Chloe, sitting on the grass cursing and pleading to no great effect. She lay there like some broken machine with all its belts disconnected. Mount imagined that if he only knew the right spot to massage he might fix her and hear the click of the cams sliding back into place and engaging the belts once again. This thought reminded him of the work of his father and the old familiar slogan from home: "The Best Sign of Love Is To Fix Something Broken." This was the truest thread that ran through his gentle Ohio upbringing. It might just as well have been stitched in the sampler above the old black stove where his mother would stand stirring something bubbling in the often-soldered pot using the shiny, often-glued wooden spoon.

He crept around in front of Chloe and tried to draw her eyes upon himself. But the lids were heavy and were wrinkled down around dark impenetrable half holes beneath which tracks of dampness meandered, making her look like she had been crying.

"Poor Chloe," said Mount. The tip of her trunk was near his hands. Suddenly something angry got into him and he struck the snout with his fist. Chloe moaned.

"There," he said. "We're even."

A little while later the spirit seemed to slouch back inside Chloe again, and she stood up and showed signs of virtue and obedience.

"Let's go back now," said Mount, and he began walking toward the distant picket wire where the other four elephants stood watching. Chloe came along behind and lay her trunk across Mount's shoulder, letting it be stroked.

"That's better," he said. "That's better."

* * *

But gradually Mount felt more and more alone, as though something good was turning bad. He couldn't have explained this, but he knew exactly how it went.

He woke up in the mornings and found the wagon empty. If Claudia had visited him the night before, she had gone sometime in the dark without his knowing, leaving the room full of mystery: something that had been true when he fell asleep was no longer true by the time he woke up. And yet there were traces of it—from the sheets the trapped sweet smell of her organs bringing forth recollections that Mount was at pains in her absence to say were real or not. He could close his eyes and hear her voice, which the dark enlarged and brought closer to him and filled with a kindness that, in the light of day, was gone. And when he was at the cook wagon for his breakfast coffee and roll, at the sight of her in her pith helmet—the brim of it nodding briskly at the level of Jack Berlin's breastbone—he would not know what to think about who she was and what she did to him.

She's telling him to sell Chloe, Mount would think. And that would bring out this feeling of being alone, leading him to take his coffee and roll some distance from the cook wagon and to sit with his back to everything, wondering what had become of Gendron and whether he had found a new elephant yet to take the place of Chloe.

That day they packed to go to New York. But they packed less carefully than usual because the trip was so short, and the gain from packing less carefully—far quicker unpacking on the other side—was thought to fully justify any chance that damage might occur during the ride across the railroad trestle into the heart of New York. Jack Berlin actually sent someone around to say, "Pack less carefully," and Mount thought to deliberately do a thing less well than he knew how to do it felt strange indeed. But that's what he did, leaving unlatched certain fastenings that he otherwise would have latched, and failing to clear the wagon shelves of breakable objects. And when they reached the other side—after unloading the train in a cavernous, torchlit space underground and marching through it to a gilded terminal, out into daylight, up a broad avenue and, briefly, sideways to a sudden, astonishing parkland where the tent was to be pitched in a vast meadow deep inside—the journey turned out not to have been so short, and the unpacking became a long series of wailed complaints about all that was broken, disarrayed and ruined, Jack Berlin going here and there apologizing abjectly and promising to set matters right at the end of the run.

At one point Mount saw him slap a hand to his forehead and cry out to the crowd of people surrounding him, "My God, are you *mindless?* No one told anybody to be so careless, did they?" But the complaining went on and on. One of the Swiss sisters was holding up a shattered porcelain doll, and the tears were streaming down her face and the faces of the other three, who clamored and pointed at its terrible cracked visage.

Mount thought: You'd think it was the fifth goddamn sister, and he felt at that instant as though Gendron had entered his mind from afar and left that statement there as a remnant of his gone-away self. Mount smiled, drifting between the past and the present.

In his wagon the only things broken were the ones that, by Gendron's account, had once belonged to and been left there by some long-ago occupant who could have been anyone: a ceramic Jesus-on-the-Cross had snapped at the knees from falling off the wall; a brown cow creamer was also dashed to the floor and in pieces; a traditional chambered seashell appeared outwardly to be intact, but rattled inside when Mount shook it; one of the several unlatched cupboard doors had banged a dent in the wall, perhaps causing the Jesus to fall. On the floor Mount noticed the small, now yellowed tooth that had once belonged to Freddie Blackhage. He put the tooth back on the shelf it had fallen from, then thought twice and put it in his pocket, where the small weight felt good to him.

"It's not so bad in here," he said, sitting on the edge of the bunk as Claudia appeared at the door.

"There's already scads of people everywhere," she said, amazed, and came in and drew the door shut behind her. "What a monstrous city this place is." She began to pick clothing up from the floor and put it where it belonged, which she had a natural instinct for doing. Mount wondered whose clothing this was—he had never before laid eyes on it and presumed it had come from some of the cupboards that he had never looked inside of and that had flown open and littered themselves everywhere.

"Is this yours?" she asked, holding up a collar. He shook his head, and she flung the collar to the floor.

"Jack thinks he's got a buyer for Chloe," she said. "They'll use her out at a place nearby called Luna Park. There's a big amusement there where pachys slide down a water chute into a pool and the crowds pay to see it. Jack says it ought to make for an easy retirement, eh? What do you think?"

Mount shook the shell and held it to his ear. "They say the ocean roars in here," he said, "but all I hear is an insect crawling." He took it from his ear and peeked inside, trying to see what it was. From behind the nearest chambered partition the slender leg of something crept in and out of view, but the whole animal didn't show itself.

"So, what about Chloe, eh?" Claudia asked.

"Well, she isn't mine," said Mount. "And how do I know what kind of a life it is sliding down a chute for people? Maybe not so bad, maybe fine. I don't know."

"Anyway," said Claudia, "it won't be for a while yet. Jack says finish the run, there's no hurry for it. That way you can get your mind ready to say goodbye."

"I feel like I let Chloe and Gendron down," said Mount.

"Never mind that," said Claudia. "It was Gendron who let Chloe down by getting himself in the thick of Jack Berlin where he didn't belong, love. Otherwise, she would have been aces and hearts."

But Mount stayed lost in thought, looking deep into the shell until Claudia clapped her hands and said she needed his help with the elephants. The sound of the clap rang back and forth off the walls of the small wagon. Mount expected something else to be dislodged by the noise and to fall and break, but he didn't know what. A spider crawled out of the shell, across one of Mount's fingers and then into space, hanging and floating.

Mother Danilecki arranged for Mount to see Semple Groves. By now this was like going to visit someone famous and ancient and wise—a legend who some people believed in and others didn't. Mount's aim was to ask him about saving Chloe from the chute.

This had to be done carefully so that Jack Berlin wouldn't know. The perfect opportunity presented itself on the second morning in New York. Mount woke up early when someone knocked at his door.

"It's me," said Claudia from outside. She came in quickly and took her clothes off. "Isn't this fun?" she said.

At first Mount thought she had been there the night before, but he wasn't sure. In his bunk, he lifted and fluttered the covers to see if her leftover smell blew out—which it did, but with only an inconclusive mildness. She came over smiling and got in with him and joined it—she and her smell. He decided she hadn't been there the night before.

"Jack Berlin's going to take me to lunch today," she said proudly. "At a place called Rudy's that Semple's brother owns." Then she reached down between Mount's legs. "Oh, what's this?" she cried. But quickly she slapped a stifling hand over her own still-gleeful mouth.

That lunch became the perfect opportunity. Mount and Mother Danilecki went back through the city the way the circus had come. Mount thought what a sight Mother Danilecki made walking the same crowded streets as the finest of New York citizens. She wore three different-colored skirts, her burlap blouse, two sweaters, a dozen brass, silver and China bangles colliding on each wrist, and nearly as many necklaces swinging back and forth, mixed together and clacking atop her heavy breasts. Mount saw how much it cheered her when people stared at her boldly. He smelled how it made her sharp perfume bloom stronger.

"All I want to do," said Mount, "is not be noticed at all."

"That's just you," said Mother Danilecki, looking straight ahead and smiling as the two of them forced oncoming people walking together to separate and rejoin once they had gone by.

Mount was relieved when they reached the gilded station and went back down into darkness, where a colored man with a hand lamp told them where they could find the train—second branching on the left to the third one on the right, and there it would be. He let Mount have his hand lamp. But Mother Danilecki suddenly stopped.

"Now, please, you go rest of way alone," she said. "Here I wait." She opened her straw basket and took out a small white kitten that Mount hadn't even known she had. She said it would keep her company, and the colored man, who had to wait there for his lamp to be brought back, said he would too.

"Go on," she said. "Dun waste no time."

Even with the hand lamp Mount missed the second branching on the left and had to double back a ways; then he mistook the second branching on the right for the third, following it as far as it went, a small lamplit room where four angry-looking men were playing cards and whispering.

But finally he got it right and found the cold, silent train reposing there like something sleeping and untroubled.

He crept alongside it as he had done once before, making his way to the final car where, Mother Danilecki had assured him, Semple would be waiting to receive him. He climbed the back platform and knocked on the door.

"Come in," he heard the voice say.

When Mount opened the door the medicinal smell of camphor wafted out. In yellow lamplight Semple was reclining on a low divan and holding a limp and camphor-saturated handkerchief in front of his nose and mouth like a veil.

"It's Mount!" he exclaimed, as though Mount was a great surprise of a Christmas gift. The handkerchief fluttered like a window curtain when he spoke. "How are you, m'boy?" It fluttered, but he held it in place. "Have a seat," he said.

"Are you ill?" Mount asked him.

"I am indeed," said Semple. "As ill as a man can be and still be alive and receiving visitors. I expect to be much better, though. I expect the off-season will revive me and bring me back amongst you all by autumn."

"That's good," said Mount, but he knew this was a lie and that Semple might die at any minute, a prospect that made Mount want to hurry the visit along and be on his way back out before it happened.

"What it is no doctor can say exactly," said Semple, continuing in the vein of illness, which Mount wanted left behind so that he could progress to the business of Chloe being sold.

"Sir?" he said. Semple looked at him like a startled ghost, wide eyed, ill shaven and confused.

"Yes, Mount?"

"Sir, I have a question about the elephant."

"Which one?" Semple asked. "I gather we now have several. Do you mean the original one that was Gendron's charge?"

"Yes, sir. That one's to be sold to a place that proposes to slide it down a water chute for public amusement. What I wanted to know was this: can you interfere with that sale if you want, and if you can interfere, would you do it please?"

"It's just a question of satisfying you, is it?" Semple asked. "It's you that wants this not to be done, and you're not here speaking for a large delegation of those who love this elephant so much they can't bear to be without her? Is that how it is?"

"Is which?"

"Is it just you alone?"

"That's right, sir."

"And how do you know it's so bad sliding down a chute? It sounds all right to me."

"I was just supposing, sir."

"Well, none of it matters a bit, don't you know, because I can't do anything anyway. You'd better go to Jack Berlin. Jack runs everything now and makes the decisions, and he is the only one who can unmake a decision he's already made."

"But what happened to you, then?" asked Mount. "Aren't you still here?"

"Well, as much as you see me, I'm here," said Semple. "But in the way of running things and so forth, I took myself out of the picture and left it to Jack. And I trust him to do what's sound and profitable— though I will say I was sorry he sacked old Gendron."

Mount wished it would go as Mother Danilecki had promised—that Semple would provide him with a great illumination which would begin to glow right there in the train tunnel and lead him through the rest of his life.

But now Mount saw that all he was was a sick old man who Mount could hardly remember knowing and who now couldn't do a thing for Chloe and didn't really care. In fact, Semple went on and said as much himself.

"All I can think of anymore is being sick. It takes up all my energy and time and interest. I'm completely devoted to it. And when Jack comes back here after such a long time gone and sees I haven't moved or improved, he just turns away and hunches up his shoulders and says he doesn't understand it. I know it's not a lack of sympathy—it's only that he isn't devoted to it the way I am. It's mine, not his. And of course he's overcome his empty arm, which makes him indomitable and intolerant all at once . . ."

Semple stopped speaking suddenly the way a person will who hears a bird in the bush outside. The room fell quiet. Mount got up and went to one of the windows and moved the curtain aside.

"Where are we?" Semple asked him.

246

"Underground," said Mount, trying to see if the light from inside threw out onto anything he recognized—the starry crystals of the granite tunnel wall.

"Then take me for a walk," said Semple, "and I'll see what I can do about that elephant."

Mount helped him up and felt how frail he was. They went out onto the back platform and stared down the tracks just as Mount had spied upon Semple and Jack Berlin doing the night he had found out Semple wasn't murdered.

"This is far enough," said Semple. "This is good."

But Mount didn't think there was anything to see. He held up his hand lamp and shined it down the tracks.

"That's hell down there, m'boy," said Semple. "I've even heard it. Hold that lamp aside and you can see the fires."

Mount did so and tried to see, but he couldn't make out anything that resembled fires. The strain in his eyes reminded him of not hearing the Old Music as quick as his father could, and of how hard he tried.

"Not the fires themselves," said Semple, "but only the shadows jumping down there."

And, lo and behold, when Mount tried again and adjusted his eyes for shadows rather than flames, he believed he actually saw them winking in the very deep distance, as though the tracks had dipped steeply down and to the side, and only then did the fires begin, their shadows reaching up from far below.

"You see?" asked Semple.

"I think so," said Mount. "So that's what hell is." He said he thought he heard something too.

Whatever Semple tried—or didn't try—to do on behalf of Chloe didn't work.

According to Claudia, reporting back from Jack Berlin, the plan was unchanged and was sure to be all for the good. Mount lowered his head and listened to this, and he let it sink in on the level of his best judgment and wisdom and decided he could accept it and agree with it. And that became the plan: Chloe was going to be sold to this amusement place and would spend her remaining days going down the water chute into the pool, pleasing the millions who would grow to love her for the giant splash she made. Mount shut his eyes and imagined the splash, the water going in all directions and getting on the spectators, who squealed and shook and laughed.

After he accepted Chloe's fate, another change came over him inexplicably: whenever he laid eyes on Chloe, everything about her disgusted him. This had never happened before; even the closest familiarity with all of her animal processes had hitherto brought forth in him only the tenderest regard.

But then one morning when he was bringing her a bale of hay, he heaved it down off his shoulder, straightened up and took a look at her and thought: My God, I've seen the fires of hell—though still not knowing for sure if he really had—and this pathetic thing is worse than that! He circled around her and looked minutely at everything and caught a whiff of every odor she produced, and the distaste steadily rose in him until his stomach and sense of balance both were afflicted. And he backed away and hurried to his wagon, where he flopped on the bunk and smelled her again in the leftover smell of himself and Claudia, since the two of them not only smelled like themselves but also, always, like the elephants.

"What's wrong?" said Claudia, coming to find him.

"It's her, it's Chloe," said Mount.

"Well, it can't be helped, I'm afraid. She's done for and sold, so you'd better make the best of it, lamb."

But then Mount explained to her how things had suddenly changed between them, and Claudia sat there patiently and listened, but then she creased her brow and shook her head, drawing her knees up close to the rest of her small body as if she had a shiver. She told him she just plain couldn't grasp how a deep affection could be modified that fast, especially if it had been true and original to begin with.

"Well, it was," said Mount. "I don't know any other way to be. It was there as I had always known it, and then all of a sudden it was gone and something new was there instead."

"What about the others? Is it all right with the others?"

"I don't know," said Mount. "We'll have to go find out."

But there turned out to be no problem with Claudia's four, only with Chloe. Mount was hard pressed to see any actual differences that could have accounted for a change arising with Chloe and not the rest.

Mother Danilecki watched the situation develop and proposed a theory that Mount was eager to hear. Like Gendron before her, though,

Claudia would stalk off when Mother Danilecki came near, returning only after the old woman was gone and pretending no interest in whatever she had had to say.

"Never mind," said Claudia on this latest occasion. "I'm sure it was the same old fish-wrap and claptrap. Wasn't it?"

Mount was coy, picking at his fingers and shrugging.

"Ah," said Claudia in a tone of triumph, "his silence is his assent." But Mount was content not to tell what was sure to be met with ridicule.

"Of course, claptrap is the rule with Mother D., is it not?" said Claudia, pressing on. "Mumbo-jumbo is the modus operandi and ingrained trait. I would go so far as to call it national character to the Poles, eh?"

This went on for quite a while before subterfuge was shed and Claudia first begged, then threatened, as a last resort, the threat being something that Mount wasn't altogether sure he was opposed to—that she would cease her nighttime visits to him and spend them on Jack Berlin instead. "Though I do completely detest the camphor atmosphere that comes with that particular realm," she said, and Mount was convinced she was in earnest.

"It was only this," said Mount, surrendering. "Mother thinks Chloe's being sold has somehow become known to her—Chloe—and that she is throwing up a barrier of disturbance that meets a like barrier thrown up by me, who is also upset at her leaving soon. And these two barriers mix and make this sudden disorder everywhere. It has the power to change my heart, she said. And that's the whole of it, I think."

Claudia smiled with what Mount wagered was just the pleasure of having gotten it out of him, and she said nothing further, which was nearly as bad as if she had laughed and rubbed his nose in how very foolish she thought Mother Danilecki was. The words themselves weren't needed for him to feel the judgment hanging heavily, and he was sorry he had given her such easy satisfaction. But she was ready enough to repay him for it, pulling shut the wagon door and peeling the sweater up over her head.

"I'd never do Jack Berlin," she said. "So put your mind to rest. Just think of that horrid flippy arm not getting even half around a girl as small as me."

But Mount was thinking instead about the one other thing Mother Danilecki had told him: "When tings like dis, better damn be careful,

249

Mount boy. Get too mixed up too close, she take her anger right inside you. And den what happen, huh?" Mount didn't know.

Because it was New York, people were always hanging around, no matter what time of day or night. The pattern was never like in a small town where people would come in ones and twos or families—and always only to see what the circus was up to. The New York people came in clumps of two or three couples, six men, eight boys, a dozen priests, two even rows of little girls holding hands. And they were often on their way to someplace else, and the circus encampment was only a point in between that was visited the way a tavern along the road was visited—an ale and then off again.

Watching the people come and go was dizzying. Jack Berlin sized up the pattern of traffic across the park and put the ticket kiosk where the greatest densities intersected. Then he installed albino Claire in the saddle of Fleeta, the whitest horse, and had her graze him leisurely near the kiosk to draw people closer and talk to them in her small white voice.

"Please come see us tonight at eight," she would say as people strained to hear her. "And bring your friends and neighbors. And come see *me*," saying "me" the loudest as though it was the best thing anyone could see.

A lot of people bought tickets, and a lot more wandered into the center of the circus camp to see what they could without a ticket and without attending a proper show. Most of what they saw was the usual tedious work going on, and if they found pleasure in that, it was only the pleasure that people who aren't working get from watching people who are.

Many of these passers-through eventually got around to spending some time near Chloe, who was sequestered from her sister elephants and hobbled and chained from each of her legs, which left her not much freedom to move. A cordon and stakes encircled her, and Mount had posted a terse sign warning, DANGER ANGRY ELEPHANT—though she looked as placid as the meekest of the people watching her.

"I don't think she's angry at all," said one man. "Do you?" But no one answered him, and no one went inside the cordon. A lot of people just stood and stared at her quietly, and she swung her head around slowly, taking in the full range of her mobility, seeming to be standing guard over something that wasn't in plain sight.

Mount stayed away from her as long as he could, but then he would feel her drawing him closer the way Claire was meant to attract New Yorkers to the ticket kiosk. With a long-handled brush he was washing Tiny, Sarah, Belle and Victoria, dipping its end like the tip of a fishing pole into the small, sudsy bucket and launching it upward to scrub each elephant in turn, each standing as still as a wall to receive his attentions.

Over his shoulder he could see a large crowd gathered near Chloe while there was almost no one watching him wash the other four—only a handful of boys with bad skin and rough clothing who might have been as much as five years older than they looked, or maybe a year younger.

"I wouldn't do that crud for anything, mister," said one of these boys to Mount, pointing at the brush.

"Well, then, it's a good thing you don't work here," Mount replied, "because if you did I'd make sure you did this every day." The boy just looked at Mount and then at his friends and led them away to go see Chloe.

Mount thought maybe it was better when there was just an elephant alone and no handler around. He wondered what would happen if he went over there and stood with Chloe inside the cordon, as an experiment. Would the crowd thin out and come back over here to see these others?

He put aside the brush and wiped his hands on his pants. Chloe was looking right at him just then, in the middle of turning her head like a beacon—which she was always doing nowadays and which Claudia said reminded her of old crazed grandmums standing out on the porches of seaside hospitals. Mount lit a cigarette from a tin of ready-mades called Noah's Ark Brand, which had a picture on the lid of the boat and the animals' heads—including elephants—sticking out.

As he looked at Chloe and felt that same sudden disgust bubbling up, he could almost hear a hollow voice from inside her inviting him to come on over and make things right again. And he thought this might be worth a try, and that Jack Berlin could still be susceptible to a sound demonstration that Chloe was her old tractable self again, all smoothed over and pacified and willing to work along with the rest—no more phlegmatic tempers to recall to anyone that she had killed two men in Texas years before.

"So, what do you say?" he said to himself, stepping out of the larger cordon where Tiny, Sarah, Belle and Victoria had soap bubbles popping and drying all over their bristled hides.

Chloe fixed her big eyes upon him in a look he took for longing, which, the more he thought about it, made the disgust subside within him as he got closer to the crowd ringed around her.

"Coming through," he said. Some people turned around and looked at him already starting to duck himself down to slip beneath the cordon. They parted and let him pass by their hips.

"Watch out, that's a bad one, mister," one man said.

But Mount told him, "It'll be all right."

And when he had got inside with her it was all right. It was like being down in a corn field outside Bolusburgh, where the wind was howling all around save for this one particular row where the stalks were higher than the rest and it was still and peaceful, the turmoil mostly distant and unheard. This was the feeling of being where you belonged.

"Hello," he said. He reached out and patted her trunk, and he felt the disgust was almost completely gone. He took the cigarette from his mouth and held it down by his side. Although they were quiet as statues, the people watching outside the cordon stayed in Mount's thoughts, where they reminded him how brave he was to be there with Chloe after everything he knew. He was in underneath her head now, and the ears closed around and made it darker and warmer there. He scratched the underside of her mouth. A boy cried out, "Have her do a trick, then," but the voice seemed small and far away. It was a private get-together, and Mount didn't care if people did grow restless and bored and go elsewhere.

"I love you, Chloe," he whispered. Her mouth came open above him and breathed down the milky-sweet hay smell upon him, which didn't disgust him at all.

But then—as unpredictable acts had come to characterize her late disorder—she did a sudden peculiar thing. She reared back her head and squirted out a laughing dash of a shriek, then she brought her trunk down hard and resoundingly upon Mount's buttocks.

"Chloe!" he bellowed. The crowd was laughing. Mount looked around and glared at them. Chloe stamped her legs and rattled her chains.

"Goddamn!" cried Mount. "Goddamn you, Chloe!" And he went in fast underneath her and thrust his cigarette up toward her mouth and into it, where he heard the ember hiss against her tongue.

The rest was swift and terrible. The crowd that had bought no tickets got to see a thing they had never seen.

Chloe first moaned eerily, her head held high and her trunk stretched straight to the sky. Then she stopped the sound and swiftly murdered Mount, wrapping the trunk around his waist, lifting him up and dashing him to the ground with a force that people watching later reported had shot up through their feet to their knees and made them shudder. Mount bounced and settled, limbs trembling and eyelids fluttering for just the briefest instant. Then it got quiet as church. And only then did people come running.

All the while the thoughts had spiralled through him, and what was coming to him was known to Mount while it was happening, and it was much too late to stop it, the mistake already far behind him—shrinking in distance like something done in childhood. The smell of the awful burn rose into his nostrils as Chloe raised him up in the aching grip of the trunk he knew could be so soft and dexterous.

"This is fast," was what he thought at the top of the lift. He looked as far as he could see, and it wasn't very far at all. As the ground rushed up he remembered everything he could and tried to be ready. He sent out signals with his bursting heart, but he was gone before they left him.

14

EDISON AT BREAKFAST

When Edison read about the death of J. Fielding Mount in the newspaper two days later, with his vivid imagination he supposed that he had actually felt the stillness after the terrible impact. He believed he might have felt this at roughly the same time it was happening, though with a reasonable delay thrown in to account for traveling all the way from Central Park to West Orange, as if the stillness were the shadow cast by a small gray cloud across streets and neighborhoods, bridges, rivers, rooftops and lawns—the same shadow moving and touching millions in all sorts of walks of life. The account in the newspaper was merely a fuller description of what he had felt two days before, adding dimension and detail, which was really all a newspaper did—told people where they'd been, in case they hadn't noticed. Because, in Edison's view, the planet was like a largish human body, and anything that happened upon it must produce a twinge of one kind or another, so that a skirmish between Indian tribes in Nicaragua or the Pope of Rome washing the feet of the poor were events, on a global scale, akin to insects gnawing on the flesh of a man's extremities— he may have felt it happen, but he couldn't always pinpoint the cause. Therefore, if an elephant dashed a man to the ground in the heart of New York, some of that energy might go through the air and be felt elsewhere as a chill on the back of someone's neck for which the cause was not discernible. This was pure science. Who could dispute that whenever something happened it changed the world in some way that people were bound to notice?

He looked away from the cold, hard print and let his eyes unfocus and felt the ground shudder underneath him and saw the dust rise up sadly, silently from around the edges of the motionless man, this image then congealing into a fulsome memory of death as the mouth and eyes of the man did strange, unpleasant things that Edison didn't think he could stand to look at any longer.

"Oh, mother," he said.

Mina looked up from scraping her soft egg out of its shell down onto a golden square of toast.

"This man is dead," said Edison. "Remember this man?" He pushed the paper across to her and pointed at the headline:

ROUSTABOUT IS MURDERED

BY TROUBLESOME ELEPHANT

IN CENTRAL PARK CIRCUS

Mina looked at the story and slowly shook her head.

"It's the same man as in Florida," he said. "That we saw with his head stuck under that elephant's foot. Same man, same elephant."

"Oh, dear," said Mina. "That's terrible. Are you sure?"

He read her lips and nodded. He was very sure. He remembered the two names, Chloe and Mount, from a story in the Fort Myers newspaper months before, under the headline, CIRCUS HIGHLIGHTS! In fact, he remembered everything he read. He could name the capital of Korea and draw its outline on a map. And one day, when he had decided that all the world was too stupid and ignorant, and complacent about it to boot, he invented a test to prove this which he based on his own compendious knowledge of world fact.

"I can pass this test myself," he boasted to one associate, "and I do not see why the rest of America can't do the same if they are well read and better educated." The associate, who saw right off that the first five questions were beyond him, nodded sadly.

"Sure you can pass it," the associate had said. "You made it up."

"Yes, but I know the answers anyway," Edison had replied.

The image of the man with the elephant foot on his head had stayed with Edison for a long, long time. It had struck him then—and was drummed in now—that this Mount must have been a woeful sort of victim. Any man who voluntarily put himself in such a position was asking for something not too promising. From his seat at the circus,

Edison had bent sideways and seen the terrified face of Mount squash and redden until it was a hot, blotted-out shadow, not even human, waiting the only way it could for something bad to happen. And Edison had thought, I'm seeing a death, and wasn't at all sure which way he wanted it to go—what, among the few possibilities, promised to be the most illuminating. Afterward, his fascination had shocked him and reminded him of a day when, in lower New York, he had witnessed a tenement fire that it shamed him to have taken such pleasure in. And in boyhood he had watched a friend go under the water of a pond and had simply sat and waited for him to come back up, as though the boy had done something akin to climbing a tree and was as happy below the water with the fishes as he would have been above it with the birds.

Reviewing these events, he felt in himself the lack of some fundamental element of sympathy.

What dies is made to die, he always thought, a half-joking scrap of cheap philosophy that pleased him both in its truth (because *every*thing is made to die) and in its callousness (because it seemed to suggest there was no good reason to care). And also: All these others die for the rest of us to see it and be affected some way—but mainly to be glad we're left behind. If there was this defect of sympathy in him, he could think of no great way in which it had harmed him or set him back in life.

After a while, when the boy did not come back to the top of the pond, Edison had felt abandoned and wandered home, saying nothing about the incident until later, when the boy was missed, whereupon the pond was dragged and the body pulled up.

"What a shame," said Mina, caressing the headline with her fingertips as though the dense black ink encompassed the awe she felt about the sudden death of the elephant man. "What will happen now to the elephant?" she asked loudly, slowly and distinctly so that Edison could make out the words.

"Oh, I shouldn't think much," he said. "After all, the man provoked it, didn't he?"

Then he brought the coffee cup up to his lips and drew off some of the sharp, hearty liquid he called "Mina's corrosive brew," but never without swearing that was exactly the way he liked it.

15
CHLOE

Grieving Mother Danilecki talked to the witnesses desperately, putting her hands on their wrists in a way she could see repelled and irritated them but that also prevented them from leaving her presence without first telling her everything she wanted to know.

And there was nothing she didn't want to know, for she had already decided she would write a letter recounting the death, and that she would send it to the true mother and father out in Ohio so that they could read how their son had died. She was looking to find a good death here, one worth telling and reading about—one that was true and terrible and brave, to fill a mother's heart with love.

She swept from one to another of the witnesses like a herding dog, responding swiftly to movements away and pulling her present detainees along in tow, bringing two or more together and setting them to talking with each other, filling the pauses with questions to one, to another, to all of them, while keeping her hands in contact, smiling up or down or straight ahead and steadily into their eyes, forbidding them not to answer.

"He was friend of mine, you unnerstan," she said. "He was friend. It hurt real bad to lose 'im."

"Sure, lady. Okay."

More than once she noticed how someone looked down at her jewelry and saw it shaking as if it were living silver or brass or wood or porcelain that was trying to escape from around her forearms or neck. And she felt her skirts in a similar agitation, layers of cotton and crinoline crashing together like opponents in the darkness around her legs and waist.

It had begun when she took Mount's arms and dragged him out while Claudia Cruikshank-West set her small self in front of Chloe and made the elephant shrink back in shame—or in something that looked like shame but was probably only the fury draining out of her puffed-up tissues. Pulling Mount, Mother Danilecki noticed how nothing inside him seemed to be connected to anything else, the bones sliding this way and that, the body having no rigidity and plainly dead. She began to shake and cry, and she thought, My boy, my boy . . . even though she knew he was someone else's. Claudia Cruikshank-West came over from the elephant and knelt down saying nothing, squeezing her knees together beside Mount's shoulder and running a hand slowly up and down his front, his chest and belly and thigh.

"Oh, bloody hell," she finally said. She lowered her forehead to his chest and the bones moved, forming a depression that remained when she raised her head back up. In the center of the depression was a yellowed tooth, the sight of which Claudia found powerfully sad. She took the tooth and put it quickly in her pocket, vowing to cherish it as a keepsake. Oh, Mount, she thought.

By then other people had come running—among them Jack Berlin— and were asking important questions that Mother Danilecki didn't know the answers to but that put the idea in her head that she should find them out and create a history of that small part of Mount's last awful day. Her shakes got smaller and faster until her flesh was like a humming-bird, whirring invisibly. She noticed all the people standing around, some staring at Mount, some staring at Chloe, but all of them pale and wide eyed—the witnesses.

Jack Berlin put his one good hand on her wrist and stared hypnotically down into her eyes and said, "What happened?" And when she did not answer him he went down in the dirt next to Mount and felt for his pulse and put his head there next to Mount's mouth to feel a breath, because he had to do something.

"He's dead," said Jack Berlin, and put his fingers to the eyelids to close them but found they were already closed. Mother Danilecki started moving toward the witnesses while forming the first questions in her mind, exactly how to ask them and in what words, her imagination already hearing fast American answers blowing like a sudden breeze across her face, drying her tears.

258

* * *

Semple Groves helped her write the letter. They sat at the table by the window in the amber-lighted railroad car that was cloaked in the everlasting dark of the underground tunnel. Semple was in his green silk robe that Mother Danilecki noticed seemed to increase in volume the sicker he became. His cough was out of control and his hair was dirty. A sick smell hovered around him uneasily, as though it didn't want to be there but had to.

"I'll give you bath," Mother Danilecki said. But he didn't hear her because he was coughing, and the violence of the fit caused the letter's first page to be ruined when his hand shook and spattered ink upon it in a string of shiny black islands. He had to start all over again.

"Dear Mother and Father Mount," the letter began, "I have news for you so tragic that it hurts to convey it."

Mother Danilecki had gone to Semple because she knew his illness had not yet damaged the gift he had for the English language. She was never more in awe of any human ability than when Semple turned her rough utterances into sentences as graceful as horses prancing, as graceful as the memory of seeing herself unclothed in the tall family mirror at home in Poznan at the age of seventeen, her father standing behind her wearing a father's proud smile and his hat held over his heart. Later she had put on her several skirts and left Poznan for good, taking three peaches and a hatpin from her mother, who dressed at home in garments so sheer that sunlight from behind would show her shamefully at an age when the grace had left her appearance and could provoke no more than a scowl from her husband, Mother Danilecki's father.

She had long ago told Semple every part of her personal story and had watched him write it quickly and eagerly, the words flowing straight across the page like city blocks being built, Semple pausing only to dart the dry nib into the ink jar or to beckon Mother Danilecki to continue, to elaborate, to retrace her steps or to find a different way of saying much the same thing as she had already said. She would never have told him any of her story if he hadn't written it down, but the pleasure of seeing the beautiful black lines accumulate could have kept her recounting things minute by minute, she herself the fuel for the saving of all her memories. Afterwards, she would close her eyes and listen to him read it back to her—her life coming out in perfect English spoken by a man.

"Your son, J. Fielding Mount, has died in the City of New York while

259

toiling ably for the Groves-Berlin Traveling Circus. The circumstances persuade me that the death was mercifully swift and painless.''

She didn't know what "persuade" meant, but she trusted Semple to choose the words correctly. Sweat formed on his forehead and his matted hair glistened close to the scalp. He had already given his best contribution, advising Mother Danilecki to lie, to make a hero out of Mount instead of a fool—which Semple said he believed Mount was. To demonstrate, he had taken a cigarette from Jack Berlin and lit it, slowly bringing the orange coal closer and closer to Mother Danilecki's tongue until she said, "Uhnh! Uhnh!" and felt the hot spot spreading and—as she imagined it—turning the usual white film brown with singe.

"Uhnh! Hokay," she said, stepping back. Then Semple crumpled in a fit of coughing and had to be helped up and back to his seat. Mother Danilecki took the cigarette from him and handed it to Jack Berlin, who had been reclining on the divan usually occupied by Semple and saying nothing, as though she and Semple were an act he was auditioning.

"If he had not been so brave, the tragedy never would have happened and you could not now count yourselves so proud as to have been mother and·father to a hero. But that is the sad way of consolation: it is never nearly enough. Still, though, it is something.

"Here is what your boy did."

This was where the letter writing had stopped, with Semple and Mother Danilecki both staring down at their hands trying to think of what it was Mount had done to make himself a dead hero. Jack Berlin sniffed and rattled the newspaper. The smell of sickness seemed to freshen and grow stronger in the silence.

Then Semple dipped the pen and began to write. Mother Danilecki shut her eyes and listened to the scratching, a comforting sound like rain on a gray slate roof, a sound of things being healed and put right again, of something sorrowful and confused covered over with goodness and sense—a transformation. She imagined the dead Mount hovering somewhere near them, reading the words as Semple wrote them, the queer smile spreading across Mount's face—wet teeth shining between thin lips stretched nearly to whiteness.

"Here," said Semple. "What about this . . . 'He saved a young girl named Saracena, the daughter of one of our aerialists, when she foolishly came too close to Chloe, one of the meanest elephants in circus history and, now, the murderer of your son. Saracena chased a ball into Chloe's enclosure, within which the beast was chained and shackled. But no sooner did the sweet child slip beneath the wire than Chloe's trunk lashed out and snatched her.' "

Mother Danilecki recreated this peril in her mind's eye and saw the small girl in Chloe's grasp. She recalled a Saracena from many years before, a plain child with one gray eye and one green who used to be able to vomit at will and who, in the role of the Wild Daughter of the Far Fijis, would pick katydids and small frogs from her thick hair and hurl them through the bars of her sideshow cage at members of the audience. Later she would capture, kill, skin and cook what was said to be a Fijian rat, though in truth a substitution was made so that what she ate was really a rabbit.

"Oh, yes," said Mother Danilecki. "That perfect." Which made Semple smile a thin-lipped smile of his own that, unkindly, led to a fit of coughing. He recovered and began to scratch again, and suddenly the sound seemed to Mother Danilecki less like rain than like the restless whisper of time passing—of the years rolling over week by week and piling atop one another like husks. She had been with Semple more than thirty years. In that time her slim, sweet body had thickened, drifting looser, the flesh unmoored from the muscles beneath. Her hard white teeth had decayed and tarnished, seeping poisonous bursts of bitterness into her mouth. And when she had finally decided to love a man, it surprised her to find she was almost seventy years old, and looking older, and that the man of her choosing was hardly finished with his boyhood before he was suddenly dead and gone. J. Fielding Mount. It confused her. She sighed, recalling the thickness of his back and the way his calf muscles tensed like twin hearts nestled upside-down above each ankle, or bats sleeping powerfully. Dear to her were the memories of spying upon him as he wrestled with Claudia Cruikshank-West. She would peer through a break between the curtain panels in the window of his wagon door, her face so close to the glass that she could smell the changes in her breath as her excitement rose and fell.

Jack Berlin lowered his newspaper and looked at her. Semple stopped composing and said, "There . . ." Mother Danilecki was crying again.

"Such a boy he was," she said.

Semple read the rest of the letter aloud. " 'It was your son who first saw, then reacted to, this dangerous situation. Without a thought for his personal safety he rushed in quickly to save Saracena. Wielding a cigarette, the only weapon he had, he dashed right in under Chloe's trunk and thrust the hot coal into her mouth. Mercifully, the elephant released the child unharmed, but before your son could retreat, Chloe grabbed him in her trunk, raised him up and threw him down to the ground, where the impact killed him outright.

" 'I know how deeply this news must wound you both. You have only the greatest sympathy of myself and all in this circus who knew your son and now miss him so terribly. You should know, too, that the elephant will be put to death for her crime. Such malevolence cannot be rewarded with continued care and feeding, but must be punished with the only just penalty. You can trust that it will be done.

" 'If there is any help I can be to you, please write to me in care of this circus. When the site of his final resting place becomes known, I will send that information to you. I remain yours in this profoundest sharing of loss,' "

Semple handed the letter across the table for her to sign, and she formed the letters one by one, meticulously, as though each was important in its own right, like the separate movements of a somersault.

"I dun wanna make no mistake," she said, looking down and squinting at the result: "Marta Danilecki."

Semple nodded. Suddenly Jack Berlin started coughing, a cough that sounded for all the world like Semple's cough. Then Semple began to cough too, and Mother Danilecki was crying again, pushing the letter away from beneath her head so the tears wouldn't fall and smear it.

This is grief, she thought, loud and evil. And the dark car filled with the sounds of all three of them and of the newspaper shaking over on the divan where Jack Berlin held it so tight.

Mount was buried very simply: pine box, a hole in the ground in a secret corner of Central Park that Jack Berlin sent someone out to find. Trees wrapped around it, and a person wouldn't know to go inside unless he was told there was something there. And now, as far as Mother Danilecki knew, the only thing there was a grave. Jack Berlin was pleased with the secrecy of it, and so was Mother Danilecki, even though she hated Jack Berlin. At dawn they stood on opposite sides of the hole when there was no one else around and the secrecy was enhanced as much as possible. Roustabouts named Harold and Tiff and Billy and Jake took the ends of two ropes and lowered the coffin. Jack Berlin read from a book of verses and homilies, by one Walter C. Horrigan, that had been found among Mount's effects and was presumed to have meant a lot to him. What Jack Berlin chose was something called "On the Turning of the Century" that had to do with losing your way and then finding it again:

> Though Any of God's Wanderers
> Can Wander into Trouble,
> A Dose of Immobility
> Can Cure it on the Double.
>
> Let's Try the Door and Make it Sound;
> Let's Turn the Rascals' Life Around;
> Let's Take the Lost and Make them Found;
> And Do it 'Fore the Night Comes Down.
>
> Though Any of God's Wanderers
> Can Take the Crooked Turn,
> The Penitents Can Trust in God
> To Pay them what they Earn.
>
> And if they Will not Earn His Love,
> They'd Better not Forget:
> He'd Sooner Cast them Down to Hell
> Than Lose a Drop of Sweat.

Mother Danilecki thought the poem sounded fine but that Semple would have read it better. Still, as Jack Berlin finished a breeze stirred through the bower and rustled the leaves and people's hair and clothing, and Mother Danilecki looked around herself and saw that the others were doing the same, being penetrated by this breeze as if it were filled with meaning and awe. Then the roustabouts all at once started kicking the dirt down into the hole, where it made a racket on the pine lid covering Mount for the final time. Mother Danilecki bent down and took some dirt in her hands and brought it up to her face, where she closed her eyes and smelled it before she dropped it down into the hole.

Claudia Cruikshank-West had been given opium by someone. She stayed in Gendron and Mount's old wagon and smoked it for days on end. The shock of Mount dying rang in her ears and made her neck feel like warm butter and her legs feel like cold gin. When Jack Berlin came in and saw her he made her open her eyes and look at him, and all she saw was his tininess and his lips moving slower and slower until the words floated out like bubbles that drifted and popped before she could hear them. He seemed to linger there for years. She wanted to lift her skirt and show him something, but she lacked the full purpose to carry out the idea. Finally he went away and she could close her eyes again. Sometimes her four elephants were stuffed inside her body along with all her organs, and there was a perfectly formed natural space in there for each of them, and they were snug and happy to be exactly as motionless as she was, and she smiled about the unity of it and let the clear thick liquid roll out of the corner of her mouth.

Or she would suddenly sit up and think of them—Tiny and Sarah and Victoria and Belle—realizing they were not inside her at all but were actually out in the world missing her and being poorly cared for or not cared for at all. And she would start to cry, rocking back and forth on the bunk until the wagon itself rocked too and somehow rocked her toward the pipe and the box of matches as though a tunnel was opening up and she was falling into its happy depths where the tears would dry like crystal candy.

She had never had opium before, and she thought it was grand.

But Belle and Sarah and Tiny and Victoria were neglected. They stood together in a clump and watched members of the circus coming and going past them on errands unrelated to their welfare. What food there was they shared, like members of a just and compassionate society, until it was gone. Then they waited patiently for more to be brought, as it always had been in the past. Their hunger grew as big as their bodies, and they tried to sleep it into a smaller size. In sleep they saw images of Claudia Cruikshank-West and of Mount coming toward them dragging hay at the end of a hook or propped high on a shoulder, and they woke up hungrier, the gas singing desperately in their hollow, aching insides. No matter how long or hard they slept, nothing was done for them. No one brought hay or water, and no one came to scratch them with a brush or to lead them out into the meadow to run through the tricks they could do without thinking and that peanuts were the reward for.

Finally, two days into this troubled period, they saw Mother Danilecki. The hunger had grown so large that it had driven Tiny and Belle to their knees. Mother Danilecki brought two boys with her, and the boys had a bale of hay apiece, which they delivered to the center of the pen and then went to fetch more. But even after this long deprivation the four elephants lived up to their training, gathering slowly around the hay in the shape of the letter x and eating delicately, neither rushing nor showing the least lack of politeness toward each other. To Tiny and Belle and Sarah and Victoria, life always felt the best when lived in tune with old habits and expectations. The great disappointment of having been neglected made it all the more important to reclaim the dignity of discipline and custom after this had been so rudely disrupted. Thus, with a satisfying ponderousness they chewed usual-sized mouthfuls of hay, and did it in time with each other. And in only a matter of minutes their heartbeats slowed to normal from the pitch of high nervousness to which they had steadily climbed the past two days. They felt the sweet warmth of each other's broad heads as the four dipped down together to eat. It all came back to them, and they added to their memories the image of Mother Danilecki bringing two boys with hay, the image becoming part of the vast body of information that sustained a life of habit and expectation. All at once the four of them closed their eyes and savored the blossoming dusky sweetness of the hay.

For Chloe everything was different. From one minute to the next, life became more terrible than the minute before. This was all inside her, like a fire, the terror of her own completely limited stillness, in which she could take no action but to see and to smell and to think—to shut her eyes and be somewhere else doing something that was now impossible for her and that she wanted so much to do on that account, such as taking three steps back and two to the side. She stood there chained and shackled double in the center of the wider circle that had been stretched around her after the thing that she did that she couldn't help doing—it hadn't been thought about but had just burst out in a furious second and been over with that fast. The person lay underneath her twinkling, and the fire burned high in her head from what he had done to her just before. And she had done something too.

She knew it was something bad. She knew no good could come. And here it was: no good. People outside the circle pointed at her. A hard bird landed on her back and crept upon it using sticklike feet that poked her. She swung her head and trunk around and tried to hit the bird, but it flew away. The people made a noise. She shook her head and was angry. The anger reminded her she was hungry. She looked down at the food near her feet. She wanted to eat some, but the sore in her mouth was much too great and the hay would have scraped against it and not been good. This was her life, then. Here she was not moving or eating or able to strike a bird on her back that was hurting her. Here she was with no one coming inside the circle to visit and say soft things beneath her mouth, reaching up to scratch. And from one minute to the next she felt discomfort, helplessness and hunger. But when, rarely, there came a cool moment of peace or forgetting, when she closed her eyes and there was only the untroubled emptiness the color of night and sleep, slowly the emptiness would fill with the image of the man underneath her twinkling, dying blue smoke still curling up from between his fingers that had burned her in her mouth. And she always knew that it hadn't gotten as bad as it was going to get. The rest of her life would become like this: the hot sore in her mouth would go on aching until it killed her, and the people outside the circle would be glad, making a noise that swelled up as big as the world when she twinkled out.

16

MAKING MOVIES

There were things Edison was not proud of that he tried to keep in the past, and one of these was the electrocution of many cats and dogs—each one, to be sure, a stray and not the beloved pet of some distraught neighbor. But, still, this was a thing of shame to him that he had undertaken, at the urging of others who worked for him, in the interest of demonstrating a fair point that he believed in strongly: namely, that admitting into people's homes a force as dangerous as alternating current—the basis for the power system of his rival, Westinghouse—would surely produce a sad harvest of accident and death that his own direct-current system would never cause.

And so it was done. An announcement would be made, and members of the press would convene in West Orange at the appointed time. With food, a dog or cat would be coaxed onto a galvanized tin plate to which electrodes were secured, and alternating current would be applied until the animal was dead. The demonstration was persuasive. Then another cat or dog would be subjected to direct current, living to bark or mewl in pain and skitter away past the fresh-killed carcass of the one done in by AC. Edison enjoyed only the part where the press boys raised their eyebrows in enlightenment. For the rest, it was terrible to watch things die or be tortured, and terrible too to see the fresh-dug holes on the laboratory grounds. But to read the news accounts that portrayed the very important differences between direct and alternating currents was ultimately gratifying, and made the cost of provoking public thoughtfulness strike his conscience a little less hard.

But he did not like remembering. And electrocution had recently been recalled to him on account of the plan of the people out at Luna Park, Coney Island, to take that elephant that had killed that man Mount and dance it onto some pieces of tin and do to it with alternating current what Edison had done a dozen years earlier to those cats and dogs. A man named Steve something had come to see him from Coney Island and asked if he thought it was possible to kill a thing that big in that way. Without saying so directly, Steve plainly was looking to Edison as an authority on electrocution. Edison was quite uncomfortable to learn that even one person on Earth could still think of him in this light when his popular reputation was so very different. He replied disingenuously that he didn't know if that was possible because he had never tried to kill a creature that big, with electricity or anything else.

"I'd rather try to hang it first," said Steve, "because I think the crowd will understand that better. But what I hear from people is that hanging an elephant can be a problem getting things to go just right. And I want to keep the crowd's attention so's it don't wander away to something else. In other words, I'm looking for a variety of backup method."

At first Edison was surprised to learn that there would be a crowd, but Steve explained that Luna Park had bought the elephant before it killed the man, and the plan to get a long and useful life out of having it slide down the water chute was all gone awry, and there was the investment still to consider and weigh against the fact that a district court judge had ordered the elephant to be destroyed by a certain date.

"If it's got to be done, I don't see anything amiss in making a profit on it," said Steve, who was speaking in a modulated shout for the benefit of Edison's bum hearing.

Edison nodded. "I suppose so," he said.

He had publicly stated many times that he didn't believe in capital punishment, and he didn't. The state had many rights over people, but one of these was not the right to murder even the lowest wretch. Yet he had lent his name and consent to a campaign to make electricity—specifically, alternating current—the method of dispatch to be used instead of hanging in state murders. And this had been done largely with a view to further establishing in the public awareness that alternating current was a lethal, inhospitable force. He had even gone so far as to suggest that the appropriate verb for this new means of execution ought to be "to Westinghouse." But if someone had gone and asked Mina to characterize his reaction upon reading of the first such execution in New York State—of a poor son of a bitch named Kemmler whom it took many applications of current to kill (Westinghouse himself was quoted as saying, "They could have done it better with an axe")—she would have had to admit he cried like a baby.

"So, this is a question of money, investment?" Edison asked the man Steve.

"That's it exactly," Steve shouted.

"And not of entertainment purely?"

"No, sir!"

"You won't be doing donkeys and apes next month?"

Steve laughed and shook his head.

Edison knew he was a bad judge of character. He looked at this Steve and had the idea that Steve could be anything—he could be the best or the worst of men, could have the kindest or cruellest nature, be generous or tight, strong or weak, genial or stiff as a shirt—and Edison would never know it for certain. All his life he had been surrounded by men and had never known who they were deep inside, and had constantly been surprised to be either benefited or harmed by some unexpectedly charitable or mean and opportunistic individual. He could have gotten up that minute from behind his acre-wide desk and gone to the gilt-framed mirror that hung on the office wall beneath his stuffed bald eagle, and stared at himself and had exactly the same thought he had when he looked at Steve: "Who lives inside that thing?" The only belief he held with absolute certainty about either himself or Steve in this matter was that he, Edison, was in a position to do a favor for which there was scarcely a prospect of being repaid by Steve.

"Yes, it's possible," he said. "I've seen that very same elephant once, and my reckoning is that six thousand volts ought to be about enough to get the job done. That's six thousand volts AC."

Steve pushed out his lower lip and nodded slowly like someone whose breathing was changing from an excitement he didn't want to reveal.

"So, how do I get that much?" he asked, taking out a gold pencil and a note pad from his inner jacket pocket. And Edison began to tell him things, feeling shameful in the role of a craftsman handing down the skills of a craft that had never truly pleased him and that he had acquired by accident, unwillingly. What kind of tin to use, how thick a wire, how big a dynamo and where it could be got, how to measure the electrical resistance of the elephant so as to be dead sure of knowing how large a current to administer.

"It's complicated, isn't it?" said Steve, looking up from his note-taking. Edison frowned, wondering what was being expressed, whether fear or awe or, perhaps, respect for Edison's encyclopedic knowledge. Or could it only have been fatigue at the thought of such extensive preparations for an act that had been foreseen as simple and easy?

"How would you like to be hired to do it?" Steve asked him, smiling and raising his eyebrows.

If the request hadn't stunned Edison so, he would have shown some indignation and ushered Steve right out the door. As it was, he only looked grief-struck and dyspeptic, declining the offer with a gentle stammer. "Oh, no, I don't think I will, no. I expect it just sounds more complicated than it is. You won't run into trouble with this, I'm sure. Just keep yourself and everyone else well away from the paraphernalia when the juice goes on. That's all."

Then Steve asked Edison dozens more questions, some of them for the second time, until Edison sent him packing with the minimum amount of requisite practical knowledge to bring about the death of a very large mammal in front of what Steve surely hoped would be a very large crowd. And all this put Edison in a foul humor that had him pacing back and forth in front of his desk mulling over one of the last things Steve had said. Which was that, whether accomplished by ropes or by alternating current, the death of the elephant Chloe was sure to be a great thing to capture on film.

"We'll get you a very fine spot to shoot from," said Steve. "We'll build you a platform up above the crowd, and nothing will be obstructed."

Edison suspected that this grim enticement was meant to guarantee his presence at the scene in the event any electrical complications arose. But what chiefly accounted for his malaise was the other man's certainty that the enticement was a good one and would work just as well as Edison now knew it had—awakening in him a slumbering, shy, but deep curiosity about death and murder, the curiosity of a spectator eager to see something quite unusual. And the reason the enticement was so well conceived was that Edison would have been much too ashamed to attend the event if he hadn't been given a purpose for attending—a pretext that would raise him above the crowd and give him something useful to do.

"I guess I'll go," he said to the empty office. "Besides, I don't have much pity for that damn elephant anyhow."

Making moving pictures had turned out to be a pretty good thing. What Edison had always hoped was that they would be used as educational tools, which was what he had likewise always hoped for the gramophone. But the fact that the public appetite was more frivolous— hot for vaudevillians and beer-hall baritones—than bent upon improving the life of the mind was both a profitable and, ultimately, an acceptable disappointment to Edison.

He called his machine the kinetograph—a camera for recording movement; the machine for viewing the film he called the kinetoscope. But to the process of making frozen life trick the viewer's eye into thinking it was animated, Edison's chief contribution might have been to encourage George Eastman to develop long, narrow strips of flexible film. The strips were the key to bringing the whole business off, and all the devices that came after—the cameras and projectors—were not much more than logical, tinkerish slaves of the perforated film (though still immensely lucrative devices if you happened to hold the patents, many of which Edison did). But all ineluctably followed from the idea that the film stock had to be bendable, spoolable and plastic, so that the ratcheting sprocket mechanism developed by Edison could advance it frame by frame past a hole through which life—as still bites of caught light—could be admitted.

The kinetoscope quickly left the realm of the arts and sciences and became an amusement, amazement—entertainment. Even Eadweard Muybridge, the great progenitor of moving pictures, showed his grasp of appetite by making a leering photographic study called "Animal Locomotion," which was nothing more than a series of plates of two nude women cavorting around throwing buckets of water at each other. So, despite the best efforts of pretense, the kinetoscope, like all new contrivances, inevitably was drawn along in a popular direction, and a practical inventor was obliged not to struggle too much against it.

So Edison didn't. He had the first moving-picture studio built, an eccentric, oblong, tarpaper-covered structure with a hinged roof opening and a foundation that rested on a pivot so that the studio could turn like a revolving bridge and track the sun across the sky. Inside this thing, which the sunlight cooked like a Dutch oven, fifty-foot rolls of film were cranked through Edison's camera as various performers possessing variable talents did odd things on a hot stage.

Fred Ott, one of Edison's long-time lab assistants, was photographed sneezing. An organ grinder and his monkey were imported from Newark and filmed (and Edison made a peculiar joke about two brave men facing one another wielding dangerous crank-driven instruments). As the organ grinder played, the monkey ran back and forth between the camera and the organ. Edison heard the shrill notes only dimly, and this gave him the idea of adding sound to movement by turning the two arts into one—maybe the gramophone could be linked somehow to the kinetoscope.

What turned out to be the most popular things were fights. Gentleman Jim Corbett performed an eighty-second boxing exhibition against a fourth-rate opponent named Courtney whom he knocked senseless on a signal from Edison's chief kinetographer, William Kennedy Laurie Dickson. Boxing went well without sound, and when large kinetoscope machines were fitted with nickel slots and installed in public places, the greatest number of nickels always landed in those with boxing matches inside. So there was frequently a fight going on in the Black Maria, as the revolving studio came to be called, which Corbett declared was the hottest, most miserable place he had ever known, and where the hardest thing he had had to do was be sure to stand in focus when he knocked his opponent out.

The next revelation was that everything could be moved. The camera could be picked up and taken elsewhere, with only a little bit of difficulty, and so great events that could not be transported to West Orange could be pursued and bagged like wild game. This prospect so excited Edison that he urged the formation of a film crew whose only job would be to roam the countryside ceaselessly and be on the lookout for unexpected curiosities to record, such as the hatching of birds' eggs or a marriage between a very old man and a very young girl. He himself would scan the newspapers and send periodic bulletins around to the kinetoscope division about what he thought the news held in store that might turn out to be worthy and photogenic.

So it was not out of the ordinary, once he had made his decision, for

Edison to send such a note to his division chief, Jim White, telling him that on June fifteenth, a Sunday, "an event of great peculiarity will transpire at Luna Park, Coney Island, and we should be there to see it done. And I would like to come along myself, and will inform you closer to the date of the curious particulars which are most strange indeed, you can trust me on that."

17

POOR CHLOE

Chloe made the journey to Luna Park on foot through the streets of Manhattan, and many bystanders stopped in their tracks and stared. Some even joined the trek for a while before going back to where they had started and resuming the lives they had left. Chloe was led by Claudia Cruikshank-West and surrounded by a rowdy cordon of song-singing Irish policemen, several of whom carried hand-lettered signs describing the elephant, her misdeeds and the fate to which she was now being marched. The general atmosphere was full of ridicule, and if Chloe had had a thought about it she would have been humiliated. As it was, she just ambled on with her head held low and her eyes dull, like an old empty ship in the midst of frolicksome catboats.

Mother Danilecki, who followed along behind, was surprised at how readily the policemen took to performing like circus people and were hardly shy at all about attracting attention to themselves. When she once strayed too close to one of them, he reached out and put an arm around her and planted a hot, beery kiss on her cheek as though she was his mother. But Mother Danilecki could easily retreat to being unnoticed because the Swiss sisters had come along too and were mingling among the policemen boldly, as if there was nothing in the world a Swiss sister liked as much as a man in a saggy blue uniform, and nothing she wouldn't do to please him for the pleasure of being near.

So men's and women's loud sounds were carried along like flags as the group went south on Fifth Avenue. The party swirled around the unheeding excuse for the party's existence, and Claudia Cruikshank-West stayed ahead of it grimly, a hostess with a twitching eyelid and a runny

274

nose who looked as if she hadn't slept for close to a year, and didn't even want to. At the start of the march in Central Park she had come out of her wagon for the first time in days and had swayed in the morning sunlight vowing revenge on the elephant. The best thing Jack Berlin could think to do was put her in charge of the exodus south. When he asked her if she was up to it, she spat at his feet and coughed and said she could "take that pachy across the bleeding Alps if it promised to die on the other damn side." So Jack Berlin nodded and said, "Godspeed," and turned his back as the four Swiss sisters galloped up and pattered around him, calling him Uncle Jack and pleading with him in phony, whining voices to let them join the entourage.

"What do I care?" Jack Berlin said, throwing up his arms. "Cut it out!" And he swatted at them with his one good hand, dispersing them in circles like flies.

Then Claudia Cruikshank-West blew her whistle and stepped off, driving the elephant hook deep into the flesh of Chloe's foreleg. And that was the start of the march. At the edge of the park the police joined up, their sergeant stating that they were there to protect both the public and the circus people from a demonstrably dangerous beast, and to see that a lawful court order was duly carried out and Chloe not somehow spirited off to continue elsewhere with her wanton and murderous life.

They took four hours to make the Brooklyn Bridge and almost one to cross it. Then the parade grew thinner going through Brooklyn, where the Manhattan police contingent was replaced by a remarkably similar one from the local borough headquarters. The Swiss sisters instantly transferred their longing to these new police, who responded as eagerly as had their brethren from across the river. At one point one of the sisters turned around and looked right at Mother Danilecki and winked. Then she took the police hat right off the officer's head and put it on herself, squealing about the warmth of it.

People came to their gates and watched the parade go by. Some of them asked, "Is that the one?" and their meaning was clear enough that whoever answered them unhesitatingly said "Yes." Mother Danilecki tried to read the faces of these onlookers as she passed, but saw almost nothing revealed in them. It was as if they all were waiting for much more information about everything, and stood no chance of receiving it. This saddened her because she thought that everyone in America was entitled, by its Constitution, to just enough information to inflame their spirits in some way.

"Dis is so damn sad, I'm tellin' you," she said to some of them, adding anguish to her voice, hoping to incite in them the first glimmer of a conviction that might possibly solidify after the parade had passed out of sight. Maybe someone would turn to his neighbor and say, "It's just a shame they have to kill that elephant," and the neighbor would say, "Well, they ought to've done it years ago, if you ask me." And that was democracy, spinning along on its differences of opinion, which were what Semple had always told her was the important thing.

"The day everyone agrees or thinks they ought to agree," he said, "I say that's the day we all take poison."

"I agree," Mother Danilecki had said.

As the trek wore on, a determined kind of quiet spread throughout the group and Claudia Cruikshank-West picked up the pace, her short legs taking more steps faster. The houses became fewer and the smell of the ocean strengthened. The sun began to go down. Mother Danilecki decided that Coney Island was very near. She had seen it on a map and knew it as a wormlike squirt of sand that lay beneath south Brooklyn like an underline.

Soon she saw the towers of Luna Park swirling up like puffs of candy. "That perfect," she said. Then Chloe slowed and began to drop loaves of waste in the road behind her. Dusk was coming on.

Coney Island hardly felt like an island at all. It struck Mother Danilecki that it was wrong to call it that. This was only the end of the land, not an island, and suddenly they were all there without warning, like pilgrims surprised by their own arriving. The somnolent road led onto it, and the sand and water crept closer in the falling darkness—a smell and a sound. If there was any deep change, it came so slow that not even Mother Danilecki noticed; it came like a sleep that takes you away before you know it's there.

Now, above them, the sky was indigo and pink, and around them the air was soft. The Swiss sisters sang spontaneously a sweet song in French, letting their voices die together at the end of each verse like a harmonic sunset, and swell at the start of the next like a new dawn. After the voices had died for good at the end of the song, there was a silence no one could bear to fill, and everyone just stopped moving.

Then the lights went on at Luna Park with a scalding hiss like the sound of cymbals and a brightness that tore the color from the sky. Mother Danilecki's breath sucked backward and she saw the candy-puff towers suddenly blazing with whorls and pinwheels and dotted lines of hot white and yellow light that, had the structures themselves been subtracted, could have lingered in the air to describe a kingdom unattainable in life.

"Ahhhh!" she said, letting her breath out. And everyone began moving again. "I'm a big big moth," whispered Mother Danilecki.

"And how's that for a welcome!" said one of the policemen to Claudia Cruikshank-West. But she didn't answer, instead swinging her hook up into Chloe's shoulder to get the elephant going.

It was a Saturday night in June, and Luna Park was just new in May. Not many people were there yet, but the man who came out to meet the entourage said the lights would draw a crowd before long. They would hum across the Brooklyn sky like a halo, and people would come out to see what the occasion was and would learn there was no occasion at all—just, in the words of the Luna Park man, "a new kind of life unlike any life they know on Earth!" Mother Danilecki wished Semple was along to see the spires and lights, but then it crossed her mind that he might find this too much like the promise of heaven, the brilliance shining in and out of everything, making it clean and gauzy and fantastic.

"You wait," said the man. "In an hour, different. Crowded. In a week, better still. And in another month, no place to sit down and rest. Just wait."

"Well, I'm sure that's fine," said Claudia Cruikshank-West, "but since it looks like there's oodles of room *now* to sit down and rest, do you think you could possibly show us where we all might do that?"

The Luna Park man, who introduced himself as Stephen Piwonka, took notice of her and smiled and nodded. He summoned handlers to come take charge of Chloe and gave the police sergeant a sum of money to divide with the rest of his men. Then he told Claudia and Mother Danilecki and the Swiss sisters that if only they would follow him he would lead them to private accommodations where they would be treated to "a level of comfort and pleasure that only the very wealthy have hitherto enjoyed."

"Anywhere is fine, believe me," said Claudia Cruikshank-West, watching the backside of Chloe be ambled off toward a monstrous cage already decorated with colorful painted panels depicting the episode of Mount's death and describing her as "the Condemned Lady Chloe, Murderess of Three Fine Men!" The cage also caught Mother Danilecki's eye, which was drawn to the three gentle faces painted within wreathlike ovals and surmounted by the words "Requiescat In Pace." She supposed that one of these was meant to be Mount, but all three looked like the faces of strangers—except for the one that looked a little bit like this Stephen character. In the painting of the death scene, Mount was the size of an underfed boy and Chloe was as big as a house. A smaller panel was entirely devoted to "The Elephant's Death Warrant," which was done as a very large scroll with Bible-like lettering. Mother Danilecki asked one of the Swiss sisters—she thought it was Margalo at first, but it turned out to be Elsbietta—to read the scroll to her.

" 'Be It Ordered,' " Elsbietta began, then stopped and said, "Look, hon, all it says is the elephant dies tomorrow, that's basically it. And it's signed to make it legal, okay?"

Mother Danilecki nodded. "By who signed?" she asked.

"The Hon. initial F. Skinner, comma initial J., which I think stands for Judge, okay?" Elsbietta put her hands on her hips and sighed ponderously because she was being torn in three directions—trying to say goodbye to an Irish policeman while also having to follow the Luna Park man and, at the same time, read something that was probably completely imaginary to an old Polish woman who would not know the meaning of most of it anyway. "Okay?" she said again. Mother Danilecki nodded.

"This way, please," called out Stephen, and Mother Danilecki could feel the deep excitement in his voice, which she believed was agitated beyond its natural register by the buzzing of the lights, audible everywhere now as though an invisible swarm of something was swirling around one's head.

"Just you wait!" he said, rubbing his hands together and grinning. Mother Danilecki turned and watched Chloe being led up a ramp and into the cage, the doors of which were swung open, splitting in half the depiction of the death scene and the face of the second of Chloe's three victims. Chloe went up the ramp like a trouper, no false starts or balks or resistance. Mother Danilecki's heart went out to her. Poor tomorrow, she thought.

* * *

If the rest of the rooms were as nice as Mother Danilecki's, they were sure to be very nice indeed. The mirror was what she noticed first: it had no splotches or flecks in it, and she stood there in the silence and stillness—lighted sufficiently by the great suffusion of brilliance coming into the room from outside—and admired herself in the glass, feeling that her skin was much better than it had looked in years, younger and softened by a glow that showed its supple depth. She opened the collar of her blouse and continued spreading it wider. She smiled, and a shiver ran down her spine. She began to unbutton her skirts.

Later—after the noise of people having fun had died away—she heard the hammering of the scaffold in her sleep, and it was not necessary for her to wake up and go to the window to see it happen; hearing was enough. The dimensions of the structure came to her: an ark of a scaffold to bear the great weight of an elephant. The timbers conveyed their thickness and density by the sound of being malleted into place. The ringing went down to the core of the wood—to the very first of its years of age—then back out into the air, across the grounds and up into Mother Danilecki's room, to her ears. Thick, heavy. Vast. She saw the scaffold rising up in her mind's eye, and hearing was all it took.

In the morning she swung her legs out of bed—a wonderful bed with a mattress as dense as the peaty earth of a Polish forest—and closed her eyes at its edge, seeing the finished scaffold before it disappeared as she awoke completely. Then she stood and went to the window and saw it there through the gap between two buildings across the midway—a prodigious instrument, exactly as it had come to her in her sleep. The gold sun struck from the east and gave the wood the look of a living thing, the necklike gibbet, for all its stubborn thickness, still having a creatury appearance—a dinosaur monster staring back behind itself to see if an elephant was coming.

She smelled the good smell of coffee from somewhere and heard the Swiss sisters out in the hall. Quickly she dressed and went down to breakfast.

Chloe liked the cage. It was big and safe and the air flowed through it. She was up above the people, who were kept a certain distance away. She tried not moving and noticed that the people also did not move when she stood as still as she could; then she tried moving and thrashing around, and the people flung their hands up and squealed and pointed and turned. But no matter what she did, she felt that the people were very far away and not important and couldn't hurt her. Her tongue felt better, and she could eat.

The food was fresh and good. The water was cold and good. She never ran out of anything, and no sooner did she soil than someone came to clean up and spread new straw. Whoever came into the cage she developed a liking for because of her liking for the cage. She had been born into and lived her whole life in the circus, and this was not like the circus. Special care was being taken with her, and she was not being made to work, only to stand in a spacious cage where she could change positions at whim and try new things to see if the people outside could be made to change what they were doing and feeling; and that was interesting and moving, better than circling the ring backwards or standing on hind legs or putting the foot on the head. Better than obeying, hearing the whistle, feeling the hook, the whip, the birch.

She liked the shapes on the outside of the bars. When the air flowed through it whispered around those shapes and took different directions, arriving at her body at different times in smaller, sharper portions that felt like particles of dust and made her hide tingle. All night the breeze did this to her, and her heart was filled with colorful sights and the ringing of colorful noises. And in the morning the sun did the same thing, bending around the shapes and splitting into smaller parts that struck her hide and filled her heart with light. And there was also a smell in the air that she had never known before, soft and moist and sweet, and this seemed like many things mixed together that she accepted as the smell of a different kind of life that was not the circus. In the moments after she soiled and before the person came into the cage to clean it up, that too was taken into the smell of the wider life and turned soft and sweet and moist.

She liked the cage and liked the place, and she could close her eyes and be happy, or she could open her eyes and be happy. She could even let go of the sight of the man lying underneath her twinkling, and she could stop knowing that nothing would ever get better.

As the sun moved higher up the side of the cage, the beams of light shifted and buzzed. Chloe fluttered her forehead and sent some thoughts out into the day. Only another elephant would have heard them.

18
THE END

When Edison and Jim White and Jim's assistant, a boy named Gilbert, reached Luna Park around noon, Edison was pleased to find two platforms, not one, provided for photographic purposes. Steve showed both off proudly as if they represented bold steps forward in platform building. The arrangement gave Edison an inspiration about how to make best use of the spare camera Jim had brought. Usually the two boxes would be stood up side by side on sticks, the first being cranked until it ran out of film and the second taking up seamlessly as Gilbert, or one of the other boys, answered to a nod from Jim White or a poke in the ribs. And while the second was cranking the first could be reloaded. But if the two cameras were deployed one each to a platform, far apart, then the film would have the benefit of two angles of view between which to intercut in assembling the final montage. Edison mused that if only there were three cameras, two could shoot at the same time and reload while the third was covering. In fact, four would be best. But there were just the two at hand. He proposed the idea to Jim White.

"Whaddaya think?" he asked. White nodded in a pondering way, as though he had independent judgment on the matter and was not just doing whatever the boss wanted, but had arrived by himself at the same exact opinion as Edison, only a beat slower and more carefully.

"Okay," he said. "I think that's best."

"I knew you'd like it," said Steve.

Jim White sent Gilbert over to the second platform with the second camera. "Which is it gonna be?" he asked Steve, pointing at the scaffold. "Are you gonna hang it or electrify it?"

"Does it make any difference?" Steve asked.

"Not to me, I guess," said Jim White. "But I'm not sure, being up this high, that I'm gonna catch all of the action once the beast goes through the trap in the scaffold, if you follow me. See, the sun'll be straight overhead, and the underside there is gonna be in deep shadow mostly, and that can trouble the exposure some." White saw a look of confusion spread across Steve's face, and this gave him pride in his own expertise. "But I guess we'll be all right," he said.

In the meantime, Edison had gone over to look at the dynamo, which was a sturdy one from a firm he knew called Bismarck Electric. An advertising sign leaning up against the dynamo said "Provided Courtesy of . . ." and gave the name and address. A man from Bismarck leaned there too and smiled at Edison in a fraternal way that needed no explaining.

"This'll do," Edison said. Steve hurried over and told him as loud as he could how a man had been sent to the elephant's cage that morning to draw a chalk-mark rectangle around where it stood so as to reckon the necessary size of the piece of tin.

"We'll cover it over with straw as a bait," he said.

"Yes, but don't weaken the contact," Edison cautioned.

"Well, I'm hoping we can just hang her, really."

For the first time Edison thought of it being a woman.

First thing after breakfast, Mother Danilecki walked down to the ocean and admired how broad and clean the newly raked beach was. She went to the edge of the water and clutched her skirts up high and waded in, imagining that each step took her closer to a sunken place where she might disappear forever, leaving the beautiful day up above her, the sky shrinking and dimming.

The Swiss sisters had wanted to accompany her, but Mother Danilecki told them no, she felt like being alone. So the Swiss sisters thought it would be a good prank to follow along behind in a cluster, sneaking in an exaggerated manner and pretending to want not to be discovered. Finally Mother Danilecki tired of their foolishness and beckoned them to join her, whereupon they turned and scampered back to the boardwalk where they found a bench to sit and sing a song upon as a way of attracting the day's first serious attention to themselves. Their voices lilted down to the water's edge where Mother Danilecki remained for most of an hour, letting the water lap over her old white feet and staring down at them until she became almost dizzy. She stood there and thought about what she would do in the fall when Semple was dead and it was time for the circus to go south again. She had a pleasing vision of herself in a cozy flat in the London theatre district, making a modest living serving tea to and reading the palms of worried actors and actresses. She could fill them with hope and cake and good advice, give them cures for colds and vocal strains and stage fright and venereal disease. It would be nice at her age to have the trade come to her instead of always having to travel from place to place. She imagined the sign gaily painted above the doorway: *"Mother Danilecki—Reader and Advisor."* She imagined also people like the Swiss sisters coming to her one by one, so she could add trouble to their hearts and minds in ways that were just and comforting to her. She would have an opportunity to bring her longer life to bear on younger people who would believe her, fear her and try to understand her—even though she was not pretty anymore and had a thick accent and spotted hands. She would have to learn to bake.

She noticed that the water had crept away from her feet while she had been thinking. For a moment she was surprised to be at Coney Island in America. Behind her a crowd had gathered around the Swiss sisters. A man's voice would begin to sing a song, and the sisters would join in and overpower it with sudden and glorious harmonies and a bewitching agreement on exactly what the words were in whatever language the song was begun in. They gave the impression of knowing absolutely everything, and Mother Danilecki stood at the water's edge facing the boardwalk and watching the crowd grow in size until it became difficult for people who wanted to go somewhere else and not be regaled by the Swiss sisters to pass. Mother Danilecki noticed that among the ones who shared this aim of getting past were several boys who hurried around and pasted up large posters on which she could see very clearly the images of the elephant and the scaffold.

The second thing she did after breakfast was go see Chloe. There were many people gathered in front of the cage, and it took some time for her to make her way to the head of the crowd. When she got there and didn't have to look over or around anyone any longer, she was struck by how peaceful Chloe seemed. A man came into the back of the cage and busied himself on his hands and knees in some task that took him completely around her. She hardly even seemed to notice him. Then the man stood up and took out a folding carpenter's measure, going around her once again and making quick notes in pencil on his shirt cuff. Then he folded the measure back up and left the cage. Chloe hadn't moved a muscle.

The crowd was as quiet as could be, as though waiting for her to do something. The quiet would stretch out perfectly for minutes at a time until someone coughed or a boy asked "What's she doing, Pa?" and the pa answered, "Nothing at all." Then people near the front would get tired of waiting and leave, and other people would filter forward and take those places.

Before too long Mother Danilecki felt herself adoring Chloe in light of what the day held in store for her and of her being only an animal without any of the usual sense of purpose that would have made it fair to judge her actions in a criminal way. No matter what she had done to Mount and those other two men, and no matter how much Mother Danilecki wished Mount was still on earth, to kill Chloe was unjust. When Mother Danilecki was a girl in Poland, she knew of a custom in the countryside of putting pigs on trial if the pigs had gotten into a neighbor farmer's crops or caused damage by knocking things down or had done other kinds of mischief. A pig would be given an advocate to argue its side before the village council while another advocate argued the side of the offended farmer. A crowd would fill the meeting hall and cheer one side or the other. The advocates wore their usual wigs and pressed their causes seriously. The pig was always ordered slaughtered, and Mother Danilecki understood this was only a complicated ritual for getting ham and bacon made in such a way that guilt attached only to the pig and not the farmer who finally did the slaughter. The meat could be eaten happily all around, and hardly ever was a pig butchered without a trial, and hardly ever a pig's advocate who won his case so the pig was set free. It was Mother Danilecki's belief that none of the pigs had actually ever gotten into the neighbor farmer's crops and done the damage they were accused of. But Mother Danilecki was bothered that Chloe hadn't had a proper trial or an advocate to take her side.

So it seemed especially fitting to stand there in front of the cage and adore Chloe on this last day of her life. Giant, simple emotions accumulated inside Mother Danilecki and were excreted through her eyes, which blurred and felt hot and strained. Chloe took a few steps toward the front of the cage, and some of the crowd instinctively shrank back. Mother Danilecki stretched forward as far as she could and reached her hand up through the bars. Chloe crept closer and brought her trunk down low until the tip of it clasped two of Mother Danilecki's fingers and lingered there while the crowd murmured.

Edison was surprised to see so many people congregating at an hour when half the world was still at dinner after church. This must be the other half, he figured. The first arrivals had lined a temporary fence erected around the area holding the scaffold. Then the crowd deepened quickly, stretching all the way back to the platform where Edison stood with Jim White and one of the cameras. And the mass of spectators teeming around the base of the platform was still increasing behind it. Vendors of taffy and candy apples and spun sugar and pig-meat coneys worked the crowd profitably, and Edison half wished he was still a young candy butcher on a day such as this when people were gathered with money in their pockets and nothing to do but spend it aimlessly while waiting for something else that was their reason for being there.

Jim White was seated with his legs dangling over the edge of the staging, both hands jammed into a black lightproof changing bag. He was loading film in the two spare magazines.

"Shouldn't we be shooting some of this?" Edison asked. He was a great believer in setting the scene so that the main action didn't seem to come out of nowhere and take the unwary viewer by surprise. Jim White nodded and said, "I'm almost finished here." Over on the other platform, Gilbert was also loading spare magazines. Edison waved to get his attention, and when Gilbert looked up Edison made a rotary cranking gesture. Gilbert nodded.

Jim White came out of the bag and put the two magazines in the space between the tripod legs. He stood up and looked through the lens and swung the camera this way and that. On the other side of the fence something glinted in the sun and caught Edison's eye. It was the giant piece of tin that the man from Bismarck dynamo company was dragging across the ground. He let the tin drop, and it lay like a square gray pool. He went back to the dynamo to fetch wires, which he measured and cut from a thick wooden spool and fastened, first at the dynamo end and then to two bolts on opposite sides of the piece of tin.

"It'll work," thought Edison.

He looked down at the tops of people's heads, some hatted, some bald and reddening in the sun. Now and then a man would look up at the platform and notice Edison staring down. If the man was with someone, he might get the friend's attention and point at Edison. Then the two of them might wave. Edison would see the lips move: "Hello, Mr. Edison!" Other heads would turn, and soon whole sections of crowd were waving up at him with cones of spun sugar and red-glazed half-eaten apples. Up in his shoulder and deep in his jaw the ache from so much waving back and smiling had begun. He was the most famous man in America, maybe in the world.

Jim White was cranking, turning the camera across a swath of people waving at Edison.

"We can use it as if they're waving at the elephant," Edison said. "You know, like saying goodbye?" White nodded and kept on cranking.

Jim White could turn at a steady speed—the speed of nature—so that people didn't move in jerks or slurs, but naturally. Some individuals just had that perfect sense of how to blend themselves with a machine, and Jim White was one of them. Edison watched the elbow pumping in and out. You could set your watch. You could say that a minute had so many Jim White cranks in it, and it would be exactly the same on Tuesday as it was on Saturday, the same at the end of the day as it was at the start. He could fetch his mind inside the process and go along with it like a friend without even having to think. He made the camera smart.

Edison saw the snout of the lens swing quickly to the back of the crowd, the gate where admissions were being collected. Some boys were scrambling over the gate while a watchman struck at their ankles with a stick. On the side where the crowd was the boys separated and blended in.

"That's good," said Edison. Jim White ran the film out and changed magazines.

"So, when do we get the main event?" he asked Edison. Edison shrugged. He looked at his watch. It was already just past one o'clock, and there wasn't an elephant in sight.

* * *

Although most of the crowd had been lured away by barkers to the place where the execution was to happen, Mother Danilecki stayed by the cage until Claudia Cruikshank-West came for Chloe. Claudia entered through the door at the back of the cage swinging her elephant hook like a police billy. She had two Luna Park handlers with her, big athletic types who towered over her on either side and wore tight-fitting blue jerseys with the letter *C* on the front.

"Chloe," Claudia said. Chloe turned her head. The two handlers tensed and crossed their thick arms in front of their chests, looking capable and magnificent as a warning to Chloe. But it wasn't necessary. Chloe remained docile. She turned herself in an economical circle, lifting and lowering her legs slowly as she came about like a railroad roundhouse. Claudia marched in underneath her jaw and led her out of the cage and down the long ramp into sunlight. The two handlers took up left and right flank positions, still tense and scowling, their arms as stiff as clubs.

Mother Danilecki caught up with Claudia, who was snorting as she walked and whose anger about everything seemed to have been fully refreshed by sleep. It was possible to see the huge gibbet rising above the level of the midway attractions.

"That's what I'm waiting for," said Claudia, pointing at the thing.

In Mother Danilecki's opinion, Chloe didn't have a suspicion as to what was going to happen. When Mother Danilecki reached out to stroke Chloe's trunk, Claudia Cruikshank-West said angrily, "Well, then, you can be the priest, right?"

The sun felt good on Chloe's back. As she walked the warmth stimulated her, and she let some good waste slide out behind. A tingling spread up and down her back legs. She continued walking at a steady pace. There were people around her. She saw them all and felt them. Two of them she knew. The tingling finally went away, and she missed it.

At first there was nothing wrong. She had eaten, and the food had not hurt her mouth. She had had water, which was cold and good. Where she walked now the dust was soft beneath her feet. But she was also getting closer to something she knew. She could hear the sound of people that was such a hum that it chilled her along her spine, and the lost tingle came back again. Something felt the same as before a performance. The sound of the people was the same, the getting closer was the same. It was like the circus that she had known her whole life, and she was going somewhere to be seen again as something different than she felt inside. And she knew she would not like it.

The very small person with the hook turned around and looked at her. The hook spun circles in the air and made a windy, whining sound. The eyes of the very small person were as cold as the good, cold water, but they caused a fire to burn in Chloe's head. If the other person she knew hadn't been there close to her and soft beneath her trunk, the new fear would have been terrible. Still, the fear grew from the sound of the crowd, the circling whine of the hook, the burning in her head that also made the tingle stronger.

Everything in life was becoming worse again. In her mouth the sore came back like a memory and brought things with it.

Jim White saw the elephant coming and signaled to Gilbert. He saw Gilbert waiting for the signal like a perfectly trained assistant. Jim White thought that if you were Jim White, you couldn't want anything more for your work than a boy like Gilbert, who was devoted and uncritical and had no ambition to advance beyond the vocation of assisting and, thus, could safely be taught everything a Jim White had to teach and would be content to wait until the very day Jim White died before daring to take his place. And even then there would be the terrible hesitation out of loyalty, and there might always be some doubt as to whether Gilbert could make the transition at all from assisting to needing assistants. One thing was sure: when the time came, Gilbert would never be so fortunate as to find another Gilbert—someone who didn't care a hoot if he stayed a boy forever.

For a moment Jim White watched Gil's arm begin to crank, striving to reach that perfect, unvarying sympathy with the inner process that Jim White always tried to teach. "At the right speed, the gears make a certain sound inside the camera. If you put your ear at this spot on the box, you'll hear it," he would explain during slow, pleasant sessions outside the Black Maria. One by one the assistants put their ears there and listened. But Gil's was the only nod of comprehension that Jim White ever believed. Gil's good, he thought as he framed the approaching elephant. He twisted the collar of the lens and felt Edison's hand at the small of his back.

The End

* * *

Chloe saw how big a crowd there was at the same time she saw the monstrous object with the ramp leading up and the long neck slanting back. Even though this was something she'd never seen before, she knew it was meant for her. She took a sudden hatred to it based on its unfamiliarity. She didn't like doing something new. Only after repeated practice did a trick lose its frightening newness and was she able to carry on without hating it. What went through her body on seeing the monstrous object was a determination not to cooperate. Whatever was planned that involved the thing, she would refuse to participate. The place was set up for a performance, like in the circus, but she had been given no practice for it and couldn't do it. When the plan to refuse occurred to her, she became calm and contented. She wrapped her trunk around the arm of the old, soft person and squeezed it nicely. The old person's other arm came up and patted her. This was nice.

Mother Danilecki was the priest. In Poland the pig had a priest who sprinkled water and held up a colorful strip of linen and swirled this in the air over the pig's head and spoke musical Latin benedictions. Then cords were spooled around the pig's hind legs and jerked up over a transom while the pig squealed from surprise. Then came the knife. By this time the priest was far enough away that if the artery shot blood, the blood couldn't stain the raiment.

Chloe wrapped her trunk around Mother Danilecki's arm. Mother Danilecki patted her. At the foot of the ramp Chloe stopped. Mother Danilecki looked up and saw the thick rope stretching down from the gibbet, ending in a vast loop. The rope was placed so that Chloe would walk straight into it.

"Chloe!" said Claudia Cruikshank-West. She swung the hook into Chloe's left upper foreleg. But Chloe stayed where she was. "Chloe, up!" ordered Claudia. Chloe let go of Mother Danilecki's arm, and when the hook came again she swung her trunk and struck Claudia full on the forehead, knocking her down. The two Luna Park handlers rushed forward and helped Claudia up. But she wasn't hurt badly. She sent them to push from behind, and each took a hind leg and leaned their shoulders in and groaned against the great weight that wouldn't budge. Claudia tried the hook again and darted away as the trunk flashed across and missed her. Slowly Chloe began to sit.

* * *

The people roared. It was one sound, mingled, distant. The people were all together; they were all the same. She lowered herself down and looked up the ramp. She saw the thick circle dangling above, very still, the air on the inside of it looking different than the rest of the air. She couldn't imagine the trick. What did they want her to do? How was it like anything she had done before? She turned her head aside and refused even to look in the direction they wanted her to go. It was not going to happen. She would not do it. She was rich in the skills of not doing certain things if she set her mind hard against them.

She could wait forever. The crowd rumbled.

"They'll have to use the dynamo," said Edison. "That beast ain't about to climb that scaffold. She's too darn smart."

They had filmed up to the point where the tiny woman had been knocked down. Then they waited for something else to happen. But Jim White took his eye from the viewfinder and shook his head at Edison and then, more broadly, at Gilbert on the other platform. The crowd was turning restless and loud. All the elephant was doing was sitting motionless at the base of the scaffold. Two rugged-looking young men were trying various comically futile leaning and prodding maneuvers, and an old, gray-haired woman wearing what looked to be fourteen skirts stayed by the elephant's head and stroked it kindly, like a samaritan.

"Nothing's happening here," said Edison.

But then the man named Steve stepped forward and whispered something to the very tiny woman whom the elephant had knocked down, and Edison saw much nodding carried on between them and knew that the alternative to hanging had been agreed upon. And so he told Jim White, who got Gilbert's attention and pointed at the dynamo, whose engine was already running loudly.

"Mother," Claudia said, "let's see if we can poke her over there to where that trough of water sits, eh?" But Mother Danilecki had resolved not to help it happen. She shook her head and said, "Not me. Remember, I am priest, huh?" So Claudia cursed her and did it herself, gently and using no hook.

It surprised Mother Danilecki how quickly and easily the thing was done. Chloe stood up and followed along, away from the scaffold, and placed herself precisely in the center of the flat carpet of gray, hay-strewn metal that Mother Danilecki knew was now to be the means of killing her. Chloe's trunk reached out for water. Mother Danilecki saw the wires.

"Start filming!" Edison hollered. But already Jim White had the last full magazine in place and threaded and was cranking at the speed of nature, his elbow as fluid as the wing of a bird.

Chloe saw the water shine in the trough and wanted some. The sun came winking off, and the water was blue, yellow, blue, yellow, and looked so cold and good. After winning not having to do the trick, she was ready for simpler performing. She stretched her trunk down toward the trough. The man by the rumbling machine hollered and waved for everyone to get out of Chloe's way. He had his hand on the handle and the other hand in the air, going like crazy. Mother Danilecki stepped back. Claudia ran. The two Luna Park young men in blue jerseys ran too. The crowd was as loud as the rumbling machine. Mother Danilecki waved and cried out. The hand on the handle moved. The good, cold water sliced up Chloe's trunk. Then the lights went on inside her. Screaming in her ears.

EPILOGUE

Father and Mother Mount told the children to go outside. Then they sat together on the wide divan with the letter between them, facing each other. They read the letter again— first Father Mount, running his finger along below the words, then Mother Mount, silently, her mouth small and gray.

"Jay's dead," said Father Mount. Mother Mount looked up into his eyes and said, "I knew this would happen." Her fingers began to tear the letter slowly, absently. Father Mount put his hand on hers to stop the tearing. He heard the children out in back asking each other questions about what was suddenly going on that was so queer. Then Father Mount said he didn't know why, but he thought they should take the letter to Bolus Hall and post it on the bulletin board next to the big glass case with the rope varieties and knot examples. Mother Mount didn't disagree.

They took a walk through town. They brought the four children with them, herding them along ahead. Other Bolusburghians looked up and waved at the Mounts and were a little bit surprised when the Mounts did not wave back. It was a beautiful afternoon in the summer. The sweetness of the corn hung lightly in the air, and the breeze was from the south.

The Mounts went up the steps of Bolus Hall and into the spacious lobby where the varnish on the wide pine planks had a deep, glad shine and a hardness that clicked under all their shoes. Father Mount stood the children back and went to the bulletin board. He took two tacks and

293

pierced the two sheets of the letter, placing them side by side on a field of empty cork. Then he stood back himself and turned to the children and told them, "Your brother's dead."

Then they all marched home.